**Also available from Charlie Adhara
and Carina Press**

The Big Bad Wolf Series

*The Wolf at the Door
The Wolf at Bay
Thrown to the Wolves
Wolf in Sheep's Clothing
Cry Wolf*

PACK OF LIES

CHARLIE ADHARA

carina
press®

Recycling programs
for this product may
not exist in your area.

ISBN-13: 978-1-335-47324-0

Pack of Lies

Carina Press
22 Adelaide St. West, 41st Floor
Toronto, Ontario M5H 4E3, Canada
www.CarinaPress.com

Printed in U.S.A.

For my mom,
who taught me to love a mystery,
but not how to solve one.

PACK OF LIES

Prologue

The unexpected part of grief was just how boring it could be. The derivative nightmares. All those empty hours spent in bed waiting for the sun to rise. How much of life had become reliving—relentlessly running the same regrets over and over in your mind until meaning slipped away like worn-loose wheels.

It wasn't that he'd expected to feel better by now. He'd just thought he might have found a different way to be sad.

Julien sat on the floor of a bedroom that hadn't been his in over thirty years, plaster dust under his nails from prying the molding away, and a stack of papers in his lap. A hazy Los Angeles sunset bled through the curtains and spilled over the pages as he carefully flipped through them, illuminating his brother's notes along the margins in golden light like messages from beyond the grave.

Downstairs the worried shuffling of his stepfather approached the bottom of the stairs, hesitated, then turned away again. Julien had purposefully waited to stop by when he knew his mother was out of the house. She wouldn't have been afraid to come up here with him. Sometimes when they spoke on the phone, he'd hear the street sounds in the background and know she was sitting on Rocky's bed, talking to him from her dead son's room. *Where are you?* he'd ask.

Home, she'd say. *Just home. Why?*

There were little signs of her in here too, now. A scotch glass on the bedside table. A half-finished biography on the bed. But in all that time she'd spent in here, the little hidey-hole behind the dresser had gone unnoticed. Julien hadn't expected to find anything there now. It had been years since either he or Rocky had been young enough to squirrel away smokes and booze in the wall.

But it hadn't been empty at all.

Julien turned to the next page and paused. Outside, a car drove past the house, music rising and falling, its bass jarring and out of sync with his pounding pulse. Instead of formulas and coded messages, someone had drawn a crude map of a mountain with a river snaking down its slope. His brother's cramped handwriting was scrawled across the middle, to the left of what seemed to be a waterfall.

Begin at the base of the wolf's tail.
Follow the backbone to the muzzle.
Pluck its fangs.

This at least was different. The only questions now—where the hell was Maudit Falls and what was hidden there worth killing for?

Chapter One

It was exactly the sort of place you'd expect to see a monster. A lonely mountain road, a forest so old it creaked. Hell, it was even a dark and stormy night. Or dark and snowy, anyway. But the way the wind was hurling restless flurries against the windshield as the trees swayed vengefully overhead was enough to put even the most assured traveler on edge.

Julien Doran had never felt less sure of anything in his life, and he'd hit that edge at a running jump about two weeks and two thousand miles ago. Right around the time he'd turned his back on everything—the shambled remains of his family, career and common sense—at the suggestion of a dead man.

He might still get lucky. He might never make it to the

elusive Maudit Falls and instead spend the rest of eternity driving up and down these mountain roads until, eventually, he'd become just another one of the dozens of urban legends the area seemed to collect like burs.

They could call him Old Doran. The Fallen Star. Forty-four years of carefully toeing the line distilled down to this one inarguably absurd decision, and told at bedtime to frighten children into obedience. Don't you know better than to throw your life away on a lie, little one? Do you want to end up like Old Doran? A man who turned down the first role he'd been offered in four years to instead take a secret flight across the country. A man who thought he could open a wound so recently closed, it still wept at the edges. A man who went looking for a monster.

Listen, they'd say. If you listen really closely, you can still hear his voice echoing through the mountains, calling out, *What am I doing here? What did I think I could change? Did I miss my turn?*

Julien glanced at the GPS on his phone, but it was still caught in an endless limbo of loading, the service having cut out about fifteen minutes ago.

"The town proper is on the other side of the mountain," the clerk at the last rest stop had told him. A woman with metallic-rose eyeshadow, a name tag that said Chloe and the unmoving smile of someone sick of delivering the same canned dialogue to every wide-eyed, monster-hunting tourist who passed through. "You'll see plenty of signs for Blue Tail Lodge as long as you stay on the main road. But whatever you do, don't get out of your car after dark. That's when Sweet Pea is his most dangerous."

Chloe had gestured with rote unenthusiasm to the huge display by the counter. A rack covered in souvenirs, and a six-foot-tall cardboard cutout of an ominous, pitch-black figure with glowing green eyes. It had hooves for feet, long, delicate claws instead of hands and the flat face of a primate, obscured by shadow. The figure was standing up on two legs but sort of stooped over, arms held awkwardly as if caught midway through dancing the monster mash.

"Mr. Pea, I presume," Julien had said, reaching out to touch one long cardboard claw. Then he pretended to shake its hand and added in a deep, formal voice, "Mr. Pea's my father. Please, call me Sweet."

Chloe's smile hadn't flickered, which was very fair. Rocky would have known what to say. He would have known the right questions to ask, the right words to use, the best attitude to strike to get Chloe on his side, talking and spilling secrets that couldn't be sold on a souvenir rack.

"Have you ever seen it?"

"Me? No." Chloe shook her head. "But my sister's ex was out hunting and swears it passed right through the campsite. Tore into his cooler and stole all his coyote traps."

"Wow. That's..." The way it always was. *No, I've never seen anything. But my dentist's kid's teacher's nephew woke up in the woods with less beer than he'd remembered packing and a missing ham sandwich. Alert the media—they walk among us.* "That's something."

"Are you in Maudit for—"

"The skiing," Julien cut her off quickly, and launched into his own canned dialogue, taking the opposite approach to Chloe, his voice a little *too* bright, smile *too* mobile, overselling his story. "I would never have thought of North Carolina for it, but a friend recommended the slopes here. He said it's snow without having to freeze your, ah, nose off."

"We get our fair share. And plenty more than that up the mountain," she said, watching him closely, the beginnings of the same frustration in her eyes he'd seen in dozens of people trying to place the face behind the glasses, the fading stubble, the lines that grief and age had carved in unequal measure around his eyes like permanent tear tracks. "I'd pack an extra pair of thermals if you're skiing Blue Tail this weekend, though. For your, *ah, nose*? There's a cold front coming." She tapped the box of single-use heat packs by the register pointedly and Julien dutifully placed a handful on the counter.

He attempted a casual nod at the looming cutout. "Why 'Sweet Pea'? Not exactly the most intimidating name."

"Well, he doesn't need it, does he? Anyone around here knows you don't want to be caught out at night with a monster like that, whatever you want to call it." She plucked a deck of novelty playing cards off the display and placed them on the counter next to the heat packs. "Everything you need to know about Maudit Falls and its most infamous residents is in here. Only $21.99. You know, something to do when you're not *skiing*." That's when her eyes had widened in genuine excitement. "Hey, aren't you…"

Of course he'd bought them. How could he not? Sweet Pea wasn't the monster he was hunting. But it was why Rocky had first come to Maudit Falls, and Julien was here because of him. Why else would he book a vacation in a town whose idea of a fun roadside souvenir was fifty-two spooky local legends? Why else had he done anything at all this last waking nightmare of a year?

Now, as he took a particularly sharp curve up the narrow mountain road, Julien wished he'd left the cards behind and bought a map instead. One a little easier to follow than what Rocky had left for him. This simply could not be the way into town. It wasn't even plowed, for goodness' sake. Just sort of tamped down, which gave the road a colorless, unfinished look. Like nature itself had been peeled back to expose a slippery layer of quilt batting. On the other hand, it wasn't like he'd passed any paths more traveled. There'd been one unmarked turnoff that couldn't have been anything but a service road. That or the perfect set for the first ten minutes of a horror film, which might still be the case considering the seriously questionable choices that had led him to—

An animal leapt in front of the car. Julien had a split second to register the huge, dark shape darting out of the woods, the twin reflection of headlights bouncing off inhuman eyes, staring directly at him, before he jerked the wheel instinctively to the right at the same time a thud rang in his ears.

Weightless slipping. The feeling of suddenly being airborne without getting out of your seat. And then the car dropped down with tooth-cracking finality, directly into the snowy ditch.

For a long moment the world felt impossibly still and silent. Empty. He couldn't hear himself breathing. He couldn't hear himself think. Julien lay against the steering wheel, dazed, pain-free and peaceful for the first time in over a year. Then, like a lever giving way, his body sucked in an agonizing gasp of air. With it, the gears of his brain began to grind once more, and it all came flooding back.

"No, no, no," Julien whispered. He disentangled himself from the locked-up seat belt and opened the door, barely thinking, and then had to catch it when the gravity of the tilted car sent it hurtling back into his shin. Julien climbed quickly out of the ditch and stumbled down the road, unusually clumsy. "Please no. Please, please, please." His hands were shaking, a low, constant tremble, and his arms felt so light, so flimsy that he had the nonsensical urge to let them float above his head, like untying two trapped balloons.

Julien squeezed his fists tight at his sides. Enough. *Do something. No one else will.* He scanned the road, walking back to where he'd swerved, looking for the animal. Not wanting to see it—needing to find it.

But there was nothing there.

Julien found the gouged snow, dark with dirt where he'd first slammed on the brakes and skidded off the road, but that was the only sign of the violence he'd braced himself for. No body or blood. No fur or feathers. No sign that he'd hit anything at all. Except he had.

Hadn't he? That awful soft thud. Not soft in volume but in texture, if sound could have such a thing. Body-soft. Maybe it hadn't been hurt. He hadn't been going fast. Not at all. Even slower than the limit, with all this snow. Maybe the animal had been able to roll over the car and just keep running?

Julien stalked from one side of the road to the other as if

he'd find some clue as to what to do now. As if the animal might have left a note with a sad face and its insurance information. He'd never hit anything before in his life. If it had been there in the road, he could call...animal control? Some sort of wildlife rehab, maybe? But would they send someone to hike into the woods at nine at night to track down a wild animal that may be injured or may be fine?

Julien blew out a long breath that clouded in the air and reluctantly walked back to the car. With no cell service it was a moot point. He'd need to hike down the road until he could get bars, anyway. He'd need a tow truck, too. The very top of the windshield was shattered and long cracks ran like roots over the rest of the glass. The rental company wouldn't be pleased.

The right front corner of the car was flattened, as well. A pool of headlight glass was sprinkled like multicolored confetti in the snow. *Congratulations! You fucked up big-time!* Oddly, there wasn't any other sign of damage in the front. Not that Julien could tell. Nothing on the hood either. Almost as if the only point of impact was the windshield. Was that even possible? If so, maybe the animal really was less injured than he'd feared.

Julien got closer to examine the roof. Even with the car at this awkward angle he was tall enough to see two distinct dents, right in the center. "What the hell?"

Julien ran his hand over one. It was about the size of his palm but distinct. More than a mere ding. As if something heavy had...what? Landed on its feet, then launched itself into the air and kept running? The paint was scratched, too. Four short contrails behind each dent.

Carefully he dragged his own four fingers down the white marks, and the back of his neck prickled as if someone was watching him.

Julien turned, scanning the road and the dark forest beyond. "Hello?"

Barely more than a whisper, his voice still sounded disrespectfully loud. It was only then he realized just how quiet the surrounding woods were. *Unnaturally quiet.* Like every living thing was collectively holding its breath.

Julien took a couple steps into the road, and his boots made a soft creaking sound on the tightly packed snow. "Hello? Is someone there?"

No one answered. Nothing made a sound. Well, of course not. What had he expected? Sweet Pea to waltz out of the trees doing his best Lurch impression? *You rang?*

Julien snorted at his own uneasiness. What did he know about the *natural* amount of noise wild animals were supposed to make, anyway? The closest he ever got to nature in L.A. was when his ex-wife Frankie sent weekly photos of Wilbur the mountain lion sneaking over her fence at night to drink out of the pool. He'd gotten one early that morning in the airport getting ready to board.

Call me back. I'm worried about you. And so is Wilbur!

He'd call her eventually. When he had good news. Or at least something better than this. If he told her he was in Maudit, he'd have to explain why, and right now he couldn't even explain it to himself. He couldn't even *think* it without wondering if the whispers were true. That maybe after years of being wound so tight, something in him really had just snapped.

Julien hauled his bag out of the car, ignoring the subsequent ache in his chest where the seat belt had bit into muscle and skin. There wasn't any sense second-guessing it now. He was either going to find what he was looking for in Maudit Falls or he wasn't. If the latter was true, he'd have proof that Rocky had been wrong, and there was nothing hidden on this mountain but superstition and perilous infrastructure. And if the former...well. He'd cross that bridge when he came to it. Hopefully in a working car.

Either way, he wasn't going to find anything sitting around alone in the dark. He'd done plenty of that these last fourteen months already. Julien began the long trek back down the road, phone in hand.

Ten minutes later, the cold air killed his battery.

"Dammit," Julien whispered. Then, wondering why he was bothering to whisper, yelled it again as loud as he could, followed by a string of every curse he knew. Considering his upbringing on the back lots of Hollywood, that occupied a significant amount of walking time.

It took another fifteen minutes of swearing before Julien finally came across the lone turnoff he'd passed before. *Maudit Falls Retreat*, claimed a very discreet wooden sign tucked back into the woods. It wasn't abandoned or a service road at all—it was some sort of place of lodging. Julien felt a wave of relief. Here there'd be people, power, maybe even a bed for the night, if he couldn't get a ride on to Blue Tail Lodge. Julien took the turn.

Even less effort had been made to clear the snow, and soon the legs of his jeans were soaked with frigid water. He began to shiver and his fingers felt thick and clumsy with cold. Despite the urge to break into a jog and get the hell out of the dark already, Julien stuck his hands under his armpits and kept his steady, careful pace. He'd hardly be able to tell people he was here for the skiing with a broken ankle. When researching the area, there hadn't been anything online about a Maudit Falls Retreat. No mention of it in Rocky's notes either. Hopefully that meant it was a small, word-of-mouth bed-and-breakfast as opposed to shut down entirely.

Five minutes later, he realized neither was true as the road spilled into a clearing in front of a large, gorgeous building.

"What are you doing hiding all the way out here?" Julien murmured, impressed despite himself. Two stories, expansive and surrounded by a wraparound porch, the retreat was a mass of polished wood, stone and glass. Most of the front seemed to be windows, and past the reflected moonlight, Julien could make out a low light inside. He tried the heavy wooden double doors, and to his relief they opened.

The lobby was even prettier than the outside—soothing in juxtaposition to the intimidating exterior. The back of the room was mostly taken up by a large wooden reception desk while to the side a couple of comfortable-looking chairs and a couch were centered around an enormous stone fireplace. Wide pine plank floors were polished to a soft gleam that reflected the light of the fire burning low. That and an old-fashioned green glass desk lamp were the only sources of light. The room was completely empty.

"Hello?" Julien called out. His voice echoed and seemed to get lost up in the high rafters. "Is anyone here?"

Julien walked up to the desk. A large painting of a water-fall hung behind it. The titular Maudit Falls, perhaps? The canvas was a violent mess of blues and purples and a lone figure stood on a cliff's edge with their arms extended, as if begging with the water, as if this very scene was where the falls had got its cursed name.

Vaguely unsettled, Julien called out again. "I've had some car trouble!"

Silence. A bed was starting to look unlikely. He walked toward the open door at the back of the lobby and peered into the darkness. He opened his mouth to call out again, but something stopped him.

Julien took a few steps into the hall, squinting into the gloom. There was an open door on the right, and he peered around the corner. "Is someone there?"

A pair of reflective inhuman eyes stared back at him and Julien yelled out, stumbling backward. The eyes jumped to the ground with a soft thud and a cat darted between his ankles and scurried into the lobby.

"Fuck." Julien exhaled and laughed at himself.

He felt a little ridiculous, but also reluctant to wander farther into the building. Because it'd be rude, and not be-cause his heart had thus far only sunk back down to the general vicinity of his throat, of course. All he needed was a working phone, anyway. Or power. Surely no one would mind that. Julien walked quickly back into the lobby and, with only a second's hesitation, helped himself behind the reception desk. The sooner he could make a call, the sooner he'd be out of here.

There was no landline. But, crouching, he found the

outlet the desk lamp was plugged into, deep at the back of a low shelf, and quickly got his charger out of his duffel and his cell hooked up. As he stood, the Sweet Pea card deck fell from his pocket and bounced out of sight. Julien knelt to retrieve it, and yelled a second time when a furry little paw darted out from under the desk and snagged the back of his hand.

"Fuck's sake," Julien sighed. "You know, so far I'm not too impressed by Southern hospitality." He got even lower to peer under the bottom shelf and sure enough found the same cat staring back at him smugly, card deck half tucked under its chest.

"If you're down there looking for a bed that's just right, Goldilocks, mine's upstairs."

A man's voice. Behind him. Julien shot up to his knees so quickly he would have smashed his head into the desk's top ledge if not for the warm, soft hand suddenly cupping his crown just long enough to act as a buffer between his skull and the wood, then gone. The only proof it had been there at all was a faint tingle where he'd been touched and the distinct absence of a painful head.

"Thanks. Hell, you sca-scared me," Julien stuttered. For half a second it looked like the man standing over him had blank, colorless eyes, as flat as the cat's. But then he shifted his weight and Julien could see it was just a trick of the light. They were a perfectly conventional gray. Nice-looking, even, though perhaps a little washed out in a pale face framed by black hair. Slightly less conventional was the dangerously short, peacock blue silk dressing gown he

wore over, Christ, nothing at all, if the cling of that fabric wasn't lying.

"My apologies." The man cleared his throat politely and
Julien tore his gaze back up, embarrassed. "I'm not up to
date on the proper etiquette for interrupting a thief. It seems
an invitation to bed only terrifies one half to death. How
disappointing for the ego." He squinted at Julien critically.
"To be fair, a keen-eyed observer might argue you looked
about three-quarters of the way there on your own. To
death, that is, not to bed."

Julien gaped, unsure what to feel more offended by first.
At least the critics had the heart to call him names behind
his back. "I'm not a thief," he said finally, because it wasn't
a crime to look old and worn-out quite yet.

"A housebreaker, then," the man said, inspecting one of
his own fingernails with a bored expression. "An interloper.
Persona non grata, though admittedly you look very *grata*
indeed from this angle."

Julien felt warmth spread down his defrosting body and
he quickly pulled himself to standing. The bruise across his
chest throbbed and he had to bite back a grunt of pain—
unsuccessfully it seemed, from the way the man's eyes narrowed with curiosity.

"You're bleeding." It was a statement, not a question,
and Julien glanced down at the back of his hand, surprised
the man had noticed.

"Your cat scratched me."

"If you're hoping to sue, I should tell you her owner is
on his honeymoon and would react poorly to being interrupted."

"Of course I'm not going to sue."

"In that case it's nothing less than you deserve, you trespassing fiend."

"I'm sorry," Julien said haltingly. "I was under the impression that this was a hotel."

The man ran his hand over the wood of the desk with a thoughtful expression. "Is this the *impression* you were under? See, I would have called it a desk, myself, but then I'm a simple, straightforward sort of soul. What you see is what you get."

"Well, I can see quite a bit," Julien muttered under his breath, and to his surprise the man grinned and just leaned back against the wall, causing the robe to slip even higher up his legs.

"And what exactly were you hoping to get all the way down there?" He seemed totally untroubled to be practically naked in front of a stranger. Maybe soaking wet, half-frozen and *three-quarters of the way* to death, Julien didn't look very intimidating. Maybe the man felt physically secure with his younger body and thick, powerful-looking thighs.

The tingling on Julien's scalp where the man had touched him intensified and he dragged an impatient hand through his hair. "I was looking for an outlet to charge my phone."

"But of course you were. I've been known to get on my hands and knees for the sake of an outlet myself. Carry on, Raffles." The man tilted his head to the side, studying Julien in a lazy, knowing sort of way. "Unless you need someone to play Bunny?"

It was the sort of over-the-top flirting men did when

they were utterly certain it wouldn't go anywhere. Teasing and unserious with no genuine interest. Meant to fluster and nothing else.

"I said I'm not a thief," Julien said tightly, suddenly feeling as weary and washed-up as he apparently looked. The crash must be catching up with him. "I'm sorry; it's been a hell of a long day."

He thrust his hand out, then quickly retreated when the man simply regarded it with a single raised eyebrow. Fair enough.

"My name's Julien. I'm on my way to the ski lodge, but had an accident a little ways up the road. My phone's dead, so I hiked down this way and saw the sign and, well, yes, I came in and helped myself to the power. I'm sorry if I surprised you or made you uncomfortable at all." He could hardly say it with a straight face. The man didn't look like he knew the meaning of the word *discomfort*. "Are you a, uh, guest here? Owner?"

"No." The man smiled sharply. He had a small heart-shaped mouth that gave his whole face a sort of pointy, foxy look. "I'm a thief." His gaze flickered toward the door with a distinct frown and Julien instinctively did, too, just as a loud banging sounded.

"What's that?"

"Some cultures call it knocking. You wouldn't be familiar," the man murmured, slipping past him with a sway in his hips that did interesting things to the silk.

Julien looked purposefully away and followed him into the lobby just as the man opened the door. On the stoop stood a woman, dripping with blood.

Julien swore and hurried closer. "What the hell!"

The woman took one wide-eyed look at him and sagged forward, forcing Julien to reach out and catch her. Her body felt cold and fragile against his and she let out a long shuddering sob and began murmuring something frantically into his chest. Julien looked over her head for help, but the man in the robe had backed away, expression closed, almost wary, and Julien felt a corresponding prickle of unease.

"Are you hurt? What happened?" he asked.

"Sweet Pea," she cried. "I saw the monster!"

Chapter Two

Of course Eli had expected it all to go tits up sooner or later. He'd just thought two weeks was a bit quick, even for him.

Though if one liked to quibble, and Eli liked little else more, it had been two months since he was first offered the job as manager of the Maudit Falls "Retreat." Some of that time had even been spent productively: reaching out to old rebel pack contacts, hiring medical staff, setting up the cabins with everything they'd need for runaways to recover, start over, move on.

Was that all interspersed with licking his own wounds, crashing his ex Oliver Park's newly wedded bliss, and drinking the happy couple out of house and home? Very much so. But that had been productive work, too, in its way. Two months ago, he'd been in no fit state to help anyone but himself to another glass of wine. This morning he'd been showing his very first hire, Dr. Mutya Capili, where the fuse box was with a fragile, foreign feeling dangerously close to pride. Well, it was a tale as old as time. One moment you're fiddling with the fuses and the next you're watching your dreams burn down. Que será, será, so they sing.

Though perhaps Doris would be singing a different tune if she, too, found herself sidelined in her own lobby watching a cop man attempt to interrogate a couple of uninvited guests spouting nonsense about some eight-foot supernatural creature lingering around the roadside like it had picked up part-time work as a crossing guard.

Most of the current spouting in question was coming from the woman, Annabelle Dunlop. She'd introduced herself last week, when she'd shown up on his doorstep the first time, significantly less bloody and ostensibly there to welcome him to the neighborhood. Eli doubted that very much. It wasn't difficult to notice her smile had only warmed when she'd realized the retreat had no interest in poaching the wealthy, outdoorsy clientele of Blue Tail Lodge, her own ski resort over the mountain. Eli had told her they were a sanctuary for people escaping bad situations. A place where those who needed to get away could receive help, catch their breath and figure out what came next. It was even almost the truth—a rarity for Eli.

Please, call me Annabelle was a tall, white woman in her late thirties with the sort of powder-soft, crepe-like tanned skin some people got when they started wearing sunblock at twenty-nine. It hadn't put much of a crimp in her obvious good looks, though. She knew it, too, from the way she kept shooting searching, sidelong glances at the man Eli had found intriguingly facedown, ass-up under the desk. Less attractive were the tangy streaks of blood dripping down the side of her face, and matting her long, heavy blond hair.

"I told you, I saw the car in the ditch and pulled over to see if the driver needed help," she was saying, holding the ice pack Eli had scrounged up to her head. "But when I got closer, I heard something, behind the trees. I followed the noise—"

"You walked into the woods?" the cop interrupted. Maudit Falls's very own police chief, David Bucknell, apparently. Also white and in his late thirties, Bucknell was a bit shorter than Annabelle, but broad. One of those people determined to counteract height with the width of their shoulders. He had a pleasant, friendly face that was currently twisted in a concerned grimace. "Alone, in the dark, toward an unidentifiable noise?"

"I thought the driver might have—have wandered off the road," Annabelle stuttered defensively, and sent another glance toward said driver.

Somehow Bucknell's expression turned even more unimpressed.

"I hadn't even gone that far when I felt a—a presence. I knew I wasn't alone." Annabelle's voice dropped to barely more than a whisper and the other humans leaned closer to her, tense and waiting. "I called out, but no one answered. The whole forest had gone quiet. I started back toward the road and heard something behind me. I could tell it was moving fast so I began to run. But it was so dark that I kept falling down." Her voice shook a little and she gestured with the ice pack at the shallow cut on her head. "I hit a branch, but I was too frightened to stop or slow down. I just—just kept running until I got here."

There was a moment of silence.

"And you never left the road?" Bucknell asked, turning to the wayward driver.

It seemed to take a moment for him to realize the question was for him. "No…? Why would I? I hiked down here to look for somewhere to charge my phone and call in the accident," he said, sounding confused. Then his eyes widened with genuine surprise as the implication in Bucknell's words sank in. "Oh! No, I didn't—I would never—"

"David!" Annabelle interrupted. "Of course it wasn't him chasing me around the woods. Don't you know who this is? Julien Doran?" *The movie star?* she mouthed without subtlety.

Surprised, Eli took a more careful look at the man. Or rather a more careful look at the man's *face*, this time. It was hardly a chore. Tall, square jawed and impeccably fit, he was white, in his midforties perhaps, and had very dark hair that glinted auburn in the low lobby lights. Handsome enough to be a *movie star* certainly. Charming enough, too, the way he immediately slipped into an obviously well-practiced bashful look and pulled out a few lines like *Call me Julien, please* and *Not a star, just an actor who got lucky once or twice.* It was a very different character from the awkward and delightfully easy-to-fluster man he'd been behind the desk.

Eli did sort of recognize him now. One of the many effortlessly attractive faces that had graced the blockbusters twenty years ago, before transitioning to guest roles on poorly lit limited series and festival darlings. Eli had even seen one of his later movies once. Some devastating art house film he'd been dragged to on a date, about a man trying to raise a baby goat in the city. It was all an allegory for the opioid epidemic. Apparently. He hadn't actually finished the thing. A well-placed hand and a couple of soft squirming sighs had convinced his date they should leave early. Eli didn't like sad stories.

Doran had changed since then. He had scruff for one thing. More coppery than his head hair, it had even faded to a pale rose in some places, giving the redhead's take on salt and pepper, whatever that was. Garnet and gold. He looked older, too. Granted, it had been over a decade since the goat movie, but there was a new, unmistakable weariness in the tilt of his head, the quiver of his hands, the scent of his skin.

Doran glanced over at Eli suddenly—he'd been studying him too long, even the most unobservant human could have sensed it—and blinked at him curiously. His eyes seemed different in person, too. Big, round and so dark they looked black. Prey eyes, Eli thought absently, biting his lip, and was startled when Doran looked suddenly nervous and ripped his gaze away.

Eli ran a quick hand over his own jaw, nose, ears, scalp. But everything was where he'd left it.

"The skiing," Doran said, answering some question Eli had missed. "I'm just in town for the skiing, but I had an accident up the mountain. An animal ran into the road and I lost control of the car."

Bucknell tensed, looking grim. "Dead?"

"No. Or I couldn't find anything like that, anyway."

"What kind of animal?"

Doran opened his mouth, hesitated. "I'm not sure," he said finally, sounding oddly regretful. "Larger than a dog, I think. And fast. Really fast."

"Sweet Pea!" Annabelle breathed. "Finally, a direct encounter!"

Eli closed his eyes to roll them unnoticed. The absurdity. As if any oft-mythologized species that had managed to remain undiscovered for thousands of years by the utmost secrecy would suddenly start flagging down cars. Eli pointedly ignored the irony as he stuck his own metaphorical flag into the fray.

"Mr. Doran, this creature you saw, be it sweet or otherwise—were they injured by the accident?"

"I don't know," Doran said seriously. "I thought I hit it. But when I got out, I didn't see anything. And it looked like—" he paused, glancing at Annabelle beside him, who was staring so intently she looked like she was seconds away from whipping out a recorder "—like maybe I was wrong."

He was clearly hiding something. Eli stepped closer, inhaling, curious, but Bucknell cut in.

"Plenty of large wildlife in the area—coyotes, black bears, deer," he said. "There's even been rumors of red wolves around here."

"I thought red wolves were practically hunted to extinction," Doran said.

"Not on Blue Tail Mountain." Bucknell shrugged. "Annie and I grew up in Maudit. I've heard the howling myself. Bobcats are out, too, around now."

Eli inspected his fingernail and sighed, telegraphing the peak of boredom. "Coyotes and bobcats and deer, oh my. The list of potential suspects grows long. Or is it potential victims? I've gotten awfully mixed up. What are we investigating again? Hit-and-run? Who stole Mr. McGregor's carrots?" He looked at the handsome one and smiled sweetly. "B & E?"

Doran's jaw flexed. "I'm sorry," he said politely. "I don't remember catching your name."

"I don't remember throwing it," Eli murmured.

Annabelle's laugh sounded a bit forced. "Oh, this is Elias Smith. He's the new manager of the retreat here."

"I heard the place was bought up a couple months back," Bucknell said thoughtfully. "First time this land hasn't had a Nielsen living on it in ninety years. Though I can't say I'm surprised after what happened last summer. Are the new owners—?"

"Based out of town," Eli said smoothly. "I'm looking after things here for them."

Bucknell studied him, assessing, and Eli felt the prickling urge to bare his teeth. As long as he lived, he'd never understand the human urge to stare so shamelessly. He channeled the urge into shifting his weight onto one hip instead, and predictably, Bucknell looked away.

"What about you, Mr. Smith? Were you outside this evening?" he asked some spot over Eli's right shoulder.

"Outside? In the dark? In the *woods*?" Eli shuddered dramatically. "Thankfully there are plenty of renovations to keep me busy indoors."

"You were renovating wearing that?"

"Oh, my goodness, no. But I had to put *something* on to answer the door. There are laws, you know." Eli winked and Bucknell smiled faintly back, amused and dismissive.

"Well, I'm going to tell park services to add a couple men this way to keep an eye out for a potentially injured and dangerous animal in the area. I recommend letting your guests know the same."

Eli cursed silently. "We're not open to guests yet."

"Your staff, then." He looked around as if hoping to catch a member of said staff who looked more like his idea of a professional. Good luck to him.

"I didn't think rangers did that sort of thing—track down animals hit by cars," Eli said.

"They don't. But the truth is—" Bucknell frowned and quickly swiped his hand over his face "—there's been a number of reports of odd animal behavior recently and we want to keep an eye on it."

"What sort of behavior?" Doran asked.

"Oh, nothing to worry about," Bucknell said hastily. "People claiming to hear strange noises. Some minor property damage. But we want to make sure there isn't a sick critter out there. So far all of the incidents have been up by Blue Tail Lodge," he added, nodding toward Annabelle. "Have you noticed anything...unusual here?"

"Besides Goody Proctor dancing with the devil?" Eli said. "No, I can't say I've noticed any animals at all."

"It's not an animal!" Annabelle erupted. "Animals don't

start fires in the woods. Animals don't carve sigils into buildings or leave piles of deer bones on your doorstep or paint the windows with blood."

Eli raised both eyebrows, but Doran beat him to it. "That sounds like, ah, people, doesn't it?" he asked with the trepidation of one being forced to alert someone to the presence of the nose on their face.

"It's no person either," she said grimly. "And now I've got proof."

Annabelle unzipped the puffy black coat she wore and pulled out a plastic box-shaped thing about the size of a large spread hand. It would have looked like some kind of clunky communicator better suited to a sci-fi movie from the fifties if not for the camouflage design. A wild-life camera. The infrared sort that hunters strapped to trees and took short bursts of images when the motion sensors were tripped.

"When the hell did you pick that up?" Bucknell demanded, sounding exasperated.

Annabelle shook her head impatiently as she turned on the little view screen on the back of the camera and started clicking through photos. "Earlier this evening. I was out tonight collecting them before I saw Mr. Dor—Julien's car."

"Them?" Eli asked, feeling cold. "Are any of these cameras on retreat property?"

She flushed and sat up straight on the couch. "No, no, certainly not."

"Because you know that our guests' privacy is very important," Eli added sharply.

"Yes, of course, Mr. Smith. But this was up the road,

nowhere near—Oh, here, look at this." She began to hand the camera to Doran, but Bucknell strode forward and intercepted it. He looked at the screen with a frown, then blew out an exasperated breath.

"Annie, what on earth—"

"No, no, look at this," she said, tapping on the screen insistently. "Does that look like a human being to you?"

"It doesn't look a whole hell of a lot like anything," Bucknell said, handing the camera off. Doran accepted it, looking at the screen with a neutral, politely interested face. Then walked toward Eli and offered it to him.

It took a moment to adjust to the camera's night vision— the silvery trunks, the stark white branches cutting across the frame like cracks in the glass—but then Eli saw it. In the back of the frame, disappearing behind a cluster of trees, a figure was running, hunched over, one long arm dangling toward the ground, the other reaching forward to disappear along with the head and shoulders behind a tree. Its form was blown out—too light for any useful detail—and the obvious, swift movement blurred its body and legs. The only clear part was the right arm hanging down. Long hand loose. Claws sharp.

It was quite obviously a werewolf.

Obvious to Eli, anyway, being a werewolf himself.

The others didn't seem to see it that way. But then there were very few humans in the world who knew werewolves even existed—a scattering of individuals "aware" because of who they loved, some government agencies brought into the loop ostensibly to help keep the secret, the unlucky few who could not be convinced they hadn't seen what they'd seen. Many of these people had been fed the same PR-packaged lines about how werewolves were just like "you and me." Average folk who also happened to possess the ability to fully turn into wolves whenever they wished. Like finding out your accountant occasionally put on a corset to go to the Renaissance fair and drink mead.

It was of course nonsense. Eli had never felt "just like" any human being, whether he was trying to or not. They were an entirely separate species living among the unaware, with their own cultures, customs, politics and histories. Their own stronger senses, bodies, hierarchies and instincts. Their own goddamn troubles, too, like how in the hell to manage a secret sanctuary for werewolves when fanatical humans are wandering around the woods hunting for monsters with cameras strapped to trees, just to name a random example off the top of his head.

The time stamp at the bottom of the screen said the photo had been taken less than two hours ago. It was impossible to tell who it was with their face hidden and their body caught in the intensely private moment of midshift. But what were they doing out there?

Eli's thumb brushed over the camera's delete button without pressing down. It would be too obvious to erase the photo now, here in front of everyone. But tempting. So tempting that his hand trembled against the screen. Every wolf in the world had a responsibility to maintain the secrecy of their kind. If that wasn't drilled into them by their own pack or the ever-watchful Preservation, they learned it quickly enough from how cruel the world was to the perceived other. But that wasn't the only reason he felt tempted.

There was an acutely raw intimacy in witnessing a wolf's shift. How slow or fast, painful or cathartic, where it began, how it ended, how much control the wolf had over "slipping" specific body parts like the claws, teeth or eyes without triggering a full-blown change—most thought it was a reflection of their most private selves. An honest, trembling declaration of everything they spent their lives hiding away. Seeing a wolf's shift midway like this, uninvited, unwelcome, on a *wildlife* camera, was…grotesque. And to hand it back to these people to pore over and dissect felt complicit.

"What do you think?" Julien murmured, standing beside him. "Here be monsters?"

"Monsters be everywhere," Eli said, and handed the camera over with a sigh.

Julien looked at him strangely—surprised, approving, grim?—but he accepted it. Their fingers brushed and Julien turned abruptly to Annabelle and passed the camera on. Eli watched it disappear into her coat again.

"So what do you do with something like that?" Julien asked. "Is there some kind of hotline? Is Agent Mulder going to be moving into the room next to mine?" He winked and suddenly looked a lot more like a movie star than the wide-eyed man who'd washed up on Eli's shores out of the cold.

Annabelle smiled a bit helplessly back, eyes bright, the forgotten ice pack hanging at her side. "As it happens, we do have an expert arriving tomorrow to look at the markings in the woods. I'm sure he'll have loads to say about the picture!"

"What?" Bucknell asked, alarmed. "What expert? What are you talking about?"

Annabelle raised her chin stubbornly. "An expert in local history who just happens to have a background in crypto-zoology."

"Crypto—tell me you're not talking about West," Bucknell said bleakly. "After the things he said to—"

"That was between him and Ian and had nothing to do with me," Annabelle cut him off firmly. "Patrick teaches at university now. He's written books all about this sort of thing and consulted with—"

"Oh, he's written books about monsters. Never mind then, our problems are solved." Bucknell rolled his eyes. "And what happens if he decides to finally write a book about Blue Tail Mountain? The lodge? Do you want this town flooded with freaks looking for Maudit Falls' own personal Sasquatch?" He took a quelling breath, glancing at Julien and Eli. He lowered his voice. "Annie, you said you were done with all this…stuff. The lodge can't take any more bad publicity and I'm, well, dammit, I'm worried about you. Ever since Ian—"

Annabelle's face turned suddenly cool. "Patrick's arriving tomorrow afternoon. If he says there's nothing unusual going on here, nothing but people being jerks, I'll let it go. There's absolutely nothing to worry about." She stood. "I'm sure Julien is anxious to get his vacation started and Mr. Smith can return to—" she glanced at Eli, eyes flickering down his body, and lightly blushed "—his renovations."

"My car—" Doran started.

"Isn't going to be in any drivable condition tonight," Bucknell said roughly. "I'll take you two to the lodge and give Liv a call tomorrow. She'll tow your rental to her shop and ought to have a set of wheels you can use in the meantime."

They said their goodbyes—Annabelle apologizing for disturbing his evening and Bucknell promising extra "presence in the area to keep an eye on things." As they opened the doors to leave, the unsettled lobby air pulled the scent of Mutya lingering in the other room just out of sight past Eli's nose. He wondered how long she'd been listening.

Just before following Bucknell and Annabelle outside, Doran paused, and turned back around to face Eli, silhouetted between the huge wooden doors, with the moon at his back. "Sorry again, about before. I shouldn't have let myself in like that."

"Next time I catch you on a heist, you can make it up to me."

"I wasn't—" Doran shook his head. "There isn't going to be a next time."

"That's the spirit." Eli winked.

Doran sighed, though Eli was sure there was a reluctantly amused twitch to his lips. "Good night, Mr. Smith." The heavy doors closed with a thud behind him. After a moment the sound of Bucknell's car started up and drove away. Eli listened to it gradually fade down the long driveway and disappear onto the road.

Two. Weeks.

"Well, fuck," Mutya said from behind his shoulder.

Eli blew out the breath he'd been holding. "I couldn't have put it better myself. Any idea who might have been out running this evening?"

"Not only can I tell you who, but I've got her in the medical bay right now."

Eli turned to her, surprised, and arched an eyebrow. "Anyone I know?"

"Not yet. But I'm happy to introduce you. While you were out here telling ghost stories around the fire, you got your first guest, Mr. Smith."

She grinned, a slightly unusual expression to pair with informing someone that there was an injured runaway on the premises, but she was a slightly unusual woman. Short, Filipina and heavily pregnant, she had a full, round face emphasized by a blunt bob and a blunter attitude. Dr. Mutya Capili was one of the first, and only, people on the retreat's staff. She'd gotten semi friendly with the retreat's new owners, Cooper Dayton and Oliver Park, last summer during a murder investigation, and when she'd heard they were buying the place, and what they intended it to be, she'd agreed to sign on as part-time medical support. Eli would have preferred someone with personal experience in what they were dealing with, but there was hardly a line out the door of wolves begging to be associated with a shelter for runaways from abusive rebel packs.

Unlike the ruling packs that dominated the culture, rebels had no territory. Other things besides property bound them together. That wasn't always a bad thing, despite what the ruling packs in charge believed. Plenty of rebel packs led stable lives, happy to be left out of the cutthroat politics of the Preservation—an assemblage of the alphas with the largest territories tasked with maintaining secrecy and managing disputes between packs.

But like anyone else, rebels could occasionally be vicious and cruel. And, considered outsiders by the majority, wolves who ran from abusive rebel packs were often left with nowhere to turn. It was one of the reasons Eli hadn't left the rebel pack he'd been in as a young man even when it became clear that the alpha, James, was leading them down a path of no return.

That was what the retreat was for, just as he'd told Annabelle Dunlop. A place where the "guests" could seek sanctuary without fear of being pursued by rebels, where they could catch their breath and rebuild before finding a new pack somewhere else. Sure, he'd left out the whole wolf pack politics bit. But she'd seemed to understand well enough. Wolves weren't the only creatures in the world who needed to escape.

"Is she injured?"

"Just a little shaken up. Not as much as the crowd you were entertaining in here," Mutya said, jerking her head at the lobby with a snort. "Seems she was running in our direction when she played leapfrog with a car in the road. Was that Julien Doran? The actor? My Christopher and I went to see one of his movies a few years back. Ooof." She fanned herself dramatically.

"He looks even better on his knees," Eli said, and the two of them walked out of the lobby toward the east wing. Behind them, Cooper's cat Boogie took the opportunity to dart between their legs and out of sight down the dark hall. Apparently she'd had her fill of welcoming visitors for the night. Eli wished he could join her.

While "medical bay" was a bit of an exaggeration, Mutya was in the process of turning it into a functioning doctor's office. Ruling packs liked to exaggerate all sorts of stories about the brutality of rebels, but the truth was it was a good idea to have medical support on hand. And not just for emergencies. One of the biggest hurdles in leaving a pack was losing its access to carefully built networks of health care, finance and legal protections hidden from the humans. Not quite as dramatic as the popular gory stories of rebel mutts forced to fight it out in cage matches or getting their canines pulled for stepping out of line, but insidious nonetheless. It had gotten harder and harder to secretly share this world with humans without the network of a pack to help. Even the WIP, the only other branch of wolves out there besides ruling and rebels, were forced to work together for some things, and they were literally lone wolves rebranded, fighting for the dissolution of packs entirely.

"Where's our guest coming from?" Eli asked.

"A rebel pack passing through west of here. She says her name is Gwen and heard rumors of a sanctuary spot opening up."

"She says?"

Mutya shrugged. "She didn't want to talk much, and I didn't push. But she did volunteer that she ran into the road because she thought someone was chasing her."

"There seems to be an awful lot of that going around," Eli mused. "She must have been running quite a long time. That photo was taken a couple hours ago."

Mutya just shrugged again. "What had the humans all in a tizzy? Haven't they ever seen a wolf before?"

Eli shook his head, then hesitated, reluctant. "She was… midshift."

Mutya hissed, stopping just outside the door to her office. *"What?"*

"She was mostly hidden behind the trees," Eli amended. "So it might in fact not portend the end of life as we know it."

"That's not how that ski lady made it sound."

"No," Eli agreed. "But she also seems to believe it's a hoofed mountain hermit named Sweet Pea, so I don't know how much luck she'll have rousing fear in the hearts of men with that as her battle cry."

He reached to open the door, but Mutya stopped him. "What are you going to do?"

"I was thinking of beginning with an introduction, then seeing where it goes from there."

Mutya made a disapproving tsking sound. "About the cryptozoologist, the photo, the cops in the woods. As ridiculous as Sweet Pea sounds to you and me, your first guest will be your last one if the whole town decides to play pin the tail on the monster in your backyard. Maybe you should call—"

"No," Eli said quickly, and she looked up at him suspiciously. He tried to look more relaxed than he felt. "Ollie and his whippet have just managed to leave for some semblance of a honeymoon this week. Let's not light the beacons quite yet, mmm? At least not until I've had a chance to inquire after our guest. Who knows, I may be one tête-à-tête away from inspiration."

She snorted. "Someday I've got to find out where Cooper found you. All right, then. Tête your tête, but don't forget I'm heading out in the morning for the next couple of days. Christopher and I need to finish moving. And if there's so much as a whisper of 'Locals Locate Wolfman' on the cover of any grocery store checkout rag, I'm not coming back." She touched her pregnant belly very deliberately and her expression dared him to argue.

"Consider your notice noted." Eli couldn't even blame her. He knew better than most how dark things could get when humans believed they'd found a monster to despise.

Eli and Mutya walked into the office. A woman of about thirty stood by the window overlooking the waterfall, wearing one of the many sweatpants and T-shirt combos the retreat kept lying around all over the place, in case of impromptu shifting. She was white with chin-length hair dyed fire-truck red, and a heart-shaped face that twisted in genuine fear the moment they walked into the room.

Eli didn't get any closer, disconcerted. Pretty much any wolf would have been able to hear them coming in. Subtly he scented the air, but couldn't pick up anything unusual. Just the adrenaline expected from a wolf who'd been running.

"Is something wrong?" he asked as gently as possible. Not a particular gift of his, admittedly.

"Sorry," the woman said after a slightly too-long pause. She shook her head as if even she was surprised at herself. "I'm just a bit jumpy. Long night."

"I've heard," Eli said, carefully continuing into the room

while still leaving her plenty of space. "My name is Eli Smith. I manage the retreat."

"Gwen. Gwen E-Evans," she added, and sounded unsure. That was natural enough, at least. Many wolves took on the last names of their pack's alpha. She might not have used this name in a long time. She might not have used it at all, for all Eli cared. He'd had about ten different identities over the course of his life, himself.

"Welcome, Gwen. Sorry you hit traffic on your way in."

"That isn't me in the photo," she blurted. Eli froze and felt Mutya do the same beside him. "Sorry. I just— I couldn't help but hear you talking in the hall, and that isn't me."

"You believe someone from your pack followed you here?" Eli asked with a frown.

Gwen shook her head impatiently. "No, no, I'm not important enough for that. Besides, I only got to town an hour ago. There's someone else out there. Someone who was already in the woods before I got here."

"Did you see them? Scent them?" Mutya asked immediately.

"N-no," Gwen said with a stutter. "It was like they were… hiding. Always staying downwind, and out of sight, stopping when I did. I even thought I was imagining it at first, but when I cut through the forest over the road, near that other big building, the one by the ski slopes, I…" She paused. "I knew there was someone there. I felt I wasn't alone."

There was a tense silence. Her words hung in the air, an odd echo of Annabelle's story. Stranger still to hear it from Gwen. Humans were constantly freaking themselves out with their muted senses and insistence on ignoring every last bit of animal instinct. Eli could easily believe Annabelle had been "pursued" by anything from a chipmunk to a serial killer out there tonight and she wouldn't know what else to call her body's natural defensive instincts but a *feeling*.

It was far eerier to hear the same thing from a wolf. Unnatural.

Who was out there wandering the woods for hours? There weren't any other wolves that he knew of in the area. The closest were the De Lucas, a large ruling pack to the south, but they had no reason to be in Maudit. And they certainly shouldn't be anywhere near the retreat's territory.

And yet someone had been caught on camera. Someone was lingering around Blue Tail Lodge. And someone was stalking wolves like prey.

Eli felt his hair stiffen slightly and his body ached to slip into a form more defensive than this. He pushed down the urge swiftly. To show either of these women what *his* shifting looked like was about the only thing that could make this situation worse than it already was. Speaking of something unnatural…

"I'm suddenly very curious to see that picture," Mutya finally interrupted the silence, and Eli hummed an agreement.

"One might even say *inspired*," he murmured.

Mutya rolled her eyes. "Well, then? Do you have a plan now?"

"Oh, *plan* sounds so stodgy," Eli said. "But now that you mention it, I think tomorrow is an excellent time to get to know our neighbors."

Chapter Three

Julien walked down the hall and tried very hard to look less suspicious than he felt. Although if anyone did catch him wandering around down here, he could easily claim to be lost. Blue Tail Lodge was enormous. Far bigger than the retreat on the other side of the mountain. Far more run-down, too. A bastardized version of a Tudor-style building, it sat perched at the very base of the ski slopes like a great big molting vulture. So close that Julien could see one of the three chairlifts from his bedroom balcony. The strange sound of its rattling had dragged him out of bed that morning and he'd sipped his first coffee of the day watching chair after empty chair in perpetual loop up and down the dead mountain.

"During the week, we only turn the one on, sunrise

to sunset," Blue Tail's owner, Annabelle Dunlop, had explained later at breakfast. "It's a beautiful ride to the top at any time of year. Even in the summer! There's a couple dozen hiking trails there, hundreds of caves to explore, and of course the old lookout tower. It's the most romantic view in all the Blue Ridge Mountains. If you're in search of that sort of thing," she'd added.

"Here on my own," Julien had said quickly, nipping that rumor in the bud. "Just hoping to do some skiing."

Her lips had curled into a slow, amused smile, and for a moment he'd worried she knew he was lying. But all she said was, "What a pity. Maybe you'll meet someone on the mountain here to change your mind."

Who? Sweet Pea? As far as Julien could tell, Blue Tail Lodge was practically empty. Sure, the larger North Carolina ski resorts like Beech and Sugar took most of the tourist trade, but Julien had still expected *some* people. The only other guests were a trio of German university students who were more interested in exploring the town than the mountain, and an older man and woman couple who wore matching ski gear, spent every waking moment on the slopes and were frankly the fittest seventy-year-olds he'd ever seen outside of Hollywood.

Well, and Professor Patrick West, who was maybe also a cryptozoologist, god help them all. But Julien had only glimpsed him arriving that afternoon before Annabelle had pounced and pulled him away while her assistant, a dogged young man named Cody Reeves, had trailed behind them like an aggressive chaperone. Julien had stood on his little balcony and watched the three of them set off not ten minutes ago, heading toward the site of the first Sweet Pea activity: carved markings at the top of the mountain by the lookout tower. It would take over twenty minutes to get there. Another ten for West to do whatever he claimed to do. Another twenty back. That made at least an hour that Blue Tail Lodge wouldn't have either of its two full-time staff members around and liable to interrupt.

Julien knocked once on Annabelle's office door, just to say he had, and then as quietly as possible let himself inside.

The office was split into two rooms. First, a small sort of waiting area with a faded sofa, chairs and accompanying side tables. It looked as bland and impersonal as the guest rooms. Julien tried the side tables' drawers, but they were both locked. Not the most encouraging sign. But what was he supposed to do? Start breaking furniture? Picking locks? He wasn't a cat burglar, for god's sake. He'd never even played one on TV.

A quick glance around the rest of the room was enough for Julien to know he wasn't going to find anything useful, or at least accessible, in here. To the left, the door that led to the office proper had been left partially open. Julien wiped his sweaty hands on his pants and stepped inside.

It was neat. Or rather more neat than Annabelle's somewhat frazzled energy had led him to expect. There was a small pile of mail, and some pens in a mug with Blue Tail Lodge printed in a different style than it was around the rest of the hotel. An earlier iteration perhaps. The bookshelves behind the desk weren't empty exactly. But they looked more like something in a showroom. Office for sale. A white stone vase here, an abstract gold wire-sculpture

there. A little brass tray holding a half-burned stick of incense which accounted for the heavy smell in the air. A small
succulent in a white porcelain pot shaped like a hedgehog.

Julien had dated a woman in set design once who'd explained to him the delicate art of filling out a background.
The complete absence of knickknacks would take you out
of a movie just as efficiently as if you'd filled the background with stuff incongruous to the characters, she'd said.
Like sound engineers needing to make sure all the diegetic
sound effects are present and true to the scene. Nothing that
was meant to be noticed, but necessary nonetheless. Objects
that supported the general identity markers of a character,
without ever straying into revealing, personal territory.

Julien wondered what she'd make of this room. *Devoid
of intimacy*, he imagined her saying with her thick South
Philly accent. She'd been nice. Smart. Sexy. With strong,
interesting opinions on the pillaged art in major American
museums and an unwillingness to be the pretty, incongruous background set to his "inevitable breakdown."

That had felt a bit harsh at the time. But here he was
two years later breaking into a stranger's office, looking for
any links to a dead man, so Julien couldn't feel too miffed
about it, really.

The downside of having the most pleasantly generic
and uncluttered office in the world was how quickly Julien ran out of ways to avoid doing some actual snooping.
He tapped his pinky against the smooth polished wood of
Annabelle's desk and stared at the closed drawers. To grasp
the little gold handle, to actually open one, felt like crossing a threshold he'd known he'd been approaching since

boarding the plane to come to Maudit. If he turned around right now, he could simply walk away with nothing on his conscience beyond entering an empty room. But once he dug beneath the surface, invaded another person's privacy, violated her trust and hospitality...

"You're the most uptight person I've ever known," Rocky had said to him once, laughing. He was always laughing. Though maybe by then, if Julien had been paying attention, he would have caught the thread of strain there, too.

"I don't think being uptight is a requirement for not wanting you to break into a condemned, boarded-up prison," he'd said. "It feels...disrespectful."

"You mean you don't want the negative publicity."

And would that be so bad? Just for a change of pace? But he hadn't said so. Because that would have caused a fight and Julien hated fighting with Rocky. Hated it to his very core.

"I just don't want you to get in trouble," he'd said instead.

Of course, Rocky had gone to the prison site anyway. Made a video, like he always did. And, as long as he skipped past the bit where the EMF meter supposedly picked up on the ghost of a murdered prisoner, Julien had even felt a little proud of the way his brother had spoken on how the horrific abuses of the prison complex were still happening today.

Not that Julien had told him that, because admiring one part felt too close to approving the other and would inevitably lead to more fighting and Rocky taking bigger risks just to prove to Julien that he could. It was easier in the end to pretend he didn't know about the videos. To pretend he wasn't one of the measly 343 subscribers to *Monster Hunt*, Rocky's blog where he chronicled his travels around the country chasing his latest mythical fixation. That summer he'd been all about hauntings—mine shafts, old theaters, abandoned sanatoriums. But before that had been the two months he'd spent in West Virginia chasing Mothman, and before *that* Rocky had spent an entire spring in the Everglades absolutely positive he'd managed to capture footage of the Skunk Ape.

For over eight years Rocky had fallen in and out of fascination with nearly every type of monster and Julien had worriedly watched every single post and secretly hoped it would be the last. That Rocky would eventually run out of creatures to grow bored of and move on to something less risky. More…real. But there always seemed to be something new to hunt.

The concept of the ghost is the only way to explain where all that energy goes when we die.

Of course, using their human forms, werewolves are able to hold jobs in key positions to control the flow of information.

They used to say the giant squid was a myth, too. It's only a matter of time until Champ the Champlain Lake Monster is next.

Rocky hadn't posted anything about Maudit Falls. Julien assumed he'd come here looking for Sweet Pea—the town did seem to take a certain pride in having its very own goat-ape-flower man—but there were no videos, or photos or mention of having gone to Blue Tail Mountain at all. Not on his blog.

Julien might not have noticed, if Rocky hadn't stopped posting entirely or even responding to the occasional comments from *Monster Hunt*'s handful of die-hard fans. But to ask Rocky why would mean admitting that he followed along closely enough to recognize all five screennames of the self-titled "Crypt Crew."

So Julien had said nothing. He'd said nothing when Rocky started acting distant, evasive and dodging calls. He'd said nothing when Rocky had canceled his upcoming hunt for the Chupacabra in Puerto Rico to isolate himself in their parents' home instead.

Then Rocky was dead and Julien hadn't said anything at all for a very long time.

If he had been less uptight maybe Rocky could have trusted him with what was going on. *Maybe if you were a completely different person, your life would have been completely different.* That way lay madness. But in the trembling, fractured aftermath of loss, every way lay madness. Every single way. Standing here in a woman's office contemplating breaking into her desk, Julien felt closer to sane than he had in the long fourteen months since Rocky's death.

The inside of the desk was nearly as bland as the rest of the room. Office supplies, some Blue Tail Lodge brochures with the same dated font as the mug. One drawer was literally empty. Granted, Julien had never owned a business himself. But part of him had expected more, well, work stuff. Didn't people usually leave some kind of paper trail? Bills? Junk mail? A Post-it note? Of course, everything could be digital now, but in that case where was the computer?

The deep bottom drawers appeared empty as well, but when Julien closed the right one he heard a rattle. There, something tucked into the back corner. He reached around for it and pulled out a statue about the size of his fist. It was different from the style of objects on the shelf. Raw un-painted wood and clearly whittled by hand, for one thing. Sort of horrifying, for another. It was some kind of crea-ture standing hunched over on animal legs.

It didn't look like the drawings of Sweet Pea he'd seen before, though, or any of the creatures he'd learned about going through Rocky's notes. While the statue did have a human-ish head, this one had elongated feet instead of hooves and catlike ears sprouting from the top.

Julien ran his thumb over the sharp tips. It seemed so out of place with the rest of the room. So unusual that Julien worried for one split second that he'd accidentally brought it in here himself. As if his own nightmares had finally overflowed into reality—the nonsensical anxieties of a first-time prowler.

It was only because he was standing there silently star-ing at the thing that he heard the click of the waiting room door opening.

Instinctively, foolishly, Julien reached for the office door and closed it almost all the way, stopping just before slam-ming it shut entirely. If someone was just poking their head in, they wouldn't be able to see him here.

But if someone came all the way into the office looking for Annabelle, well, they might wonder why Julien was in here. With the door practically closed.

I came in looking for—My new rental is ready and—I was just going to leave a note about—I got lost so I—

All of his premade excuses tripped over one another unhelpfully as he stared through the crack at the slowly opening door...

...and saw the half-dressed manager from the night before step silently into the waiting room. Eli Smith—because apparently *that* critical information his brain had no problem remembering in a state of panic. Of course, the man was significantly more dressed today, wearing an absurdly oversize dark green sweater and some kind of voluminous pants tucked into heavy boots that really should have been making more noise than they were.

Julien waited for him to call out to say something and licked his suddenly dry lips in preparation. *No, just me in here, I'm afraid! Are you looking for Annabelle? Me, too. What a coincidence, we're both here on perfectly innocent errands. I was just going to leave her a note...*

But Eli did not call out. He stood there for a long moment, then softly closed the door behind him, took a couple steps forward and reached for the locked side table drawer. Like it had for Julien, the drawer stayed stubbornly closed. But instead of moving on, Eli dropped into a crouch, blocking the drawer from sight. Two seconds later Julien heard it open with a rattle.

What. The. Hell.

Had he picked the lock? Was he *breaking in*? Julien tried to think of what to do. Go out there and give up any hope of remaining undiscovered? Confront him? And say what? There's not enough room in this caper for the two of us?

While Julien stood frozen with indecision, Eli continued to poke around inside the drawer, but shut it without removing anything. He rose, walked to the center of the room and stood absolutely still again. Closer now, Julien could see him take a deep breath and wince dramatically as if something disgusted him. Was he... What was he doing? Without taking a step, Julien leaned minutely forward.

Eli jerked his head around to look directly at Julien as abruptly and unerringly as if he'd called out his name.

"Fuck!" Julien gasped, taking a couple stumbling steps backward. He tripped over the open drawer, which just made him swear again and reach down to clutch at his throbbing shin.

"Up to your old tricks again, Raffles?" Eli said, and Julien almost fell over himself a third time. The man had somehow crossed the length of both the waiting room and office to sit on the desk's edge, inches away, without Julien hearing him approach. "And not even twenty hours later, too. Even I've gone straight longer than this."

"I wasn't—I was just looking for Annabelle. My car is ready and I needed a ride into town," Julien stammered, straightening hastily. "What are you doing in here?"

"Corporate espionage," Eli said in the same lazily indifferent tone as ever, but his gaze was sharp, studying Julien, the room and, of course, the incriminatingly open drawer. "I heard they have the codes to hospitality in here. Did you happen to find it while looking for Annabelle in her desk? Or is this another electrical outlet–based escapade?"

Julien felt his face grow hot. "I saw you," he said boldly, and Eli made a strange face, gone as quick as it had come.

"What do you think you saw?" he asked slowly.

Julien opened his mouth, but hesitated. The truth was not a whole hell of a lot. Eli had just opened a drawer. So what? So had he. But there had been something else there, too. A glimpse of the different way the man moved when unobserved. A strangeness to the way he'd stood so still. Unfortunately, Julien didn't know how to say any of that.

"You were...looking in drawers. Locked drawers," he remembered suddenly.

Something in Eli seemed to relax. He pushed himself to standing and took a couple of languorous steps toward Julien until he was directly in his space. "That drawer wasn't locked."

"Yes, it was. I just—" Julien's mouth snapped shut and Eli smiled.

"Oh dear. Is this what they call an impasse?"

Julien shook his head, but didn't know what he was disagreeing to exactly. He couldn't seem to think clearly, distracted by how...near the other man was. It was strange, wasn't it? Standing this close to someone? Eli couldn't be taller than five foot nine or so, a good five inches shorter than Julien, and everything from his floppy hair to the fuzzy folds of his sweater said soft, delicate. But still Julien's heart was racing as if he was standing nose to nose with a lion.

Ridiculous. A beautiful man was standing close to him and forty-four-year-old Julien Doran, who had two marriages—and two divorces—to his name, was as sweaty-palmed and wobbly-kneed as a kid at his first middle school dance.

"Um——" Julien heard himself say eloquently. He cleared his throat. "Why are you here?"

"Oh, the same reason as you, I expect. Let's both say it on the count of three," Eli murmured. "One, two——"

Julien felt the whittled creature being plucked out of his slackened grasp a moment too late to hold on to it. He made a belated attempt to grab it back, but Eli slipped around him like smoke.

"That belongs to Annabelle," Julien said uselessly. "We should——I was just about to put it back."

Eli hummed, but otherwise didn't look up from the statue. "What does this look like to you?"

"I don't know. Sweet Pea in a pair of cat ears?"

"Cat ears?" Eli repeated incredulously, looking almost offended. Then he laughed, a clumsy sort of huffing sound at total odds with the elegant way he moved and spoke.

"I said I don't know. This isn't my sort of thing," Julien said. "What do you think it is?"

"Do you believe in monsters, Mr. Doran?" Eli ignored the other question, still spinning the creature carefully between his fingertips.

Julien snorted softly which finally made Eli look up at him with a faintly curious expression. "Not the sort with cat ears." He hesitated. "Ah, do you?"

Eli smiled that sharp little smile. "The only visitors I like going bump in the night are the ones that make me breakfast in the mornings." He stood abruptly, placed the statuette back in the desk and closed the drawer.

"What——" Julien began, then quickly shut up when Eli, well, *prowled* toward him. There was really no other word for it. Julien took a few hasty steps backward, and then a few more when Eli didn't slow, essentially herding him back into the waiting room.

"I'd appreciate it if you stopped...manhandling me," Julien said between gritted teeth.

"Please. When I handle men, or individuals of any gender for that matter, it involves a great deal more touching and less of whatever this is." He plucked at Julien's jacket. "Now tell me once more: What exactly are you doing in here?"

"I was looking for—"

The door to the waiting room opened and Annabelle walked in followed by a man Julien had only seen from a distance. They both stopped abruptly, obviously shocked that the room wasn't empty.

"And here she is," Eli said. "Mr. Doran was just telling me he was looking for you."

"Oh," Annabelle said, gaze darting between the two of them curiously. "I hope you weren't waiting long."

Julien shook his head. "No, I—Not long." He glanced at Eli half expecting a contradiction, but Eli just raised an eyebrow as if to say *go on.* "My car is ready, and I hoped someone might give me a ride into town."

"Of course! Cody can take you right away. You didn't see him come in? He was supposed to meet us here with David."

Julien's throat itched and he traced the back of the couch with his pinkie. "Chief Bucknell? Um, why—"

This time it was a relief to hear Eli's despondent sigh cut

him off. "Not our dogged patrolman again. What errant wildlife is he after now?"

The man behind Annabelle snorted softly, which he hastily turned into a cough. "We ran into David on our way to the activity site. He told us about the incident last night."

"Oh, I'm sorry. This is Patrick. Professor Patrick West, the cryptozoologist I was telling you about," Annabelle announced proudly before introducing Julien and Eli.

"The business card says anthropology department, actually," the man corrected good-naturedly, shaking Julien's hand then reaching over to do the same with Eli. "They don't pay me to go looking for cryptids quite yet."

"Will the myopia of academia never end," Eli murmured, and moved to drop his hand almost as soon as they touched, but Patrick held on.

"Have we met? You look very familiar."

Eli smiled and blinked slowly. "If that's the line you use on Bigfoot, no wonder you're still looking."

Patrick laughed. "Thanks for the tip."

He didn't look much like a professor. But then, Julien's only concept of that came from the screen. Patrick was white, tall and approaching forty, at a guess. Blond, with glasses and obviously fit beneath a high-quality snow jacket, he looked like the hero of some inexplicably popular adventure series. The scientist who starts the movie awkwardly babbling data and ends it vine-swinging across an unpassable gorge with the heroine in one hand and his wire rims in the other. From the reluctant way he finally released his hand, it seemed like Patrick was interested in doing that swing with Eli.

Julien cleared his throat. "So, what does the expert think?"

"We didn't make it to the site," Annabelle said. "David said the snow is coming down too hard at the top of the mountain, so we've postponed until the morning."

"But now I get to see the photo," Patrick prompted, and Annabelle clapped her hands in excitement and walked across the waiting room, pulling a key ring out of her jacket pocket. Julien couldn't resist looking at Eli, but he seemed perfectly calm.

"I'm so excited to get your opinion on this, Patrick. I think I've finally found proof." Annabelle bypassed the side table nearest to the door and went to the one Eli hadn't opened. She unlocked it, keys jingling against the metal drawer handle. Far louder than whatever Eli had used to get in.

"I try to record where we've already had activity. Fires. Bone piles." While she spoke, Annabelle pulled out the camera from last night, pressed a button and frowned, words slowly petering out. "That's..." She flipped it around, opening something on the bottom, and cried out. "It's gone!"

"What do you mean?"

"The SD card is missing. Someone took the picture!"

Chapter Four

"Is it me, or did we just do this dance?" Eli said, leaning against the dark wood paneling.

They'd moved, or been moved, to the lodge's breakfast room. A wall of windows, frosted with snow, overlooked the bottom of the slopes, while what smelled like ten years of breakfast sausage grease coated the tables and chairs. It was thick and distracting and Eli felt a headache sparking to life behind his nose bones. Of course, it wasn't just the stink making him want to go home.

Bucknell had arrived shortly after Annabelle had discovered the SD was missing and had promptly corralled them away from the *scene of the crime* for questioning. *Crime* because Annabelle had not merely misplaced the card as Professor Bigfoot had gently suggested and was quickly disproven when she went to check her laptop and found it gone as well. That's when the yelling had really begun, and, as if waiting in the wings for his cue, her assistant Cody Reeves had come charging in ready to fight, rounding their numbers up to precisely five more people than Eli ever hoped to see in the middle of a heist.

It had taken Bucknell a while to convince the hotheaded Cody no one was attacking Annabelle and he could put his fists back down. Frankly, Eli still wasn't sure he wasn't going to go off again and had elected to stand with his back to the wall, while Bucknell, Annabelle, Cody and the professor sat around the table. Interestingly, Doran had opted to stand as well, albeit about as far from Eli as he could get.

"It's okay, Annabelle. All of Blue Tail's files are backed up on my drive," Cody was saying. "We'll be up and running again soon." He was young, white and tall with buzzed brown hair, big ears and a bright red snow patrol jacket pressed deep with the smell of motor oil.

"Not the picture," Annabelle said miserably. "I was so close."

"But Bucky here is going to find the card and it's all going to be fine." Cody handed her a second tissue, straight from his pocket.

"I'm about thirty years too old for nicknames, kid. I've told you to call me Bucknell. Or Chief, if that's easier to remember," he said, sounding amused, if a little tired. "Who has access to the office?"

"Apparently anyone who wants to walk in, *Bucknell*," Cody said pointedly, and shot an accusing look over to where Eli and Doran were standing by the wall, an absurd amount of space between them.

Doran shifted in place. "If you mean me, then yes. I admit I went into the office. But I never touched the laptop or opened that drawer. I was only in there looking for Annabelle."

No stammering, no blushing, no blinking. This wasn't the same guilty man Eli had caught elbow-deep in his host's desk. Actor, Eli reminded himself sharply.

And a quick study, too. This time he'd neatly avoided admitting knowing the drawer was locked. The office had been choking with incense, so he couldn't track Doran's movements through the room or, embarrassingly, notice him there at all. When Eli had realized he wasn't alone in the office, any annoyance at his own carelessness was outmatched by surprise at exactly who was peeking out at him from behind the door.

He'd only been teasing the man last night about being a thief to watch his pretty blush. It was patently absurd to think a famous Hollywood actor would be going on a petty crime spree in a sleepy mountain town.

Or so it had seemed yesterday. Today, after seeing Doran's big doe eyes blinking guiltily at him, that carved *shifting* wolf clutched in his hands, well, Eli wasn't so sure. There was a chance he'd been played. Rare occurrence though it may be, it was still possible. But to what end? He glanced over at Doran and found him studying him intently back.

"And what about you, Mr. Smith?" Bucknell asked, and Eli looked away. "You'll forgive me for asking, but I don't believe I caught why you're here?" He seemed more muted today. Older in the twenty short hours since his last inter-rogation. But that might have just been because he was sat across from Cody, the human iteration of a bull calf.

"A return mission." He twisted his wrist in the air with magician-esque flourish and produced his own, far more elegant alibi—a convenient pack of playing cards. "I found these after you all left last night and assumed someone dropped them?"

"That's mine," Doran said, striding across the room. He reached for the box, but Eli held on.

"How peculiar. I thought you weren't interested in *this sort of thing.*"

"I always try to educate myself on the local culture," Doran said, and then with a little emphasis added, "I enjoy knowing *what's going on.*"

"Then what a joyless life you must lead," Eli murmured, but released his hold on the deck. Doran shoved it out of sight and into his pocket.

"Are you serious?" Cody asked. He stood up, rattling the wooden chair, and just barely avoiding tipping it. "You're trying to say you came all the way over here to return some cards?"

"Cody—" Annabelle soothed.

"I'm sorry, Ms. D, but come on. That's c-crazy!" He flinched slightly and glanced at Annabelle as he said it with an odd expression flitting over his face too quickly to parse.

"Are you implying that I have some reason to lie?" Eli asked politely.

"Not at all," Cody said tightly, taking a step toward him. "I just think it's interesting that you left your own tanking business in the middle of work hours to let yourself into the competition's office while the boss was conveniently out, and just happened to be passing through at the exact moment all our files were sabotaged."

"Tanking? Competition? Sabotage?" Eli repeated, perplexed. "I had no idea the hospitality industry of one-road-in-one-road-out Maudit Falls was so ruthless."

"If you have nothing to hide, you won't mind being searched."

Eli tucked his hands behind his back hastily as his claws prickled. "So that you can confirm I didn't sneak into an office and mysteriously pick the drawer's lock because the success of my business depends on the blurry image of a mythical creature?" he asked with an admirable amount of incredulity considering that was exactly what had happened. "Yes, I can absolutely see why that's far more believable than cutting out of work early to see a cute, famous actor again."

Somewhere to his left, Doran made a small incredulous sound under his breath, but Cody just shrugged. "Who else could it have been? You have to admit it doesn't look good. We practically caught you red-handed."

"Not yet," Eli murmured quietly. "But try to search me and I may soon be."

"What did you just say?" Cody demanded. For a moment it honestly looked like Cody was about to cross the room, which would be very bad indeed. Mostly for Cody. But for Eli, too, as far as maintaining his defenseless persona went.

Then Doran stepped forward, situating himself a little between them. "I was already in the office when Mr. Smith walked in." His dark eyes were unreadable, but there was a faint clench in his jaw.

Eli tensed, waiting to be set up. *He picked the locks right in front of me. I saw him take the card. I say we all search him. I'll get his legs.*

"He didn't go near that drawer, and we were only in there for a minute before Ms. Dunlop and Mr. West joined us. In fact, I'm the only one here who was in the room alone." Eli raised an eyebrow in surprise, studying Doran's profile, but the man didn't so much as glance his way. "I think it's fairly obvious I'm not hiding a laptop on me, but if you want to search, I understand," Doran added, raising his arms so that his close-fitting long-sleeve shirt rose and a sliver of skin above his waistband peeked through.

"No one is searching anyone," Annabelle interrupted. She shoved away from the table. "Mr. Smith, please accept my apology. Cody didn't intend to accuse you of anything. Did he?" She shot her assistant a sharp look.

Cody hesitated. His face said that was exactly what he'd meant to do, but what came out of his mouth was a begrudging "No."

"No. Of course not," she agreed with a hint of warning in her voice and a calm sort of resolve that hadn't been there before. "Now, I'm sure this has all been a simple misunderstanding. I'd like to move on, please."

"Can't do that, Annie," Bucknell said, piping up at last. "There's been a crime. I'll need to file a report and—"

"No, I don't think there has," she said firmly. "I'm sure I've just misplaced them. Like Patrick said."

Professor Bigfoot looked surprised to be called out from

where he'd silently been enjoying the show, but just said, "Seems reasonable. I do it all the time myself."

Bucknell shot him a frustrated look, before turning back to Annabelle. "Are you sure that's what you want?"

"Maudit is a good, safe town," she said. "We don't get break-ins, do we."

They shared the long speaking look of friends who had known one another for years.

"All right," Bucknell said finally. "But I'll want to look through the office again with you. Make sure nothing else was…misplaced."

"I'll help," Cody said immediately, glancing at Eli. "There are some very valuable items in there."

That seemed unlikely to the point of absurdity, but it was as good a line as any to feign insult. It was always nice to enter as a burglar and leave as the wronged party. Second only to not being noticed coming and going at all. "On that note. I hate to flee the scene, but I'm getting the strangest feeling that I've overstayed my welcome."

"Oh, not at all," Annabelle exclaimed, shooting Cody an annoyed look. "Please don't rush out."

"You have inventory to account for. I wouldn't want to be accused of being a distraction. There's an overabundance of accusations going around as it is."

Annie offered to walk him out and they left the others behind. On his way out, Eli cast one last curious glance at Doran only to find him studying him intently yet again. Eli wiggled his fingers goodbye and winked—Doran quickly looked away.

It was snowing outside, but not as badly as he'd expected.

Eli took a deep breath of cold winter air with relief. Ice, rocky dirt, sleeping trees, car exhaust, the mildew of someone's winter boots, various humans, some familiar and some not, a bobcat making off with someone's trashed fries.

"You must think we're horrible people," Annabelle said glumly. "Cody's normally not like that. He just feels..."

"Overprotective?" Eli guessed, clearing the scents from his nose and opening his eyes.

"Of who, *me*?" Annabelle asked. She sounded more surprised than he thought that deserved.

Eli just shrugged. "Isn't that what all the old poets sing? Boy likes girl. Girl likes monster. Boy flies into rage when girl's monster photo disappears from her locked desk. Play on, sweet bard."

Annabelle let out a throaty laugh. "Would you call that a rage?" she mused. "Anyway, I was going to say he feels useless."

"Is he?"

"Not at all," Annabelle protested. "We run the lodge together, these days. After Ian left I was...well. Part of me just wanted to burn the whole mountain down. Cody wouldn't let me."

"Ian's your ex-husband?" Eli guessed.

"In everything but. We never actually got married. Ian said he didn't believe in it. What he really didn't believe in was merging resources," she added wryly. Then, "Boy meets girl. Boy persuades girl to invest everything she has into buying a business and building their happily-ever-after. Boy decides maybe this isn't how he wants to spend the rest of his life after all, thanks anyway, good luck with that."

"Mmm, I've heard that one before," Eli said.

"Me, too. But I still danced along until the very end." She stared out over the mountain. "He had this…quality to him, even when we were kids. He could convince you that any moment was meaningful. A turning point you'd spend the rest of your life looking back on thinking thank god I took that risk. *These are the choices that separate the special people from the crowd,* he'd say. Except people were only special when Ian needed them to do some foolish idea that served him. Every single shred of gut instinct could be screaming no, don't, but then Ian said you'd be crazy not to. *Don't you want to matter in this life? Don't you want to be worth anything at all?* And the next thing you knew you were signing your life away."

"What a delightful human being," Eli said mildly. "Where is this paragon? Enjoying a veritable buffet of just desserts, one hopes."

Annabelle laughed. "I have no idea. We're not in touch. Last year he cleared out his accounts and told me he was too smart to never make it out of the mountains. In retrospect I suppose that was another reason Ian insisted on not getting married. Quick and painless exit."

"Doesn't sound particularly painless to me. Did you both grow up here then?"

"Mmm, the four of us," Annabelle said. "Patrick, David and I. Ian moved here high school junior year."

Eli arched an eyebrow, surprised. "Professor Bigfoot is from Maudit?"

"That's right. Although good luck getting him to admit it. I think he likes acting like we're just another one of his anthropological studies. But the four of us were friends, once."

Eli hummed. "I didn't get the impression he and Bucknell were particularly close."

"No," Annabelle agreed. "It was Ian who brought us all together. He was just one of those kids who always had a group around him. Every other week of senior year he'd dare us to spend the night up in the lookout tower at the top of the mountain, scaring each other shitless."

"One of his infamous foolish ideas?" Eli guessed.

"No," Annabelle said seriously. "Those were some of the happiest days of my life. We all had such lofty, ridiculous plans then. David was going to be a big-shot senator and Patrick was going to be a famous author and Ian would build them up. Make them believe it until we started talking like it was inevitable. Like our dreams had already come true. There isn't a drug in the world that can compete with the ego rush of being sixteen, happy and naive, you know?"

He did not. Eli had spent most of his teenage years focused on surviving one season to the next. Although, he supposed, occasionally that had required its own sort of naivete. "I can imagine," he said vaguely, and turned the conversation back away from himself. "What was your dream back then?"

"Mine?" Annabelle said as if surprised.

Eli shrugged. "Didn't you build any castles in the sky sitting in your castle in the sky?" he asked.

Annabelle was quiet so long, he half expected her to ignore the question. "Before your bosses bought it, the retreat was the last bit of land around here still owned by the Nielsen family. Do you know much about them?"

Most likely more than Annabelle did. Now dead, Dr. Nielsen had been a wolf, and a fairly influential one back in his day. Not in the sense of controlling a large pack—in fact, he'd defied expectations of the time by isolating his small family here on the mountain—but he'd been one of the original developers behind the AQ, or alpha quotient. A test that theoretically determined what strengths and weaknesses a wolf would bring to a pack dynamic.

A growing contingent of wolves believed it was nonsense, of course. Antiquated, problematic pseudoscience as unreliable and biased as any IQ or personality test. But Eli had never met a wolf who hadn't taken it. Either out of pack tradition or just to see. Nielsen himself had grown obsessed with the theory of manipulating an individual wolf's alpha quotient, growing more and more secretive with his research.

As far as Eli knew, after a series of murders at the retreat—then run by his last remaining family—all of Dr. Nielsen's research had been seized by Trust agents. He could only assume it had been passed on to the greedy paws of the ruling packs by now. The Preservation loved nothing better than the possibility of legitimatizing a hierarchy.

"I know most of this mountain used to belong to the Nielsens," Eli said to Annabelle.

"That sums it up. The father was some sort of scientist and his children ignored us entirely, so of course Ian was completely fascinated by them. Honestly half the reason I think he dared us to camp on the mountain was to force

Dr. Nielsen to come yell at us to go home." She pursed her lips. "We wouldn't even be doing anything wrong. I have no idea how he'd know we were out there. But every time without fail he'd show up bellowing, like we were possums in his trash. I hated it. Hated how enamored Ian was with him most of all. I wanted to own all this land so no one would ever be able to make us leave again." She smiled. "Oh, and so that Ian would be enamored with me instead. Like I said, the delusions of puberty."

"Here's to living half the dream, anyway," Eli said.

Annabelle's smile twisted. "Yes, isn't it wonderful. A failing business, Sweet Pea scaring away any chance of guests, everyone around me acting like I've lost my mind—I've really managed to manifest something here."

Eli studied her. "May I ask you an honest question? What makes you so sure there is such a thing as Sweet Pea?"

"I've seen it out in the woods," she said immediately.

"Last night, you mean?"

"Oh goodness, no. It's been years," Annabelle said, surprising him. "The very first time the four of us were on our way to the tower one night, back in high school. It was just a glimpse through the trees, but I'll never forget the sound it made as it was standing. Like the mountain itself was falling down. David was the only other one of us who saw it. Then later he changed his mind, as soon as Ian and Patrick said they hadn't." She rolled her eyes.

"Hmm," Eli said neutrally. "And was that the last time for you as well?"

"For a while. But when we moved here I—I noticed things in the woods. Holes in the ground, markings on the trees, that horrible *clacking* sound. I was so frightened, some days I couldn't go outside alone. But Ian said—" She shook her head.

"He didn't believe you?" Eli guessed.

"No. At first he said it was just the sounds of living in a big place like this and I'd get used to it. But I didn't. It just got worse. Of course it didn't help that I only ever heard the sounds when he wasn't there. Ian thought I was manipulating him. Trying to make him feel guilty for going out. Then after he left it got worse. I started feeling it follow me around, everywhere I went. And then came the fires, and the bones and the blood. And once—" She hesitated. "Once I woke up and it was in my room. Just... standing there in the dark. All I could see was its shadow but I knew it was watching me."

Eli's claws prickled. "How horrific," he said, honestly. "Did you tell someone?"

"I told everyone. I screamed it all over the lodge, which did wonders for our bookings, let me tell you. A little piece of professional advice—if you want to get good reviews on the travel sites, don't tell all your guests a monster broke into your room to murder you in your bed."

"Or make reports of stolen property in front of famous actors with the power of publicity?" Eli guessed.

Annabelle snorted and shook her head. "Now you're catching on. I don't know what Cody was thinking, honestly. He's the one who's always insisting we don't report. That we can't afford any more bad press. You'd think he'd know better." She eyed him. "Look, it's okay that you don't believe me about Sweet Pea. No one does. Well, Cody says he does, but I know he's just humoring me, the big softie."

Eli bit back his opinions on Cody's relative softness. "Annabelle, let's say you did indeed see something in the woods as a child. What makes you think it's the same…creature standing over your bed? Rooting through your drawers. Isn't it possible that there's a person out there who's taking advantage of your fear to fuck with you?"

She looked at him pityingly. "Trust me, if you'd seen what I've seen, you'd be able to tell the difference between a human being and a monster, too."

What could he say to that?

"Tomorrow morning I'm taking Patrick to the first activity site," Annabelle said. "I think you should come along."

"Why?" he asked carefully.

"Because you live here now, Mr. Smith. And whether you believe in it or not, there is something out on the mountain, and it's not going away."

Julien stared out the passenger-side window, relieved to be driving away from the lodge. Patrick the cryptozoologist or professor or whatever he was had offered to give him a ride to pick up his car, claiming he needed to grab some things in town.

Privately Julien suspected he was just looking for an excuse to get out of there as well. The atmosphere had been awkward after Annabelle and Eli had walked out. Bucknell was quiet and distant, staring after them with concern, while Cody became almost obsequious in his attempts to assure Julien he never meant to imply a man like *him* had stolen anything. Julien had been half-tempted to tell the truth, that he had been rifling through the drawers just to see the look on his face. Not that his snooping had done any good. But what had he hoped to find? A file titled *Cover-up*? *Murders A-Z*?

The most suspicious thing in there was the manager of that retreat and Julien had risked his own alibi to leap to his defense. Perhaps it would have been smarter to stand back and watch what happened the way Bucknell had. To see what might be revealed. But the thought hadn't even crossed his mind. For one thing, Eli was about the only person he was sure hadn't stolen the card and laptop. More importantly, he'd seen the way the man's hands had been clenching behind his back and the slight tremble in his body when Cody had demanded he be searched. It made him feel…something. Annoyed, at the very least. He had no patience for bullies like Cody.

"Strange day," Patrick said, startling Julien. It was almost dusk and the falling snow was distracting in the way it appeared so suddenly in the headlights.

"Was it? I hadn't noticed," Julien said dryly. "I guess you're used to this sort of thing in your line of work."

"Teaching? The closest I get to theft is a bit of plagiarism here and there."

"Ah, no, I meant the other thing."

"I know. I'm not sure what Annabelle told you, but ninety-five percent of cryptozoology is comparing casts of footprints people bring me. Insider tip: always bet on bear."

"Thanks," Julien said. "I'll keep that in mind."

Patrick grinned and some distant part of Julien's brain noticed he really was a very good-looking man. He wondered if Eli had thought so, too. "You probably get sick of hearing this, but I'm a big fan of yours. What was that one with the sculptress and the stalking?"

Julien tried not to wince. His first proper movie over twenty-five years ago. He'd been nervous as hell to work opposite Penny Carr. A brilliant actress cast as the lonely, bitter, withered artist whose success was a distant memory at the ripe old age of thirty-fucking-nine, god help them all. "*Antiquity*."

"Right. My sister Rebecca wore that DVD out." He added a wink as if Julien didn't remember he'd been twenty and naked for his three short scenes.

There was a long silence, then Patrick said in a rush, "Are you here doing research for another movie? I won't tell anyone. Well, maybe Rebecca. But she can keep a secret."

"No," Julien said shortly. Then, "I'm—I'm not working on anything right now. Just here to get away."

He felt Patrick's gaze on him for a long awkward moment and almost cringed at the gentleness in his voice when he finally broke the silence. "Well, it's a good area for that."

"Have you stayed at the lodge before?" Julien asked a bit desperately.

"A few times. And twice at the B & B in town. If you ever have a hankering to see a peach plush rug, that's your chance." Patrick winced. "Once at the motel off the highway. I do not recommend. Woke up with all sorts of mysterious bites, none of which I'd want to take a cast of, if you know what I mean."

"Not the Maudit Falls Retreat?" Julien asked, not nearly casually enough. He felt Patrick shoot him another curious glance.

"I haven't had the pleasure, no. It was some sort of superexclusive couples counseling center until a few months ago, I think. I didn't know it had been sold."

Julien hummed. That explained why Rocky hadn't stayed there.

"Have you met Mr. Smith before?"

"Just last night," Julien said. "After the accident."

"He's..." Patrick trailed off and Julien finally looked over at him. Then looked away when he saw the thoughtful expression, the glimmer of interest in his eyes.

You should see him in silk, Julien thought. He cleared his throat. "So why do you keep coming back to Maudit Falls? I'd think there are bear tracks all over the world."

"This area has a bit of a reputation for people like me."

"Teachers?" Julien asked wryly.

Patrick laughed. "The *other thing*. Appalachia has an incredibly rich and complex history of folklore. A large number of the legends originated with the local indigenous tribes, particularly the Cherokee people whose nation is just southwest of here. Some stories were brought over by early colonizers of course. Others are as recent as the UFO craze of the late '40s. Then of course there's the biblical influence—" He stopped and glanced at Julien. "Sorry, I went into lecture mode. I'm boring you."

"Not at all," Julien said.

Patrick laughed like he didn't believe him. "Anyway.

I'm not here for myself this time. Annabelle and I...were friends. We've known each other thirty years."

Julien looked at him, surprised, and more than a little curious about that pause. "I didn't realize. Lucky she has a friend with so much, um, background in, you know, this sort of thing." A strange expression flickered across Patrick's face and Julien worried he might have insulted him. "Sorry, I didn't mean to sound rude."

"Not at all," Patrick insisted. "I'm just feeling some good old-fashioned guilt. It's been a long time since I've visited. Annabelle and I had fallen out of touch. I had no idea things had gotten so—" He shook his head. "I probably still wouldn't know if Cody hadn't reached out."

"Another old friend?" Julien asked doubtfully.

"I wouldn't say that," Patrick said wryly. "But he seems to think I'm the only one with the credentials to convince Annabelle to give up her Sweet Pea crusade."

Julien frowned. God knew he thought Annabelle was wasting her time, too, but something about the idea of them conspiring behind her back left a bad taste in his mouth. Apparently, Patrick noticed.

"It's not like it sounds. He's just worried about her. We all are."

"Because she believes in Sweet Pea?" Julien asked, confused. "Isn't that—that is, I thought—don't you?"

Patrick laughed. "A bit pot kettle black, you mean? It isn't the belief, no. Not on my part, at least. She and Cody have been working on this big deal to sell the lodge for over a year and apparently she's suddenly changed her mind. Which is odd because before it was her who was desperate to sell and her ex who convinced her not to. Cody's been—" He hesitated and then glanced at Julien almost guiltily. "Sorry, this isn't what you wanted to talk about."

This was exactly what Julien wanted to talk about, and he had to clench his hands into fists to stop himself from yanking the emergency brake and demanding to know everything Patrick did. Desperately he tried to think of something to say that would get him to keep going. "I don't mind. Actually after this afternoon it'd be nice to know what's going on."

"Oh, I doubt that has anything to do with it," Patrick said dismissively. "Unless... Are you sure Mr. Smith didn't go into any drawers?"

"I was with him the entire time," Julien said. Not technically a lie. "Anyway he doesn't really seem the type." *That fucking was.*

But surprisingly Patrick made a sound of strong agreement. "He'd be a terrible thief. Those aren't exactly the sort of looks that blend into a crowd."

"I don't understand what he has to do with not selling the lodge, though," Julien said a bit impatiently, trying to push Patrick back on track and away from thoughts of Smith's looks.

"Oh, Cody's convinced that someone's cooked up all this Sweet Pea stuff to sabotage the deal. The whole reason he's invited me here was to help him convince Annabelle that Mr. Smith is seconds away from snatching their only ladder out of this money pit away for himself. Unfortunately for him, now that I've spoken to Annabelle, I'm not convinced there isn't something going on. And I certainly won't be making a determination about that until I've seen these activity sites."

"That's good," Julien said, surprised to find he meant it.

Patrick grinned at him. "You still think I'm ridiculous, don't you."

"No," Julien said hastily. "That's not—" He stared out the window. It was just getting dark enough to catch his reflection in the glass. "My brother was really into this stuff," he heard himself say. "If he were here, he'd be drilling you for every last drop."

"Well, if he wants some book recommendations, let me know." Patrick paused. "That was a very unsubtle plug, just so we're clear. The books I'm recommending are my own. Well, one of them is. The others I'm more of a contributor on, but still."

Julien opened his mouth and his throat closed. An awkward beat passed before he just nodded and managed a gruff "Thanks. What, uh, sort of books?"

Patrick looked pleased and not a little surprised that Julien was interested. "The most popular is one I cowrote with a colleague of mine: *Evolution of the American Monster*. It's our attempt to separate out the conventional cryptids from the more fanciful ones."

"Conventional cryptids?" Julien asked.

"Oh, you know. The Loch Ness Monster. Bigfoot. The ones where there's no real compelling evidence why they shouldn't exist. I'm a biological anthropologist in my real life, so my main interest is distinguishing what creatures have evolutionary precedent and which are just…well, folklore."

"So the fanciful cryptids are stuff like mermaids, were-wolves and vampires?" Julien guessed, studying Patrick's face carefully. "You don't, uh, believe in those?"

Patrick just laughed, apparently unbothered by Julien's wariness. "It'd be pretty difficult to make a scientific case for mermaids. Although—" He launched into something about an Aboriginal myth called the bunyip and the rest of the ride was spent back in lecture mode.

It wasn't a long drive off the mountain, when there weren't animals leaping in front of cars or scantily clad men flashing their impressive upper thighs. In less than an hour Julien had made it to town, waved goodbye to Patrick with a list of titles in his pocket to "pass on to his brother," picked up his new rental car and was utterly stumped on what do next. He didn't want to turn right around and go back to the lodge. It was winter dark, so still early, and the thought of sitting around the dining room making small talk with no idea how he was supposed to move this theoretical investigation along was excruciating.

Julien walked up and down the charming Main Street. It was that strange week between Christmas and New Year's when time ceased to feel real and the town was decorated accordingly. The trees were strung up with lights and many of the shops had painted their windows. One of the book-stores had the same cardboard cutout of Sweet Pea as the gas station in its display, although this one was wearing a jaunty snowflake scarf and a pair of reindeer antlers. Julien bought two of the books Patrick had mentioned to add to the pile, signed an autograph for the cashier, then bought another she recommended herself.

He saw the fit, older couple Mr. and Mrs. Miura from the lodge sitting inside one of the cafés and considered saying hello and telling them what had happened at the lodge. They were sitting in the window table—he was telling some quiet story and she reached out to sweep the fall of hair off his forehead, and Julien changed his mind at the last minute. It felt violent somehow, to interrupt their contentment with his neediness. *Can I sit with you? Just for a bit? Just long enough to not feel so alone?*

Julien found a bar that served food and ate dinner by himself. He tried to read one of the new books under the table, but kept losing focus, watching the people pass by on the street instead—faces illuminated under the tree lights.

Eight years ago he and Frankie had been at a New Year's Eve party in San Francisco when Rocky had called from a compound in the middle of the Emerald Triangle. It was his winter break and he'd told everyone he was staying at school. "Getting a jump on those senior year applications" had actually meant going Bigfoot hunting and landing himself in the middle of a drug feud.

Sometimes when Julien woke up at three in the morning choking with fear, it was that New Year's Eve he was reliving. Dreaming of a world where he hadn't picked up. Or Rocky hadn't called. He had to remind himself that's not what had happened. That Julien had driven the five hours north to bail him out and rung in the New Year yelling about irresponsibility and selfishness and never again. And because Rocky knew him better than anyone in the world, he'd seen right through it all.

I'm fine, Juley. Nothing's going to happen. I promise, okay?

It had been his therapist who'd urged Julien to go into Rocky's childhood room. The first time Julien had been in there since his death. They'd shared the room once, for the brief five years their lives in that house had overlapped. He'd been the one to teach Rocky where the molding could be pried away. The little hidey-hole that was the perfect size to hide smokes and a six-pack. Which was how, almost fourteen months after Rocky's death, Julien had found the notebook, the flash drive and the map of Blue Tail Mountain.

He'd booked the first flight out he could.

Now what? What exactly did he expect to find? Where did he even begin?

Rocky wouldn't have come here looking for trouble. Just like he hadn't been looking for a meth lab when he'd tracked the Mothman into a hidden outpost in the mountains or trying to catch that sheriff in the Everglades on tape running an extortion ring. *They destroyed all my footage, Juley! I had four whole seconds of the Skunk Ape on there. I swear! You have to believe me! For real this time!*

Every single violent crime, fraud scheme, cover-up and payoff Rocky had ever stumbled into had been circumstantial. Because it was the Ningen and the shape-shifters and the motherfucking Loveland Frog that he cared about. It always had been.

Julien put the book away and pulled out the deck of cards, spreading them out on the table. Rocky would never have broken into Annabelle's office looking for murder. He would have been out on that mountain hunting for Sweet Pea. So that's what Julien would do, too. At least for now.

Chapter Five

Eli was in fur when he heard the car pull down the driveway. He'd been about to run the property boundaries and had just shifted with relief—stretching into the full length of his spine, yawning widely until his jaw popped and settled with a thrum of pleasure that resonated from the tips of his ears to the pads of his paws.

It was peculiar to think some wolves resented this. That there were those who even resisted the need to shift daily, putting it off or spending as little time in fur as possible. His ex, Oliver, could get like that sometimes. Too wrapped up in the narrative of it all. Tangled in his own history as one of the most feared wolves on the Eastern Seaboard. Yawn.

When they'd been together, Oliver had been fascinated by why Eli was so comfortable in fur, and how he could so easily blur the lines between shapes to suit his needs. Every wolf Eli had ever known besides his sister and himself only had the two forms—a slightly oversize but otherwise average wolf, and an upright being visually indistinguishable from a human. Fur and skin. Of course, there were those who could "slip" their claws, eyes and teeth while in skin without triggering a full change, but these were small, localized shifts that often had more to do with defensive instinct than deliberate control.

Eli's body had always been a bit more...fluid.

He could slip any part of himself he chose at any time. Lengthening his human jaw to a snout or shifting a furry ear to the top of his head was as easy as flexing a muscle or straightening a joint, and unlike his fellow werewolves he didn't require a full transformation from one form to another to do so.

If Eli needed to jump higher while in skin, he slipped his leg muscles to those of a wolf. When he had to grab hold of something while in fur, it was effortless to slip an opposable thumb from his paw. And if he wished to horrify humans and wolves alike, he simply had to let his body drift somewhere in between the forms and rest there in its most relaxed state. A nightmare. A sacrilege. A curse.

"Your slipping must be why you're always so at ease in fur," Ollie had decided eventually, and Eli had let him think so rather than risk telling the truth. Better to be seen as an oddity to be protected than a monster even among monsters.

Only a select few even knew about his particular peculiarity, anyway. There were too many ways an ability as *unique* as his could be exploited. And had been, before Ollie's grandmother and then-alpha, Helena Park, had swept in, plucked Eli from the depths of the darkest hole of his life and secreted him away on their estate to lick his wounds in hiding for years. He rather thought managing a top secret sanctuary in the middle of the mountains would involve a similar sort of isolation, but apparently not.

The car parked in front of the retreat. As he watched from the tree line, a man and woman stepped out. He felt the stiff guard hairs down his back stand up a second before the newcomers' scents registered. Wolves. No one he recognized, which wasn't ideal. Though there were plenty of scents he did know that he didn't want to catch stepping out of that car either.

Eli growled very softly and watched the woman whip her head around to stare directly at him. The man was slower, reacting to her rather than hearing anything himself, but he also zeroed in on Eli behind the trees.

"Elias Smith?" the woman asked.

Eli hesitated. It went against every instinct to shift into skin to go greet a potential threat. On the other hand, it was a lot harder to play innocuous in all this muscle, tooth and fur. Not to mention a depressing inability to flutter his eyelashes. But needs must.

He shifted, purposefully slowing the change to look awkward and pained, and even threw in a couple of tortured whimpers. He hoped Helena had continued to keep his secrets after leaving her pack, otherwise this whole dramatic performance would be pretty embarrassing.

The wolves waited patiently for him, watching with

neutral expressions. When his last joint was in place, Eli trotted down to greet them, adding a little wobble in his step for good measure.

"We apologize for interrupting your run," one of them said genially. She was a tall, willowy Black woman impeccably dressed in an all-black suit, with a slightly crooked jaw, strikingly beautiful almond-shaped eyes, and short silver locs that looked out of place on her twentysomething face. The man beside her was intimidatingly large, white, bald and far more casually dressed in tight black hiking clothes. He didn't recognize either of their scents.

"I'm afraid I've already bought all the Mary Kay I can handle," Eli said.

The woman laughed lightly while the man's expression didn't change. "My name is Nia and this is Brett. We're here on behalf of the De Luca pack. May we?" She nodded at the retreat door.

"Be my guest." Eli made an elaborate gesture for them to enter and followed, quickly excusing himself to put on clothes. Nudity between wolves was inconsequential, of course, but he wanted a moment by himself to think and ideally locate some backup in case things got ugly.

The De Lucas were a ruling pack whose territory extended right up to the border of Maudit Falls. While nowhere near as famous as the Parks or Nguyens, Celia De Luca had been on something of a power rise in the last few years, rapidly acquiring territory and incorporating smaller packs into her own. He knew there'd been some sort of run-in between Celia's second-in-command brother and Oliver last summer during a murder investigation that had resulted in the brother's merciless and oft gossiped-over demotion, but he couldn't imagine why she'd send an envoy here now. Somehow he doubted it was to bring him a welcoming fruit basket.

Unfortunately Mutya had left that morning and he couldn't find Gwen, so Eli returned to the lobby with no one but Cooper's cat Boogie trailing at his heels.

"There," he said flaunting the thigh-length sweater he'd left by the back door and a thick pair of socks he'd thrown on. "Now we can look like we're going to *three* very different parties."

The man, Brett, had taken a seat by the fire while the woman, Nia, was on the opposite side of the room, admiring the large painting behind the desk. Unless Eli stood directly in front of the fire, less than a foot from the flames, he would be unable to keep both of them in his line of sight.

He stood by the fire and the sudden, intense heat sent a paradoxical flash of goose bumps over his bare legs. Worth it for the flicker of irritation in Brett's face.

"I know we're not supposed to mind the snow much, but try telling that to my toes!" Eli said cheerfully. Boogie jumped on the couch beside Brett and stretched her body cautiously forward to scent him as he eyed her neutrally.

"Weren't you living up north before this? Canada, wasn't it?" Nia asked.

So they'd looked into him. Hopefully that was where the trail had ended. "Yes, with Helena. You know, the *Parks*." He emphasized the pack name that should strike a healthy dose of wariness in any wolf.

But Nia just smiled. "Not anymore. We heard you left Helena recently and joined the pack of her grandson Mr. Oliver Park and his, ah, human mate, Dayton. They do seem to keep busy, don't they? Tell me, are even half the rumors about them true?"

"I have no idea. I begged and begged, but they never let me watch. Some people can be so *conventional* in the bedroom."

Nia's indulgent smile bordered on a grimace and she neatly changed the subject, gesturing at the painting behind the desk. "An interesting subject choice."

"It came with the building."

"Along with many other things. I understand the previous owners took very little with them when they left. Strange, don't you think? Nielsens have controlled this territory for a hundred years, but one visit from Oliver Park and his human and they decide to leave it all behind. Although perhaps this mountain was ready for a change."

Eli shrugged and tried not to focus on the feeling of his leg hair curling in the heat. "I don't know anything about that. I was just hired to get the place up and running."

"Yes, as a sanctuary for the rebel runaways. Celia is aware of Oliver's plans. Very admirable."

Brett spoke for the first time. He had a surprisingly soft, gentle voice which didn't make what he said any less threatening. "Which is why Celia is very reluctant to take a complaint to the Preservation."

Eli blinked. "On what grounds?"

"Mr. Smith," Nia chided gently. "The whole town whispering about a monster in the woods? Your neighbor hiring a self-proclaimed cryptozoologist? Reports of *unnatural animal behavior*? And now one of your runaway wolves has been captured shifting on camera?"

"Where did you hear that?" Eli asked sharply.

Nia spread her hands, the picture of amiability. "Your little mountain here is practically Celia's neck of the woods. She takes a keen interest in this place."

"Is Celia's neck this long? I didn't think so," Eli said politely. Sweat was beginning to form at the backs of his knees.

"An ill-kept territory is every wolf's concern," Brett said softly, removing Boogie from where she'd begun to inch into his lap. "If this little vanity project has drawn this much human attention already, how bad do you think it will get when rebels start pouring in?"

"What's happening over there has nothing to do with the retreat," Eli said.

"Then what is happening over there?" Brett stood with a grimace, looming over the room. *"Sweet Pea?"*

Eli didn't have an answer to that.

"If the problem isn't dealt with, Celia will take a complaint to the Preservation," Brett continued. "You may be something of a Park pet, but I don't think even Helena will intercede for you on this. There's no love lost between her and rebels."

"And who can blame her when even well-intentioned attempts to help them bring such danger to us all?" Nia shook her head sadly. "One of those rumors I mentioned is that Oliver and Dayton have quite a lot on their plate at the moment. They may be relieved to have the Preservation take a troublesome territory like this off their hands."

"And give it to who, De Luca?" Eli asked acerbically.

"I understand why you want to make this political, but for once it's not," Nia said. "I have my issues with the Preservation. As does Celia. But maintaining our secret supersedes everything else. Surely you agree with that."

Eli tilted his head. "Certainly. But I would be more inclined to believe you if Celia's primary issue with the Preservation wasn't her lack of invitation to join. A key territory like this, the only thing separating De Luca from Helena Park's empire, once the home of *the* Dr. Nielsen himself... well, one wonders if Celia would be quite so concerned with silly human superstitions if acquiring the mountain wasn't the only thing standing between her and putting *her issue* to bed."

Nia studied him, dark eyes disappointed, and then let out a heavy sigh. "You don't know the first thing about this territory, Mr. Smith. It wouldn't be so shameful to admit you're out of your depth and walk away. I imagine it wouldn't be the first time." She signaled Brett to the door. "Think about it. Sometimes plans just fall through. Wrong place, wrong time, wrong person in charge."

Fortunately, they left after that. Unfortunately, as far as parting shots went, it was a haunting one. Eli sat on the couch with Boogie twisted on her back in his lap, staring at the fire, thinking. When was the last time he'd been the right person for a job? For a job he wanted to do? He couldn't seem to remember. Somehow that made Nia's words feel more insightful than he would have liked.

"Are you all right?"

Startled, Eli turned to find Gwen watching him from the dark hall.

"What good are winter nights if not for getting melancholic?" Eli said lightly, a bit embarrassed to have been caught off guard for the second time that day. He was losing his touch. "Would you like to join me?"

Gwen hesitated then padded silently in and curled up in the chair opposite him. "Those were De Luca wolves," she said more than asked.

Eli arched an eyebrow. "You're remarkably quiet."

"Sneaky and rude, you mean. Whenever my pack needs someone to eavesdrop, they send me. My old pack, I mean." Gwen's faintly sad smile turned anxious. "I hope you don't think that means I'll spy on you, though. I wouldn't."

Eli shrugged and didn't bother to point out she already had. It's not like he wouldn't have done the same. "I had a similar role myself when I ran with rebels. Don't worry yourself."

"You were a rebel?" Gwen asked, sounding surprised. "I thought... Well, I heard them say you left Helena Park's pack to be with her grandson and his human lover."

Eli barked out a laugh, surprised. "What a delightful *Design for Living* that would be. But alas it wasn't quite as dramatic as all that." Or maybe it was. After all, it had taken four murders, a long-lost sister and a good deal of blackmail to get him to leave one pack for another. But that was another story. "Helena Park was my alpha until recently, yes, but before her I was with a rebel pack out west."

"Was it...bad?"

"Not at first," Eli said, which was putting it mildly. In actuality it had felt like belonging for the first time in his life. He'd have sacrificed anything for the chance to join them. In fact he had. "I was happy with them for a long time. I suppose that's what made it harder to notice when things got bad."

Gwen hummed, a sympathetic sound. "I thought I was lucky to be with my pack once, too. That we were special somehow. That we were…going places. Took a while to realize the alpha was going places, not me. All I was good for was hiding behind doors."

"I suppose we all had our jobs," Eli mused. "Though some were distinctly dirtier than others."

"That's one way of putting it. What did you do? With the rebels?"

"Oh, stole things, mostly."

Gwen gasped softly under her breath. "Really? From—"

"Just unaware humans, of course," he said. And aware humans. And other rebels. And the wealthiest ruling packs around, most of whom now held seats on the Preservation and absolutely could not realize who and where he was. And pretty much anyone who could either afford it or had something his alpha James particularly wanted.

"Shit, that's…" Gwen bit her lip and peered at him from under her lashes as if deciding something. "I used to help my alpha blackmail people," she blurted, then blushed. "An-anytime she wanted something from someone, I had to go find some dirt on them for her. It was a horrible thing to do, I know."

Eli felt a prickle of uneasiness followed immediately by

guilt. On his personal metric of loathsome, blackmail was high. But that might have to do with the fact one could find enough dirt on him to build a small island out of the Mariana Trench. There were after all people who considered letting yourself into strangers' homes a worse crime, and Eli had never felt particularly bad about that. "I suppose we do what we think we have to in order to survive."

"Sure. Until I realized my alpha thought she had to have power over all those people in order to survive. Most people can't tell the difference between what they want and what they need."

He hummed neutrally though personally he found the people who confused the two were often those who'd never really known real, desperate, life-or-death need.

"It's why I finally decided to get out for good," Gwen was saying. "What about you? What made you finally leave?"

"It'd be more accurate to say I was left," Eli said, looking down at Boogie and stroking her softly under the chin. "Terrible job security in petty crime."

There was a silence and when he glanced back up Gwen was watching him with a rueful grimace. "You're right to be wary. But I swear I'm not going to blackmail you."

"The thought didn't even cross my mind," Eli lied hastily. "It just isn't a particularly good story. One day my pack took something we shouldn't have. The alpha sold us out to some humans. There was some bad trouble. Helena Park saved me and offered me a place with her pack. I lazed around there for a number of years then took this job under Oliver Park and his mate, Cooper. That's all."

It sounded absurdly simple said like that, and he could see Gwen was still hurt. She wanted more. Expected it, even, after she herself had been brave enough to begin to share her own past with him. But there was nothing else he could say. It was a lonely life living so many lies. Every little bit of intimacy contingent on exposing a secret that put him at risk.

He couldn't possibly explain the way he'd felt when he'd first seen James and his pack of rebels without revealing too much of his upbringing before. Couldn't fully explain how James had immediately put him to use, stealing from the most powerful ruling packs around the country without revealing his slipping abilities. Couldn't explain how James had traded a chained, slipped and monstrous-looking Eli to human hunters in exchange for his own freedom without reopening wounds that had only just begun to close and were still infected and raw.

There wasn't much he could bear thinking about from that time. But he still remembered Helena crouching over him, a lump of ill-fitting, unmatched flesh and fur on the floor, and promising she would never ever use him the way James or the humans had.

"Why should I believe you?" he'd asked.

"Because I don't need you. I never will."

Almost pathologically cold, Helena. And yet it was the only thing she could have said that he'd believe. The Park pack was one of the most powerful ruling packs on the continent and Helena held an untouchable seat on the Preservation because of it. She had spies across all three factions—royal, rebel and WIP alike—and even deep within the Trust, the supposedly neutral government agency that investigated crimes against wolves. Helena needed a wolf that could contort his body to enter any home and pick any lock like the queen needed a petty thief to access the royal coffers. Nor had she seemed to mind that he'd spent most of his youth with the rebels stealing from rich ruling alphas like her. If anything, it had entertained her to hear which of her peers he'd robbed, who secretly showered in fur and who talked in their sleep. There was a strange sort of safety in being an amusement—unnecessary and ornamental. So he'd stayed with her, gotten better and gotten on with, if not life, then at least the act of living.

It was shocking how much time could pass that way. For years he'd wake up, run, eat, walk, get lost in stories, walk, run, eat, walk, run, run, run, sleep. Then do it all again in the morning. Every day filled with little pleasures to make himself feel well. To avoid the ever-watchful chasm of his past, his pain, his own nature. Until one morning Eli realized *feeling okay* had turned into the longest, most time-consuming passion of his life.

Maybe it had been foolish to leave that behind. But a collection of good days makes a good life like the same short story over and over makes a good book. And when his carefully constructed world had unexpectedly imploded last summer with James's murder, he'd taken the opportunity to write his own fresh start.

Breaking away from Helena's padded kennel, joining Oliver and his pretty little whippet's pack... He'd wanted *good* this time. Sometimes, in his most maudlin moments, he wanted to *be* good. Which had, in its own circuitous way, led him to believing he could possibly be responsible for a place like this. How hopelessly arrogant. How utterly laughable. Never mind the humans, De Luca, or the Preservation; Eli couldn't even have a properly empathetic conversation with a fellow rebel wolf without wrapping himself in lies on lies on lies.

"What are you going to do?" Gwen asked, pulling him out of his increasingly morose thoughts. That question again.

"As much as I hate to admit it, De Luca and her henchmen may be right," Eli mused. "For all the ruling packs' sins, they're unmatched in their ability to put supernatural rumors to bed."

"Oh no, you can't!" Gwen said immediately, then bit her lip worriedly. "It's just that I don't know where I'd go if this place closed. I mean, I'd figure it out. I have before. But I'd rather not have to be on my own again. I know that's stupid, but I... I *hate* it."

"Not at all," Eli said, a little startled by the vehemence in her voice at the end. "Most of our kind do. But you needn't worry about that. Even if the Preservation gets involved, you won't have to leave."

Of course, Eli himself would need to be long gone by then. He simply couldn't risk the eyes of the Preservation on him. Not now. Not ever. Nia and Brett didn't seem to have any idea who he was in his previous life, but many of his old marks still held power in that world. How long would it take for them to start asking questions and making connections? Would Helena still protect his secrets then? Even her power had limits. In theory. Anyway, he didn't like the idea of sticking around to find out. Oliver and the whippet could find a different, better choice to manage their project, and Eli would simply start over again as someone new. Just like he had countless times before.

"I'm sorry," Gwen said. "I feel like I've brought a mess to your door."

"Unless you're the one playing the enigmatic role of Sweet Pea to frighten Annabelle to death, then you haven't done a thing wrong."

"You think that's what someone's doing?" she asked.

Eli looked at her sharply. "As opposed to there really being a Sweet Pea?"

Gwen shook her head quickly. "No. No, of course not. I meant, what if it's not about frightening them at all? What if it's a scheme to get, I don't know, tourist attention?"

"Then it's a scheme going poorly. The business seems to be running into the ground."

"The opposite then. Sabotage. Who might want them to fail?"

"Besides the competitive business on the other side of the mountain with even less 'guests'?" he said wryly.

To his surprise, she growled. "Doesn't it make you angry? They're going to blame us for this. Some fool puts us all at risk by fucking around with humans and instead of figuring out who and why, all De Luca does is use the opportunity to grab more territory. It's everything that's wrong with ruling packs these days."

Eli shrugged. He tended to avoid emotions like anger until he was already running a brisk forty miles per hour in the opposite direction of any problem. Nursing a lifelong grudge didn't hold quite the same appeal without a long life to live. "It's terribly tiresome, yes, but De Luca won't get away with it. When it comes to uncovering a plot, the owners have some experience. They're Trust agents, you know."

Gwen's eyes flashed and she pulled away from him. The scent of her fear made his claws prickle. "The Trust? They can't know I'm here! Weren't you listening? I've—I've done things! Recorded people and helped set them up, and it won't matter that I didn't want to, they'll take me away!"

"Oliver and Cooper aren't going to care about all that," Eli said. "They don't even need to know."

"Would you take that chance in my shoes?"

Well, no. Not in a million years. And if it were any other two Trust agents in the world Eli would have already run. He supposed it was hypocritical of him to be planning his own escape route and judging her for doing the same.

"Perhaps... I could look into it," Eli said hesitantly. "Try to figure things out myself first."

Gwen blinked at him, her face relaxing a little. "Really? And then you wouldn't need to call the Trust?"

"Not if I'm successful," Eli said, warming to the idea. If he could figure out who was really playing peekaboo between the trees and prove that it had nothing to do with the retreat, De Luca would lose any ability to make a complaint. Gwen wouldn't get spooked by the Trust and Eli wouldn't have to run. Oliver and Cooper could remain blissfully unaware on their honeymoon until it was time to come home, at which point Eli would have masterfully averted catastrophe and they would count themselves lucky to have invited such a responsible wolf into their pack and entrusted him with the running of the retreat.

After all, it was merely a matter of tracking down what amounted to a petty vandal, which didn't sound very hard. He had plenty of experience with criminal investigations. Nearly always from the other side of things, but still. Surely that still counted for something. He knew it wasn't Sweet Pea and he knew it wasn't him, and that put him two major suspects ahead of everyone else involved, which wasn't a bad start. Annabelle had even invited him to join her the next morning, which couldn't be a better opportunity to try on his sleuth hat.

It seemed absurd, a monster going monster hunting. But why not? Just for a couple of days. What could possibly go wrong?

The next morning was gloomy. Everything was fogged with gray—the sky, the air, the snow—and there was a slight bite in the wind that warned of worse weather to come. It was the sort of day that begged you to stay home in bed.

Not that bed was a very nice place to be at the moment either. Julien had spent most of the night staring at the moonlight moving across his ceiling. The countryside was supposed to be so dark, but in fact the moon seemed brighter here. Maybe because of the snow or the lack of competition with city lights. A couple times Julien considered getting up to close the curtains, but then he'd have nothing to keep him company outside his own sleepless brain, aching like a bruise. Running shorter and shorter loops. Arriving nowhere.

He'd stayed up late poring over the books Patrick had recommended. The couple of times he did manage to drop out of consciousness, fleeting and dissatisfactory, he'd dreamed of animals running across the road, reflective eyes, Eli Smith standing at the edge of a waterfall fluttering his fingers *goodbye, hello*. It was easier in the end to watch the moonlight.

By morning, the weather had become dangerously foggy for skiing, so Annabelle invited the entire lodge to accompany her and Patrick on their hike to the activity site. At this point "everyone" consisted of a mere six guests, but it was still convenient for Julien, who had agonized over how he might ask to join them. Mr. and Ms. Miura politely declined, deciding to spend the day in town, which left Julien with Annabelle, Patrick, Cody and the trio of German university students who seemed to find the prospect of monster hunting too amusing to pass up.

They gathered by the ski lift. It was the quickest way up the mountain, Annabelle explained, that could also accommodate the entire group. "Then there's a trail at the top we can take to the site. It's about a twenty-minute hike until the—oh, Mr. Smith!"

Julien turned along with everyone else. Sure enough, Eli was walking toward them from around the lodge, impossible to miss in a retro snow jacket in geometric neon orange, teal, purple and lime green.

"Jesus," Cody muttered beside Julien. "If there is such a thing as Sweet Pea, I hope he's color-blind."

"I didn't think you were coming," Annabelle called, apparently delighted.

Eli just smiled demurely. "Someone recently reminded me it's good manners to acquaint yourself with the local milieu. And if there's one thing you must know about me, it's that I can't abide rudeness."

"That's the spirit," Patrick laughed.

Annabelle continued to explain how they were getting there, what to expect at the top and why they were going, but Julien wasn't paying attention anymore. He drifted as casually as possible over to Eli, who stood a little distance from the others with a politely bored expression.

"What are you doing here?" Julien whispered. "Or did somebody else drop their poker chips?"

Eli smiled without looking around at him. "Worried I've had a change of conscience and decided to tell everyone I caught you with your hand in the proverbial cookie jar?"

"No," Julien said quickly. Although that was one explanation for why his heart had started beating a little faster when Eli had arrived. "I have nothing to hide."

"Neither do I," Eli purred. "Look at us. Two open books."

"Sure. Except yours is written in code. And invisible ink. And has one of those paper snakes that pop out and scare the shit out of anyone who picks you up."

Eli made that odd huffing sound again. "I assure you, Mr. Doran, I've never received a single complaint from those blessed enough to pick me up."

Annabelle saved Julien from coming up with a response

to that by waving them over to the lift. "Come on now, boys! Fall in line, we're heading up!"

Everyone else had already gotten into pairs while they were talking, so Julien supposed he'd have to ride up with Eli, which was bad luck. He was too distracting, for one thing. Julien had to muster all his focus for deflecting insults and sexual innuendo and cryptic comments, which embarrassingly didn't leave much room in his head for anything else.

Worse, it was dead obvious Eli didn't believe in Sweet Pea. And while any other day of his life Julien would have said that was a good thing, it did put a damper on his own resolution to approach this goose chase like Rocky would have: seriously. The thought of asking Annabelle sincere questions about her encounters, talking to Patrick about his books and really, genuinely trying to believe that there was some kind of humanoid creature walking among them was, well, embarrassing, at the very least. And frankly unbearable in front of someone like Eli. Julien felt a chill up his spine picturing the heights his eyebrow would climb in judgment.

In fact, Eli had a slightly skeptical look on his face already as he watched Annabelle and Patrick get into position for the chair.

"Shall we?" Julien gestured.

Eli followed him, quiet for once, but winced a little when the chair slapped into Annabelle and Patrick, picking them off the ground, and began the long ascent up the mountain.

"You're not afraid of heights, are you?" Julien asked.

Eli shot him a scathing look. "Heights have nothing to

do with it. I simply object to being locked into a cage held together with tape and spit, and dangled over death's maw to passively await the whim of fate."

"Sounds like you're afraid of heights," Julien said as two of the German students were picked up and carried away and they shuffled forward to replace them in position for the lift. Though to be fair, Eli wasn't entirely wrong. Like the rest of the lodge, the lift looked like it had seen better days. Worse days, too, from the patched-up rips in the cushioned seat.

"I spent my adolescence on rooftops. I'm not—" Eli let out a strange, muffled yelping sound as the chair knocked into the backs of their thighs and scooped them from the ground. Julien grunted as he felt Eli's hand clamp down desperately tight on his upper thigh. A shocking thrill raced up his leg and Julien felt a swooping sensation in his belly that was immediately eclipsed by alarm when the chair started rocking violently.

"What the hell are you doing?" Julien gritted out, grabbing on to the chair a bit tightly himself. Eli was squirming in place, trying to pull his legs up under him so that both feet were flat on the seat. "Don't move or we'll fall."

Eli froze, one knee half tucked up to his chest, the other jammed into Julien's hip.

"Hey! Stop fooling around up there!" Cody's voice echoed out from a couple chairs back.

"Sorry! We're good!" Julien called back, then lowered his voice. "Are we? Good?"

Eli nodded tightly, staring straight ahead, and then belatedly added, "Yes. Fine."

"All right," Julien said. He twisted around for the safety bar and then cursed when the grip on his thigh sharpened painfully.

"You said no moving," Eli said, voice edged with panic.

"It's okay," Julien said gently. "Let me just…" He pulled the safety bar down over their heads so that it could block their bodies from slipping forward off the chair. It was a little awkward with Eli's knees up, and Julien almost suggested he put his legs back down, but one look at his colorless face nixed that idea.

They sat in silence for a minute. The constant thrum and click of the steel cables interspersed with Annabelle's cheerful chatter echoing oddly against the mountain and drifting back toward them.

"Sorry," Eli said, startling Julien. His voice was very quiet, a little unsure. Julien didn't like it.

"You're fine," he said briskly. "I take it you're not a skier."

Eli huffed. "I know exactly two things about skiing: rich people do it and you're never supposed to cross the tips. That's more than enough to determine it's not the extracurricular for me."

Julien couldn't help smiling. "Fair enough. How long have you lived here?"

"Is this your clunky attempt to distract me from the fatal drop below us?"

"Bruising drop, maybe. We're not even twenty feet up yet."

Eli shook his head, but Julien felt him relax slightly.

"Today will be my thirteenth day living in Maudit Falls. Are you a superstitious man?"

"Not at all."

"Let me guess," Eli said, eyeing him. "A man like you, the world built for his pleasure, must believe we make our own fate. Masters of our own destiny."

"I hate to know what I've said to deserve that judgment," Julien said mildly.

"Not true? Then what pulls at your compass, Mr. Doran? What philosophies keep you safe and warm at night?"

"I don't know," Julien said. "That we're all just animals fighting nature, I guess."

Eli gave him a strange, piercing look. "Are we. And who's winning?"

"Never bet against the house," Julien said with a shrug, and Eli made that huffing sound again.

"I've always thought of your sort as more impractical. More inclined toward magical thinking. Actors, that is," he added belatedly.

"What, Macbeth and break a leg, you mean? Those aren't superstitions. Just good sense." Julien tried for a relaxed smile. "Although maybe I shouldn't have said break a leg up here. Might have tempted fate."

"Might have tempted it when you said Macbeth."

"Only counts in a theater."

"My mistake. I thought we were in one on account of all the lines you've been feeding me."

"*Me?*" Julien asked, genuinely taken aback. It seemed the small talk portion of the ride was over. "What lines? When?"

Eli gave him an assessing look. "Why did you defend me? In the sausage room?"

"The *sausage* room?" Julien repeated, beginning to feel like another mountain echo. "All I said was the truth. Or is that why you're so offended?"

"Why didn't you tell the others you saw me going through that drawer?"

"Why didn't you tell them I was up to my elbows in Annabelle's desk?" Julien waited a beat. "Is this another one of those things you were talking about before? An impasse?"

Eli's eyes narrowed, before he made a rude sound and turned away, clearly signaling an end to their conversation. But he didn't stop gripping Julien's thigh, and Julien didn't move his leg a centimeter the rest of the way up the mountain. He didn't want to rock the lift.

Disembarking at the top was much easier. Julien put the bar back up at the last possible moment and Eli leapt onto the snow with frankly astonishing grace.

"Beautiful." Patrick applauded, waiting beside Annabelle.

"It's only a mile-and-a-half hike to the tower," Cody said. "We'll be walking an old Forest Service road. It's pretty flat and we keep it plowed for emergencies, but don't be stupid. It's still winter, and slippery."

Somehow Julien was pulled into the head of the group with the German students, who introduced themselves as Ahmet, Claudia and Jonas. The three of them had just finished some sort of internship thing in D.C. and were delighted to inform him they'd put their heads together and figured out who he was on the lift ride up.

"I thought this country would feel bigger," Ahmet said seriously. "But you are the third movie star we've met so far."

By the time he'd finished answering their questions about winner-take-all urbanism, what it was like to live in L.A., and barbecue food, they'd made it to the tower.

"Welcome to Blue Tail Lookout," Annabelle announced, flourishing her hands. It was a slightly hilly outcrop that had been cleared of all but a handful of young trees. "We're about five thousand feet up, so even without climbing the tower, the view's pretty impressive."

Julien looked around for Eli and saw him still meandering up the road. He and Patrick had fallen farther and farther behind as they'd walked and no wonder with those deliberate, delicate steps. He wondered what had led someone so apparently uncomfortable with nature to such a rural, isolated life. It seemed like every other time Julien had peeked over his shoulder as they'd hiked, Patrick was grabbing Eli's elbow in a steadying grip.

"Terrifying, isn't it?" Annabelle said.

Julien turned to her, startled, and then beyond to take in the view. "Oh. Yes, it is."

In truth it just looked like most American mountains on the East Coast. Rolling into the mist, edges softened by dense forests, gray with winter's trees. In the clearing itself were a couple small brown sheds with heavy-duty-looking padlocks, a propane tank on a concrete slab, and one tall, narrow satellite tower situated a little farther up the hill from the shed and used by the "…National Weather Service to collect data for forecasts" Annabelle explained. "And then, of course, the main attraction, the lookout tower it-self."

A little ways away stood a forty-foot monstrosity. The bottom was an open structure of crisscrossing steel poles built around four flights of stairs that zigzagged up the center and topped by a square cabin made entirely of windows that glinted in the sun.

"The Forest Service built her in 1946, and she's still the third-tallest tower in western North Carolina," Annabelle said. "The cabin stays locked year-round. But you can just about see into Tennessee from the top step. Back in '77, Benny Dobbs went on the run after killing five people; he spent a week barricaded in this very tower."

"Some say his ghost is in there still. And that he's just waiting for some poor sap to wander into the cabin to be the hostage he needs to finally make his escape," Patrick said from behind them. He and Eli had caught up at last. "Same old stories we used to tell as kids, huh?"

Annabelle smiled, but it didn't quite make it to her eyes. "We wouldn't want to forget our history, would we?" She clapped her hands. "Now, who wants to go up?"

The students scrambled forward and immediately started racing up the steps.

"It's icy!" Cody yelled after them, and cursed under his breath. "That thing's a death trap and should be torn down."

"And yet Blue Tail Tower will outlast us all," Patrick said smoothly, looking around. "God, this place doesn't change. Annabelle, remember when Ian dared us to climb the satellite tower? Now, *that* was a death trap. You were the only one who made it to the top."

She smiled, and this time it looked genuine. "Because I was a competitive little shit who'd rather die than lose."

"Were?" Patrick teased. "Maybe something finally has changed on the mountain."

"When were you last here?" Julien asked.

"Oh, three or four years, probably," Patrick said.

"It was more recently than that," Cody spoke up unexpectedly. "Two summers ago. The week before Ian left."

There was an awkward pause. "That's right," Patrick said eventually. "I can't believe that was only last year."

"Have you heard from him recently?" Cody asked. He had a strange, almost mocking expression, but Patrick just laughed.

"I'm the last person Ian would get in touch with."

"Second to last, I think," Annabelle said promptly. "Cody, go collect the camera. You know where it is. I'll take them to the markings."

Cody hesitated, then nodded. "Sure thing, Ms. D. Be back in a minute."

Patrick watched him go and murmured, "I see the church of Ian Ackman still has followers among the younger generation."

Annabelle tsked very softly under her breath and to Julien's disappointment quickly changed the subject. "I have about thirty-five motion-sensor cameras around the mountain now and try to check them every three days or so. Down the hill a bit is where I set up my very first."

"Why here?" Eli asked, looking around. "One would

think a being intent on secrecy would avoid hubs of human activity."

"Oh, but it's not," Annabelle said. "The tower is closed to the public during the winter and the access road stays gated. Only the weather data folks and a few people who work for the town have the key, and hardly anyone hikes this way these days. Besides," she added. "I have proof Sweet Pea was here. Come look."

She led them up the hill toward one of the sheds and around the back. Four lines were carved directly into the wood. They were straight down the center of the wall, about six feet long, tightly clustered and perfectly parallel to one another.

Julien stepped closer and ran his hand over the gouges without touching. It reminded him of the scratches on top of his car roof and he felt a trickle of unease. "Black bear?"

"It's a similar size," Patrick said, snapping pictures with his phone. "But no bear could have done this."

"What do you mean?" Annabelle asked eagerly. "How can you tell?"

"Watch." Patrick fit his own fingers into the grooves where they began, a short distance above his head, and then traced them all the way down to where they stopped near his ankles, slowly bending over and eventually shuffling into a wide squat as he went. "Now try to imagine a bear doing that same movement with no hesitations or need to readjust." He stood back up. "Whatever made this had the hips of a bipedal—"

"Like Sweet Pea," Annabelle interrupted excitedly.

"Without more data I wouldn't be comfortable making

that call. There are many bipedal cryptids reportedly seen around this part of the country. Sweet Pea, yes, but also Sasquatch, Mothman..." Patrick hesitated, an odd expression on his face. "Humans too, of course."

"Which is exactly what I've been saying," Cody said, rejoining them. "Someone is trying to scare you, Ms. D. Mess with your head." He glanced at Eli, who stood a little ways away from the rest of them, examining his fingernails like he was barely paying attention.

"Then it's a good thing it's not working," Annabelle said. "Isn't it?"

Cody's expression didn't shift, but he did hold out the camera. It was identical to the one that had been stolen—same sturdy little box, with nylon straps hanging and camouflage print. "Only twenty-eight new pictures."

That sounded like a hell of a lot to Julien, but Annabelle made a small, disappointed sound as she started flipping eagerly through them on the camera's back screen. "Dammit. Deer, birds, owl, more deer and—that's odd. Nothing at all yesterday." She sighed and this time didn't offer to pass the camera around to anyone else. "I'm going to set this up again before we head back. The west side of the tower this time, I think. Do you want to come see, Patrick?"

Patrick shook his head. "Actually, I'd love to take a couple samples from these markings, if you don't mind."

"I'll help you put it up, Ms. D," Cody said quickly. The two walked away over the hill and Patrick pulled a roll of wide, clear tape out of his jacket pocket.

"No casts?" Julien asked, genuinely curious. Eli had also

stayed behind and was drifting closer to the shed at last as Patrick laid a long strip of tape down one of the gouges.

"Not yet. This is in case any biological traces are left behind. Hair, skin, nail. If this wasn't man-made, of course."

"Forgive me for saying so," Eli said, "but for a cryptozoologist, you don't seem very keen on pointing fingers at any cryptids."

"Because I'm not a cryptozoologist. I'm a biological anthropologist with a healthy sense of agnosticism." Patrick winked and laid another strip of tape. "Any real scientist will tell you that one of the most important tenets of modern science is acknowledging just how little we actually know. How much we may never know. Not in this lifetime."

"I don't think Cody will be pleased to hear that," Julien said, and felt Eli look at him curiously.

Patrick just laughed. "I don't think Cody is pleased with much of anything at the moment. But I'm just here to follow the evidence. Sometimes, yes, the easiest explanation for that evidence is human mischief. But other times...well, even the most hardened skeptics admit we've only identified a fifth of the species in the world. Who's to say what's hiding just out of sight? Maybe some larger animals. Maybe some creatures with intelligence comparable to our own." Patrick prepared another tape strip, the *scritch* as he yanked it off the roll suddenly loud.

"Spooky," Julien said for lack of anything else to say.

"Actually, I find it exciting. I mean how incredible would it be if we weren't actually alone in this world?"

Julien blinked. "I've never thought about it that way."

All those years he'd viewed Rocky's obsession with monsters as his way of disconnecting from the real world, from his family, from him. Now he wondered if his brother had simply been trying to escape the same loneliness that haunted Julien. It was a depressing thought.

"What about you, Eli?" Patrick asked. Apparently on a first-name basis now. "Do you believe humans are the only intelligent life on the planet?"

"I've never considered humans generally intelligent, no." Eli smiled a secretive sort of smile back and Patrick grinned, white teeth sparkling.

Julien cleared his throat. "How'd you get started in all this?"

"An anatomy background, actually. I've always had an interest in evolutionary morphology of vertebrates. The ways we've evolved to walk. All the compelling stories a body can tell us about who we are and where we come from. Like Eli's, for example."

Oh, for Christ's sake. Not one missed opportunity. Julien glanced at Eli, who just raised an eyebrow. "How kind of you to notice."

Patrick chuckled. "I *meant* most people learn how to walk on the balls of their feet then transition to heel-to-toe around two years old. But some people never make that switch for a variety of reasons. Like you. You're a toe-walker." He hesitated somewhat pointedly, then winked. "Not that it's the only compelling thing about you, of course."

Julien fervently wished for the appearance of Sweet Pea

just then. No such luck. He waited for the inevitable flir-
tatious response, but Eli's expression was unusually blank.

"How interesting of you to say so," he drawled. "On that
note, I think I'll toe-walk around and acquaint myself with
this infamous view before we head back."

Julien watched him go, noticing his steps were a bit
more flatfooted than before, and made sound for once
as he stomped through the snow. He felt the urge to say
something—*Does he seem upset to you? Why did you upset
him?*—but he wasn't sure if he meant it as a question or an
accusation. He also wasn't sure it was any of his business
either way.

"I'll, uh, leave you to it," he said. Patrick just smiled distractedly, intent on his work once more, and examining
the tape as he peeled it away from the wall.

Julien wandered the clearing. He couldn't find Annabelle or Cody. But he did see Eli standing about twenty
feet down the hill from the tower where the clearing came
to a steep drop-off, standing alarmingly close to the edge
and staring out over the neighboring mountains.

Julien ought to keep exploring the area. Maybe get a
look at where that camera was. The man had only been
here thirteen days. What could he possibly know? But Julien felt oddly reluctant to leave. He took a step forward.
Stopped. Took a step back.

"Make up your mind already. All this wavering is making me seasick," Eli called from below without bothering
to turn around.

Julien approached to stand beside him. "I just didn't want
to sneak up on you."

"Worried I'd fall?"

"Nah, I just didn't want to steal your signature move," Julien said easily, and Eli huffed that odd laugh then shot him a considering sidelong glance. Julien looked away, peering out over the cliff's edge. Maybe he should have been worried. It was a dizzying drop. "This doesn't make you nervous? Being this close?"

"I told you, I'm not scared of heights," Eli said absently. "It's the hanging I don't like. That—" he searched for a word "—feeling of suspension. Trapped between falling up and falling down."

Julien considered the horizon. "I get that."

"Really? You don't strike me as the sort of man who's ever felt trapped."

"Well, then I guess it's like the old adage says—you can't break into an office with somebody one time and expect to know everything about them."

Eli turned to him suddenly, surprising Julien into facing him as well. "What are you doing here, really?"

"Skiing," Julien said automatically.

"Fuck off," Eli snapped, which shocked Julien enough for him to take a step back. Eli closed the space between them with a new intensity. He seemed different, like this. Focused, sharper. "What did you mean before, that Cody wouldn't be happy?"

"He's the one who called Patrick here," Julien said. "I don't think it's any secret he wants him to convince Annabelle that there's no such thing as Sweet Pea and that it's a person behind everything."

"That person being me, I suppose," Eli said. "And what about you? What do you have to do with this?"

"Nothing," Julien insisted.

"You've never been to Maudit Falls?"

"No."

"Or met Patrick West before?"

"No."

"Or De Luca?"

Over thirty years of theatrical training stopped Julien from blinking. "Who is that?"

Eli studied him for a long silent moment. "Are you here to threaten the retreat?"

Julien frowned, genuinely perplexed. "No."

"Then why are you always following after me? Watching me?" Eli murmured so quietly Julien's gaze compulsively dropped to his lips, as if he could catch them moving and know if he'd imagined the words or not. When Julien looked back up at Eli's eyes, his expression had changed to something paradoxically both curious and knowing. "I suppose that's one possibility," he agreed, though Julien hadn't said anything.

"Wh-what?"

Eli took another step forward, and this time Julien didn't retreat. Eli's eyes seemed brighter today beneath long black lashes. Like they were reflecting the misty mountain sky itself.

He'd look beautiful on screen, Julien thought recklessly. Light and dark. Soft and hard. Film loved a study in contrast. Though he wasn't sure even a camera could capture the promise of danger peeking out beneath all that pageantry.

"Tell me—" Eli began. Then paused as the wind shifted directions and blew his soft hair away from his forehead, where a faint crease had appeared in concentration. He backed away, lifting his face toward the sky, and stood almost eerily still, much like he had in Annabelle's office.

"What's wrong?" Julien asked. He felt confused. Dizzy from how abruptly Eli had retreated and left him alone on the edge. "Mr. Smith? E-Eli?"

"Hey! Hey!" Behind them, one of the students had started yelling down from the top of the tower. Julien looked back and up, trying to block the sun from his eyes to see Claudia waving and pointing. "Hey! There's smoke! Fire!"

Before she had even finished speaking, Eli took off, running. Julien didn't stop to think. He bolted after him. Up the hill, across the clearing, down the other side and into the woods.

Eli was disarmingly fast, but easy to follow in his ridiculous jacket, and soon enough it didn't even matter. Julien could smell the smoke, too. Hear the dull roar of something burning. See the light that was the wrong color, wrong direction. Like a sunset in the middle of the day.

Seven small burning pyres of branches and brush had been set up between the trees. The air, hazy with smoke, burned Julien's eyes, and he had to squint to find Eli stomping on the burning branches. Julien found the closest pyre and did the same—kicking it down to hiss and pop as the snow smothered the flames. Within a couple minutes, Patrick was there, too, doing the same, and then the three students, until all the fires were hissing to nothing beneath their boots.

"Who would do this?" Jonas asked. "So close to the trees."

"Would the forest burn? With all this snow?" Ahmet added.

"No, it's unlikely," Patrick said, coughing. "But some fires can keep smoldering all winter and catch again when the weather dries out. Not to mention how dangerous it is for the wildlife in this—"

"What in the hell!" Cody gasped, running up to join them, Annabelle right behind. "What's going on here?"

"You know as much as we do," Julien said, holding back his impatience. They'd taken their time getting here. He looked for Eli, but it was incredibly hazy still. Smoke and steam hung heavily in the air over the slush and mud.

"How did anyone even find dry wood up here?" Cody asked.

"It's not. Look at all this smoke," Annabelle said. "They must have used an accelerant. Just like last time."

"This has happened before?" Julien asked as he finally located Eli standing behind the tree where three of the seven pyres had been built.

"A few times, yes," Annabelle answered. "It's all part of the increased activity. Fires, lights, the markings and—"

"Piles of bones. You mentioned that before," Eli said. His voice sounded odd, flat, and Julien started to walk toward him. "What sort of bones usually?"

"Oh. Deer, I think," Annabelle said. "That's what David said. He's the hunter, so I trust he knows."

"I don't think this one's a deer," Eli murmured as Julien came up beside him.

There, at the base of the tree, half submerged in slush and mud, was a filthy, yellow, greenish rib cage. And there, right above it, a human skull.

Chapter Six

Eli couldn't get the smell of smoke out of his nose. He'd washed, shifted, run the territory border, shifted again, washed again and still it lingered, contaminating everything. Like seeing the world through a brightly colored strip of gauze where mysterious shadows passed in and out of his vision. Things he should have recognized, but didn't beneath the haze of smoke. After hours and hours of it, his head ached.

It had been dusk by the time he'd gotten back to the retreat. Bucknell had brought them all down to the station to take their statements and photograph the bottoms of their boots in the vain hope of distinguishing tracks. Laughable, really. The site had been a muddy mess by the time they'd stomped the last fire out. They stood no better chance of isolating a boot print than Eli did of scenting who had set light to those pyres in the first place. Never mind anything else useful like who'd been playing with human bones. All he knew was they had been buried once, dug up and arranged beneath that tree, and weren't very old. Oh, and that whoever they were had been murdered, of course. At least that's what it seemed like from the buckshot still embedded in the ribs, right where the heart had once been.

Unexpectedly, Gwen had been excited by the development when he'd filled her in on the afternoon's find. Eli had been pleasantly surprised to find her waiting for him in the lobby nervously when an officer had dropped him off after the questioning. It was nicer than he'd anticipated having someone notice he was gone. Not the same as pack. But a wolf whose life had mirrored his own in just enough places to be wary of marked cars coming down the drive. Although he couldn't quite relate to her optimistic take on the skeleton's discovery.

"One morning of investigating and you've already had a major break in the case! I knew you didn't need to call the Trust," she'd said.

"I wouldn't hoist the banner quite yet. We don't even know who was killed. Or why. Or by whom."

"But that doesn't matter! You said the bones were old. Or at least older than when you or I or Dr. Capili got here. De Luca and her bullies can't possibly blame this on the retreat now."

That was true. So true he couldn't explain why he'd left the police station more tempted to call Oliver and Cooper than ever. Preferably from a red-eye on his way out of Dodge.

He didn't like how any of this felt. The over-the-top staging of the remains. The lodge's cast of characters, who were shifty even by human standards. There was a wrongness in the air, like the hour leading up to a thunderstorm, and Eli had the creeping urge to run for cover.

But with Oliver and Cooper came the Trust, and he couldn't do that to Gwen.

"You're not going to give up now, are you?" she'd asked, and when he'd hesitated betrayal had flickered in her eyes. Disappointment. Defeat.

"Right after my first major break? Darling, I'm just getting started."

Gwen's relief was so obvious it'd made Eli's heart ache. No, not pack. But he was beginning to feel responsible, perhaps even protective of her nonetheless. Which is why, a few hours after dark, he'd tugged his shoes back on and made his way over to Blue Tail Lodge to continue his investigation.

Eli stared up at the building, looming against the night sky, and listened to Cody shuffling around his room. He'd been the one to bring the cryptozoologist in, he was the one intent on framing Eli, so that was where Eli would start. If Julien Doran was telling the truth, anyway, which seemed…

Eli slipped his right ear to fur to eavesdrop more easily on the room four balconies away from Cody's, where Doran was currently singing in the shower. Curiously upbeat for a man who'd just uncovered a murder while on vacation. Eli wondered what Ollie and Cooper would make of that. Something suspicious, probably. But then Cooper saw everything as suspicious. Peculiar, nervy bastard, Eli thought fondly. He would call them when this was done. Once he knew what was going on and could prove he was perfectly capable of looking after the retreat. That he was *not* the wrong choice.

Park pet, Brett had called him. It had rankled more than it should have. Cruelties with kernels of truth usually did. He'd gone complacent these last years hidden away, existing on the perimeter of Helena's den like an outdoor cat. But he'd lived many lives. It was time to remember another Eli. One who didn't make foolish mistakes like prowling in front of men like Patrick West or not making absolutely certain a room wasn't already being rummaged through by some stupidly handsome and constantly underfoot tourist like Julien Doran.

Eli's ear twitched, irritated. The difficulty was he didn't know if Doran was trouble or not. He couldn't figure him out. He was unpredictable, like a thorn between the toes. Merely aggravating one step, disastrous the next. Not to mention constantly there watching him so intently with those dark eyes that always seemed to *want*.

What exactly it was he wanted, was the question.

Cody finally turned the lights off and left the room. Eli slipped his leg muscles with a sigh and leapt for the balcony directly below, catching hold of the wooden ledge easily and pulling himself up with only the slightest creak of boards. Then he balanced on the railing and did the same again to get to Cody's room.

The sliding glass door was unlocked—they always were, on the third floor—and Eli let himself inside with a soft *whoosh*. Even with the smoke still haunting his senses, the room was overwhelming. A barrage of scents hit him the instant he stepped onto the carpet. Food, sex, sweat, cigarettes, mud, mice—layers and layers, new and old. It was difficult not to start sniffing everything at once. Like walking into a carnival and forcing oneself to stare at a single flashing light bulb.

It was a suite of rooms. A bedroom attached to the balcony; a corner kitchen that consisted simply of two tall cupboards and a mini-fridge-microwave combination better suited to someone's dorm; a living room that had been turned into a makeshift office with a slightly dated desktop computer whose screen saver of a twisting colored ribbon threw strange shadows onto the wall.

It wasn't messy, exactly. Not to the eyes, anyway. Cody's clothes were folded in drawers and hung up in the closet, hangers all going the same way. The desk was clear of papers. The bed was even made, almost too neatly going by the military corners and the oddly solitary pillow centered on the full-size mattress.

But everything reeked. Sheets stale with sex, and clothes put away unwashed. The trash bin wasn't overflowing, but there was an orange peel taking to mold at the bottom. Eli found the boots Cody had been wearing that morning stuffed under the bed, still crusted with soot, dirt and damp.

It was odd. Almost childish, in a way. As though hygiene began and ended with appearances. Cody seemed a bit old for that, but what did Eli know? A good part of his own twenties had been spent believing he was some sort of Wolfy Robin Hood, because a man he thought loved him had told him so. You were never too old to be foolish.

It didn't look like Annabelle had exaggerated how much of the lodge responsibilities Cody had taken on, though. The desk drawers were packed with files, papers and countless overdue bills. From the looks of things, Annabelle was something of a penniless millionaire: although the land itself was valuable, the lodge was hemorrhaging money and badly in debt.

Eli made sure everything was back in its place and before closing it ran his hand under the bottom of the drawer—an old habit that had turned out lucky a couple times in the past. He'd once found a dime bag of diamonds tucked under an alpha's couch. It seemed he was going to get lucky again when his fingers brushed the edges of a piece a tape. Carefully he peeled it back and removed what Cody had been hiding.

"Snotty little bastard," Eli murmured, looking down at what was undoubtedly the SD card to a camera. He'd taken the damn thing himself and then had the audacity to demand Eli be searched. It was almost impressive. But what reason could he have taken it for? Eli plugged the card into the desktop reader. He was tempted to just grab and go, but there was no point alerting Cody to the fact someone had broken in sooner than absolutely necessary.

Never take more than you came for, Prisha used to say. A brilliant wolf who had been part of the rebel pack when Eli had joined all those years ago, uncommonly naive and new to...well, more than even she knew.

Prisha had helped train him. How to slip a claw into a lock just so, how to scale a wall, how to lie. She'd been the first to see the turn their pack was taking and jump ship. Before she left, she'd invited him to join her. They'd make a good team, she'd said, the two of them, at least until they could find someone better. He wondered sometimes what life would have been like had he gone. If he'd paid more attention to what she'd really been trying to say.

And never give more than they have was the second half of her oft-repeated words of warning. Ah well. He was listening to her now.

Eli woke the computer and slipped the SD card into the attached reader. He'd delete the photo of the wolf—perhaps try to get a closer look himself, now that he wasn't limited by the two-inch camera screen—then put the card back under the desk. If his luck held out, it would be a long time before Cody even noticed it was gone.

But the picture wasn't there.

Eli frowned, clicking through the images. These were different pictures. Different card. Different day. Different location, too, though easy enough to recognize seeing as he'd only just been there that morning, digging up bones. It seemed Annabelle—or someone—had set up a camera at the edge of the lookout clearing.

It appeared to be summer, with the mountain backdrop awash with green, and Eli could see the shed to the left, conspicuously missing the claw marks. Most interesting were the two people the camera had caught lingering by the bottom of the tower stairs. One was a man Eli had never seen before. White, dark-haired, glasses, forty-ish, good-looking in an awkward sort of way. In most of the photos his hands were a blur, as if he never stopped moving them. Gesturing, pointing, touching the arm of the woman he was meeting. And her Eli did recognize. The wolf from the De Luca pack—Nia.

On the ground between them sat a blue backpack. What was a De Luca representative doing having clandestine meetings on the mountaintop? What was Cody doing with pictures of them secreted away in his desk drawer?

In the last photo, both Nia and the man had turned away from the camera and were walking up the tower stairs. His hand, clear and still for once, hovered over the small of her back as if protecting her from falling. Eli snapped a shot of that on his phone, then did the same for the other photos as well. He carefully put the SD card back where he'd found it and set the computer to sleep once more, screen saver ribbon twisting in the dark.

When he was certain the hallway was empty, Eli slipped his ear back to skin and left Cody's rooms through the interior door. As long as he was in here, he wouldn't mind another look through Annabelle's office. A better look this time without any interruptions.

As he passed Doran's room, he could hear that the shower had stopped but the singing continued. It seemed he wouldn't be running into him tonight, Eli thought, and tamped down anything silly like disappointment.

He walked into the stairwell at the end of the hall at the same time another door on the floor below opened and someone began to climb the steps. Eli quickly retreated back into the hall and made his way down the other end to the small elevator, but it was already whirring away, light lit up red like a warning.

Fuck's sake. For a deserted failing business, this floor certainly led an active nightlife. The footsteps in the stairwell were getting closer now. Pinned between the approaching people, Eli knocked quickly and repeatedly on the only door he knew would open.

"Eli?" Julien stood there, shocked.

"I need to talk to you," Eli said, and pushed inside, startling Julien into stepping back into the room. The moment the door closed behind him, Eli leaned against it. Somewhere down the hall, the elevator doors opened.

"What's wrong?" Julien asked, concern and confusion etched across his face. "Are you okay?"

"Of course, I just…" Eli trailed off. And for one single, rare moment he felt genuinely speechless.

Julien was still quite wet from the shower. Hair damp and ridiculously tufted like he'd just scrubbed it with a towel. Eli saw a single droplet of water that had escaped rolling down the side of his throat and over the curve of his collarbone, only to be caught in his chest hair, faded rose-gold like his beard.

Eli dragged his gaze back up to Julien's face.

"Goodness me, Mr. Doran. Should you be answering the door like that after what happened today?" he said, throat a bit dry. "There may be unsavory characters about."

Julien rolled his eyes. "Yes, I know. One just barged into my bedroom. Why are you here?"

Eli could hear the two murmuring voices still lingering by the elevator doors, even after they'd closed. He looked around the room for a reason to stall. It was dimly lit—only the small lamp by the bed and the light from the bathroom were on. Fairly neat, too. Eli noticed an empty suitcase inside the open closet, and a handful of button-downs hanging above.

"I wanted to continue our conversation from before," he said, absently flicking through the boring shirts, all in dark colors, all sized a bit too wide for Julien's rangy frame. "Don't big-time movie stars have someone to help them pick out clothes?"

Julien stepped neatly around him, grabbed the soft black-and-gray flannel shirt Eli was fingering out of his hand, and put it on a bit deliberately. Unbuttoned and paired with the towel he looked...well.

"Ridiculous," was what Eli said, anyway.

Julien folded his arms over his chest as if he was self-conscious. "You came here to talk now? At this time of night?"

"I don't know about you, but my afternoon was murder." He kept one ear on the elevator voices. They were too hushed with too many walls between them to distinguish words, but his guess would be a man and a woman. "Or have you already forgotten the poor shot bastard in the woods. Typical Hollywood."

Julien stilled. "Shot?"

"Didn't you notice the buckshot in the rib bones?"

"Poor Ian Ackman," Julien murmured under his breath.

Eli stilled. "Annabelle's Ian? You think the remains are her ex?"

Julien looked startled. "How did—yeah. Yeah, I do."

"And which card of Maudit Falls facts led you to that conclusion?" Eli said, all of his attention on Julien now, senses on high alert. "In fact, how do you even know that name? Because somehow I doubt the owner's ex-lover is the sort of information to casually come up while booking an innocent vacation."

"I must have heard Annabelle—"

"Please," Eli hissed. "Let's skip along to the true part. Why the hell are you really here and before you answer let me warn you if you so much as breathe a word that *rhymes* with skiing you're going to wish you were wearing something thicker than a towel."

Julien considered Eli, dark eyes unreadable. Finally, haltingly he said, "Approximately fifteen months ago Ian Ackman up and left the woman he'd been with for twenty years, the town he'd grown up in and the business he'd pushed her to buy. The problem is he didn't arrive anywhere else. He completely fell off the grid."

"What does any of this have to do with you? Don't tell me you're moonlighting as a private eye. Acting can't be going that badly."

"My brother was concerned that no one was taking it seriously and started looking into it himself. They were friends."

"And where's your brother? The room downstairs?"

Julien blinked. "No. But he stayed at Blue Tail right after Ian disappeared. I came here as a favor to him."

"To continue his investigation incognito? What's the matter, did he burn all his own bridges?"

Julien pursed his lips. "Close enough. The cops weren't

interested before. Wouldn't even list Ackman as a missing person. Said they had 'proof' he was alive. But now there's a body and I think someone in this town killed him. I'm here to find out who."

"Why are you telling me this?"

"Because you've been here thirteen days," Julien said simply. "You didn't kill Ian, you're the only person I know for a fact didn't steal that SD card, you're clearly a quick thinker, and—" He hesitated, running a restless hand through his damp hair. "And on that mountain today I watched you put fires out without hesitation simply because it needed to be done and it didn't even cross your mind to wait for someone else to step up instead. Your turn."

Eli raised an eyebrow. "I didn't realize this was a game."

"Yeah. *Guess Who?* And I don't want to play anymore. What's your story, Eli Smith?"

The murmuring voices from the elevator had long since disappeared. The footsteps in the stairwell had walked past this room, too, opening another door at the far end of the hall and going quiet. Eli could brush Julien off and leave the lodge now unnoticed.

But would that be what was best? Julien was apparently a man on a mission, and unless Eli gave him some sort of explanation, he'd probably continue asking and ending up underfoot. It was his MO. What's more, Julien might actually be helpful. Eli frankly didn't care who'd killed Ian Ackman, if that was indeed him they'd found on the mountain. Unless it had something to do with who was behind the renaissance of Sweet Pea. Then he was very interested. Were the two connected? He couldn't see an obvious connection. And yet it seemed like too odd a co-incidence to not be.

"All right then. I did go into Annabelle's office to get that camera," Eli said, and smirked when Julien's jaw dropped.

"You—but—why?"

"Not because I'm trying to sabotage Annabelle's business, whatever Cody might think. I have no need. We host very different clientele."

Julien frowned. "As in hers exist and yours don't?"

"*As in*, the retreat's purpose is to be a sort of safe house for individuals leaving bad situations with nowhere to go. I can't give you any more specifics than that."

"Right." Julien's expression looked a bit grim, but he was nodding. "No need. I understand. The night of the accident, you said your guests' privacy was important. You're worried who might be on that camera and where that information could go."

Eli controlled his surprise at how quickly Julien had picked up on where he was going with that. "Yes, that's right. Only, as you know, the card was gone before I got there."

"Which makes me think there was something else on there besides, well, whatever that thing was Annabelle showed us," Julien said, and Eli hummed a noncommittal sound. "Whether it has to do with your retreat or my murder is unclear. Who's De Luca?"

"Why do you ask that?" Eli asked sharply.

"You said the name De Luca. Right before you asked me if I was trying to take the retreat. I just wondered what they had to do with this."

Eli hesitated, considering if he was about to take this too far. But Julien was an unaware human. What harm could it do? "Celia De Luca is a businesswoman of sorts, with ties to this area. She isn't pleased with what we're doing with the retreat."

"Why not?"

"Apparently she thinks we'll draw the wrong sort of attention. Although I also suspect she's interested in…buying the property herself. And might still get a chance to do so, if we're forced to shut down. You look upset."

Julien's face had gotten more and more tense as he'd spoken. "The *wrong sort of attention*? You mean the wrong sort of people."

Eli shrugged. He'd meant human attention of course, but that was probably true, as well. It was unlikely there'd be quite this much pushback if it was a retreat for wolves running away from ruling packs. Not that such a thing even existed, as far as Eli knew.

"Like it's something to be ashamed of, being hurt, needing help," Julien was saying angrily. "What the hell does she want to be there instead, a second luxury resort? 'Cause this place is so clearly flooded with guests."

Eli took an impulsive step closer, cautiously scenting him. Julien's heart rate was up, he was all heat and adrenaline, and Eli felt his own pulse quicken in response. "Perhaps she thinks it's more…respectable on this side of the mountain. Except for the teensy little issue of murder. But I'm sure she'll find a way to blame the retreat for that before long."

Julien hummed in agreement and then gave Eli an inscrutable look. "Look, I have a proposition for you."

"I accept. But you'll have to take that shirt back off first. I don't fuck people in flannel."

"Ah." Julien coughed, face flushing immediately. "I meant it sounds to me like the sooner this murder is cleared up, the better for your retreat. Maybe we could...pool our information."

Convincing the mark they want to give it to you is always better than taking it for yourself. Another one of Prisha's favorite maxims. As always, she was absolutely right.

Eli pretended to consider that and watched Julien shift his weight nervously. "I guess that makes sense," he said slowly. "If only to avoid finding you under my kitchen sink or hiding in my shower."

Julien laughed in an embarrassed way, but looked relieved. "Great. That's—well, it'll be nice to hear someone else's opinion on this stuff finally. Should we get started tomorrow morning?"

"It's a date." Eli smiled softly and Julien stuck his hand out as if to shake, before snatching it back.

"Oh, you don't like that, do you? Well—" He reached out to tap Eli's upper arm in a friendly sort of way and his eyes widened slightly. "Oh," he said under his breath, hand lingering a millisecond too long, fingers finding the grooves of not-insignificant muscles.

Julien's mouth parted slightly, eyes abruptly, impossibly blacker. There it was again. All that restrained *want.* Eli felt the thrill of it race along his skin like an electric current. Felt the desire to preen, show off, tease until *want* tightened to *need* and snapped into *take*. There were a lot of things Eli planned to find out about Julien. But first and foremost, how he liked to fuck.

Julien blushed and pulled away. "Sorry. Back home, people pay trainers a lot of money for arms like that."

"I spend a lot of time walking on my hands," Eli said, and stepped into his personal space. Eli rested three fingers on the center of Julien's bare chest, feeling his heartbeat as intimately as his own. Slowly, giving him time to say no, Eli dipped his hand under the unbuttoned flannel to trace the same muscles of his arm. "How much do they pay for sartorial advice? Back home?"

"What?" Julien choked just as Eli slipped the flannel off his shoulders and let it fall to the floor.

"Doesn't matter. First tip's on the house." He traced back up the arm and down his ribs until he hit the towel riding low on his hips. "Second tip may cost you, though."

Eli let his finger trail along the edge, to the center of Julien's belly, and looked up at him through his lashes.

But Julien wasn't moving. He was just staring at him, as if stunned.

Frowning, Eli gently withdrew his hand. When Julien still didn't move, he took a couple steps back.

For fuck's sake. Had he—? How the hell had he read this wrong? The way Julien tracked him across every room, the way his heart raced when he got near, the way he'd been *feeling him up*. Well, clearly there was some other reason for it because he sure as shit hadn't been thinking about sex.

God, it was time to go. Never take more than you came for, indeed. What a colossal fuckup.

Eli took another step back and his back pressed up against the door. "I'm sorry, I thought... It doesn't matter. I apologize for making you uncomfortable," he said, stiffly reaching behind him for the handle. "I'll see you in the morning, okay?"

Julien was still staring at him with wide eyes, but as soon as Eli managed to crack the door he made a distressed sound, stepped forward and reached for Eli's hand. "Wait, please..."

He was barely touching Eli's knuckles, the slightest brush of skin on skin more than any pressure, but Eli let the cracked door fall shut again. The soft click sounded impossibly loud in the silence.

Julien looked down at their hands still resting on the handle. He trailed his fingertips down the fleshy curve between finger and thumb, over the sensitive pulse point of his wrist and then slowly up the inside of Eli's forearm, pulling back the sleeve of his sweater until it was bunched up above the crook of his elbow. He hesitated there for a moment, frowning down at where he was tickling the thin skin, then suddenly pressed his thumb down into the muscle just below and pulled Eli's arm up over his head to press against the door.

Eli couldn't resist the slightest growl, instinctively resistant to having his flank vulnerable and yet yearning for more. It couldn't have sounded like more than a vibration to human ears, but Julien met his eyes all the same.

"Is this okay?" he asked with a little more grit in his voice himself.

Eli nodded, but Julien continued to look at him expectantly and his grip on Eli's arm loosened, which wouldn't do at all.

"Yes," Eli said. "It's more than okay."

Julien's thumb went back to massaging slow circles into the tender muscle, studying it intently. His face was so serious he was nearly frowning. It gave him a stern, analytical look that was distracting enough that Eli didn't even notice Julien's other hand until it landed on his hip. That thumb didn't waste any time finding its own sensitive spot just beneath his belly, and within seconds Eli felt pinned against the door by those two points of pooling heat, as securely as if Julien had strapped him down with rope.

Eli opened his eyes—when had he closed them?—and found Julien watching his face with a faintly approving smile. He leaned forward, and Eli licked his lips and tilted his head in expectation, but Julien moved past him and pressed his just-open mouth against the crook of Eli's elbow and dragged his teeth over the skin. Eli groaned and his head tipped back, hitting the wood.

"Is this okay?" Julien asked into his body.

"Yes," Eli choked out, and Julien began to suck and tongue at the spot with the occasional nip in between. His hand was wrapped around Eli's wrist now and pulled it straight so that he could mouth his way up his arm. Eli's hips jerked forward, seeking more contact, but the hand on his hip forced him back against the door and Julien straightened back up.

"This is nice," he said. "Surprisingly...silky. Would you like to pull it up for me?"

It took Eli an embarrassingly long time to realize he was

talking about the sweater. With one hand still trapped, he gripped the hem and tugged it above his chest. Julien drank him in, dark eyes darting from his rather defined pecs to his soft, pale belly, then reached up and rolled one nipple under his thumb. Eli whimpered, hitting his head back against the door again, harder this time.

Julien made a disapproving sound and tugged Eli's trapped wrist down until he was cupping the back of his own head with his hand. "Can you keep that there?"

Eli nodded silently. He felt uncommonly slow, dazed by how succinctly Julien had taken control of his body. With both hands freed up, Julien began to play with both nipples concurrently—urging them into tight points and then plucking at them lightly, then not so lightly. Experimenting with different touches while studying Eli's body, every minute reaction and sharp inhale, when he flinched away and when he began to grip at his own hair.

"Please," Eli said, unable to take it anymore. His trapped dick ached and he tilted his hips forward again, leadingly.

Julien looked at him and seemed startled. Had he really been that focused on his chest?

"Hurts. Please," Eli whispered again.

Julien's hands slid immediately down his belly and undid his pants, carefully tugging them up and over Eli's erection straining in his briefs, and letting them fall to his knees. That helped ease the pressure a bit, but his hips still twitched restlessly, begging for touch. Any touch.

Well, maybe not any, Eli amended when Julien began to rub teasingly at the insides of his thighs. Julien was staring at his body with such an odd expression on his face that

Eli felt inexplicably shy. He absolutely refused to squirm away or hide, but couldn't stop his arms from trembling where they were still pinned behind his head and holding up his sweater.

Julien's fingers brushed lightly over his dick, tracing the line of it behind the fabric, then cupped his balls. "You're so hard," he said wonderingly, squeezing lightly.

"I need to come," Eli said. "Please let me."

Julien's gaze flickered up to Eli's, eyes huge and so black it was difficult to tell where the pupil began. He leaned forward, almost crowding Eli against the door but not quite, and nudged the side of his face with his own, nipping at his earlobe.

Then he pressed his thigh against Eli's dick. "Rub."

Eli's knees wobbled and he almost fell, but Julien caught him, hands grabbing his hips and then sliding around to his ass. They slipped up the back of his briefs from the bottom and massaged the naked flesh there as Eli began to rut into his leg frantically, their chests just barely brushing, Julien's short hard breaths against his ear.

When Eli felt Julien's fingers slip into his crack, pull him apart as he bit at his jaw, he came unexpectedly. As if the orgasm that had been building steadily, heavier and hotter within him, had suddenly burned through its last restraint and plummeted free fall down the length of his body, leaving nothing behind but smoldering ash.

What...the fuck. He wasn't even undressed. He hadn't even made it into the room. And yet somehow his ears were ringing, his muscles were goo and he was docilely allowing Julien to gather him up and lead him to the bed, where he collapsed face-first into the mattress. Somewhere over the edge, he felt his shoes and socks come off, gently followed by his pants. The cool air on his feet and legs was so blissful that it suddenly felt imperative that he get naked right now and *good god* why was he still wearing a *sweater*?

"Shh, shh," Julien said, helping him pull the rest of it all off, and then left the room. Eli's ear twitched as he tracked him entering the bathroom, running some water and then returning, the bed dipping beneath them. A moment later he felt a gentle wet washcloth clean him and the coolness of someone blowing lightly on his back.

"Oh," Eli groaned, and heard soft laughter though it sounded a bit strained. *Oh. Right.* Eli glanced over his shoulder. Julien was sitting on the edge of the bed, twin spots of color high on his cheeks, gripping the towel that was still modestly bunched in his lap, looking at Eli's body and then away as if not sure he was allowed.

Eli tilted his hips invitingly, and was gratified to see Julien's eyes widen so dramatically it was almost funny. "Go ahead. You can if you want to."

Julien's whole face flushed and he coughed on a choke. "Um, no. Thanks." Then in a rush added, "Not that you aren't—I just don't have stuff for, uh, that, here, now."

Eli raised an eyebrow, feeling a bit more like himself now that Julien was blushing and stuttering and order was being restored in the world. "I wasn't saying you could fuck me," he said, amused.

"No, right, of course not."

"Not like that."

Julien snapped his mouth shut and his eyes darkened.

Eli spread his thighs slightly and tilted his hips up again. Hesitantly Julien got up on the bed and placed the towel to the side.

"Fucking hell," Eli murmured, genuinely startled. "Do people often invite you to jump in them sans prep with that thing?"

Julien looked a little embarrassed but his voice was wry when he said, "Not often, no."

"Although now I understand how the towel was staying up."

"Okay." Julien rolled his eyes, but he looked more relaxed as he crawled over and then decisively put a strong hand on the small of Eli's back and pushed him down firmly.

"Mmmmph," Eli grunted, burying his face in the pillows. His teeth sharpened and his muscles rippled, wanting to shift, and he pulled everything back into place. Now that he was sated, the feeling of someone dominating him tickled wary defensive instincts. But as surprisingly strong as Julien felt, Eli only needed to flex to reassure himself that he could overpower him, if necessary.

Not that it was going to be necessary in the least since aside from that hand on his back, Julien wasn't even touching him. Eli looked over his shoulder again to find him slowly stroking himself, watching him.

When their eyes met, Julien bit his lip but didn't look away. "I want to come on you. Is that okay?"

Eli nodded. "Yes."

And Julien picked up the pace. The sounds of his soft panting and slapping skin in the otherwise silent room was oddly exciting. Illicit, somehow. Eli dragged one knee up to the side so that he was practically presenting himself to be taken.

Julien gasped, "Jesus. You're—"

"Yeah," Eli agreed. Because whatever he wanted to say, he probably was. "Tell me."

"So *pretty*." It was less than a whisper. Definitely not meant to actually be heard, but Eli couldn't help preening a bit, arching his back. Julien's hand moved to grip his shoulder, instead, and Eli thrust lightly against the mattress to move his ass. He wasn't going to come again, but there were definite rolling swells of pleasure cresting somewhere deep inside.

"I want it. Mark me. I want to smell like yours." Oops, maybe not that. But either it still worked in translation or Julien hadn't even noticed because his breath was coming in short gasps now. "Please, give it to me. I want to be so pretty for you."

Julien grunted and Eli felt the first splash of heat on his ass before the hand on his shoulder moved suddenly, grabbing the back of his neck. Eli reacted without thinking, twisting his head and biting down on the threat. He tasted Julien's scent against his tongue, and stopped just in time to avoid breaking the skin.

Julien grunted and finished, jerking so hard he knocked into Eli's body a couple times by accident, then collapsed on the other side of the bed on his back, wrist sliding out of Eli's mouth, teeth scraping skin.

They both lay there panting. Julien from exertion, Eli from nerves. He'd let his canines slip to something way too pointy to pass as human for a moment there, and he waited for the horror, the fear, a fist—anything to confirm whether or not Julien had noticed.

After a long moment Eli glanced at Julien as subtly as possible, but the man didn't seem to be alarmed or on the verge of demanding answers. He just seemed a bit dazed. Staring up at the ceiling with wide eyes, one hand—not bleeding, thank god—resting on his rapidly beating heart. He hadn't caught sight of the teeth then. Now the only thing to worry about was if Julien was upset Eli had *bit* him like some kind of skittish animal.

Eli pushed himself to sitting. "Well—"

"Thank you," Julien said at the same time, then blushed. "Sorry, what were you going to say?"

Well, see you on the slopes. But that seemed a bit harsh now with those big dark eyes staring at him so intently. Also...*thank you?*

"Can I use your shower?" Eli asked instead.

"Oh! Yes, of course. Do you want me to—" He started to get up and Eli quickly stood.

"I think I can find it. Good sleuthing practice for tomorrow."

"Right. Hot water to the left. Cold to the right. Just, you know, one less for the caseload," Julien said, wincing and shaking his head a little as he spoke, as if he regretted it, but was powerless to stop.

And with that sparkling exchange, Eli retreated into the bathroom.

Yeesh. So top marks for the sex and participation points at best for the post-coital conversation. Though to be fair,

Eli hadn't exactly been his usual droll self at the end there either. He felt oddly flustered by the whole thing. That had been far too sloppy of him, biting like a brand-new pup. Was Julien acting oddly? Had he seen something after all? No, surely not. When humans did manage to notice the existence of wolves it leaned more toward screaming than bumbling repartee over the plumbing.

The truth was he'd felt uncomfortably…seen by Julien in ways that had nothing to do with being a wolf. It had been unbearably exciting by the door for reasons he hadn't realized others could see in him. Things he certainly hadn't expected a man like Julien to have picked up on, anyway. They'd only met a couple days ago. And in between a busy itinerary of breaking and entering, monster hunting, fire fighting and body discovery, had managed approximately five minutes of non-antagonistic conversation cumulatively. Hardly soul-baring stuff. But somehow Julien had plucked at threads Eli had allowed be woven into a simpler, safer pattern a long time ago.

Eli wasn't sure he liked it. And yet he felt a delicious swoop in his stomach imagining doing it again. Julien might follow him into the bathroom, tell him to keep his hands up, keep washing his hair, while he did anything he wanted to his body.

Eli lingered in the shower thinking on that.

Well, and why not do it again? He wasn't one to get precious about sex. Quite the opposite. For him fucking was comfort, distraction, fun. An easy way to feel better when life felt bad. At least that's what it could be with Julien. The man was mouth-wateringly hot with an eye-watering cock and apparently predisposed to be compatible in bed. Even better, he was only here for a limited amount of time. Eli didn't have sex with the same human more than once. It was a good rule that avoided the risk of feelings and prying questions and dreary breakups when they determined he was hiding something.

But Julien was leaving town on his own accord. And he already knew he couldn't trust Eli. They'd be spending time together investigating a murder, god help them all. They could have some fun while they found their answers and then go their separate ways.

He couldn't have any more slipping or fucking *biting*, but at least Julien seemed as cynical about all the Sweet Pea nonsense as Eli was. It was easier to get by unnoticed with humans like that who'd rather file just about anything under "quirk" rather than entertain the possibility that they'd been quite efficiently lied to for thousands of years. So Eli wouldn't need to be *too* careful. Have your cake and get your cake eaten too, if he was lucky.

Eli got out of the shower and quickly dried off, slipped his twitchier bits back and forth until they were soothed and walked back into the bedroom fully convinced and ready to get off again. Right now, preferably. But Julien was asleep.

Propped up, he sat against the headboard, hands clasped in his lap like he was waiting for an appointment. He'd slipped into a pair of boxers and laid out a selection of sweatpants, T-shirts and underwear options on the bed as if in offering. That was...oddly sweet. Even if they were still some of the most boring clothes Eli had ever seen.

Eli put on some sweatpants and folded up what remained.

He wasn't trying to wake Julien, really, but if he jostled the bed a few times, accidentally, of course, and it happened to wake him, that would be fine.

But Julien didn't stir once. Not even a twitch. Honestly, how this species continued to survive without the least bit of self-preservation was beyond him.

Eli sighed and went to put the leftover clothes in the dresser, but the top drawer was already full. Books, papers, notebooks, charcoal sketches. Words leapt out at him. *Windigo, Chupacabra. Werewolf. Nagual. Michigan Dogman. Werewolf. Ningen. Dover Demon. Dybbuk. Werewolf. Werewolf. Werewolf.* Monster after monster interspersed with images of fleshless, fanged women. Slinking creatures with glowing eyes and dripping claws. A wolf howling at the moon.

Eli dropped the clothes and ran.

Chapter Seven

Julien woke up, heart pounding in his throat, alone and aching all over around three a.m. His neck was so stiff the pain seemed to radiate up through his entire skull. Even his jaw cracked as he yawned and he walked to the bathroom, shuffling awkwardly because his spine was lodging some serious complaints, all of which were valid.

How embarrassing to pass out sitting upright like an old man in front of the TV. He was almost grateful the nightmares had woken him tonight. Almost. His insomnia had been particularly bad since arriving at Blue Tail and part of him was surprised he'd managed to sleep at all. Of course, sex always put him out like a li—

Julien stopped in the middle of washing his hands. "Oh no."

He rushed back into the bedroom as if Eli might have

been tucked away in a corner stealthily amused, as was his custom. But of course no one was there. Had he even said goodbye? Or had Julien just come and then tipped over like an asshole? Like one of those insects that died at orgasm. No, that was being too generous. At least their mates got a nice post-coitus meal out of it. He hadn't even offered Eli a beverage.

"Fuck." Julien sat on the end of the bed and ran his hands through his hair. Well, that was that. Decades of simmering curiosity and wondering *what if* had finally culminated in completely fumbling one of the hottest encounters of his life. Just as he'd always suspected.

It wasn't that Julien didn't know he was bisexual. Maybe he'd realized a tad later than some, but so what? He didn't have hang-ups about it either. He might not be out in a public way, but most of the people he loved knew. Being bi had never been the scary part. But being bad at it?

Desire and experience were different games. He'd been monogamously married to cis women for the majority of his adult life. Out of his three nonconsecutive years single, he'd spent one of them at the bottom of such a pit of grief he wasn't having sex with anyone, and the other two he'd just been, well, *nervous*. Being a man in your forties and relatively famous meant people treating you a certain way, having certain expectations. Especially the ones who wanted to sleep with you. *Especially* especially the ones who wanted people to know they'd slept with you.

Julien Doran Sucks Dick was a headline he could shrug off and laugh about. Hell, he might even frame it on his wall. *Middle-Aged Man Julien Doran Gave Me the Worst Blow Job of My Entire Life, Spit Up on my Dick and Then Started Crying* was a little long for a headline, but the perfect length for a coroner to write under "Cause of Death."

He'd been scared last night, too, obviously. But the moment Eli had reached for that door, the idea of losing the chance to touch him was worse. He'd been operating on instinct and a prayer with that one, and it had been a rush. For a man like *that*, all quick and biting and sly, to stand still for Julien, to look at him with nothing but honest desire in his eyes was intoxicating. Too much so, apparently, since he'd keeled over immediately and Eli had taken the chance to run like a shot.

Well, of course he had. It had probably been the worst sex of his life. Julien hadn't even been brave enough to give him a hand job. He hadn't even taken his underwear off, for fuck's sake. Too worried that it would be obvious he hadn't done this before. Just ordered him around, made him ride his thigh in his clothes like a teenager, came on his back and immediately cosplayed *Weekend at Bernie's*. What, no morning sex?

Jesus, what if Eli reconsidered working together? What if things were just too awkward between them to continue? He couldn't let that happen. Eli was precisely the sort of help he needed in this. He'd only just begun to see that on the mountain yesterday. Even just the prospect of maybe not being alone with this miserable, suffocating *thing* every single minute of every single day—

Julien felt a tightening in his throat. Ah, god. Enough of that. He'd gotten here on his own, he could keep on the same way, if that was how it had to be. Would he rather do it with a sharp-witted, good-hearted, quick-thinking, sexy-as-fuck manager of a haven for disenfranchised people, who, oh right, apparently had access to information Julien had crossed the country looking for? Well, yeah. He also would *rather* have gotten Eli's briefs down and sucked him off better than anyone else ever had in his entire life, but here they were.

Julien pulled at his own hair and groaned loudly. *I never even kissed him.* Somehow it was that thought that propelled him into action. Well, all right. He owed the man an apology, that was all there was to it. Maybe if he explained—

Julien winced. What? *Sorry for the shitty lay? Come across any clues while you were fleeing into the night? Also, can we please try again?* God no. He'd go over there, at least. They did say they'd get to work in the morning. Then he'd play the rest by ear.

Julien stood—now that he'd decided on a course of action, he wanted to get started right away—then remembered it was the middle of the night and sat back down. The really smart thing to do would be to get back to sleep. This was a conversation best had while well rested.

After seven hours of sitting in bed replaying every second of the evening, which was equal parts agonizing and arousing, and reading through Rocky's notebook trying to determine what he could and couldn't share, Julien knocked on the door of the retreat with coffee and pastries in hand. Then knocked again. It was snowing a little and the air was that sharp, wet cold you felt in your throat. It seemed silly not to walk right in—it was a lobby, after all—but Julien wanted to avoid previous mistakes. If he demonstrated he was capable of learning and improving, who knows, maybe Eli would extrapolate from there. Or at least that's what he'd like to demonstrate if anyone was even home.

Julien took a step back to look for something louder than a knock—a doorbell, gong, boom box to place on his shoulders—and saw something flash by from the corner of his eye.

He turned to face the empty parking lot. "Eli?"

But no one seemed to be there. Julien turned back to the door and saw it again. Now he was sure something had run past. Julien walked down the porch steps and into the snowy parking lot.

"Hello? Is someone out here?" It was the same feeling he'd had out on the road, that strange quiet, like the world was holding its breath. This time Julien held it, too. His heart was beating fast and his hands tingled. He curled them into loose fists and rolled onto the balls of his feet in preparation. *Check me out, Patrick West.*

Julien scanned the driveway, the tree line, the hill, the little cottages down the hill, under the porch, over the— there. Slight movement at the corner of his car's shadow, the very edge of another shadow was moving. *Breathing.*

"Hey!" Julien yelled. "I know you're there. Come on." He stalked forward across the parking lot, slippery with fresh snow. "Why are you—" Julien rounded the car and stopped. Nothing. There was nobody there.

"What the fuck," he murmured. There were tracks in the snow. Feeling extremely out of his element, Julien crouched to get a closer look. He had done a film once where his character had crash-landed in the Arctic and developed a Captain Ahab–inspired obsession with a polar bear. It had involved a lot of crouching down like this, looking haunted and then going careening off through deep snow. Of course, Julien had never actually seen a single footprint. They'd added those in post.

These were…an animal. Not a deer. Probably. And went in the direction of the tree line. That's all he had. Julien stood back up without looking away from the woods. Morning sunlight peeked through the tangle of branches and glinted off the snow, giving the illusion of movement. It was eerily easy to feel like something was standing just out of sight, watching him back.

"Looking for someone?"

Julien gasped and fumbled the coffees, dropping one to the ground and spilling the other when he instinctively tried to grab it. "Shit, shit, sorry. I didn't hear you there."

He turned around to find a woman was standing less than a foot from him. She was white, young and rather beautiful with cherry-red hair and cheekbones that stayed prominent even without smiling. She also had a hideous bruise on one leg, easily visible since she was apparently only wearing a thigh-length T-shirt, a pair of flip-flops and nothing else.

Julien took a couple steps away from her, putting some space between them. "Are you all right?"

The woman tilted her head, staring at him with an oddly blank expression. "Of course. What were you looking at?"

"Oh, I thought I saw—" he glanced back at the trees, but the watchful feeling was gone "—an animal. But it was probably nothing."

"It's never *nothing*," she said. "The question is if it's a dangerous something or not."

"Am I likely to see a dangerous something around these parts?"

The woman smiled suddenly, and Julien had the oddest feeling of relief. He hadn't even realized he'd felt tense before. "I guess that depends on why you're here."

"I wanted to talk to Eli. Eli Smith, the manager?"

"You didn't want to book a room," she said more than asked.

"Not exactly," he said vaguely, distracted by wondering if it would make her uncomfortable if he suggested they continue this conversation inside. But he was cold just looking at her. What was it with this place and wandering around half-dressed? "Do you, ah, work here?"

"Not exactly," she said with another smile.

Before he could react to that, the retreat's front door opened and Eli sailed out across the parking lot. "Thank you, Gwen. I can take this from here."

She ducked her head in an almost old-fashioned way and walked past him. "Sorry about the coffee."

"What did you say to her?" Eli demanded as soon as she disappeared inside the retreat.

"What? Nothing," Julien said, confused. Eli looked a bit wild this morning. Hair tousled and eyes boring into Julien with...suspicion? What did Eli think he'd been saying to her? Did he not want anyone knowing they'd hooked up? Jesus, did he think he'd been asking *her* out to coffee right here in his backyard?

"Then what were you talking about?"

"You. Dangerous animals," Julien joked, and was surprised when Eli took a stumbling step away from him.

"Do you think you're funny?" Eli hissed, his voice cold.

"No...? We—I thought there was a big animal behind my car. But I think it ran into the woods." He looked at the tree line again, half expecting to find something watching them, but there was no one.

"What animal?"

Julien shrugged. "Why, do you think it was Sweet Pea?"

Eli ignored that and brushed past him, stooping to pick up the fallen coffee cup.

"I dropped that when Gwen came outside. Look, all I told her was I wanted to talk to you. I didn't tell her ab—I didn't tell her why, if that's what you're worried about. I'm not here to spread your business around your, ah, business."

"Then why don't you tell me why you are here," Eli said evenly.

"Oh." Julien looked down at the bedraggled remains of his nice gesture. "Um, you said what goes bump in the night should bring you breakfast. So."

Eli stared at him with a cryptic expression. It definitely wasn't Julien's imagination. He was definitely acting different this morning. Shut off, wary, pissed. Afraid? Maybe it wasn't about Gwen at all. Maybe last night had been worse than he'd feared.

Julien racked his brain for what else could have happened. Did Eli regret it? It was obvious he hadn't been planning for that to happen. Jesus, had he felt pushed into something? Julien felt sick at the thought. He convulsively squeezed the pastry bag and felt a jam tart burst inside.

"I'm sorry I passed out on you like that last night." He blew out a puff of air, visible in the cold. "I had a good time. I hope you did, as well. But if you, ah, didn't, I'm really sorry about that, too."

Eli tilted his head and after a moment stepped closer, inhaling deeply. A tiny frown on his forehead. "The sex isn't the problem. The sex was…good."

Well, he could have done without that hesitation there, but it was the first win in a while and Julien's stupid little heart still did a stutter of happiness. *Hey! We were long-pause-good! We did that!* "Wow! I mean, that's gre—good. That's good. Um, what is the problem?"

"You lied to me."

"Wha-at?"

"Investigating the lodge, Ian Ackman, working with your brother to solve his murder. In a word, bullshit."

Julien's face went numb. His heart had shut up, too. "No."

"Yes," Eli snapped. "I'm not someone you can lie to, Mr. Doran. It isn't done, it isn't wise and it isn't good for your health. Last night you said you were done playing games, so let's stop. I'm going to ask you for the last time, why did you come to Maudit Falls, and if you try to fuck me around one little bit, you're going to long for the days when a dangerous animal was the worst thing in this parking lot."

Eli had prowled closer as he spoke. His eyes were so bright and so cold they almost glowed, like blue ice catching dawn's first light, and Julien felt…alive.

"My brother, Rocky, died last year in an accident." Julien looked down at the empty coffee cup still held haphazardly in Eli's hands. It was dripping—warm, almond-brown droplets staining the snow. "I've been seeing this grief counselor and she gives me these little homework assignments. A couple weeks ago the assignment was to go somewhere I associate with Rocky and apologize to him. Let him apologize to me."

Julien reached out and nudged the lid so that Eli held it upright and the dripping stopped. He laughed self-consciously and forced himself to look back up at Eli. "Goofy, I know. But I thought, why the hell not? I went to our old room that we'd shared at our parents' house. There's this little hidey-hole behind the molding. Perfect for a kid to stash stuff in. I looked in thinking I might find, I don't know, thirty-year-old weed? But instead there was all this stuff about Blue Tail Lodge and Ian Ackman."

Julien hesitated, speaking carefully now. "Rocky had stayed there after Ian went missing. He'd become sort of... obsessed with finding out what happened to him. It felt like he'd left those notes there for me to find. I mean, I was the one who hid stuff there. Not Rocky. He never worried about getting in trouble."

Eli's expression was unreadable, or maybe Julien was just much worse at reading him than he'd thought. "Did your brother know Ian Ackman?"

"No, I lied about that," Julien admitted. "I didn't know how to explain without sounding—" He cut himself off. "The truth is I came here to finish what Rocky started. I know that might be ridiculous, but honestly it felt like a better way to apologize than sitting in a bedroom he hadn't even slept in since he was fifteen, waiting for forgiveness from someone who isn't there."

And it was the truth. Or at least it was all the truth Julien could make sense of. He couldn't begin to know how to explain the rest. The haunting guilt that had driven him here. The anger at Rocky for chasing after monsters and forcing Julien to put aside his disbelief to do the same. He couldn't tell Eli about that part, even if he knew how.

"How did you find out about all this, anyway?"

Eli grimaced slightly but didn't look away. "I didn't. I was referring to the trove of supernatural literature in your dresser."

"Oh," Julien said, embarrassed. "That's Rocky's. Most of it, anyway. He was really into that kind of stuff. He actually believed in—" he flapped a hand "—whatever the creature of the week was. Compared to him, Annabelle looks like a hardened skeptic."

"Don't tell me your brother thought Sweet Pea killed Ian Ackman."

"No, not this time. But it is why he first came to Blue Tail. Rocky traveled all over looking for, you know, ghosts. Yeti. Shape-shifters. Monster hunting, he used to call it. I thought reading his books would help me think like him, retrace his steps."

Eli's expression had gone very blank, and he turned to look at the retreat. "Well? Has it?"

"I'm not going to suggest we add Mothman to our suspect list, if that's what you're asking," Julien said dryly.

Eli's shoulders seemed to relax a fraction, as if up until now he'd genuinely been worried Julien was going to do exactly that. Christ, just how bad had that drawer looked last night? Bad, if it had literally driven Eli screaming into the night. Not to mention his reaction this morning, which had been...confusing, now that Julien thought about it.

Because that hadn't just been anger in his eyes. That had been fear. And he didn't have a clue why Eli would be afraid over some silly old books.

"I—I don't really believe in any of that shit, though," Julien said, studying Eli's face. "I mean, if that's what you're worried about."

"Why would that worry me?" Eli said, tilting his chin up a little imperiously, and Julien realized something else—he was still afraid.

"I don't know," Julien said cautiously, searching for something to say to put Eli back at ease, the way he'd been last night, smirking and confident and not at all concerned that the man he'd just gotten naked with was currently traveling with *An Abridged History of Exorcism in the West*. There was a whole spectrum of belief between Julien's eye-rolling dismissal and Rocky's gleeful passion. Just because Eli appeared as cynical as him didn't mean he wanted to be around that sort of stuff. "My brother once got kicked out of a bed-and-breakfast for packing a Ouija board. You don't have to be a full-on believer like Professor Patrick West to get weird about supernatural things."

To his relief, Eli made his odd little huffing sound and his shoulders dropped farther. "I do try to keep my devil worship and amateur murder investigations strictly separate. I'm a purist like that." He paused. "You didn't go on these...monster hunts before? With your brother?"

"I've never done anything like this before in my life," Julien said bluntly. "And I can't imagine I will again. It's funny, the whole reason my counselor wanted me to go back to our old room to apologize was to help me accept my *new normal*. Talk about a backfire. Last month the most abnormal thing grief had me doing was drinking an extra couple glasses of wine at night. Now I'm running around after cryptozoologists and digging up skeletons and—and—having vacation sex with strangers."

"On the other hand, who are we to question the process," Eli drawled, surprising a real laugh out of Julien.

He tore restlessly at the edge of the pastry bag. The crushed tart had stained the bottom dark red, and his hand felt vaguely sticky. "The thing is, losing Rocky didn't even change much of my life. We had one conversation that whole last month before he died and it was just a stupid, ten-minute fight. Honestly, so much of the day-to-day stuff has stayed the same that sometimes I don't even believe it really happened. I think he must just be ignoring me again. Like if he was really gone, I wouldn't see colors anymore or be having the same exact small talk about the lottery with my corner store guy."

Julien wished Eli would look away. Say something. Give him permission to stop talking. Hell, maybe even threaten him some more. But instead he just stood there listening with careful focus. As if Julien wasn't just telling his version of the same old tired story everyone had. As if Julien was the first person in the whole world to ever experience loss so it mattered, *actually* mattered, in the real sense that gravity and entropy and inertia did. As if his own private little sorrow was something no one could possibly ignore.

"Some weeks feel so familiar, so *normal* that I forget he's dead and then I remember and—" Julien paused, vocal cords painfully tight. He forced the words out anyway. "I don't know why that's harder for me, somehow. The remembering."

Julien cleared his throat roughly and swiped his fingers under his eyes brusquely, horrified that they were stinging. The crinkling paper of the pastry bag was so loud in the silence and there were still no birds. Even now that the animal was surely long gone. "Jesus, sorry. That was a lot. I'm kind of an emotional guy at the best of times."

"And these haven't been the best of times," Eli said.

Another laugh burst out of Julien's mouth. "No. Not really."

Eli fiddled with the empty coffee cup in his hand. "I'm sorry. About your brother. And for possibly overreacting this morning. Just a little."

"You're good. You've got a right to know who you're getting into bed wi—business with," he corrected hurriedly. "Detective business. That is, if you still want to work together."

Eli shot him a sharp look. "I'd look like a real villain if I said no now."

Julien smiled, feeling lighter, hopeful. "You always do. No offense. A really gorgeous villain, though. One of the slinky sort in great clothes and judgmental eyebrows." Eli raised one of the eyebrows in question. "Exactly like that, yeah."

"If this is your idea of buttering me up, scrape it off. I'm not agreeing to team up just because of a little flattery. I'm not that easy."

"I doubt anyone would ever think that of you."

"And I'm definitely not agreeing because I feel guilty about yelling at you, forcing you to talk about your grief and making you cry."

"I don't remember it happening *exactly* like that."

"I have my own reasons for wanting to figure out what's going on, remember?"

"Yes, I do," Julien said, seriously this time. "I care about that, too."

Eli eyed him for a long moment. "All right then. Let's solve a murder."

Finally, Julien could breathe. He inhaled shakily, the cold air clearing his lungs, giving him strength he hadn't had, the smell of spilled coffee in his nose. "Should we take this inside, swap stories, plan our next move? First move?"

Eli was already shaking his head. "We can swap whatever you wish in the car. I want to get back to the top of the mountain and take a look around that tower before the snow takes out the roads."

"That might be soon, at this rate." Eli's hair had already collected a large amount of snow. It looked...poofier, somehow, the way the flakes kept getting caught on the outermost layer. "Do the roads often go out?"

"Motto of the mountain, or so I've heard. Come for the murder, stay because inclement weather and neglected infrastructure make it impossible to leave."

Julien hummed, gaze drawn once more toward the tree line. "Do you think it's safe to be in the woods?"

"Because we're two amateurs involving ourselves in a murder investigation that we know nearly nothing about with an obscene degree of confidence?"

"You really know how to make a man feel like a Hardy Boy," Julien said wryly. "But no, I meant in case of animals. Should we bring bear spray?"

Eli waved that off. "We'll be fine. I'm going to shi—ft into sturdier clothes before we go. Will you be warm enough in that?"

Julien nodded, glancing down Eli's unusually subdued outfit, and couldn't stop a soft inhale, mouth instantly dry. "You're wearing my sweatpants."

The slightest, most fascinating pink appeared on the tops of Eli's cheeks and across the bridge of his nose, like a little sunburn. "Ah. Yes, I am. Thank you for the loan. Mine weren't exactly travel-appropriate last night."

So he'd worn them home, slept in them and not taken them off all morning? Julien felt a cautiously hopeful little flutter in his chest and a much bigger flutter some ways below that. Eli had said the sex was long-pause-good. Julien could improve on that. Julien wanted to improve on that. He was flushed with the excitement of finally having direction, an ally, a source, a second chance. He'd forgotten what that felt like. Worse, somewhere along the line he'd forgotten that he'd forgotten.

Julien took a step forward so that he was standing inches from Eli. Close enough to hear his breath catch. "I'm not as slick with the sartorial advice as you are, but—" he ran his hand up the inside edge of Eli's leg slowly, giving him time to pull away "—if you're looking for an amateur's opinion, I think you make even my clothes look good." Julien's fingers brushed the edge of Eli's dick hanging loose along his thigh.

Eli's eyelids dipped slightly and he licked his lips. "Oh," he said softly.

"Mmm-hmm." Julien brushed him again and felt Eli begin to respond, hardening very gradually under his touch, the soft cotton between them. Julien leaned closer, pulse in ears, and dipped his head down to meet Eli's—

"Wait."

A hand on his wrist gently held him still. Julien stopped and looked up from Eli's lips to meet his eyes.

"I think we should just keep this professional," Eli said. He looked a little flushed, but tense. Determined.

"Professional?" Julien echoed.

"Or as professional as a couple of Hardy Boys can get, you know what I mean," Eli said, then hesitated. "Look, one-night stands are fine and dandy, but if we make this into a habit, you're going to start thinking you can trust me, and I wouldn't want that. I *don't* want that, because I'm telling you right now, I don't trust you. We've both got too much riding on this to take those sort of chances."

"Right, of course. I understand," Julien heard himself say, even though he didn't. Because what else was he supposed to do, tell Eli that he *could* trust him?

He pulled his hand away, but Eli's grip on his wrist lingered a moment before letting him go and his gentle touch throbbed. Julien looked down and noticed a bruise there he hadn't seen before. From where Eli had bitten him.

At least he'd have that, Julien thought, and pressed down on it hard with his own thumb. The small, quick pain helped ease the pounding in his head.

"It's not that I didn't enjoy it," Eli said suddenly, sounding frustrated.

"Hey, hey." Julien forced himself to look back up into his eyes. "You don't need to explain anything to me. You say you want to keep it professional like the Hardy Boys, my only question is who's Frank and who's Joe."

Eli huffed and gave him a slanted look. "Well, I do have darker hair."

"*And* you're the brains of this operation. Which is why I'm grateful to have you on my side, Frank," Julien said, and he wasn't even lying.

He was more grateful than he could possibly tell Eli. Even though this was all he was allowed. Even though his wrist ached in sync with his heart.

Chapter Eight

Heel-toe. Heel-toe. Heel—fuck it.

Eli clumsily tripped on the snowy service road and glanced at Julien out of the corner of his eye, but he was staring straight ahead, toward the tower, apparently lost in his own thoughts. Eli allowed his feet to slip into a more natural—and blessedly quiet—position. He and Julien had driven as far as they could and parked outside the locked gate. A rusty metal sign hung from a chain in the center stating *Closed for Season* had made Julien a bit nervous, and Eli refused to find that disarming in the least.

He wasn't sure what to think of Julien's story, exactly. It wasn't that he didn't believe him. As they'd driven, Julien had readily told him all the details he'd managed to dig up about Ian Ackman. Moved to Maudit as a teen, was described as a charismatic but impulsive man who had a knack for making friends and losing money. After high school he'd worked a string of jobs in town, before settling into his career as Annabelle's partner. Unlike him, she'd come from wealth and had paid off most of his debts before moving them both out to Blue Tail Lodge.

In a way this was the beginning of Ian's disappearance from the world. The two of them had spent increasingly little time off the mountain as the stress of a failing business took its toll. By the time he was supposed to have left town, Ian Ackman hadn't had any friends or family left to report him missing. No one but Annabelle, who'd claimed he'd left her and shown Maudit Falls Police the letter to prove it. Apparently Bucknell hadn't bothered to look any further. Apparently it was an open secret that Ian Ackman had been planning to leave her for years.

Julien even answered the occasional questions about his brother that Eli peppered in. He sounded like your run-of-the-mill paranormal-obsessed human. He'd drowned in a boating accident just over a year ago. The guilt on Julien's face when he talked about him was so painful Eli frequently had to look away.

It made sense, in its way. Way more sense than the paranoid worst-case scenarios Eli had been cooking up as he'd spent the entire night pacing, replaying the moment he'd opened that drawer over and over. He'd even broken down and called Cooper around four in the morning. Thank god, the whippet hadn't picked up and Eli wasn't quite so far gone as to leave a voice mail. Of course he'd started ringing back with a vengeance in the car, but near the top of the mountain Eli lost service again. Perhaps by the time he got back down to the retreat, Cooper would get the hint and let it go. Hope sprang eternal.

The only part of Julien's story that did bother Eli was the sheer relief he'd felt to hear it. How quickly he'd wanted to accept it as the truth. How the first thing he'd done when Julien had burst into his private misery was to demand answers like a betrayed lover. The clever thing would have been to feign ignorance and play along with whatever Julien thought was wrong until he could pry the truth free from the inside. When was the last time he had ignored an opportunity to work his own angle? And over what? A pretty face? Stern, demanding hands? The tantalizing possibility of a phenomenal fuck? Absolutely not.

Eli liked Julien. He wanted him to find what he'd come to Maudit looking for, because he knew what it was like to reach for someone who wasn't there and grab hold of the first thing you happened to touch instead. That thing could drag you to hell if you didn't figure out how to let go first.

But Eli had already done his time down below the last time sexually compromised feelings had convinced him to ignore his gut. It was one of the many reasons he didn't get involved with humans beyond a single one-night stand here and there. Not even the nice ones. Not even the funny ones. And especially not the ones who went looking for monsters whether they believed or not.

They came to the tower clearing and paused. There pulled to the side of the road was an official-looking vehicle with *Maudit Falls Police* stamped aggressively over the doors.

"Looks like we're not the only ones with murder on the

mind. How tedious." He sighed, but inside he felt antsy. He didn't like the idea of anyone noticing him take an interest in this murder, least of all Bucknell. He quite liked his status as eccentric on the fringe. Out of the loop was out of the snare.

Julien didn't look particularly pleased either. "I thought they closed up the scene yesterday. With all this snow coming down, what could they be doing?"

"I hope you didn't want to form this dynamic duo because you were under the misapprehension that I'd provide forensic insight."

"Nah, I was just drawn to your straightforward, plain-talking manner," Julien said. "Do you want to look around the clearing or turn around and try another time?"

Truthfully Eli wanted to slip into his far more sensitive nose and try to pick up any hints that Nia, or another wolf, had climbed that tower recently. But he couldn't put it quite like that. "I want to go up."

"The tower?" Julien frowned. "Why? Annabelle said the cabin on top is locked."

"Means, motive and opportunity," Eli said airily, counting off three fingers. "Isn't that where they always begin? I hear the view is to die for. Maybe that's where we'll find our means."

"Be serious," Julien said. "I couldn't help but notice when we were pooling information in the car that your end was a little shallow."

Eli laughed and began walking. "Thirteen days, remember? I'm just trying to catch up to you."

Julien stopped him with a hand on Eli's arm. Not a grab,

just a firm touch that stilled him as easily as it had last night. Eli looked up into Julien's dark eyes. "Listen, Rocky left Maudit…different. More convinced that there was real evil in the world than he'd ever been before. Less than a month later he was gone. So whatever it is, whatever you know, you can tell me, because *nothing* is more important to me than finding out what happened."

Eli rocked on the balls of his feet a moment, considering. "Remember Celia De Luca? The woman who's trying to turn people of influence against me, destroy the retreat and steal Christmas? The day before yesterday, a couple of her representatives showed up on my porch."

Julien looked shocked. "What? Are you okay?"

An odd first reaction, but Eli still felt a ridiculous, pleased sort of warmth. "Yes, of course. But they…knew things. About what's been going on at the lodge. Annabelle's cameras," he said carefully. "I think they might be getting inside information from someone there."

"Hmmm," Julien hummed thoughtfully. "Is that why you broke into Cody's room last night?"

Eli's jaw dropped. *"What?"* He snapped his mouth shut and took a wary step back. "What in the hell makes you think I would do something like that?"

"You can save the sanctimony. I've seen you breaking into someone's drawers once already. And I was there doing the same thing." Julien looked at him intently. "Remember, nothing is more important to me."

"How?" Eli asked flatly.

"There had to be some reason you were wandering the halls at night and Cody is the only one on that floor with

me. At first I thought you really were there just to see me."
Julien's cheeks went pink. "But I think it's pretty obvious
now that's not the case."

"Julien," Eli whispered. "I didn't—"

Julien shook his head. "It's fine. Honestly. I just hope
you didn't feel like you—like you had to. Do that. To stay."

"Absolutely not," Eli said vehemently. "I could have left.
I stayed because I wanted you." They both winced at the
past tense. "I—"

Julien held up his hand. "Seriously, it's fine. I was only
worried you thought you didn't have a choice. And if anything like that ever happens again, which I know it won't,"
he added hastily. "But if it does, you can just tell me what
you need. You're not trapped with me."

Eli blinked and hastily looked down. He didn't think
anything was slipping, but he felt…precarious. Better safe
than sorry.

"Here," he said, taking out his phone and pulling up the
photos he'd taken last night. "Cody had an SD card hidden
in his desk. Not *the* card. Different. I don't know what I'm
hoping to find in the tower exactly. Maybe nothing. But
she—" he tapped the screen before handing it over "—is
one of the De Luca reps who showed up at my door. Based
on the leaves and the unmarked shed, I think this was taken
sometime last year."

Julien examined the pictures for a long couple of moments. "Fifteen months at least. That's Ian Ackman."

"Perchance me hears the plot thicken," Eli said, grimly
satisfied. "Are you sure it's him?"

"When I was looking into his background I found a couple of photos of Ian online from when he and Annabelle first opened Blue Tail. It's him." Julien ran a finger over the screen absently. "Why would Cody have taken these?"

"Blackmail?" Eli guessed. "Proof that Ian was meeting with someone? Something to show Annabelle?"

"You think they were having an affair? Isn't she a little young for him?"

Eli snorted. "You're not serious."

Julien's face flushed and handed the phone back over to Eli. "Well. I just mean, what about De Luca?"

"You think Nia might be acting as a representative here, too? Perhaps. De Luca would love to get her claws on the—" He hesitated, looking down to tuck his phone away. "Into a business here on the mountain."

Julien hummed with interest. "Ian might have been meeting her to negotiate some kind of deal behind Annabelle's back."

"Another blackmail-able offense," Eli agreed. "So, Cody caught Ian doing something bad in business or pleasure up here and has held on to the photos to prove it. You want to take a look in that tower yet?"

"Views to die for," Julien agreed, gesturing him forward. They crossed the clearing quickly, trudging through the quickly gathering snow. Eli peeked at the stark claw marks on the shed door as they passed, drawn to the blatant threat of a wolf. He worried for a moment that Julien would want to examine them again. But Julien didn't even glance over there. He seemed as eager as Eli to get to the top of the tower as they began to climb the metal stairs.

"Tell me about De Luca," Julien said suddenly, and Eli

would have preferred they'd just gone to look at the clawing.

"What do you want to know?"

Julien tapped on the metal railing restlessly as they got to
the first platform and turned to walk up the second. "Well,
you make her sound sort of...mafia-esque."

Eli laughed. "She's not." Maybe it would be easier to say
so rather than describe the intricacies of what it meant to
alpha a ruling pack. But the last element of chaos he needed
dropped into this mess was Julien feeling obligated to contact some agency claiming to have uncovered a mob war in
the mountains. "She's the head of a conglomerate, I guess.
You know, the *other* organized crime."

"She holds controlling stakes in a bunch of unrelated
businesses," Julien confirmed.

Well, maybe it was easier to explain ruling packs to humans than Eli had thought. "Yes, something like that." He
sighed a bit petulantly. "I don't know the details. I'm afraid
I'm not very corporate-minded. Imagine me climbing the
stairs of a high-rise right now, in a suit, ordering people
about. It's just not who I am."

Julien shot him a wry look. "Mmmm, something tells
me you are whoever you want to be at any given moment.
In fact, I've seen you become at least three different types
of people in the last hour alone."

That surprised a laugh out of Eli. They climbed in silence for a moment. Then Julien said, "What you're doing
with the retreat, though, that's... I'm glad you decided to
skip the high-rise and apply that Machiavellian brain to
the powers of good."

"Now you're just being mean, and I can't begin to imagine why," Eli said archly. They started on the third flight of stairs.

"When I was a kid, my mom and I stayed in a place like your retreat once," Julien said after a moment. "Just for a couple days. But it was...the difference between swimming across the entire ocean toward land you can't see and swimming to a boat waiting way out on the horizon. Mind you our boat had a whole lot less windows and stone fireplaces. More of a dinghy, really. But it was still something solid under our feet."

"Just the two of you?" Eli asked.

"Oh yeah. For a long time. Mom didn't marry my stepfather, Skip, until I was twelve. Rocky was born a couple months after that."

"Twelve years is quite an age difference."

"Yeah. Helpful, though. Mom and Skip are both in the business. Filming is weird hours, so it was really lucky for them I was old enough to take care of him." He cleared his throat. "What about your family? I'd love to see a baby picture of you."

"Trust me, you wouldn't recognize me," Eli said, which was an understatement. They crested the fourth and final flight of stairs onto the platform just outside the glass cabin's steel door.

"Any siblings?"

"I have a twin sister. We're extremely different."

"Twins! I can't imagine the scheming. You must have terrified your parents."

Eli turned away from Julien to stand by the railing and

look out at the mountains. "How tall did Annabelle say this was?"

There was a pause and Eli glanced back in time to catch Julien grimacing, where he lingered by the cabin door as if he realized he'd pushed too hard, crossed some line. But all he said was, "I'm not sure she did. Forty feet, maybe? The mountain's just under five thousand, though. I guess you really aren't afraid of heights, huh."

Eli shook his head and walked back to join him. "Not as long as I have something solid under my feet. I didn't always. Have that either." Even just that small bit of truth, of *exposure*, sent his heart pounding absurdly. But Eli forced himself to meet Julien's eyes and then moved toward the door, leaning close and allowing their arms to brush together firmly as he passed him. It was how he'd offer comfort and affection to another wolf. Julien probably wouldn't get anything out of it, but Eli wanted to nonetheless. Maybe he needed to feel it himself. It had been a long three days.

"Unlocked," he said, trying the door. "That's lucky."

The moment he opened it, he caught the scent. Cody was getting to his feet quickly. Had he been…sitting? Kneeling? Eli looked around, sniffing subtly, but there was no one else there or any clue as to what he'd been doing.

"What are you two doing here?" Cody asked with a slight edge. He seemed caught off guard and he smelled nervous.

"We didn't get a chance to climb the tower yesterday with everything. So we thought we might sneak back for a peek," Julien said. He sounded friendly and unconcerned. He either hadn't picked up on Cody's discomfort at all—

possible; Eli wasn't too clear on how humans noticed things without noses—or he was a hell of a lot better at acting than that goat movie had advertised.

"Yeah, well, unfortunately the cabin is closed to visitors," Cody said. "It isn't safe."

It seemed a whole lot safer up here than the slippery metal steps with an easily jumpable railing between you and death, in Eli's opinion. There was nice, solid planking for the floor and four walls that were almost entirely window grids with only a low bench circling the room. The bench had accumulated decades of graffiti. Some was carved directly into the wood, but most of it was done in marker. Outside the snow seemed to be coming down in aggressive, billowing swells. As if angry that they were encroaching on its home territory in the sky.

Eli drifted away from the others, ostensibly to look out the window but actually to get a sniff around before they were booted out. It was the graffiti though that kept catching his eye. All different colors and sizes. Words Eli could read. Words he couldn't. Words he'd rather not. There was art, too. Doodles of faces, pretty designs, funny little illustrations of animals, and an array of breasts, balls and dicks that was genuinely impressive, both in variety and number.

"Listen," he heard Cody say very quietly to Julien across the room. "You guys can't fuck in here or whatever. Annabelle would freak. No one's supposed to come into the cabin ever."

Julien's blush was borderline audible. "We weren't— we're just here for the view."

"Yeah, okay," Cody said, and Eli could hear his smirk without turning around. "Nice *view*."

"Is that why people usually come up here?" Eli asked, tracing one of the carvings on the bench—a heart with the initials A and D. "To fuck?" He turned around to look at the others staring at him with wide, surprised eyes.

Cody recovered first and shrugged in a way meant to broadcast all the disenchanted maturity of twenty-five. "That's one reason. You wouldn't even begin to believe the other shit I've seen on this mountain. Turns out freaks roll uphill, too."

"How long have you worked here?" Julien asked.

"Six years. I used to do ski patrol over school breaks. That was when we had, you know, actual groups of skiers to patrol." He ground the toe of his boot against an anatomically unlikely etching. "I can't wait to get out of this place."

"What's stopping you?" Eli asked politely.

Cody shot him an annoyed look. "And leave Annabelle here to fight her demons alone? You'd like that, wouldn't you? Except I would never abandon her like that asshole did. We leave together. Just as soon as she signs those fucking papers and sells this cursed shithole, we can start our lives together."

"A multimillion-dollar cursed shithole," Eli murmured.

"What's that supposed to mean?" Cody demanded.

"Just admiring your loyalty," Eli said.

"I hope your buyer hasn't been turned off by this business yesterday," Julien said hastily before that comment had time to ripen. Pity. "You're selling to De Luca, right?"

Eli felt the distinct urge to kick him in the shin, not this again, but Cody just looked confused. "No. Who is that?"

"No one," Eli said.

At the same time Julien said, "Oh, my mistake. I forgot that's who's interested in purchasing the retreat."

Cody seemed to swell right there in front of them, breathing in deeply. "Now that Annabelle gets that Ian's not coming back, we can both get out of here. No more waiting on spoiled tourists, no more debt and no more Sweet fucking Pea. If *anyone* thinks he can sabotage that, think again."

"Is that why you're pressuring Patrick West to convince Annabelle it's not Sweet Pea?" Julien asked.

Cody just snorted. "Pressuring? Yeah, right. Don't let the 'oh, I'm just here to follow the evidence' act fool you. Dude doesn't believe in Sweet Pea any more than you do."

"He certainly visits a lot for someone not expecting to find anything," Julien said.

"Oh, he expects to find *something*—Nielsen's treasure."

For one long moment the only sound was the soft icy brush of snowflakes hitting the window glass. Cody had a smug look on his face, and for once Eli thought it well earned. There weren't a lot of opportunities in life for melodramatic announcements and he'd handled this one quite well. Even Julien looked taken aback. Unnerved.

"Forgive me," Eli said at last. "I thought Dr. Nielsen was a scientist, not a pirate. Was he apt to bury treasure?"

"He was super fucking rich, that's what he was. Not to mention a total paranoid freak. So yeah, probably."

"The treasure is money?" Julien asked, which seemed like an odd question.

Cody seemed to agree since he stared at them blankly. "As opposed to what? Gold?"

Julien opened his mouth then shut it, like even he didn't have the fortitude to follow that up. Instead he asked, "Did Ian and Annabelle know that's why Patrick kept coming back to Maudit Falls?"

"Ian sure did. They used to go looking for it together. Gridding out the land, digging up the mountain—sometimes they wouldn't come back 'til morning."

"Ian thought there was actually treasure on Blue Tail?"

Cody smiled in an unfriendly way. "Why else would he be spending all that time in the woods?"

The *whoop-whoop* of a police horn broke the silence and Cody rolled his eyes. "Bucky's calling. He hates coming up here. Annabelle told me he's scared of heights." He snorted. "You better go before he puts on the siren."

It was quicker going down than coming up. Sure enough, there at the bottom in the clearing Bucknell greeted them with a lazy salute. "I was wondering who left their car by the gate."

"That's mine," Julien said. "Should I not have parked there?"

"Don't much matter now," Bucknell said. "You're not going to be moving it anytime soon. Tire's out."

"*What?*"

Bucknell shrugged. "Looks like some kind of puncture. I can drive you all back down to the lodge. But I'm afraid you'll have to find your own way from there, Mr. Smith. I have to stop in and have a word with Annabelle."

It was interesting, the way Julien and Cody both went very still. Not so dissimilar from wolves first catching the scent of blood in the air.

"Well, you have us on bated breath, Mr. Bucknell," Eli said. "I take it from your theatrical pause that you've identified the remains?"

"We have. Carter Lourde. Hiker who went missing four years ago. He and his buddy were doing the Appalachia Trail. The buddy twisted his knee and went home. Said Carter wanted to keep on. Family reported him missing a couple weeks after that. Said he never made it to the next check-in point. You remember it, don't you, Cody?"

Cody didn't seem to register the question. There was an awkward pause as he just kept staring at Bucknell and then, "What? Yeah. Yeah, I remember."

"What's the matter, kid? You're looking a tad green over there," Bucknell said sharply.

"No, I—I thought they were looking for him up north, in Virginia."

"That's true. On account of the buddy saying they didn't split up 'til somewhere over the border. Needless to say, we'll be following up on that lapse in memory."

"You're sure?" Julien asked. "I mean, it's definitely this hiker guy?"

"Ninety-nine percent only because I'm not the sort to say a hundred. We ran his plates. The titanium ones in the arm. Carter had an old playground fracture. It's him." He slapped his hands and rubbed them briskly in the cold. "If we don't get on the road now we'll be spending the night in the tower and any local can tell you that's bad luck."

"If the moon catches you up Blue Tail, he'll steal your love away," Cody said distantly.

Bucknell sent him a sharp look. "That's right. Where'd you hear that?"

Cody shook his head. He still looked a little unwell. "Just something Ian used to say."

"Of course he did," Bucknell muttered. "Well, today that's one bit of Maudit folklore I can get behind. Nobody's going to want to be stuck up here during a storm like we've got coming. Not even the moon."

Chapter Nine

The Moon is a popular figure in Maudit folklore dating back to…

Julien tossed the playing card on the table in front of him. Useless. All of it. The answers he was looking for weren't in these Sweet Pea cards, Patrick West's books, or even, he was beginning to fear, Maudit Falls at all. After everything that had happened that morning at the retreat, everything Eli had told him, Julien had felt like progress was finally being made. But what did a fatal spat between hikers have to do with his brother, the map, *anything*?

Julien flicked another card onto the table where they'd gathered informally in Blue Tail's breakfast room. Bucknell was speaking with Annabelle in the corner. Cody, for once, wasn't hanging on her like a scarf, but couldn't seem to fully leave either. He kept futzing over this and that, leaving the room and then returning five minutes later to do it again, all while casting long looks at the two of them. The other guests seemed restless as well, all of them lingering around the room over long-empty dinner plates as if waiting for something.

Or maybe they just had nowhere else to go. The snow was sheeting outside now and it had taken Bucknell twice as long as it should to drive them all to the lodge, the roads were that bad. Julien thought it was odd for North Carolina, but according to the ever-helpful Bucknell some of the mountain towns around here got eighty inches a year at least. It seemed like Blue Tail was trying for the whole thing in one night.

Julien shot a hopefully subtle look across the room where Eli sat entertaining Mr. and Mrs. Miura, doubtless trying to charm a ride out of here. He'd been quiet on the car ride back with Bucknell and Cody. Not that they could openly discuss anything then. But Julien had still craved some glance, some moment of connection to assure him that Eli was still with him. It seemed unlikely. In order to solve a murder, one typically required a murder to solve and Julien's had just gone up in smoke, no disrespect to the unfortunate Carter Lourde. He'd been so sure they'd found Ian Ackman and that finding his killer would be the key to understanding everything. Now he couldn't even be sure the man was dead.

The chair across from his scraped across the floor and Eli sat. "I've just had the most interesting chat with Sara Miura. Apparently she and her husband, Jun, have run into our alleged treasure hunter Patrick West before. He's been staying in town for the last week at least. Seems like a rabbit, to me."

The way Julien's heart was beating out of his chest was a good reminder of just how quickly and quietly the man moved and it took a minute to register what he said. "A rabbit?"

"An odd thing to keep under your hat," Eli said. Paused. Grinned. "Unless you're playing tricks."

"You—you still want to do some digging?"

"Well, of course I do. Some nefarious type is parading around the woods in a Sweet Pea suit, our list of potential culprits has just grown by two, the retreat remains in peril and the mystery of the missing camera remains." Eli eyed him critically. "Unless this is your way of telling me you'd rather lay down your own shovel."

For a moment, Julien was too relieved to say anything. "No, not at all. Hardy Boys *never lose their nerve*. Ah, what do you mean the potential culprit list has grown by two? West and who?"

"Ian Ackman, of course," Eli said promptly. "Now that the man's officially missing in action, once more."

"You mean if he isn't dead he might still be...around? Here?" Julien whispered, glancing around the dining room, but no one was looking their way. "Why would he do that?"

"Why does anyone go off the grid?" Eli replied. "To hide from someone. Or something." He tilted his head, gaze drifting over to Bucknell and Annabelle in the corner. "She doesn't sound very relieved, does she."

"Sound? When'd you manage to eavesdrop over there? I

thought you were talking to the Miuras," Julien said, suddenly feeling self-conscious that while he'd been sulking Eli was apparently running recon all over the lodge.

Eli looked confused for a moment. "Ah, no. But if I thought I'd stumbled across my ex-lover's bones and then found out I was wrong, you could expect a little less calm, collected conversation in the corner. One small *woot*, at least."

"To be fair, we don't know if she ever even thought that was Ian Ackman," Julien reasoned. "Just because I jumped to conclusions and dragged you along with me."

"Cody jumped, too," Eli said firmly. "You heard him in the tower. *Now that Annabelle gets that Ian's not coming back.* He couldn't have been more shocked if they told him that was his own rib cage out there."

Julien barked a laugh and Eli met his eyes with an answering smile.

"You should stay here tonight," Julien heard himself say, and Eli's face went peculiarly blank. Shit. "I mean, the roads aren't really safe, and if you stay we can talk about this more privately." Double shit. "I mean, I think it would be a good idea to recap. I'd like to get your take on what Cody said."

"Yes," Eli said after a moment. "Mad scientists, buried treasure, a monster in the woods. All that's missing are a few meddling kids and he'd have quite a story."

"You don't believe him?"

"I didn't say that. You'd heard Nielsen's name before?"

Julien looked away from Eli's piercing gaze. "Mmm, the name popped up in my brother's things." When he glanced back, Eli was still studying him, head tilted slightly. "What?"

Eli blinked slowly. "Just thinking about how out of everyone in this lodge you send up the most red flags and yet here I am prancing after you like a horny bull."

"Well, there's no one here I'd rather have at my back, Ferdinand," Julien said, and Eli flashed a very toothy smile before his eyes flickered to the left. Julien followed his gaze in time to catch Patrick West redirect toward them.

"Gentlemen, mind if I join you?" he asked, already pulling out the chair directly next to Eli's. "Quite a bad storm out there."

Julien did his part by agreeing. They made the requisite comments about climate change, and then Patrick got to the point. "Terrible news about that poor hiker. So young, too. All it takes is one bad patch of service and you're suddenly the most naive animal in the woods. And there's more than one bad patch in these mountains."

It seemed Bucknell hadn't told anyone how Lourde had died. Julien wondered why.

"Cody mentioned you've spent a lot of time up the mountain yourself," Eli was saying. "Have you ever run into a stranded soul?"

"Oh, once or twice. Nothing drastic. Folks wandering off the trail to follow the sound of a waterfall and think it's child's play to retrace their steps. Couples who sneak off to hook up in the woods."

"In the woods?" Eli repeated, looking appalled, and his gaze drifted over to meet Julien's. "How...coarse." That sounded less like a condemnation and Julien felt a traitorous spark of want. A spark that was doused with all the subtlety of a fire hose when Eli looked back at Patrick and said, "Is that what you and Ian Ackman were really doing out there? Hooking up?"

To his credit, Patrick barely reacted. His eyes only slightly narrowed while Julien hastily reattached his jaw. "Did Cody tell you that? I admit I'm impressed; I didn't think he had the imagination."

"Oh, he doesn't," Eli said. "Cody insists that you and Ian were hunting for buried treasure. I assumed he'd gotten the wrong end of the euphemism."

"Nielsen's secret fortune?" Patrick asked with a surprised laugh. "Not that old story again."

"So you've heard of it?" Eli asked.

"Not only have I heard of it, I was there when it first got told. Back when we were kids, the four of us were obsessed with the Nielsens. I hate to say it, but there probably isn't a rumor about that family that we didn't spread ourselves."

Eli hummed. "If the two of you weren't spending the night where XXX marks the spot, what were you doing?"

"There was no *two of us*. There never was." Patrick studied Eli with an expression Julien didn't quite understand—offended and amused at the same time, maybe. An expression Eli probably got a lot, come to think of it. "Do you honestly think having an affair and—" he waved his hand "—digging for gold sounds more realistic than believing in the existence of creatures science has yet to identify?" He laughed again, but this one sounded slightly strained, forced. "Is it really so difficult to accept that there are people who genuinely believe in the possibility of something more?"

Eli blinked slowly. "On the contrary, I'm nearly always in a state of wanting more, myself," he murmured. "But you wouldn't catch me traveling back to the nucleus of my childhood trauma and pitching tents with a man I clearly despise for a mere *possibility*."

Patrick smiled wryly. "Ian and I weren't always enemies. But I see your point. It isn't particularly easy, coming home."

"Then why keep coming back here and not, oh, I don't know, where do supernatural creatures usually congregate? Somewhere less snowy, one would hope." Eli shivered slightly. "Tell me what's so irresistible about this place. The nostalgia? The pretty views? I want to know what Patrick West finds *compelling*."

"Besides you?" Patrick asked.

Eli's lips curled in a slow secretive smile and he tilted his head just so. "Not unless you came all this way for your something more with me."

Patrick was staring at Eli for all the world like that was *exactly* why he was here and who could blame him? If Julien were the one Eli was looking at like that, charming and playful, he would, too. Hell, he'd go anywhere for a chance of more with Eli. Not that more was an option being offered to him.

Julien hastily arranged his own expression into what he hoped was casual, unaffected observation and not anything embarrassingly childish like jealous, jilted and horny. Little that it mattered since no one was even looking in his direction, anyway.

Patrick shook his head slightly then, as if deciding something, said, "Sweet Pea is a curiosity, a shadow myth. He can't definitively be traced to any known people, identity group or text."

"What do you mean, shadow myth?" Julien asked. Partly out of genuine curiosity. Partly to remind them that he was in fact still here.

"Oh, just a phrase some of us came up with a while ago. It's a bit silly, really. But imagine folklore, legends and myths as sort of shadows that cultures leave on the land. They're not perfect representations, but you can get a general idea of the shape of a culture, what mattered to their people, by studying their myths. There are certain consistencies of value reflected there. Of course, like shadows, myths overlap and meld together as communities mix through whatever means and stories are appropriated. But the point is every shadow requires something to cast it."

"Every story needs a storyteller," Julien said.

"Right. Sweet Pea stories are like shadows that lead… nowhere. At least nowhere we can see, as of yet. They're a completely different style from the legends of the Cherokee tribe here in western North Carolina. There's no recognizable roots in any of the newcomers who either settled or were forcibly brought to the area. Nor in any of the relatively newer cultures that evolved here, isolated in the mountains. You can think of it as an outlier separate from the plethora of Appalachia folklore, unclaimed by any group, rife with idiosyncrasies, storytelling rhythms, character roles and archetypes that don't align with the established lore of any known culture, and yet still somehow seeped into the consciousness of the town. A shadow with no one behind it."

"So that makes it seem more likely he's based on a real creature?" Julien asked.

"Some people think so."

"Did Ian Ackman?" Eli asked.

"Ian Ackman didn't think about anything but himself. The day he finally left was a relief for everyone," Patrick said sharply. Then he blew out a breath and smiled at Eli with chagrin. He really was very handsome like that, Julien noticed again. But this time there was something off-putting about it—a little too lacquered, a little too inviting. "God, listen to me. I'm sorry, I didn't mean to snap. I think you might have been right. Maybe it is a bad idea, returning home. Even for views that are far more than merely pretty these days."

Patrick's shoulder moved like he was placing his hand on Eli's leg under the table, and Julien stood up so suddenly he nearly knocked his chair over. Both Patrick and Eli stared up at him with surprise.

"I—" Julien started, realizing he had nothing to say. Fortunately the lights chose that moment to flicker and everyone in the room seemed to pause, waiting. But they stayed on. "That's not a good sign."

Eli glanced out the window. It was getting dark, both with heavy snow and the sun's losing battle to winter. "No. Speaking of home, I'm beginning to worry I might not make it back to mine."

"That's right. You don't have a car," Patrick said. "I'm more than happy to give you a ride."

"I'm afraid that won't be possible," Annabelle said, joining them. She placed a friendly hand on Patrick's shoulder and hovered at the head of their table with an apologetic look. If she had heard him bashing Ian she didn't show it. "It seems like they've closed the road down the mountain tonight. Mr. Smith, I've asked Cody to prepare you a room."

Eli made dissenting noises, but Annabelle cut him off. "No, I insist. The town's got their hands full plowing the roads in town. They won't even make it up here until morning. Even David's staying. He's gone on to radio it in now. And goodness knows we've got the room."

Julien gathered the cards back up off the table and looked down as he shuffled them as if it required his entire attention. He didn't need anyone to see his relief. So what if Patrick had given Eli a ride back? It wasn't his business. Except the roads were way too dangerous to drive. And Patrick may or may not be involved in Ian's disappearance. And the thought of him hearing those needy, bitten-off whimpers Eli made right before he came made Julien's skin feel about three sizes too tight. Not because he was under the delusion that those belonged to him alone. He just didn't think Patrick would appreciate them the way they deserved.

The lights flickered again and this time the whole building seemed to sigh in defeat as all the ambient sounds of every electrical device running whirred to a stop. This time the lights didn't return.

"It looks like we're having a good old-fashioned slumber party," Eli murmured as the room erupted into sound, guests chattering nervously, caught in the adrenaline of a blackout.

"Everyone, everyone, please don't panic," Annabelle called out over the room. "I'm sure the power will be back up soon."

"What about our rooms?" Mr. Miura asked. "Will we be able to get in?"

"The locks are all battery operated. You'll be fine. In the meantime, our fridges run on a generator, so we'll still be able to provide some light dinner. And we have games and an assortment of books in the front room—"

"Maybe now's the perfect time to start that poker game you wanted, Mr. Doran," Eli said far louder than his usual corner-of-the-mouth drawl.

"Poker?" Mrs. Miura piped up. "Do you play?"

"Um," Julien said, glancing at Eli for any clue as to what the man was up to.

"He tries. They're always playing on movie sets, in their trailers, waiting for their scene to shoot. Isn't that right?" Eli said, turning to Julien. "Who did you tell me fleeced four hundred dollars off you? Some big name. But I suppose money doesn't matter much to movie stars."

"How interesting," Mrs. Miura said with the look of a woman who knew she was about to clean house. "I'm happy to play a couple of hands, if anyone else is up for it."

"Annabelle? Patrick?" Eli asked.

"I should really find Cody," she said distractedly. "Make sure the generator has enough gas. But I'll set you up with some battery lanterns in here first."

"Will you be playing, Eli?" Patrick asked.

"Oh, I have a terrible poker face. Can't tell a lie to save my life," Eli sighed mournfully. "But I'm happy to watch you all. Blow on your cards, if you really want to get lucky."

Julien fumbled the shuffle.

"Then how can I resist an offer like that?" Patrick laughed.

Before long Eli had roped the others in as well until Julien was dealing to Mrs. Miura, Patrick, and the three students, Ahmet, Jonas and Claudia, who seemed less interested in the game than finding out what "big name" he was giving his money away to. Mr. Miura opted to sit nearby with a book, ostensibly reading but more likely setting up a front row seat to watch his wife finance their vacation.

Julien tried to keep his eyes on the poker and simultaneously figure out what the hell kind of game Eli was playing and if he was supposed to be doing anything to help. Eli didn't look like he needed much help, laughing with Patrick, pointing at his cards, asking easily overheard questions and all in all making a win for the man impossible.

Fortunately for him they had to stop when, after the flop, Jonas abruptly asked which was better, two pair or a full house, and by the time Julien had explained that and handed the deck over to Mrs. Miura for a new deal, Eli was standing. "I should call the retreat. Make sure they've battened the hatches in my absence. Unless you don't think you can play without my good luck charm," he added.

Patrick waved him off, clearly having figured out he wasn't going to win a single hand with Eli at his shoulder saying things like *Never trust a man wearing diamonds* and

What is a Jack, exactly? 'Cause this one seems awfully cozy with your queen. "No, no. Business calls, I understand."

Eli finally met Julien's eyes, giving him a cryptic look. "Very well. *Don't go anywhere*, I'll be right back."

Right. *Right.* Now, those were instructions he could work with. Julien gave him a quick nod and Eli drifted out of the room.

"Well, now that everyone knows the rules, should we make this interesting?" Mrs. Miura said, cutting the deck sharply on the table.

An hour later they were on their fifth hand, Julien was down over two hundred dollars and Claudia had just dealt the river when something about the card caught his attention. In the center, where all the little facts were printed, was an ink illustration of a figure knelt at the edge of a cliff with his head bowed, one hand on the ground in front of him, the other reaching out pitifully toward a loosely rendered waterfall. The words under the image simply said *Little Blue Wolf.*

Julien's pulse quickened in recognition. This was the same scene as the painting in the retreat. The same words in Rocky's notebook. "Patrick, have you ever heard of this? Is it another Maudit monster?"

"Hmm?" Patrick barely glanced up from studying his own hand with a frown. He was down around a hundred dollars himself. "Oh, Little Blue. In a way. It's another shadow myth—involving Sweet Pea, actually. Some say it's how the mountain got its name."

"Shadow myths?" Claudia asked, and Patrick explained everything he'd told Eli and Julien earlier.

"Stupid," Ahmet said. "That is your proof that Sweet Pea is real? Just because you people can't find the culture means that the culture did not exist? No. It's far more likely that they were eradicated by genocide, disease, forced assimilation, or any of the other ways cultures have been forced to disappear in this world."

"You're absolutely right," Patrick said with a hint of praise, and Julien could easily see what sort of teacher he was. "And many believe that's exactly what happened. Then there are those who believe the original storytellers behind Sweet Pea weren't eradicated at all. That they're just…hidden. A shadow culture, if you will."

"You're saying that like it's unheard of," Claudia said with a frown. "There are communities around the world that choose to remain separate for all sorts of reasons."

"Separate, yes. Not hidden entirely. That takes serious effort. A lifelong commitment of silence from every member for generations. A reason to want to stay under the radar."

"What, like some kind of secret society in the mountains?" Julien asked, forcing a laugh.

Patrick shrugged, and he leaned in over the table, lowering his voice theatrically. "Or out here living among us, with nothing but shadow myths like Sweet Pea and Little Blue to hint at their existence at all."

The others laughed, but Julien hastily looked away, feeling suddenly ill. "Do you know it?" he asked, tapping the image of the person and the waterfall. "Do you know what this story is?"

"Not well," Patrick said. He hesitated, rearranging the cards in his hands, then continued, "The Little Blue Wolf left his pack and climbed to the peak to watch the hunters on the other side. There he met the monster in the mountain, who offered him shelter for the night in his mouth. All night the wolf was nervous and slept restlessly, but when the sun rose all was well. He left the mouth and when he was almost all the way out the monster bit down and stole his tail. Without it, he could never go home or be a wolf ever again. He died of loneliness."

"So it's another moralizing story about sex," Claudia muttered. "Yes, wow. So idiosyncratic."

"I can think of another reason no culture wants to claim that story," Ahmet added.

"I thought you said Sweet Pea was a character?" Jonas asked.

"That's the monster. Historically he was known as the Monster in the Mountain Who Smells of Sweet Pea. You know, like the flower? But obviously that was shortened to several different, snappier nicknames over the years. Sweet Pea is just the alias du jour. It's technically the Little Wolf Who Smells of Bluebells, too. Almost all of these shadow myths identify characters by some sort of scent profile. Like I said, they're...unusual."

"So are you here looking for Sweet Pea or for some secret, isolated community in the mountains?" Mr. Miura asked, speaking up for the first time since they'd sat down.

Mrs. Miura made a small disapproving sound and shook her head sharply at her husband.

"Neither, sir," Patrick said. "I'm just here as a favor to an old friend. And to find out who, or what, is starting these fires." He looked at Mrs. Miura. "I take it you're not a big believer in these things?"

"I believe in demons exactly enough to not go poking my nose into their business," she said evenly, then laid down two kings in the hole to make four of a kind. "Now, are we playing or not?"

Somewhere, from the back of the lodge, someone screamed.

At first, Julien didn't understand what he was looking at. He had followed the sound along with everyone else to the other end of the lodge and into a large kitchen, which presumably didn't usually look like this. Cupboards were open and food was ripped out of the fridge and thrown around the floor. There was a horrible chill in the air; every window in the room was wide-open and snow blew inside from the dark. Even with the wind, Julien could smell the gasoline that was leaking from a tipped fuel can on the floor.

Next to it lay Annabelle's crumpled body.

"Oh my god!" Patrick yelled, reaching her the same time as Julien. They crouched beside her, trying not to step directly in the gas, and Annabelle's eyes flickered open.

Julien exhaled in relief. "What happened? Are you hurt?"

"It was in here. In the room with me," Annabelle gasped. She pointed to the door behind her on the other side of the kitchen. "It pushed me down as it passed."

Julien left her with Patrick and the others, hurrying out of the kitchen and into the pitch-black, empty hallway. He knew the left just circled back around toward the breakfast room, so Julien went right, toward the lodge's back entrance, shoved open the door and ran directly into a warm body. Julien didn't think. He just wrapped his arms tight, hooked an ankle and took them down to the ground, landing on top. The person made a small *oh* sound Julien would recognize anywhere.

"Eli?" Julien pulled back slightly. Sure enough, Eli's cold-flushed face stared back up at him. Hair splayed out in the snow like some kind of reverse halo. Fitting seeing as he looked like a dark angel, seductive and divine.

"You sound surprised. I hesitate to ask who you were hoping to straddle to the ground," Eli murmured, shifting slightly beneath Julien's body, the warm press of him a sharp contrast to the frigid air. He sounded a little breathless, but not hurt or frightened. Julien suddenly felt the overwhelming urge to push him into the snow just to hear the way his breath caught in his throat again.

Feeling himself flush, Julien hastily scrambled back up to standing, and then reached out a helping hand, but Eli had already hopped to his feet in that oddly light, graceful way of his.

"Would you believe I thought you were Sweet Pea?" Julien asked, brushing the snow off himself while Eli did the same.

"I leave you with Patrick West for five minutes—"

"Someone just attacked Annabelle in the kitchen."

Eli stilled, then took a deep breath. "No one came out this way."

"Are you sure?"

"Mmm. I—"

Raised voices drifted out of the open door. Exchanging

a look, Julien and Eli made their way back to the kitchen. Someone had placed an electric lantern on the center island, and it cast odd shadows against the walls. Annabelle was standing now with Patrick beside her. Bucknell and Cody had joined them, and the students and Mr. and Mrs. Miura had disappeared.

"Enough is enough, Annie. This can't go on," Bucknell was pleading. "I can't help you if you don't tell me what's going on. You have to—"

"I don't have to do anything," Annabelle snapped. "Why won't you listen to me for once instead of telling me what to do all the time? All of you!" she added, shrugging Patrick's hand off her shoulder. "I told you it was nothing."

"Is this nothing?" Bucknell shook the red plastic fuel can, and it sloshed loudly, nearly empty. "What if you hadn't interrupted them? What if someone had lit this place up?"

"Oh, don't be stupid, David," Annabelle snapped. "I was taking that out to the generator. I dropped it when so-someone shoved past me in the dark."

Bucknell looked away, obviously frustrated, and saw them standing in the doorway watching.

"Where'd everyone else go?" Julien asked.

"Upstairs in their rooms," Annabelle said. "David practically told them to hide under the bed and wait to be burned alive."

Bucknell frowned. "I sent the rest of the guests upstairs as a precaution. Where'd you two come from?"

Julien gestured toward the hall while Eli delicately hopped over the pool of gasoline and crossed the room directly to the sinks, for some reason. "I went to see if I could catch whoever it was."

"Any luck?"

"No one. Eli said no one passed him coming out the back door either."

There was an awkward pause and Julien's own words sank in. He looked guiltily over at Eli, who was still ostensibly studying the wreckage around the kitchen, though his shoulders had stiffened, and he'd gone somewhat still. "I mean—"

But Cody spoke right over him. "So there was no one lingering out the back door *but* Mr. Smith," he said with barely contained triumph in his voice. "Kind of like how there was no one else in the office when the laptop and card were stolen but Mr. Smith. Am I the only one who can see one plus one equals two here?"

"Thank you, Inspector Clouseau," Eli said, turning around at last, eyebrow arching so high, Julien winced. "I hate to complicate your equation, but many hallways have a pesky habit of going *two* directions. Just because our visitor didn't pass me doesn't mean there wasn't one."

"That would mean whoever it was went left, farther into the lodge," Julien said. Nobody liked that.

"We should all partner up. Search the place," Patrick said after a moment.

"Absolutely not," Annabelle said firmly. "My guests aren't here to *search the place*."

"Annie's right. The best thing to do is for everyone to return to their rooms, lock your doors and stay there.

Cody, Annabelle and I will make sure there's no one in the building."

"What's the matter, David? Don't trust me?" Patrick asked lightly.

A complicated expression flickered across Bucknell's face too quickly for Julien to understand. "I just thought you already had plans." He didn't make a big deal of looking directly at Eli, but his eyes did flicker in that direction.

Eli didn't appear to notice. His gaze was slightly unfocused and he was drifting closer to where Cody stood by the window. Julien couldn't imagine why. From Cody's steadily reddening face, neither could he. Suddenly Eli stooped, reaching under the kitchen counter, forcing Cody to stumble backward. When he straightened, he held something in his hand. "Did you drop this?"

Cody's face spasmed. He reached out to snatch it away, but Eli was too quick, pulling it just out of reach. Julien recognized the small carved wooden figurine from Annabelle's desk. He opened his mouth to say...what? *Hope my fingerprints aren't still on that!*

But fortunately, Annabelle beat him to it. "That's mine. I have no idea how it got in here."

"Is that one of Ian's creatures?" Patrick asked curiously, looking over Eli's shoulder. "God, I'd forgotten he did those."

Julien cleared his throat. "What is it?"

"Nothing. A—a memento, really. Ian carved them for fun. I held on to one or two when he left." Annabelle forced a self-conscious laugh and reached for the statuette. This time Eli let it go. "How pathetic is that? Maybe you're right, Cody. Maybe I…" She trailed off, frowning in confusion.

"Something wrong?" Eli asked lightly, but he was watching Annabelle with a very intent expression. Julien took a closer look, too, and realized with a jolt that it wasn't the same statuette at all. Raw wood, palm-sized and also clearly whittled by hand, this wasn't the same creepy monster as before. This one was rougher, more crudely done, and seemed to be a perfectly ordinary wolf rearing up onto its hind legs.

"I've never seen this before," Annabelle said slowly.

"Perhaps it's a newer piece. A little welcome-home present," Eli murmured.

"You think it was Ian?" Annabelle asked incredulously. "Here in the kitchen?"

"Is there some reason you don't?" Eli asked, but Annabelle just shook her head and looked back down at the wolf.

"Does it look like Ian's work?" Julien asked.

Annabelle scoffed. "He's a hobbyist, not Dali. I'd hardly say he had a signature style."

"What about this?" Eli asked, plucking the electric lantern off the counter and holding it up toward the wall over the sink. "Does this seem like his style?"

There beside the window someone had carved a word directly into the light green plasterboard: *Thief.*

Everyone in the room broke into surprised chatter. Bucknell strode forward to examine the wall, pulling a small flashlight from his belt, Annabelle sagged against the counter, just barely held up by Patrick at her side, and Cody… Cody was staring at the carved wolf that Annabelle had dropped to the floor. At the center of it all, Eli just stood there surveying the chaos with a smug look on his face.

Theatrical bastard, Julien thought, and had the sudden, inappropriate urge to kiss him.

"Anyone steal anything recently?" Eli asked, which shut the room up pretty quickly.

"Who the hell do you think you're talking to?" Cody exploded, stepping in front of Annabelle.

"The same person for whom this brand-new bit of wall decor is intended, of course. I don't think it's a leap in logic to suppose whoever was in this kitchen, be it man or myth, believes someone in this lodge has stolen from them. It seems to me that the simplest way of finding the accuser is to identify the accused. So..." He paused and tilted his head at Cody, blinking innocently. "Is this the part where I demand we strip-search you?"

Cody's hand shot forward toward Eli in a wild punch. Julien cried out, and stepped forward to stop him, but he was too far away to get there in time—

Smack.

Eli caught Cody's fist inches from his face. There was a ringing silence of shock. Cody tried to yank away, but Eli didn't let him go. He didn't even sway.

"I don't like to be hit," Eli said. His expression was uncharacteristically serious, and the lantern hanging limply in his other hand threw strange shadows across his face, making it look a bit sharper, strange. Julien felt an involuntary shiver run through him. "Don't ever try it again."

Eli released his hold on Cody, who stumbled backward, slipping slightly in the gasoline.

"All right, that's enough of that," Bucknell said, stepping up to them.

"Oh, fuck you," Cody snapped. "Fuck all of you! I'm so done with this shit." He stomped out of the kitchen.

"Cody, wait!" Annabelle said, belatedly, but he'd already disappeared.

"Let him go, Annie," Bucknell said, touching her arm gently.

"But what if he leaves? It's too dangerous to—I'm sorry, I can't," Annabelle said, pulling away from him, and hurried after Cody.

Bucknell stared after her for a moment, expression worried.

"Mama Annabelle runs to kiss the booboo better while you and I are left to clean up. Just like old times," Patrick murmured. "And here I thought she wouldn't be able to find someone less willing to grow up than Ia—"

"Don't," Bucknell interrupted. "Just don't."

Patrick's eyes glittered, but he shrugged and placed a hand on Eli's shoulder. "Are you all right?"

Eli's answering smile trembled so pitifully that it seemed impossible he'd been the one to humiliate Cody less than a minute ago. "A little shaken up. I think I need to lie down, actually."

"I can walk with you," Julien said hastily, itching to push Patrick's hand off Eli's shoulder where it still sat, gently rubbing soothing circles, petting him like an animal.

"Good idea. You two better head to your rooms. Patrick, looks like a spot on patrol duty just opened up."

Patrick looked like he wanted to protest.

"I'd also like to take a look at your monster kit. See if there's anything I can use to get some samples off this." Bucknell gestured at the *Thief* carved into the wall.

"Right. Of course, no problem." Patrick squeezed Eli's shoulder. "If you need anything, anytime, my door is open."

Eli blinked gratefully up at him. "Thank you."

Patrick patted his back one last time and turned away. Eli met Julien's gaze and winked.

Something loosened inside Julien's chest. "Right, we'll leave you to it!" He consciously pulled back on the cheerfulness when the others looked startled. "Be careful."

"Don't worry, Mr. Doran," Bucknell said. "This is nothing but low-life scare tactics. No one here is in any real danger."

They said good-night, and Julien and Eli walked in silent agreement across the lodge, up the three flights of stairs and down the dark hall until they got to Julien's door.

"Want to come in for a minute?" Julien asked, already holding the door open for Eli, who wordlessly entered.

As soon as the door closed behind them Julien blew out a breath. "What in the ever-loving *fuck* is going on?"

"I couldn't have put it better myself," Eli mused. "Did I miss anything beforehand? A communal sipping from the cup of delirium, perhaps?"

"No, no, nothing like that, Jesus. More myth talk and Mrs. Miura won two hundred and forty-five dollars off me. Thanks for that, by the way. Mind telling me whose drawers you were rifling through while I covered for you?"

Eli shot him a look, half appraising, half delighted. "You know, you're getting awfully familiar for a stranger I picked up on vacation. I thought it was a good idea to poke around the myth man's room. I had a theory. I was wrong. Even the greats, et cetera et cetera."

"A theory that Patrick West isn't being honest about what the hell he's really doing here because it sure as shit isn't convincing Annabelle to sell?"

"Call me a cynic, but when someone asks what's more believable, having an affair while searching for untold riches or tromping around the woods chasing after fairy tales, my answer will always be sex and money." Eli sighed and looked out toward the balcony window and the moon that kept the room from total darkness. "That said, I didn't find anything connected to Ian, Nielsen, or what the hell he was doing in town last week."

Julien acknowledged that with a neutral hum and studied Eli's face draped in shadows. "Mmmm. Why a wolf?"

For a moment it didn't seem like Eli had heard him. Then, without turning away from the window, he asked, "Hmm? Why a wolf what?"

"Ian's carving. Do you think it's...significant? Like a calling card for some kind of group or—or something..." Julien trailed off as Eli shot him a skeptical look.

"Don't tell me you're back on your mafia theories," he said.

"No, but...what if the wolf itself was some sort of message?"

"Well, I don't think the intruder unintentionally dropped the most conspicuous clue since Cinderella's glass slipper, if that's what you're saying. It's a message certainly, but whether it's shorthand for *I'm watching you. Best wishes, Ian*, or something else entirely, I don't know."

"Cody does. He couldn't take his eyes off it. I can't believe he took a swing at you. Nice moves, by the way. Consider me thoroughly intimidated."

Eli brought back the same tremulous smile he'd turned on Patrick. "I don't know what came over me. God, I was terrified."

"Save it," Julien said bluntly. "Unlike the rest of them, I haven't underestimated you since I washed up on your shores one night seeking shelter and ended up as a whetstone to sharpen your tongue instead. I just didn't realize your hands were twice as quick as your mouth."

"I have no idea what you mean. I promise you, my mouth is the most dangerous thing about me," Eli said, absurdly innocent and wide-eyed for one unnatural moment, before he grinned, a brief flash of teeth in the moonlight. "Besides, you're one to talk. I can't remember the last time I was tackled to the ground. An amateur sleuth and a trained fighter? I had no idea you were so versatile."

"I'm not. A fighter," Julien added a touch too quickly, and felt his face heat when Eli huffed. "But my stepfather was a stuntman. I can take a man down."

"I bet you can."

Julien stared at him and Eli stared back, eyes glinting. Belatedly Julien reached for the light switch on the wall. The flick was loud in the suddenly quiet room, but the room stayed dark, and Julien remembered the power was still out.

"Well." He cleared his throat. "Where have they put you?"

Eli examined his keycard. "Three doors down to the left. Neighboring Cody, as it happens. Perhaps we may mend fences yet."

Julien frowned. "I don't like the idea of any of us being alone tonight."

"As you insisted on pointing out, I'm tougher than I look."

"I'm not. This whole undaunted exterior is a carefully constructed facade. If at any point during the night you hear someone screaming, it's the real me. Feel free to come meet him. Bring that dangerous mouth of yours."

That was when Eli reached for him. Their bodies met and Julien's arms automatically went around Eli at the same time he felt Eli's hands slide up his chest, skirt over his throat and into his hair, where they clenched and tugged until their lips were almost touching.

Julien stopped him. Because he'd never forgive himself if he didn't at least try. "Eli," he breathed, looking down at his beautiful face with all its contrasts of light and dark, delicate and deadly. "No complaints. Not one single one. But...you said we shouldn't do this again. I can't trust you. You can't trust me."

Eli shook his head, denying something—what he'd said then, what Julien had said now, himself. "But do you want me?" he asked softly, which wasn't really an answer, but

Julien hadn't really asked a question, and he could feel the words on his skin.

"Yes," Julien choked, and his hands slipped daringly down Eli's back until his fingertips brushed the top swell of his ass. *More than I should. More than I thought I still could.* "So badly."

"I can work with that," Eli hissed, and shoved him backward against the door. Julien hit the wood with a rattling thud that could absolutely be heard up and down the hall. Probably downstairs, too. Hell, they might have caught Sweet Pea's attention, for all Julien cared. At that moment, all he could think about was the sight of Eli dropping to his knees and crawling toward him with that sharp, almost predatory focus.

"Fuck," Julien groaned, and Eli pressed his face up against his dick through his pants and hummed an agreement. He nudged and mouthed at Julien a few times as if assessing the position of him like this, hard and trapped, then suddenly sat back on his heels.

Julien watched, his entire body taut with anticipation and arousal, but Eli didn't move. Just knelt there, looking up at him, a little coy, a little hungry. Slowly, deliberately, Julien undid the button and zip of his pants. Eli's eyes flickered with excitement.

"Is that what you're waiting for?" Julien murmured, squeezing himself roughly. "Do you want to suck me?"

He expected a smart-ass reply, but Eli's lips just parted passively and he squirmed slightly in place on the floor. Julien took off his heavy-knit sweater and dropped it in a neat pile at his feet. "Here. Get on that."

Eli knelt up on the padding obediently, still looking up at him. Julien maneuvered his pants down just enough to get his dick free and fisted himself slowly. Eli's gaze dropped, but when Julien tsked, he immediately looked back up. "I'd like to watch your pretty face while I feed you my cock. Can you do that?"

Eli blinked slowly and paused long enough that Julien actually stopped midstroke, arousal abating as the silence grew. "Yes," Eli said finally, simply.

Julien studied him, worried he'd gotten this horribly wrong. Again. "Are you sure? We can do something else. Whatever you want," he said recklessly, and hoped he meant it. "Or if you changed your mind—"

Eli reached up and gripped Julien's hand, cutting him off. "I haven't. But I don't like...speaking. During sex. Is that a problem?" he asked in a disinterested tone that might be convincing if Julien's fingers weren't going a bit tingly from the tightness of Eli's grip. Clearly it had been a problem for someone before and Julien's distant anger at that thought untangled the last of his nerves, replacing them with an odd sort of protectiveness.

"Would it bother you if I talk?"

"No," Eli said immediately, and Julien bit back a smile. "No more than usual," he snipped.

"And if I ask you questions, will you nod or shake your head so I know you're good?"

"Yes, fine," Eli said stiffly.

"You can pinch me if it's urgent. I don't like being pinched, so there's no chance of misinterpreting that. Okay?"

Eli opened his mouth, but Julien brushed his thumb over his lips to stop him from speaking.

"Okay?" he asked again.

Eli's gaze softened to something pleased and very nearly shy. He nodded and Julien was surprised by the pulse of arousal that simple movement sent through him. Usually he liked nothing better than wringing a loud and desperate *yes* from his partners. Finding this spot and that tone and every single touch that made a particular person's body begin to babble. Apparently Eli's silent consent was just as thrilling. Either that or Julien was overcome with how efficiently they'd actually come to an agreement, for once.

"Then I don't see any problem with that at all," he said, and tapped the head of his cock on Eli's lips. "Now suck."

Eli groaned and eagerly took him in. Not all the way, Julien certainly didn't expect him to, but more than enough. He tried to stay still and patient as Eli's tongue got acquainted with all his most sensitive spots. Suckling the tip, then pulling off to lap at the shaft and flick that one place that made his knees wobble. When Julien really started to throb, Eli began to bob his head, finding his own greedy rhythm while doing his best to keep his eyes fixed obediently up.

"God, you've got a smart mouth when you're on your knees, too," Julien croaked.

Eli's lips curved into a quick smile around him and Julien couldn't resist running his hand over his head, combing his fingers through his hair and then taking a careful grip at the root. He didn't try to control his moment, just rode the motion, felt the softness of his hair, the warm brush of his cheek against his wrist.

Just like everything else Julien had seen him do, Eli was sinfully good at sucking dick. And no wonder, since he clearly enjoyed it. The sounds he was making alone—all desperate gulping and helpless whimpers—would be enough to get Julien off and his hips twitched forward, pushing just that little bit deeper into his throat. Eli groaned, sending a merciless vibration through Julien's balls.

"You like that?" Julien asked, and carefully rocked forward again. "Choking on me? Taking what I give you?"

Eli couldn't add much in the way of nodding to the frantic pace he was taking now, but his eyes slipped shut and he had maneuvered his own dick out to stroke in time with his sucking. Julien couldn't really see from this angle, and he felt an ache that had nothing to do with his fast-approaching orgasm. Was he really going to let a second chance, a second chance with a man like *Eli*, slip through his fingers? Or rather *not* through his fingers?

Julien nudged Eli's moving elbow with his toe gently but firmly, and Eli's eyes sprang open, beautiful and bright in the darkness.

Julien cleared his throat. "Save that for me. I want you coming in my hand tonight."

Eli's body shook as he made a broken sort of mewling sound, and that was it for Julien. He gasped a warning, and Eli retreated until just the tip rested on his tongue, which he flicked with assassin precision. Helplessly, Julien emptied his balls in his mouth, head rolling back to slam painlessly into the door. He didn't think he'd ever feel pain again. He couldn't even remember what pain was, at the moment.

"God," Julien said, stunned, and looked down at Eli, who had sat back on his heels again with a sharp, self-satisfied smile. He might have looked as calm and collected as a cat if not for the rigid dick poking out from his waistband.

"Come here," Julien said, patting his thigh, and Eli stood gracefully. That self-contained watchfulness was back and when Julien reached for him and pulled him close, Eli spun in his arms until they were pressed front to back and deftly laced their fingers together so that he could be the one to control Julien's hands over his own body.

Fine by him. What problem could he possibly have with Eli's round ass pressed up against him, his sweet-smelling hair just under his nose or his surprisingly soft hands on Julien's, showing him exactly how he wanted to be touched. Moving one up his belly and chest, brushing over tight nipples, and the other down, to cup his hardening dick.

Julien began to massage him there wordlessly through his briefs, and Eli made a small helpless sound as his eyes closed and his head tipped back against Julien's shoulder. He dropped that hand, allowing Julien to stroke and tease him on his own.

"That's it," Julien said. "Let me."

Eli shuddered slightly against him and his left hand inched Julien's incrementally upward to land on his collarbone. Julien let him control the pace of that, moving where he was moved, while his right hand continued to palm him, then carefully pulled his pants and underwear the rest of the way down. Eli's breathing increased and their left hands took a somewhat larger leap, so that Julien's was now resting around the base of Eli's throat with Eli's own hand holding it there still in a trembling death grip.

Julien turned his head and pressed a kiss into Eli's hair, wrapped a hand around his cock. "Is this for me?" he said, testing the weight and texture, experimenting with different grips, then dipped to tease his balls the way he liked himself.

Eli nodded slightly, licked his lips.

"Very nice," Julien said, and watched Eli's swollen lips part slightly and his eyelashes flutter shut against his cheek.

Julien pulled his hand off Eli's dick, gripped his chin and gently swiped his thumb over his mouth, forcing those lips farther apart for just a second.

Eli's eyes opened and he stared up at Julien hungrily. Julien did it again, slower this time, and when Eli opened wider, he fed him his two fingers. Eli instantly began to suck on them, eyes slipping closed again in pleasure and making small, pleased noises.

"Jesus, you like to use your mouth." Julien pulled his fingers away slowly and watched Eli chase them, lapping at the tips until he couldn't reach and dropped his head back with a frustrated growl so animalistic it was honestly shocking. Julien laughed, half startled, half horny as hell that he could have such an effect on him. Watching all those layers fall away made him feel more powerful, more in control than any receptive mouth or vulnerable throat.

God, he wanted Eli to remember him. Remember him like he was right now with the flattering light of good sex to soften the mistakes they'd make down the line.

He took hold of Eli's dick and began to stroke him off. It was absurd to have felt nervous about this. Bodies were bodies. As similar and as different as people were.

"That's it. Fuck my hand now. You earned it," Julien added as Eli thrust into his grip, grunting. "So good for me on your knees, looking up at me like I asked, swallowing my—"

Suddenly Eli moved their left hands up to squeeze his own throat under the chin. His whole body trembled and he made a small, strange whining sound before biting down on his lip viciously and beginning to come. With no better options, Julien caught it in his hand and murmured gentle nothings all the way through, until he gave his final twitch and slumped against Julien's chest.

Julien held him upright and studied the only sliver of face he could see beneath his own chin. Perhaps it was the angle, but he looked…different like this, relaxed and mindlessly nuzzling at Julien's neck. Of course, Eli would be the only person whose features got sharper post-orgasm, unlike every other slack-jawed plebian in the world, Julien thought fondly, and without thinking, pressed a kiss to his brow.

Eli's eyes opened immediately, catching the moonlight in such a way that it was hard to tell the iris from the whites, then abruptly shrugged out of Julien's arms. He stepped deliberately away, keeping his back turned and running his hands over his own hair, face and chest as if nervously smoothing wrinkles out of his very body.

"Well," Eli said finally, without turning around. "That was…"

Julien would have given nearly anything for him to finish that thought. *Yes? That was…wonderful? An erotic journey that will linger in the mind long after the curtain has closed? An engaging story impeded by uneven performances as one principal vastly outshone his costar?*

But it seemed the reviews wouldn't be coming in. That was fine. Julien had done more with less.

He tentatively touched Eli's back. "You okay?"

Eli finally looked at him with a small, wry twist to his lips. His eyes were closed off again. "Okay? I would have suffered less losses down the hall with a sign on the door saying *Sweet Pea, Do Your Worst*."

"What do you mean?" Julien demanded, alarmed. "Did I hurt you?"

"Only my mystique. My reputation as an enigmatic character may not have survived all that…exposure."

"Oh." He felt an immense wave of relief. Eli couldn't have put his bombastic walls back up faster, but surprisingly that didn't bother Julien. He liked this version of him, too. It was starting to get hard to imagine a version of Eli he wouldn't like. "Don't worry about that, I still think you're baffling."

Eli huffed and belatedly reached for his pants. "I should get going."

"I'd feel better if you stayed tonight. Safety in numbers, and all that," Julien said hastily, and held up his hand. "You can tell your enigma I'll be a perfect gentleman. Please," he added, and mentally kicked himself. Hell, speaking of showing way too much of oneself.

Eli was eyeing him way too closely. "All right. For the sake of safety. There's monsters about, you know."

Julien suppressed a grimace and gestured at his filthy hand. "I need to…"

By the time he'd cleaned up, Eli had curled up in the center of the bed and was lightly dozing. His eyelids only just cracked open when Julien pulled back the covers as if this was old routine for them, as if there was nothing to worry about, or bad coming with the dawn.

It seemed like the simplest thing in the world to lie beside him.

Chapter Ten

The power was back on, but the clock had reset to a flashing midnight. Eli watched the red numbers and imagined a countdown, counting backward from twelve. As soon as he hit zero, he would get up and go. Go to his own room where he could shift and rest and maybe even reflect on his own choices, just for a change of pace.

When he hit zero, Eli started the count over from twenty. Then fifty. Then seventy-five. But his body was beginning to protest, and when he counted off the last numbers from one hundred on slipped claws, Eli forced himself to get out of bed.

Behind him Julien didn't stir, curled up on himself in an uncomfortable, protective-looking position, a stern look on his face even in sleep. He looked a bit like one of those children who frowned when frightened, and Eli suddenly disliked the idea of him waking up alone. Just until morning then. But he would still need to shift, and soon.

Eli deliberated, but the promise of fresh outdoor air and all the smells it brought with it beat out a warm bleached bathroom any day of the week. He closed the curtains to the balcony and then slipped outside unnoticed, opening and closing the glass door with a soft *whoosh*. It wasn't the largest space, but relatively empty at least. No chairs or tables to maneuver on all fours. Just the same flowerpot that was on all the balconies, tucked in the corner with its single dead stem sticking up out of frozen dirt. There was a good inch or so of snow collected across the wood boards, but the icy unpleasantness under his toes faded as he dropped into his shift. The instant relief felt so sweet he almost whimpered. He hadn't been in fur since, when? The day before yesterday? No wonder he was all out of sorts, making poor choices and losing control.

Sure, that was why. And it had absolutely nothing to do with stupidly handsome Julien, or the way he'd laughed out loud at the very idea that Eli was anything less than dangerous, or his easy acceptance of Eli's inability to maintain, well, *Eli* during astonishingly good sex, or the astonishingly good sex, or the way Julien's eyes lit up in a way that was nothing like a wolf's whenever Eli was saying something particularly absurd, or biting, or…anytime he spoke at all, really.

Eli shook his body, disgusted. *He wouldn't have looked at you like that if he'd actually caught you slipping into a monster right there in his arms.* Eli didn't need to imagine the revulsion, fear and violence that would have filled his eyes then. He'd seen it before in others.

He'd seen a shadow of it in Cody's eyes that evening, and he didn't even know the extent to which Eli was different. In theory. Eli was beginning to suspect someone in this circus knew a hell of a lot more about werewolves than they were letting on. The gasoline had wiped out any hope of catching the scent of the kitchen intruder, but Eli would bet anything that claws had carved that word into the wall.

Thief. It would help knowing what had been stolen. Nielsen's maybe mythical treasure? That would rule out De Luca and her minions, if there even was such a thing. She had no need for money. Blue Tail Lodge's territory, on the other hand? That was far more likely to be on her wish list. But the place was about two seconds away from foreclosure anyway, and if anything, this campaign of horrors seemed to be pushing Annabelle further and further from any rational decision making and convincing her to stay.

Eli stretched his legs out behind him one at a time, thinking, and sniffed absently at the dead flower in its pot.

Then there was Cody. One might say he had stolen the life Ian had had here. Cody and Annabelle were clearly involved somehow. There was something vaguely possessive in the way she watched him, scolded him, ran after him. A dynamic that apparently echoed what she'd had with Ian. And though she might not have the same intensity of feeling for him that she had for Ian, Cody still seemed pretty certain that wherever Annabelle and her riches went, he would be able to follow. He might even be right.

That is, unless Ian was alive.

There was no question that Cody had been the most worked up in the kitchen. Though interestingly that had begun before he'd seen the word on the wall. Eli had caught the scent of Cody's anxiety as soon as he'd walked in and it had skyrocketed the moment he'd seen that statuette.

Which raised a whole other question: What was Ian Ackman doing carving werewolves?

He could be closer to the De Luca pack than those pictures had shown. He could even be a wolf himself. Which would explain his ability to disappear without a paper trail. Ruling packs held that power and more. He could have been meeting with Nia in the tower to buy a new life, away from here. It would have required money. Quite a lot of it, in fact. And somehow Eli didn't think Annabelle had spotted Ian a loan so that he could leave her behind. He might have stolen the money from Annabelle. And instead of an affair, Cody might have taken those photos as evidence that money was leaving Blue Tail. But if Ian was the thief in question, who—

Eli heard a sharp cry from the inside the room. He stood into skin as quickly as he could and fumbled the door open, fingers clumsy from the abruptness of his shift. Julien was sitting at the far edge of the bed, with his back to him, bent over with head between knees, breathing heavily.

Eli scented the dark room for danger, but they were alone. There was nothing but the stinging smell of fear so strong and unappealing it almost overwrote the sex lingering in the air.

Eli padded toward him and then stopped a couple feet away. "Julien," he said cautiously.

Julien jerked upright with a small gasp and looked over his shoulder at Eli, black eyes wide and wet. "You're— I didn't realize you were still here," he said, and hastily swiped at his own face.

"What's wrong?" Eli asked.

Julien shook his head quickly. "Nothing. Everything's fine."

Eli hesitated, but Julien's hands were trembling where they were clutching his thighs and his heart was beating so quickly it made his own hurt. Eli slowly walked closer and sat down on the bed's edge beside him. They sat like that in silence for a moment.

"It's really nothing," Julien said finally, without looking at him. "I'm not even actually upset. I just get nightmares sometimes. And then I wake up like this." He laughed harshly and added under his breath, "Reason number three hundred and eighty-two why I can't do one-night stands, because this is honestly humiliating."

"How often?" Eli asked. Julien just shook his head. So, often. "Do you want to talk about it?"

"God, no," Julien said, voice cracking. He covered his face and ground the balls of his hands into his eyes and blew out a long breath. "Fuck. Sorry. I'm just...so tired."

"Go back to bed," Eli said, touching his shoulder.

"I'm probably not going to be able to sleep again," Julien warned, but didn't resist as Eli gently pushed and prodded him until he was lying back under the covers and then crawled over him back into his own spot. He hissed when Eli's body brushed his own. "Christ, your feet are ice."

"Warm them up," Eli suggested, and Julien tangled their

legs together until Eli's feet were trapped between his. They lay like that facing one another, and Eli listened to Julien's still-pounding heart as his feet slowly warmed.

"Where were you?" Julien whispered in the dark. "Were you going back to your room?"

Eli studied his expression, his dark worried eyes, then shifted closer until he could press his face against Julien's chest, flushed hot from his nightmares. The hair there tickled his nose, and he nudged Julien over onto his back so he could rest his cheek flat over his heart instead and felt Julien's arms wrap automatically around him. "No. Not tonight."

Eli's eyelids began to droop shut, lulled by Julien's warm fingers moving in long, exploratory strokes up and down his back.

"Be careful of West," Julien said suddenly, and Eli opened his eyes again.

"Hmm? I told you there was nothing suspicious in his room."

Julien's hand had paused and was lingering on the dip of Eli's lower back, drawing circles into the skin with his thumb. "I believe you. But just don't…drop your guard around him. Please."

"Ah." Eli snorted and rubbed his cheek over Julien's chest hair, almost relieved that he was behaving so predictably for once. "You mean don't drop to my knees for him."

Julien's hand flexed against his spine and he hastily said, "No, that's not it. Of course you can, ah, do that with whoever you want. I know we're casual." He shifted in the bed as if uncomfortable, jostling Eli. "Temporary partners in the amateur sleuthing business. Hardy Boys who hooked up."

"Let's stick with casual," Eli said. "Catchier. Fewer allusions to incest."

"The point is I know it's not my business. But as your, um, casual, I would be careful of Patrick. Some of the stuff he was saying earlier—I don't know. It gave me a bad feeling."

"Stuff about me?" Eli asked curiously.

"I think so. Maybe. I don't know anymore." Julien laughed shortly, chest jumping under Eli's cheek. "Ignore that. Just nightmares catching up to me."

"About your brother?" Eli asked.

Julien hesitated, hand drifting to Eli's tailbone absently. "Sometimes," he said eventually, and his thumb dug into the muscles there.

Eli arched into his touch with a groan. "S'nice."

"I bet. What do you need all these knots down here for?"

"To tie my tail on," Eli joked sleepily. It was something Helena always used to say while playing with the Park great-grandchildren. *Here's where we'll tie your tail on when hunters cut it off. Here's where we'll paste back your ears.* Honestly, brilliant alpha or not, how she was allowed near kids at all was a mystery, though it did explain a lot about the adults she'd raised.

After a moment Eli realized that Julien had stilled. "Why'd you stop?" He pushed into his hand.

"Sorry." Julien started massaging him again. "I might have just realized something."

"Important?"

Julien pressed a kiss onto the crown of Eli's head. "It can wait. I'll tell you in the morning."

Eli hummed, honestly relieved. He was half-asleep as it was. Body more relaxed from even that quick shift than it had been in days.

"I'm sorry," Julien whispered into his hair.

"F'what?"

Julien was quiet, his big warm hand working over his skin, and Eli's heavy lids drifted closed. He could listen like this just as easily. He just had to wait for Julien to speak and then he could finally get some sleep...

...It was the crying that woke him. Eli opened his eyes, grimacing in the strong morning light. Hours had passed and he'd managed to maneuver all the way onto Julien at some point. He had to crane his head back to see his face.

Julien was staring at the ceiling with a distant, thoughtful expression on his face, but glanced down when Eli moved and smiled faintly. "You're awake. Good. I thought of something last night."

"You're not crying," Eli mumbled, surprised.

Julien's eyebrows shot up. "I guess I deserve that. But no, waking up crying usually requires sleep first."

"Someone is," Eli said, rolling off Julien and sitting up, pulling the top sheet with him. "You don't hear that?"

Even with his weaker human ears, surely he heard something. They were huge, gasping, rending sobs. Choking. Miserable. Eli stood and walked to the balcony, pulling open the glass door.

Whoosh. The smell of blood and raw meat was overwhelming and Eli growled automatically, eyes fluttering shut. His skin prickled and his hearing went watery as he swayed—

Arms wrapped around his shoulders. "Easy. Deep breath," Julien murmured, turning him away from the cold air. Eli pressed his face into Julien's shoulder and breathed, carefully through his mouth, until he felt steady on his feet again and the crying no longer echoed through a tunnel.

"Are you okay?" Julien asked above him.

"Sorry. Dizzy," Eli murmured, then took one last breath and stepped back. Julien's arms fell away. "Never mind me. Go." He nudged him toward the open door, and when Julien turned, Eli covered his nose and followed him outside. Together they peered over the balcony ledge.

There. Just below, Annabelle Dunlop knelt on the snowy pavement weeping over a man's body, his limbs twisted at funny, cartoonish angles, head sunken into itself, like a smashed toy. Snow a dark, deep blackish ruby next to the bright cheerful tomato of his snow jacket.

Cody Reeves was dead.

Eli and Julien dressed as quickly as possible, speaking very little. Julien seemed distracted and distant. Disturbed by the sight of Cody's broken body perhaps, or maybe even reminded of the death of his own younger brother, who couldn't have been far from Cody's age himself.

By the time they got down to the breakfast room, the other guests were already gathered, pale-faced and shaken. The students whispered in German to one another in the corner, Mr. and Mrs. Miura sat by the door holding hands and not speaking, and Patrick West paced by the window but walked over to Julien and Eli as soon as they entered the room.

"David took Annabelle inside," he said in a hushed tone that still seemed to carry around the room. "He's trying to radio down the mountain to tell them there's been a murder."

"Murder?" Julien asked. "Are you sure?"

"Seems that way. His, uh—it looks like someone stabbed him before he fell over the balcony railing."

Eli hissed and tucked his hands behind his back as his claws prickled. "Stabbed? With what?"

Patrick shook his head. "I don't think David has found a weapon yet."

Bucknell entered the room with the faint odor of death drifting in on his clothes. "Mr. Smith, there you are. I stopped by your room, but you didn't come to the door."

Eli shrugged, ignoring the implicit question. "Here I am. Were you able to make contact with the outside world?"

"Yes. Unfortunately, it seems we're going to be handling things on our own for a little bit. The roads are impassable at the moment, so it's going to be a while before anyone can make it up here. I'd like everyone to stay inside so as to preserve the crime scene as much as possible."

"Can we go to our own rooms until then?" Mrs. Miura asked.

"Yes, ma'am. If you're on the second floor, that's fine. Just as long as you head straight there and don't wander around. Anyone on the third floor, I'd like to speak with you first."

"I assume you're speaking to Julien and myself," Eli said.

"I believe we're the only ones up there." The only ones left, anyway.

"*Were* you on the third floor last night?" Bucknell asked.

Eli blinked. "Excuse me?"

"As I said, I stopped by your room late last night and you didn't seem to be there. I'm curious as to where you might have gone after your fight with Cody."

"*My* fight?" Eli protested.

At the same time Julien said, "He was with me."

"All night?" Bucknell asked.

"Yes. All night," he said firmly, surprising Eli. He didn't think—well. At least Julien didn't seem that upset. Tense and annoyed? Yes. Darting a quick glance at Patrick West, as if he simply couldn't help it? That, too. To be fair, Patrick did look stunned, staring straight ahead as if trying to make sense out of what he was hearing.

"All right," Bucknell said at last, without judgment. "And did you—either of you—hear anything last night between ten and approximately twelve thirty last night?"

Eli frowned. "What makes you think that's when he was killed?"

"Because that's when I went to check on him," Annabelle said, standing in the doorway to the breakfast room. She'd clearly just showered and her long hair hung wet and still dripping around her face, leaving slowly growing dark patches on her baby blue sweatshirt.

"Annie—" Bucknell said gently. "I thought you were lying down."

Annabelle shook her head. "Co-Cody said he was going upstairs at ten. I knocked on his door at twelve thirty, but he didn't answer. I thought he was just ig-ignoring me. I have a key, so I went inside, but he wasn't there." She inhaled shakily. "He must have already been outside. Lying there in the sn-snow. All alone. What if he was still—and I didn't keep looking for him? What if he was lying there dying and—" Annabelle's voice cracked.

"No," Bucknell said. "You can't think like that. There's nothing you could have done."

"Particularly seeing as Cody wasn't dead yet," Eli said.

The others all turned back to look at him.

"What makes you say that?" Patrick asked coolly. Apparently he was all recovered from his shock and moved on to the hurt feelings stage.

"Last night I stepped out onto the balcony for some air. I don't know the time exactly, but I'm certain it was later than twelve thirty. There wasn't anyone down there."

Annabelle exhaled, staring at him with wide eyes. "You mean…"

"I don't know where Cody was, but he wasn't dead when you dropped by his room."

"You might not have noticed him there," Patrick suggested. "Why would you? You'd have to have been looking pretty intentionally at the ground in the dark."

Eli shrugged. "I'm certain I would have. I remember looking down at the snowfall. And the moon was bright enough." He wasn't really sure if humans could smell that much blood or not. But no sense risking it.

Bucknell however was frowning. "I thought you and Mr. Doran were together all night."

"We were," Eli said. His nose twitched helplessly as if

something dangerous was just out of range and he had to fight down the sudden impulse to run. "I only stepped out onto the balcony for a moment to get some fresh air."

"Outside. Sometime after twelve thirty. In the middle of winter," Bucknell said flatly.

"Yes, remarkably the great outdoors remains the best source of fresh air regardless of the season."

Bucknell turned to Julien. "Did you notice when Mr. Smith left the room?"

"Um," Julien said, glancing at Eli a bit nervously. "No, but I'm sure he was just on the balcony. I had—I was awake when he came back inside."

"But you have no idea how long he was out there?"

"Does it matter? What do you think I was doing? Leaping from balcony to balcony in the dark, in the snow, three stories up?" Eli asked as incredulously as possible considering he'd done exactly that twice in the last twenty-four hours. "What possible reason would I have to kill Cody?"

"No one is saying you did, sir," Bucknell said calmly. "But I would suggest you begin telling the truth now."

"I'm not lying."

Bucknell stared at him for a long moment, then sighed, as if disappointed. "I ran a check on your name last night. And there doesn't seem to be any record of a person matching your description existing. Eli Smith, isn't it?"

"Elias," Eli said automatically.

"I checked that, too," Bucknell said. "There's no matching driver's license, record of employment, or even birth certificate under that name."

Eli could feel Julien's gaze on him but didn't, *couldn't*,

look at him right now. The rest of the room didn't offer up a pleasant alternative either. Every guest was staring at him with a morbid sort of fascination in their eyes. No doubt they thought they were watching Bucknell corner a killer. Annabelle even took a couple steps backward and let Patrick wrap a protective arm around her shoulders. Foolishly, Eli felt a pang of hurt at that.

"I changed my name."

"Legally?"

"No," Eli said tightly. "Is an aversion to paperwork the slippery slope that leads one to murder?"

"So you have records under…?"

"Genet," Eli said, and hoped to god that whoever Bucknell had checking these records of his couldn't be reached for rebuttal anytime soon. "Nelson Genet."

Beside him Julien made a small sound and Eli finally couldn't resist looking at him any longer and found him staring right back. His heart was racing and he smelled a bit like excitement—impossible to tell if it was the good kind or bad—but his face was completely and utterly blank.

"I don't see what any of this has to do with the murder."

Bucknell scratched his head absently. "Most likely nothing. I just find it interesting, that's all. Yesterday evening Cody told me Mr. Smith followed him to the lookout tower and demanded to know the name of the buyer interested in the lodge."

"What?" Eli hissed.

"He firmly believed that you, Mr. Smith, would do anything to sabotage that deal. Shortly after that, the two of you got into an altercation and I discovered that Elias

Smith is a false identity. I went to your room to ask you about it and you were not there. In fact, it seems during the time of the murder, your whereabouts are unknown."

"On the contrary, I was making my presence extremely known *thereabouts*," Eli said, gesturing vaguely toward Julien's body. "And for the two minutes I wasn't hanging off this one's dick, I was on the balcony."

One of the students made a squeaking sound and Julien was blinking very rapidly, but Bucknell's expression didn't change. "I'd like to take a look at this balcony."

"What do you think you're going to find up there, a rope swing to the scene of the crime?" Eli drawled.

Inside, however, he was panicking. There'd been snow on the balcony floor when he'd shifted. Had he left paw prints? Had he walked around enough to confuse the tracks? Maybe for a city mouse like Julien, but Bucknell was a hunter, wasn't he? That's what Annabelle had said. Wolf tracks on the balcony of a three-story building wasn't a smoking gun, but they were hardly going to assuage anyone's suspicions either.

"Is there some reason you don't want me up there?" Bucknell asked, and Eli opened his mouth, but Julien spoke instead.

"It's my room. If you're looking for permission, I'll take you up there to look around myself."

"All right then," Eli said, spinning on his heel and walking out of the room. "Fine. Let's all go take a look at this balcony. Why not? I have nothing to hide."

"Mr. Smith," Bucknell called after him. "I'd rather—"

But Eli had already crossed the lobby and was hurrying up the stairwell. Eli tried to think as he turned onto the third-floor hallway, slowing his steps. There wasn't much point anyway. He wouldn't be able to get into Julien's room. He'd have to wait at the door for the card key. Then he could probably push forward again, walk out on the balcony, make use of some of those flat-footed stomps the others seemed so fond of…

Julien brushed past him walking down the hall, quickly unlocking his room door and disappearing inside.

"What—?" Eli ran to catch it just before it fell shut again, remembering not to breathe through his nose just in time. He didn't have a second to spare going all dizzy again. Inside the room Julien had pulled open the top drawer of his dresser and was rifling through the books and papers there.

"I'll tell you later," he said without prompting, and not one to look a gift horse in the mouth, Eli left him to it and walked out onto the balcony, pinching his nose shut and trying to breathe as shallowly as possible.

All Bucknell had done was cover Cody's body with a bunch of plastic tarps, hoping to preserve the crime scene. The snow on the balcony was a mess from when they'd run out that morning, but a single paw print had survived. Eli stepped on it hastily, and looked around for anything he'd missed.

He heard Julien open the room's door and immediately start saying something about wanting to put the sex paraphernalia away before everyone and their mother came tromping through. God, the man was a natural born liar and it turned Eli on like nothing else.

His eye caught on the flowerpot in the corner. It looked

different somehow. The dead stem. That's what it was. There had been a single stem there last night, and now it was gone.

Closer up, he could see the dirt had been disturbed, and something stank just out of sight. With his sleeve, Eli scraped the first few layers of soil away, newly loose.

It was bad luck he found the knife just as Bucknell stepped out onto the balcony.

Framed for murder. Didn't do it! Locked up at a ski lodge. If anyone asks, my name's Nelson Genet.

Eli tried to send the text to Cooper, but the message failed. Not enough service. So much for reaching out if he really needed help.

They'd put him in Annabelle's office, in the end. "Just until the roads are open," Bucknell said almost apologetically. But it was clear Eli had no choice. As soon as Bucknell told the others he'd found the murder weapon stashed away on the balcony, the same balcony Eli had blatantly run up to tamper with, he was fucked.

"Someone planted that there," Eli had said, knowing there was no point. Someone in this lodge had murdered Cody Reeves and Eli couldn't have fought harder for the title of most suspicious if they were offering prizes to the winners.

He sent another text to Mutya asking her to "shift the retreat to skin" in preparation for possible visitors and to warn Gwen what was happening. Based on her fear of the Trust, he'd assumed the blackmail she'd been involved with for her old pack was restricted to wolves. But there was always a risk something would pop up on human databases, too.

His text to Mutya wasn't delivered either, of course, but hopefully would go through before anyone showed up with a warrant. Eli would be long gone by then anyway. He couldn't afford to stick around. Innocent or not, Eli's paper doll identity was frayed too thin to stand up to any sort of real inspection. Clearly, since Bucknell had already called bullshit on the name.

If he was arrested, it wouldn't be long before the Trust was flagged, and then the Preservation would have eyes on him and the whole house of cards would come tumbling down. Cooper and Oliver would suffer since he was their responsibility. Helena might even get knocked a few pegs down from the top when it came to light she'd knowingly sheltered a rebel thief and the bane of her peers' pasts.

How long would it be before someone asked what he'd done before that? Where he'd really come from? What he really was?

Eli curled up tighter under Annabelle's desk. He couldn't risk getting in fur right now, so just soothed himself by slipping bits here and there. How had everything gone to shit so quickly? He didn't want to leave the retreat. He didn't want to leave Cooper's ragtag pack of misfit toys.

Stranger still, he actually missed the way things had been yesterday. Even with the encroaching threat of the De Luca pack and lies flying this way and that, Eli had been *enjoying* himself. Breaking into rooms again, charming his way into information, catching Julien's eye across the room as if they were accomplices working the crowd together. It was ridiculous to feel some kind of loss there as well. But then, Eli had lost track of the number of people who had told him that's exactly what he was. A ridiculous creature with a skewed sense of what really mattered in life.

He wouldn't say goodbye to Julien before he went. Imagine if he did. *No, I can't explain why I'm running. Yes, it's true, this isn't my name. No, I have no idea what's going on, but I just wanted to...what? See your frowny face one more time?*

For all Eli knew, Julien thought he was guilty, too. He was, after all, the only one who knew Eli had the skills to break in and out of the rooms. Had been operating under his own mysterious agenda, this entire time.

Eli slipped his claws directly into the rug, snagging the ugly nylon. It didn't matter what Julien thought of him after he left, anyway. Unless it meant he would stop looking for the truth. But surely someone would figure out what was going on eventually. Cooper had formed the embarrassing habit of not resting until justice was served or whatever naive worldview kept him poking his nose into everyone's affairs all the time. Perhaps, if Eli asked him to pass on any findings to Julien... Just so he'd know, for his brother's sake and not because Eli needed his name cleared, of course, which in itself was an absurd concept. But then he'd forgotten—Cooper wouldn't be his alpha anymore either.

A wave of sick, clammy fear washed over him. The nauseating dizziness of being without a pack, a grounding point. What was it that the one time he really did need to run was the one time he really didn't want to? Irony, maybe. Or just the same self-destruction as always from a slightly new angle.

In the waiting room, the door to the hall quietly unlocked and opened. Eli hastily slipped everything into skin
and sat up, sniffing the air. His breath caught at Julien's
now familiar scent just before the man himself walked in
and looked around nervously. He startled when he caught
sight of Eli peeking out from behind the edge of the desk.

"Jesus," Julien whispered. "That bad?"

"That depends—did you bake me a spoon cake?"
Eli asked, heart pounding with excitement he probably
shouldn't be feeling.

"I didn't have time. Some of us have been working,"
Julien said, lowering himself to the floor next to Eli with
a grunt. "Cody made an impromptu trip up the mountain
after he attacked you. That's where he was when Annabelle
went by his room last night. Ahmet, Claudia and Jonas were
on their own balcony smoking and saw him come down
the ski lift. You were absolutely right. He wasn't dead yet."

"Nice of them to share after I was already dragged to
the dungeons," Eli muttered.

"Wouldn't have done you much good with the way you
dug up the murder weapon. Or was there some other reason you ran upstairs ahead of everyone else?" Julien asked
pointedly.

"Oh, did you notice that? I thought you'd be too busy
shoving past me to cover your own sins."

Julien bit his lip as he studied Eli's face. "Is this another
impasse?" he asked finally.

"Seeing as only one of us has been wrongfully placed
under desk arrest, forgive me if I don't view our situations
as equally grim. Notice how I'm assuming you know I

didn't kill Cody," Eli added, and winced when it sounded a lot less blasé and a lot more desperate than he'd intended.

"I know," Julien said immediately, flapping his hand like the idea was ridiculous.

"Well, I've always said you're far too trusting," Eli said to distract from his helpless smile.

Julien snorted. "You have no idea." He abruptly reached into his pocket and pulled out the deck of Sweet Pea cards.

"Oh, excellent, I could go for a nice round of Go Fish," Eli said sarcastically, then stopped when Julien pulled a small sheet of folded paper out from between the cards.

"I wanted to grab this in case Bucknell decided to search our roo—my room." Julien stared down at the paper for a long moment, as if now that it was out he wanted nothing more than to stick it back in the box.

"If that's a note confessing your undying love for me, I've got to warn you, I don't think I'll be around much longer. States to flee, identities to burn."

"And they call me melodramatic," Julien said with a quick smile. "I bet you anything that whatever he went up there for is what got him killed last night. We just need to figure out what Cody found up the mountain, and you'll be out of here."

"Oh, is that all? Well, let me pack my bags now."

Julien handed Eli the paper decisively, though there was a slight shake in his fingers. "Here. I think he went here."

Eli hesitantly accepted it and unfolded what looked like… "Why, Mr. Doran, is this a treasure map?"

"I don't know," Julien said. "I found it in my brother's notes on Maudit."

Eli hummed, studying the paper. It looked like the photocopy of a crude drawing of the mountain with *Maudit Falls* labeled neatly at the bottom. In different handwriting, near the center of the page, someone had scrawled what seemed to be a list of instructions.

Begin at the base of the wolf's tail.
Follow the backbone to the muzzle.
Pluck its fangs.

"Does that mean anything to you?" Julien asked, and Eli looked up at him. He had a careful sort of expression on his face. Watchful. Guarded. Everything Eli assumed his own face was.

"I don't know what this means," he said carefully, mouth dry and the same sensation of danger stalking him just around the corner. But there wasn't really. Just more of the same sort of lying he did all the time.

Julien held his gaze a beat longer, then nodded. "Neither did I at first. I didn't know if it was a map or riddle or hell, maybe I should be keeping an eye out for wolves running around the mountain." He laughed briefly and Eli tried to smile. It felt unnatural on his face. "Then last night Patrick told me one of Maudit's myths. Little Blue Wolf and the monster in the mountain. Have you—do you know that story?"

Eli blinked. "I may have heard of it. I'm not sure," he said slowly. He might not have grown up around other werewolves, but it was hard to escape the seemingly never-ending misadventures the Little Wolf Who Smelled of

Bluebells. He'd liked to trail after Helena sometimes when she took her great-grandchildren out into the woods and told them grim tales of Little Blue getting into various predicaments, losing bits of himself and dying a little more inside each time. As far as Eli could tell it was all just a warning not to forget they were wolves first or ever give that up, though that could very well be down to Helena's telling. She wasn't particularly maternal, but extremely... traditional. "Let me guess, Little Blue loses his tail to the monster in the mountain?"

"Got it in one," Julien said, and shuffled through the Maudit cards. "Long story short, the monster bites down on the tip of the wolf's tail after he spends the night in his mouth."

"Kinky."

"Here," Julien said, tossing one of the cards at Eli. "Look familiar?"

Eli twitched in shock. It was a similar image to the painting in the retreat. A figure begging, reaching longingly toward the falls. The same painting Nia had commented on when she and Brett had visited, which meant... well. Maybe nothing. Maybe everything. The scene was titled *Little Blue Wolf.*

"What if it really is a treasure map?" Julien said quietly, urgently. "If the falls are the Little Blue Wolf's tail, then the base of the falls—"

"No," Eli said. "Those are behind the retreat. I've been all over that lake and under the falls themselves. There's nothing there."

Julien deflated slightly.

"Rivers empty into mouths, don't they? What if the lake is the monster's mouth, the river is Bluebell's tail and the base—"

"Is somewhere up the mountain. Wherever the head-waters are," Julien finished.

Eli flicked the card around between his fingers. "Granted, it's been a while since I brushed up on my limnology, but I doubt that's going to be a precise point on the map."

"It doesn't need to be. I just need to follow the river up-stream until I cross the backbone."

Eli dropped the card. "What does that mean? You're going there? Now?"

Julien nodded impatiently as if he wasn't agreeing to the most foolish plan Eli had ever heard. "My brother left this for me to find. He wanted me to go there. It's the entire reason I came to Maudit. Then Cody took an impromptu trip up the mountain and it got him killed. Which means the murderer must know what's up there, too. They could be destroying the evidence right now."

"Very noble. One question. You and what guide?" Eli snapped. "Because I've seen what you call hiking, and the only upside is you won't even complete step one until the snow melts, which should at least make steps two and three a bit easier."

"Cody's dead, someone's planted a knife on you and the authorities are on their way. The same authorities who didn't notice Ian Ackman disappear, filed every weird thing that's happened on this mountain misogynistically as An-nabelle's hysteria, and allowed Bucknell to sequester you away in here on some very shady legality. Do you really trust them to protect you?"

"Of course not," Eli said quickly, though he could hardly explain he didn't plan on sticking around that long.

"How seriously do you think they'll take a treasure map based on a folktale? This could be my last chance. I have to at least try."

Eli looked into Julien's eyes, dark and pleading with him to understand. "Fine. I'm coming with you."

"What? No, Eli—"

"You wouldn't be able to track the river on the clearest of spring days, never mind in this snow. And if what you say is true, and there is something at the end of this map that helps identify Cody's killer... As fond I am of your hands, I'd rather not place my fate in them while I wait around here."

There was also the small matter of a possibly murderous wolf out on the loose. Eli couldn't just let Julien wander into the woods without one natural set of defenses. He'd be utterly helpless.

"All right," Julien said at last. "I can't pretend I wouldn't appreciate the company."

Eli took one last look at the map and handed it back to Julien. "Now that we've settled that, is it time to stage an office break? There may be gold in them there hills."

It was the simplest thing to walk out the back door of the lodge. Julien wasn't sure where the others had gone, but it was well out of sight. Of course, considering the chaos that had met Bucknell's announcement that Eli had been placed under arrest, it would have been surprising to find the other guests sitting around playing pinochle. Based off the expressions on their faces alone, Julien would guess Mr. and Mrs. Miura were somewhere snowshoeing their way out by any means necessary. A big part of Julien wished he could join them.

The ski lift was running; Julien wondered who had turned it on and when. Or maybe Cody had never gotten a chance to turn it off last night. Maybe he'd planned to go back up the mountain and had only returned to the lodge to…do whatever it was that had ultimately led to his murder.

It was an easy enough ride to the top of the mountain, although Eli still insisted on pulling all his limbs up onto the seat until he was doing something more akin to squatting than sitting. Far less nerve-racking was following him through the snow single file, and watching the competent, sure-footed way he moved. If this was what walking on your toes got you, maybe they should all give it a go.

Eli told him headwaters in the mountains often just came from melted snow that fed into multiple tributaries that then fed into the river, rather than some clearly bubbling fountain secreted away like Shangri-La. He would be able to get them to the stream farthest up the mountain, however, and they could walk that until they saw something meeting the description of a backbone.

Eli said he knew where the stream was because of a map they had in the retreat and Julien didn't argue. He couldn't risk the wrong question right now.

More and more he'd felt like they were walking toward

a precipice and a fall they wouldn't survive. But what could he do now to change things? He'd come here with one goal and was close, so close to reaching it. Everything else—the murder, Eli, his razor-sharp silver tongue, the way he squirmed and whimpered before he came, the soft whuffing sounds he made in his sleep—that was unexpected, peripheral. It had to be.

"I was worried for a moment." Eli interrupted his anxious thoughts. "Back in the lodge when the mob pulled their pitchforks, I wondered if you might think I killed Cody, too. I'd completely understand if you had, of course."

Julien avoided the unspoken question. "Maybe I do think that. Maybe I'm just choosing to ignore it for now because I need you and your divining rod to track this stream to the treasure."

Eli looked over his shoulder at Julien and wiggled his eyebrows. "Isn't that a coincidence? I'm avoiding all sorts of important things for the sake of your divining rod, too."

Julien snorted and Eli turned to face forward again.

"I'm thankful, though. That you're helping me," Julien felt compelled to add. "I couldn't have done this without you."

Eli was quiet for a beat, and when he spoke he almost sounded embarrassed. "Yes, well. Like I said before, I've got just as much reason to figure out what the hell is going on as you do. I'd rather not have to leave this place. I just got here."

Julien frowned. "There isn't any...danger of you getting fired because of all this, is there? I mean, I'd be more than happy to talk to the owners of the retreat if you need someone to vouch for you. Who are they again?"

Eli shot him a small smile that made Julien's stomach flip. "You're sweet. But no, it's not the threat of termination I'm concerned by. It's more that..." He hesitated, and for a long moment there was only the sound of their boots wading through the snow.

Then, speaking so quickly he sounded breathless, Eli said, "I don't want to let them down. I don't want De Luca to use me as an excuse to take the retreat away from them. I don't want them to think maybe reb—the retreat is more trouble than it's worth, just like everyone said it would be. At this point it would be better if I just go away and stop tarnishing the place. I really should have known I'd be utterly inept at this 'doing good' thing."

"Hey." Julien couldn't stop himself from touching Eli's arm and bit back a smile when Eli immediately tangled their fingers together and held on. "We're going to figure this out. I don't think anyone could ever see you as inept. Not at anything. You positively ooze...ept. And besides," he added hastily lest anyone dwell on that witticism, "they can hardly expect you to handle something like this any better than you have. Solving murders isn't in the job description, is it?"

"With Ollie and the whippet? It should be," Eli muttered. "They get mixed up in murder themselves on a quarterly schedule."

"Murder? Those are your bosses?" Julien asked, heart skipping when Eli nodded. "Are they dangerous? Are you in danger?"

"It's nothing like that. They work for one of those very official investigative government agencies. Solving murders is very much in *their* job description."

"A government agency? You mean like FBI or something?"

"Or something," Eli agreed, but he dropped Julien's hand as he said it.

"Do they—" Even though they weren't touching anymore, Julien still felt Eli stiffen. He changed directions. "How'd you end up working here?"

"Oh, I dated Ollie back in the day. Then he married Dayton, I lived in their house for a couple months and they offered me this job. Not exactly in that order, but you get the idea."

"That sounds...cozy," Julien said. "You're close?"

"They're my family now," Eli said as if it was as simple as that. He turned to eye Julien curiously. "Do you think that's strange?"

Julien considered that. "No. No, I guess not. I sort of think of Frankie, my ex-wife, as family. We got together as kids and stayed married twenty years. I hope she's always in my life. Actually I introduced her to her current wife, Natalia, who was a grip on one of my sets. Don't know if I'd spend months living with the two of them. But—" He shrugged. "Frankie moved back in with me for a couple of weeks after—after Rocky died. Just so I wasn't, you know, alone."

"She sounds lovely," Eli said gently.

"Yeah, the best," Julien said, and just barely bit back the impulse to blurt out how much Frankie would like Eli, as if he was a five-year-old introducing his friends. Except one friend had divorced him and the other had pretty adamantly stated that they were nothing more than a one-night stand. That had happened twice. And almost certainly wasn't happening again. Unless it did?

"What kind of celebrity are you, anyway?" Eli was saying. "Only one divorce? Still on good terms? I'm positively disillusioned."

"Er, two divorces actually. But Marla's great, too," he said hastily when Eli twitched his eyebrow into a position that honestly said more than most Shakespearean monologues. "We were only married for three years. I met her right after Frankie and I called it quits. It was a strange time in my life and she has this superpower of making the craziest schemes seem reasonable."

"What happened, did she get you into a cult? Religion? Oh no." Eli's voice went soft and horrified. "She didn't— she didn't get you framed for murder and then drag you out into the wilderness looking for buried treasure, did she?"

"First off, would we say *drag*?" Julien laughed. "Second, no. She's just very...effervescent. Boundless. Up for anything always. We met zip-lining in the French Alps. The problem was I was behaving like that because I was going through something; she's like that all the time. She's a photojournalist in São Paulo now."

Eli's expression had turned distant, thoughtful. "You've been married most of your life."

"Mmm-hmm," Julien said, a little strained. "I guess I'm a commitment sort of guy." Then he heard himself and added, "Not that I have to be. I mean, it really depends on what the other person wants. I can keep it casual, too. In fact it might be nice to do things differently, if the opportunity, uh, was there."

Fortunately, Eli didn't even seem to be listening anymore. "Do I spy with my little eye the elusive backbone?"

"No need for sarcasm," Julien muttered, then realized Eli wasn't talking about him. Up ahead was a procession of boulders left behind by some shifting glaciers, like the tide marks its place with stones.

"Don't suppose you know which way west is?" Julien said, and Eli rolled his eyes and walked to the right.

"I agree, by the way. You couldn't have done this without me," he said over his shoulder. It was a much shorter walk to the muzzle, less than two minutes, and Eli and Julien came to a stop again. There, at the end of the boulder line, was a small sloping cliff face of about twelve feet topped by a triangular slab of stone jutting out of the mountain.

"Is that the muzzle?" Julien asked, staring up.

"As opposed to what, Little Blue's party hat?" Eli looked around. "You know, we're not too far away from the tower, I don't think. Two or three miles. Come on. We should be able to climb over here on this side; it's less steep."

"*Climb?* You think there's something up there?"

"Some sort of den, at least," Eli mused, poking around the rock face, for what, Julien didn't know. Ideally an elevator button.

"How do you know that?"

Eli glanced at him quickly and then away again. "Well, there's nothing down here, is there? Come look at this. I think this is the easiest path. If I go up first, all you need to do is put your hands and feet where I do."

Julien watched him brush extra snow away and test how wiggly various bits of mountain were. "You're different out here, you know."

Eli's quick hands faltered for a moment, then without turning away from the cliff face he asked, "Oh? In what way?" with a chuckle tacked on the end. It was the first time Julien had heard a sound like that from him since the ultra-fake laugh he'd bestowed on Bucknell the first night they'd met. Julien wished he hadn't said anything.

"I don't know," he said hastily. There was a tense moment of silence. "Maybe not different. Maybe it's more that you're just as debonair and confident out here in the snow as you are in silk and that's different from most people I meet. It's nice. Not that you need my approval, obviously. I just think you're... Well, inside and outside, I think you do Nelson Genet proud."

"Ah," Eli said flatly. "I wondered when we'd get to that." He turned to face Julien with an expression so sharp it tingled. "Go ahead. Ask what you really want to ask."

Julien shrugged a bit nervously, but he wanted Eli to know he knew. At least about this maybe they could be honest. "I'm not *asking* anything you don't want to tell me. I just wanted to say that you embody him well. The way you talk, the way you dress, the way you move your eyebrows and your, ah, hips—it's Nelson Genet all over. Seasons thirteen to twenty-two. Not the later stuff when he went through that monk phase, of course."

Eli was staring at him, as close to shocked as Julien had

ever seen him. "You watch *This Time Tomorrow*," he said at last. "You, with your snobby art films and sad, boring goat movies, watch soap operas."

"Yes, sort of," Julien said, flustered. *Sad, boring?* "I told you my mom was in the industry, too. Honey Doran. She's—"

"The Countess Moira Esseintes. Your mother is the actress behind the Countess Moira Esseintes on *This Time Tomorrow*."

"Well, I think she lost her title sometime around season twenty-seven in order to—"

"Marry Joe the veterinarian, that two-timing bigamist bastard, I know," Eli hissed. He seemed angrier about this than Julien had anticipated. "That show means everything to me. I've watched it since I first learned what a TV was. It taught me how to be like people. I—" He snapped his mouth shut like he was afraid to say too much.

"Based chunks of your personality off of one of the characters?" Julien said wryly. "Yes, I can see that now. I thought there was something familiar about you. But I didn't put it together until you said his name."

Eli had that wary look in his eyes again. "It's not a lie," he said eventually.

"What?" Julien frowned. "What isn't?"

Eli hesitated. "When I was younger I—there weren't people like me around. Not many people around full stop. But there was an old man who lived by the—nearby." He rocked on the balls of his feet almost nervously, stumbling unusually through the words. "Every day he watched *This Time Tomorrow*, so I, ah, did, too. Nelson was... As soon as I heard him, I thought *that*. That's the kind of human I want to be. But I'm not lying or *acting* or whatever. This is really me."

"Of course it is," Julien said, confused. "What are you talking about?"

"What am *I* talking about?" Eli echoed a little shrilly. He took a step toward him. "I don't understand you, Doran. You clearly know I'm giving out false names left and right. You just said yourself that I'm embodying a fictional character. I fully admitted that I had to steal a personality off the TV. But none of that makes you the least bit suspicious that this is all a front for something?" He gestured at himself. "That I'm lying to you about what I—what kind of person I really am?"

Julien blinked at him. "Eli...you manage a clandestine safe house for people in trouble, pick locks, break into third-story rooms, go faint at the smell of blood, move like a martial artist and can track a stream up a mountain in the middle of winter from memory. I sort of already figured you were hiding some personal shit."

"You could smell the blood?" Eli asked weakly. Julien ignored him.

"But you also watched a soap opera as a kid and said, 'I am going to be that subversive, provocative, poison-tongued old queen.' Not Brock Elmwood, not Cecily DeFoe. But Nelson Genet. That tells me more about *who you really are* than anyone who wants to pretend their personality was just handed down by the gods like a—"

Eli grabbed the back of Julien's neck and tugged him down. Faster than he could realize what was happening,

Eli's lips were on his. Julien caught up quickly enough. He wrapped his arms around Eli and pulled him closer until he was forced to bend backward a bit, pressing the lines of their bodies together. Eli kissed like he did everything else—teasing, clever and graceful. A partnered dance between the wicked and the divine.

His hands combed through Julien's hair, holding him with strangely thrilling strength, and Julien grasped him beneath his thighs, lifted him up against the slightly sloped cliff face and pressed up between his legs, pinning him there.

"Oh!" Eli gasped, and Julien took the opportunity to deepen the kiss and swallow the resulting whimper and every other secret little sound he made after that, too. They kissed until it wasn't cold anymore. Julien had the absurd, delirious thought that they'd kissed all the way into spring, and the murders and the lies and all of Rocky's secrets that were Julien's secrets now had melted away with the snow and he could just be here with Eli like this. Kissing with nothing between them.

But Julien couldn't hold him forever. Eli slipped out of his hands, feet touching the ground again as they separated, and it was still winter.

"What was that for?" Julien whispered.

"Just angling for a set tour of *This Time Tomorrow*. Now that I realize you have connections."

Julien laughed and, carefully, hesitantly, brushed his mouth lightly over Eli's. Once, twice. When the third time led to nibbling his lips, and tasting the heat just inside, Eli abruptly pulled away.

"God," he groaned, squeezing his eyes shut for a long moment. "You make me want to fuck right here against this cliff and that would be a very bad idea."

"Right, terrible," Julien said faintly, suddenly overwhelmed by images of exactly that. He cleared his throat. "Should we get a good look inside the wolf's muzzle? Unless you'd rather make out some more first. I can go either way, really."

Eli huffed like that amused him and then turned to climb the small cliff side. "Just...follow me."

Thankfully it was a lot easier than Julien had feared. Twelve feet wasn't very far to go and Eli had charted a pretty simple path that wasn't too steep and fairly easy to follow as long as Julien didn't get distracted by Eli's ass moving above him. Of course he made the mistake of looking up anyway, and had to restart a couple of times. But that was okay, too, because Eli always hopped back down beside him and gave him a quick kiss that was supposed to be encouraging, but only made Julien want to fall to the ground again.

At the top, below the triangular "muzzle" stone, there was a narrow ledge and, just as Eli had predicted, some kind of den or small cave. The entrance was only about three feet in every direction, and Julien crouched down to try to get a look inside.

"What are the chances something isn't already sleeping in there?" he asked.

"I doubt it," Eli said vaguely, crouching beside him. He crawled forward a little, sticking his head into the den, and then jerked back suddenly.

"What? Bear? Is it a bear?" Julien asked, already jumping to his feet and trying to drag Eli up with him without pulling them both off the cliff.

"No, will you—" Eli shrugged him off. "There aren't any animals in there. At all. What do you deduce from that?"

"That they're all out here with us? That's worse," Julien said.

"They don't feel safe in there. Either due to too much activity or something on the inside isn't what you want to be hibernating around."

"Never mind, *that's* worse," Julien said immediately.

Eli made his huffing sound. "Are you going in first this time or am I?"

Julien looked at him, alarmed. There were very few things he'd rather do less than crawl into a tight, dark cave in the woods that animals were too scared to sleep in. But he'd faced a lot of terrifying possibilities in the last three days. And one of them was staring at him now, with a glint of challenge in his eye, waiting to see what he would do.

"Right," Julien said gruffly, and cleared his throat. "I'll go first. Don't let anything with sharp teeth follow me."

"Then how am I supposed to see what's in there?" Eli complained, and flashed him a smile.

Julien crawled into the dark den entrance. It did smell rank in there. Oddly sulfuric, heavy, wet air; dead, winter dirt; and the sweetness of rot, all combined into a heady sort of perfume. The den's ceiling rose after the first four feet and it opened up into something a little more cave-like than burrowed tunnel. Julien could probably even stand if he stayed bent over quite a bit, but that seemed far more painful and awkward than crawling.

Behind him, the dark figure of Eli was sitting apparently quite comfortably in a full crouch, the flexible bastard. Suddenly he turned his phone light on, momentarily blinding Julien.

"The fangs," Eli said, gesturing around the space. "Preplucked."

Julien blinked until the spots cleared and his eyes adjusted. There were multiple rock piles around the wall, but Eli was right. It was pretty obvious someone had already gone digging at some point. All around the cave rocks had been tumbled and scattered haphazardly and there were several piles of dirt, long since dried out and faded. Closer to the mouth of the cave, over a dozen backpacks were tucked against the wall, as if any moment now a group of schoolkids would be by to collect them. Toward the back, empty, rusted cashboxes had been stacked in front of what looked like a dark pile of fabric.

Julien crawled closer to the shadow behind the pile of cashboxes and heard Eli murmur a warning, just before he saw it. The second human skull in two days.

"God," Julien said, jerking away immediately. He felt a wave of nausea and took a deep steadying breath. The fetid air didn't help at all. This body was a good deal more… preserved than the hiker out in the woods. It looked like a dusty prop left behind from a mummy movie.

"Will the real Ian Ackman please stand up," Eli said behind him, sounding only mildly curious.

"How can you be sure it's him?" Julien asked, shuffling

backward toward Eli and the mouth of the cave until he could no longer see that horrible grinning face.

"Sure? Not at all. But I believe this is what those in the business call *a clue*." Eli tossed a familiar-looking blue backpack at his knees, unzipped and open. The same one that Ian had been holding in Cody's photographs. The ones of him and the De Luca representative. It landed with a *thunk* and a brick of cash fell out into the dirt.

"Oh," Julien said. Because what other response was there to that much money? The backpack was stuffed with fifty-dollar bills banded neatly together in thick stacks. So not full of half-completed chemistry homework then. "He did it? Ian found Nielsen's treasure?"

"Never bet against sex or money," Eli said, unzipping a second backpack and flicking through yet more cash with lightning speed before moving on to a third. "My guess is he was trying to launder it through De Luca's pa—company. You can't just show up with this much money one day. Nielsen still has family out there. It would have gone to them."

"How much—"

"Two million, five hundred and sixty-five thousand," Eli said promptly. "If each backpack has the same number of stacks."

Julien blinked. "How can you possibly know that?"

Eli held up a wad of cash and waved it in Julien's direction. "See this? The brown currency band means five thousand dollars a stack. Twenty-seven stacks in this bag. Nineteen bags total."

"I see," Julien said. "And you have currency band colors memorized in case of...?"

"I hooked up with a bank teller once," Eli said, then flashed Julien a smile. "I have a longstanding fascination with safes."

"Of course you do," Julien said fondly, then heard himself ask, "Do you ever come out to California?"

Eli blinked at him with such a startled expression that Julien nearly took it back. But his lips were still tingling from their last kiss.

"I mean, would you want to? Come out there for a visit? When the retreat is up and running, of course, and all this mess is behind us."

"Doran, you shameless reprobate, are you attempting to arrange a cross-country booty call with just over two and a half million dollars of untraceable cash and a mummy playing witness?"

"No! Not a—not for sex," Julien protested, and Eli raised an eyebrow. "I mean, yes, obviously I would very much like to have more sex with you if you also want to. But not just that. I'd like to keep in touch, see you again, you know. Maybe come visit you sometime if I'm not on Maudit's most wanted list after this. Or if you ever feel like following up on that longstanding fascination with soap operas, I could show you around town."

Eli looked down, fiddling with the zipper of the bag. "I don't think that would be a good idea."

The cave suddenly felt much smaller and Julien had the overwhelming urge to get out. Perhaps he had a touch of claustrophobia after all. "Right, okay. I'm sorry. I didn't mean to— Sorry. Forget I said anything." His voice sounded way too strained to keep talking, so Julien bit his tongue and focused on returning the fallen cash back to the backpack at his knees. "So what do we think, was Cody killed because he found Ian's body?"

Eli didn't answer. When Julien finally risked a look back up, he was zipping one bag and reaching for another, shoulders hunched as if hiding. "Of course we've had fun. You're occasionally amusing and god knows I could write a book of things I want to do with those enormous hands of yours. But I'm just not interested in a relationship right now," he said as if continuing an argument in his own head. Julien felt a flicker of hope.

"Me neither. I'm not looking for a relationship at all," he said hastily.

"So says Mr. I'm a Commitment Sort of Guy."

"No, really. You have heartbreaker written all over you, for one thing. The sort of man who keeps a bank teller in every port, I bet."

Eli was shaking his head, but he was smiling softly, as if he couldn't help it. "If that's the case, is it wise to get involved with such a lothario?"

"More good news here. My therapist says I'm way too quote 'mired in my own grief to be emotionally available' end quote. Be honest, you're tempted now, aren't you? If not, I can talk about my multiple divorces again and really bring it home."

Eli was openly laughing at him—that clumsy huffing that had somehow gone from strange to charming to his favorite sound in the few short days they'd known each other.

"So you don't want me around for sex and you don't want me around to date. What is the purpose of this hypothetical visit then? Don't tell me there's a mystery afoot in Tinseltown and you're getting the dream team back together."

"God, I hope not," Julien said. He forced a smile, but Eli's words had made his chest ache a little. "Are those the only options then? Or do you think you might be able to pencil me in as a friend?"

"Oh." For one brief moment, Eli looked startlingly young before something like regret twisted his mouth and he hurriedly grabbed the last bag and began to open it in jerky movements. "You don't even know me."

"But I'd like to," Julien said carefully. He was walking a thin line now. "There isn't anything about you I wouldn't like to know, I think."

Eli shook his head, but it didn't seem like denial, just disbelief. "You're sweet, really, but you don't understand what you're talking about."

"I might know more than you think," Julien said, heart pounding so loudly he didn't understand how it wasn't echoing around the entire cave. "Eli, I—I need to talk to you."

He couldn't say it. He didn't *want* to. Because talking about it meant thinking about it and Julien spent every raw, endless night skirting around his memory's torn-up edges of that final phone call. Rocky's voice on the line. *I found something. Something big. For real this time.*

Now wasn't the right time to tell Eli anyway. Not when there was still so much of the puzzle missing. He could make up some excuse. Eli wasn't even fully paying attention, anyway, as he emptied the backpack stack by stack. They could go their separate ways with no hard feelings—just two people who'd managed to have some fun in the strangest of circumstances. Julien could be a good memory, if he kept lying. He could be someone Eli caught while channel-surfing late at night. *See that guy there? Believe it or not I once went monster hunting with him in the mountains. He was sweet.*

Julien took a deep breath. "I wasn't entirely honest with you before. There's another part of the story."

Eli didn't look up. He'd pulled a thick leather-bound notebook out of the bag and was flipping through the pages distractedly. "Isn't there always."

"After he left Maudit, my brother called me. He—"

Eli stopped suddenly on a page and was reading with a small frown.

"What's the matter? What is it?"

"I think this notebook belonged to Nielsen. I keep seeing his name, and there are some formulas, I think. But it's gibberish mostly. Like some kind of code—" He turned the page and his whole body went still, his face completely, unnaturally blank.

"Eli?" Julien asked tentatively. His ears were ringing faintly. *Too late, too late.* "Did you find something?"

Eli didn't do anything for a moment. Then he tilted the book toward Julien.

There, plain as can be, was the same crude drawing of the mountain Julien had spent weeks poring over. The same river snaking down the slope. The same little doodle of a wolf in the bottom left corner. The only difference was the page in Eli's hands didn't have the three cryptic lines on how to find the cave—his brother's cramped scrawl across the center.

"Rocky must have found this when he was here. Taken a picture."

"Just of this page?" Eli asked quietly.

The silence between them went on forever.

"No," Julien said at last. "He left me a complete copy. I read it all."

Eli's eyes flashed a breathtaking luminous blue and Julien's breath caught painfully in his chest.

"It's true," he breathed, amazed. "You really are a—a werewolf?"

Eli spun on his knees and scrambled into the tunnel faster than should be possible. Julien jumped after him. "Wait! Please!"

A strange clacking sound like rocks falling on rocks echoed around them. *Oh god, was it caving in?* Julien just managed to grab Eli's ankle and tried to pull him back to safety before they were crushed, but the flesh and bone moved oddly under his hand. Then suddenly his leg twisted in a way that didn't make sense and shot back to kick Julien in the chest, hard.

Julien let go of Eli's ankle, wheezing and shocked, but he couldn't stop now. He dragged himself toward the entrance, blinking in the bright sunlight. Eli was standing at the ledge already, but spun around when Julien jumped to his feet and made a terrifying snarling sound.

His face was...different. Utterly, inarguably inhuman. His eyes still glowed, and his open mouth flashed sharp fangs. *Fangs.* Actual long, sharp teeth that hadn't been there before glinting brighter than the snow.

"Eli?" Julien whispered. He tentatively reached out. To do what? Touch? Hold? Check that he was really there and not a hallucination Julien was having while he lay dying under a collapsed cave?

It didn't look like he'd get the chance to find out. Eli sidestepped his hand, knocking some snow over the ledge to the ground below, and swayed slightly. Julien instinctually grabbed his jacket, to steady him, but Eli *growled* at him.

"Don't touch me."

Julien released his jacket and took a step backward. "Okay, just please don't—"

A loud popping sound echoed around them, and Julien felt something burn his arm. "Ow, fuck," he said, looking down.

Almost as quickly, the burn was gone and same spot felt piercing cold. Like an icy breeze had found some small hole in his sleeve and was whistling in with a vengeance. His arm was wet, too. Dripping. And a throbbing was starting there in the bicep and radiating all the way up into his brain. Julien tentatively touched his jacket where it looked shiny and torn, and was hit by a wave of nausea.

"Did you shoot me?" he asked numbly, shocked.

"Shut up," Eli hissed. He was looking around them frantically. His hair was sticking up strangely, too, moving around without a breeze. Julien blinked, trying to make sense of it, but he felt woozy and confused. Eli tilted his strange face back and was making some sort of snuffling sound now, similar to what he'd done in his sleep.

I'm never going to watch him sleep again, Julien thought groggily.

"I'm sorry," he whispered.

Those luminescent blue eyes looked at him, colder than the winter air in his open wound. "Stop spea—"

Another popping noise exploded nearby, and Eli shoved him over the edge of the cliff.

Chapter Eleven

If the moon catches you up Blue Tail, he'll steal your love away.
Wasn't that what the people of Maudit Falls said? Well, the
moon was out, they were stuck up this mountain, and not
one of the emotions Eli was feeling right now came anywhere close to love. Not even a little.

Eli sat with his back up against the wooden bench in
the top cabin of the fire tower watching Julien's unconscious body across the room. He'd been out for a long time.
Maybe he'd lost too much blood. Maybe Eli shouldn't have
thrown him over the edge of a cliff. It had only been a little one, though. With snow at the bottom. And he didn't
see what other choice he'd had. As soon as it became clear
someone was intentionally shooting at them, Eli had known
they either had to jump or crawl back into that tomb to

wait, cornered and trapped, for death to find them like it had Ian Ackman.

Not that they were in much better circumstances now. He'd managed to drag Julien under the cover of the trees, sling him over his back and run the relatively short distance to the fire tower. Up here at least there was shelter and a lockable door, the advantage of height, and the ability to hear anyone trying to climb the stairs well in advance. That and he'd simply not been able to carry Julien much farther. Stronger than most humans didn't mean he could lug six foot three inches of dead weight all the way down the mountain while an armed killer stalked them in the growing dusk.

Of course, he almost certainly could have shifted and outrun the shooter all the way to the safety of the retreat if he left Julien behind, but...well, he hadn't. Eli'd rather be anywhere else but sharing air with the lying bastard. But leaving Julien alone and unconscious would be a death sentence, and Eli couldn't bring himself to do that. Yet. At least not until he had a better idea of what was going on.

Eli watched the slow, even movement of Julien's breathing in the moonlight. Once he'd been sure the gunman wasn't going to kick down the door, he'd examined Julien's injuries, a small bump on the back of the head and a bullet graze that shouldn't leave more damage than a deep scar. The arm certainly had bled a lot, though, and Eli's hands hadn't stopped shaking as he'd torn up Julien's shirt and wrapped the wound. He'd had to close his eyes multiple times, because of the way the blood looked under his nails and not because Julien's face looked so innocent unconscious.

Now he knew that wasn't true. Because Julien knew. He'd *known*. The entire time he'd known and lied and lured Eli in like an animal to a trap. But why? A hunter would have killed him by now. He'd certainly had plenty of opportunities while Eli slept in his bed. Unless getting his guard down was only half of the plan and convincing him to travel back to the West Coast had been step two. He would have been helpless caught in Julien's own den, just like he had with the humans who had kept him before. Only instead of his dead ex-alpha James leading him into a cage, Eli would have walked into this one all on his own.

The second thing Eli had done was check Julien for weapons, but he'd only found that ridiculous deck of playing cards, which he'd confiscated out of spite. Then he'd bound Julien's hands together with what remained of the shirt and settled down across the tower room to examine Nielsen's notebook cover to cover. No more surprises. No more lies.

It was a mess of formulas and coded messages interspersed with personal concerns about raising his daughter away from a large pack, his paranoia over the growing interest from the Preservation in his work, his befuddled disappointment with the human son who took after his mother. It wasn't exactly How to Stalk and Kill Werewolves 101, but anyone who read it could see Nielsen was either a terrible practical joker, deeply delusional, or a wolf.

When he'd gotten all he could from the notebook, Eli dealt himself a game of solitaire. Finished one game. Started another. Tried not to think too much about what would happen when Julien woke up, when the gunman decided they couldn't wait any longer and made their next move, when Cooper and Ollie found out he'd ruined everything, when the Preservation found out he'd exposed them all and played right into the hands of the worst possible human— someone too rich to be bought, too famous to be silenced, too conniving, manipulative, two-faced, duplicitous—

Across the room Julien made some groaning noises and began to move, slowly at first, then with real panic when he realized his arms were bound. Eli couldn't help wincing when Julien managed to roll his injured arm into the bench ledge and cried out in pain.

"Stop wriggling."

Julien froze and stared in the wrong direction. "Eli? Is—is that you?"

Eli rolled his eyes. "Yes. Stay on the ground. You've only just stopped bleeding as it is."

Julien lay still, but Eli could see his gaze darting around the cabin, trying to adjust to the dim moonlight. "Where are we? Did they tie you up, too? What happened?"

Eli placed another card down, flicking the corner with a soft *snick*, and watched Julien frown as he recognized the sound. "We're in the Blue Tail Lookout Tower. I'm not tied up. I carried you here after an unidentified gunman began shooting to kill." He placed two more cards. *Snick. Snick.* "You know it's strangely invigorating, this honesty thing. I feel as splayed open and laid bare as a frog pinned to the dissecting table."

"Hold on, you did this?" Julien asked, holding up his bound hands. "What the hell, Eli. Why?"

"Why have I taken extra precautions with the man who targeted, manipulated and lied to me for some as of yet unknown reason? Guess."

Julien's face twisted as if in disgust. "I didn't—I would never hurt you. I swear."

"It's a little late for that, don't you think?" Eli said.

There was a long moment of silence.

"You're angry," Julien finally said.

"Well spotted. With whip-sharp emotional intelligence like that, it's difficult to believe you're twice divorced."

"I want to explain. Everything. But first I need to know if we're in danger."

"Define 'we,'" Eli growled, letting it sound as inhuman as he wanted.

Julien went quiet again and Eli scented the air for any spikes of fear or revulsion. But the room smelled much like it had these last few hours—of blood and dust and Julien and the lingering weariness he wore like a pall.

"So that really happened," Julien said eventually. "I didn't imagine it."

"Spare me," Eli sighed. "It was a lovely performance, but the curtain's down now. You weren't surprised. You've known the entire time."

"I didn't," Julien protested. "I swear."

"Who told you about me? About the retreat?"

"No one!"

"So it's a happy accident that your first night in town you broke into a haven for wolves?" Eli demanded, voice rising despite his best efforts. "And it's a total coincidence that you latched on to the only wolf around? And it's nothing but a giant fucking fluke that you've been walking around with a copy of the unabridged diary of a narcissistic wolf this entire time?"

"That doesn't mean I believed it was real!" Julien struggled up to sitting with hands bound in front of him. "How could I? I thought *wolves* was a gang or code word for something. Not actual *werewolves*. Even Nielsen doesn't use the word *werewolves*! Do you know how insane I feel saying that out loud? Is Sweet Pea going to waltz through that door next? Maybe we can get a round of poker going."

Julien laughed a little hysterically. "It doesn't make sense. How come no one knows about this? How many of you are there? How can your eyes light up like that? Real animals don't do that, do they? Is it like, magic? Is magic real now? Vampires? Ghosts? I mean, listen to me! I can't believe I'm actually—"

Snick. Eli placed another card down and Julien trailed off. "It's so boring listening to other people debate the unlikelihood of one's own existence, don't you agree? Don't bore me again, Doran. Please."

Julien opened and closed his mouth a couple of times. Then, "I'm sorry," he said softly.

Eli waited for more—excuses, questions, fear, anger—but nothing came. Unsettled, he gathered up the cards on the floor and shuffled them. "Why are you really here? Because I'm guessing coming to Maudit in search of justice for the dead is as fictitious as your ski trip."

Julien bit his lip and Eli's heart sank as the last hope he'd held on to shriveled. "My brother, Rocky, called me about a month after he got back from Maudit. He said he'd found something. Something big. *For real this time.* A conspiracy of people who looked human but—but weren't." Julien paused, expression intent and curious, but didn't ask the obvious question burning in his dark eyes.

"And?" Eli said when the silence stretched on. "I presume the conversation didn't end there."

Julien blinked, then laughed—a short, harsh sound. "I didn't give him the chance to continue. I can't tell you how many times I've gotten calls like that. Rocky was always convinced he'd *found something, for real this time.* Proof of alien tech in the military. Some lab in Wisconsin he was positive did experiments on a kraken in the lake. All it ever meant was within a week I'd be bailing him out for a trespassing charge or paying damages to an irate homeowner whose yard Rocky had dug up looking for the bones of the Michigan Dogman. I was so tired of it. Tired of fighting with him over *nothing.* Fairy tales. We argued and… that was the last time I ever heard his voice. Three days later he was dead."

Uneasiness prickled down Eli's spine. "You said it was an accident."

"Undetermined, officially. According to the Coast Guard, fourteen months ago Rocky took a boat out on a perfectly clear night and didn't come back. They found the boat first. His bo—his body a couple days later, miles away. He'd hit his head and drowned. They can't tell if the hit happened before or after going into the water. It didn't make sense to me. Where was he going so late? How did he end up in the water at all? It wasn't storming, he wasn't drinking, the boat wasn't damaged."

Julien hesitated as if carefully searching for the right words. "Two weeks ago I found a copy of Nielsen's notebook hidden in Rocky's things. He'd scribbled some of his own notes in the margins. The riddle on the map. Ian Ackman's name. Celia De Luca. Sweet Pea and—and the word *werewolf*."

Outside the wind had picked up and panels of glass all around the tower room creaked, horribly loud in the silence. "You came here because you think wolves killed your brother."

"Except there's no such thing as werewolves," Julien whispered. "Everyone knows that." He looked down at his bound hands, flexed the fingers and exhaled shakily. "The thing about Rocky is every make-believe monster he thought he'd found was usually covering a real one. I thought I'd come here and find a cover-up, or cult or, hell, one of Patrick West's shadow societies living in the mountains. Even the most hackneyed *This Time Tomorrow* plotline seemed more likely than some secret cabal of supernaturals. I never once expected to find out he was right. And I never expected to find...you."

Eli closed his eyes. Without the fear, he felt so unbelievably tired suddenly. So alone. He just wanted to go home, but there was no such place. And he could feel Julien watching him, waiting.

"Eli? Do you—do you believe me?"

He opened his eyes and saw Julien flinch. He supposed

they were probably glowing, again. But he couldn't be bothered to hide anymore. "Yes. It makes sense now."

"Does it?" Julien said incredulously. "Because none of this even feels real to me."

"You know I thought it was strange how quick you were to tell me that you were investigating Ian Ackman's disappearance. Now I get it. Of course you didn't want to play detective with me because you thought I was *a quick thinker.* You just heard me say De Luca's name. It was the very first thing you asked me about. You thought I was involved. Didn't you?"

Julien didn't say anything, and Eli laughed without amusement. "God, we really have been living different experiences these last few days. I noticed you seemed a bit squirrelly the first time. I just didn't realize you considered it sleeping with the enemy."

"That's not true," Julien said immediately. "I mean, yes, you clearly knew more than you were telling me and at first I did want to find out about the De Lucas. I'm sorry for that. But the rest of it wasn't a lie. And I thought maybe… maybe you were afraid of them, too. That they were the past you were hiding. I wanted to help you."

"You wanted to use me. All those oh-so-innocent questions about the retreat, my bosses, groups that might use a wolf as their symbol. As soon as you made the connection to Little Blue's painting you waved Nielsen's map under my nose and said fetch. I can't believe I actually thought you'd come to the office to ch–check on me. I can't believe I thought you wanted to be my friend."

Julien made a sound, but Eli continued over him. "Well,

save your sorrys. You haven't done anything wrong. You looked me right in the eye and said there's nothing you wouldn't do to solve this case. *Are you sure, Eli? Remember, you can't trust me, Eli.* Of course it helped that I was too busy humping your leg like a dog to listen—"

"Stop it."

"What's the matter? Does it offend you to know you've been getting off with a *monster*?"

"No!" Julien reeled back, as if repelled. "Don't say that. I never—"

"Oh, relax. You haven't hurt me," Eli said, hoping to god Julien couldn't hear his voice shake. It was embarrassment, anyway. Not hurt. "Not even a little bit. If anything, I have to admire a job well done. I've pulled more cons in my life than I can even remember, but I don't think I've ever managed to make anyone look quite as ridiculous as you have me."

"What was I supposed to say?" Julien yelled. "'Hey, I just met you and you're obviously lying to me about a ton of stuff, but what's your opinion on *werewolves*?' You're the one who said we don't know each other. You're the one who said you couldn't be trusted—"

"I can't! So why did you have to involve me? Why couldn't you have just left me alone? I wish you'd left me alone."

Eli threw the cards down in front of him, sending them fluttering around the cabin, and stood. He hurriedly crossed the room, dropping his jacket and toeing off his shoes unthinkingly, ignoring whatever Julien was saying so very urgently in the background. He unlocked the door, and stepped outside onto the platform. The cold fresh air was an immediate relief and Eli breathed deeply as he found the stairs and began to undo his pants. He could already feel his body leaning into a shift, aching for the familiar comfort and safety.

It was probably because of the way he was suddenly dropping in height that the bullet missed him, sailing over his shoulder and clanging against the metal railing with a bright spark.

Eli hit the ground in fur and scrambled on all fours back up to the observation deck. Another *pop-clang*, *pop-clang* rang out around him and he saw bursts of light in the corner of his vision. Inside the tower room, Julien was yelling. Eli reached the door and was just realizing he'd need to slip a thumb to get back in when it swung open from the inside.

Eli pushed past Julien's legs and heard the door slam and lock behind them. He slid into the bench, claws scrabbling across the slippery wood floor and spun to face the door in a defensive position, haunches up, teeth bared, snarling, but the outside world was silent. No more gunshots. No footsteps on the stairs. The danger remained below.

Julien stood with his back pressed up against the door, staring down at him with wide eyes. Eli waited for him to say something, but Julien seemed to be in some sort of state of shock. Eli knew what he must look like. He hadn't had time to take his clothes all the way off and he felt them hanging strangely on his body now, making it fairly difficult to mistake him for just some random enormous black wolf that had taken advantage of the chaos to book a room for the night. So be it. Eli had never in his life been ashamed of being a wolf, and he wasn't going to start now. It still didn't feel real to Julien? Well, Eli could be of use there, too.

He bounced on his front paws for momentum—muscles, flesh and bone slipping, aching like that first perfect stretch of the day—then quickly stood up into skin. Julien made a small terrified sound, but otherwise didn't move, rooted to the spot. Now he reeked of fear.

Good, Eli thought viciously, and tried to feel it as well.

Julien's whole body was trembling and the blood smell was sharper than before. There were great big smears of it on the floor, bench and door. Even as they stood there, a couple more droplets fell from his fingertips to soak into the wood by his feet. He'd clearly reopened the wound while struggling to get to Eli. To help him even while his own hands were bound.

Eli adjusted his skewed, torn clothing and walked up to Julien, who continued to just stand there. He flicked a single claw out to slice the tie around his wrists, slowly, deliberately, letting Julien see just how sharp and long and *part of him* it was, then slipped the claw back to a dull nail. "You're bleeding again."

Julien blinked, looking away from Eli's hand and down at his own sleeve as if confused. He touched it and looked back up at Eli, eyes wide like a child's. Or like a man just woken from a nightmare.

Eli sighed. "Take your jacket off and sit down away from the windows. It doesn't look like we're leaving anytime soon and I'm not dragging your anemic body around again if the castle is stormed."

Julien reached for his zipper obediently, but his fingers were too clumsy and he couldn't seem to grip the tag. After a few fumbling attempts, Eli unzipped it himself and tugged it off as brusquely as he could while staying careful not to touch him.

"Sit," he repeated, and Julien wobbled his way down to the floor with his back to the bench while Eli knelt beside him. He began to redress the wound, listening to his dangerously frantic heart rate.

"You—" Julien said at one point, but that was all he could manage before falling silent again.

At least now Eli could be certain that Julien really didn't know more about wolves than he'd admitted. It would be impossible to fake a reaction like this. Surely that was a relief, no matter what it felt like.

"Do try to get it together, Doran," Eli said as he worked. "I need your focus."

Julien blinked at him, then nodded, almost like an afterthought. It reminded Eli of last night and Julien gently and immediately offering a way to communicate without speaking. No doubt he'd be reading all sorts of shit into that now that he was comparing Eli to what *real animals* do and don't do.

Eli shoved aside the fresh wave of sharp-edged discomfort. "The way I see it, we have two options. Wait it out in here until someone comes looking for us in the morning, or make a run for it out there now. How well do you see in the dark?"

There was a pause like Julien was trying to piece together the question. "I wear glasses to drive at night," he said eventually.

What the fuck. "In here it is." Eli tightened the knot around Julien's bicep and heard his soft grunt of pain.

That at least seemed to snap him out of it. "You want to wait here? While—while a killer circles below?"

"Do you have a better plan? Outside we're at the disadvantage. There's only one predictable route out. It would be like shooting fish in a stairwell. Even easier if you're moving slowly in the dark."

"Do our phones still not have service?"

"Now, why didn't I think of that?" Eli said sarcastically. "Look, I don't relish the thought of spending another night with you either, but as long as we're in here, we're safe. That's a dead-bolted steel door. Short of explosives or one of us opening it ourselves, no one is getting inside. But I can't do anything against a gun long-distance."

Eli finished the last knot and stood up, moving across the cabin. "Someone will come looking for us eventually. The shooter can't stay out there forever. The eagerness of their trigger finger indicates they know it, too. All we need to do is play out the clock."

Thankfully Julien didn't argue, just nodded slowly and put his jacket back on. All by himself this time, though his hands were still shaking. Eli put his own shed clothes back on and sat on the floor across the room, mirroring his position. "It's going to be a long night of waiting. Sleep if you want," he said, and Julien let out a strangled sort of laugh.

"You're joking."

"Well, don't cling to consciousness in the hopes of any scintillating conversation on my end," Eli said.

"I'm sorry I can't spare you my waking presence. I'm just a little worked up right now what with the *gunman*, and the hole in my arm, and you—you—" Julien was gesturing to the floor, then up, then down again, presumably referencing the shift. "And you expect me to sleep?"

"Right," Eli said. "You can take first watch then. Wake me if you die."

He lay down curled on his side with his back to Julien. He considered slipping his ears to fur, but didn't. Although he could hear even better like that, it would be fairly useless at the moment. Anything that escaped the muting effect of the snow was obliterated by the howling wind. And Julien's chattering teeth were loud enough as it was.

He couldn't really afford to sleep, of course. Someone had to keep apprised of this unholy mess. They were trapped in here for the night. On the other hand, they were safe in here for the night. In fact, this could even be considered a nice little calm before the storm. Eventually the cavalry would arrive, and that's when it would really get bad. For one of them, anyway.

It seemed inevitable now that the Preservation would send someone in, first and foremost to deal with Julien. What if he told them about Eli's slipping? What had he actually seen? Eli had slipped his claws to cut his ties, but practically any wolf could do that. He'd slipped his ears when Julien was shot. That was...not good. But Julien had been frantic and confused and *bleeding*, so maybe he hadn't noticed. Eli had slipped a good deal of his musculoskeletal

structure trying to get out of the cave as quickly as possible. He'd been terrified to find himself suddenly staring
into the eyes of a stranger, thinking that a ghost of his past
had caught up to him at last. That was very bad indeed.
But would Julien even know how unnatural that was? Or
did it all just look like one big horror show to him?

And to think, when they'd been hiking through the
woods, Eli had felt like things might actually work out.
Maybe they really could figure out who killed Cody and
Eli wouldn't have to run this time. Maybe they'd figure
out this Sweet Pea mess so that the De Lucas had no case.
Maybe they could put this whole disaster to bed before the
Preservation had any cause to look his way at all. It would
be a close call, certainly, but Eli had thrived on those once
upon a time. For just a moment, sitting there in that cave,
his biggest worry had been how to tell Julien he couldn't
possibly keep seeing him; his biggest fear realizing how
much he wanted to anyway.

Not that any of that mattered now. He hardly recognized
the people they'd been this afternoon. Julien had been playing a role and Eli had been playing the fool. It was painful
knowing he'd been pursued because he was at best a pawn
and at worst pitiable. But it was a pain Eli had felt many
times before from people he'd trusted a great deal more.
Julien was just a man he'd met this week who'd made him
laugh and come and promised nothing.

Eli had no reason to be this hurt. No reason at all except for the raw and tender nervousness he felt whenever
he focused on Julien's too-fast heart; the shameful, animalistic urge to protect his belly and snarl at the horror in

Julien's eyes when Eli had shifted; the knowledge that the question of whether or not he might ever trust Julien with who he was had been taken out of his hands before he'd even thought to ask it. If he never heard the word *monster* again, it would be too soon.

Eli dragged a claw through the soft wood of the bench wall, cutting a line through someone's doodle of Sweet Pea.

"What was that?" Julien whispered urgently. "Someone's here."

"No, it was nothing," Eli said, then, because he wasn't that cold-blooded, added, "Just contributing to the decor." He carved another loud line through Sweet Pea in a nice surly X to demonstrate. Above it was that same A+D in a heart that he'd seen before. Ackman and Dunlop? Annabelle and David? Anywhere-but-here and the ghost of Benny Dobbs? Eli considered clawing it out, too, and immediately felt absurdly childish. He folded his arms, which didn't help.

"Who do you think is out there?" Julien asked, barely louder than the wind.

"I don't know."

"Celia De Luca?"

"What? No," Eli said, genuinely taken aback. "God, no."

"Why not?"

"Well, for one thing, if a wolf had wanted to kill us on that cliff side, at least one of us would be dead by now." Eli paused, listening to the slight catch and restart of Julien's breath. Eli wasn't breathing much himself, waiting for Julien's response, but the silence stretched on. "Not to mention the whole benefit of being the alpha of the largest pack around is you have plenty of good little wolves to do your dirty work," he pushed. "A pack I've never been a part of in my entire life, by the way."

This time Julien just hummed softly, as if in mild, polite interest and, frustrated, Eli rolled over to face him.

Julien was also curled up, mirroring his position on the floor and watching him. When their eyes met, he smiled in a shaky way that seemed almost sad. Either that or very, very cold. Although his jacket zipped up under his chin and the hood was pulled up around his face, he was still shivering badly.

"Out of questions already?"

"Not quite," Julien said with that same sad, quivering smile. "But I don't want to bore you. Not when it's been such a dull day already."

Eli snorted despite himself.

"Thank you, by the way."

"For what?" Eli asked warily.

"Oh, pushing me out of the way of gunfire. Getting us both to shelter. Not letting me bleed out on the floor even though you're squeamish and would have been a lot happier if I'd remained unconscious."

"Don't be absurd," Eli said. "I'm not squeamish."

Julien made an amused sound under his breath. "I'm not sure how you're supposed to thank someone for saving your life."

"Save mine next time and I'll show you." The words slipped out and hung in the air for a moment, and too late Eli heard the innuendo. He curled up on himself a little tighter, bracing for a reaction, but Julien didn't seem to have noticed. He just picked at the wood floor with a distant, thoughtful look on his face.

Then a small branch hit the window outside and Julien jerked in place, looking at the door immediately. "Is that—"

"Wind," Eli said, and Julien blew out a long breath.

"Someone must be desperate to make sure we don't tell what we know if they're willing to stay out all night in this weather."

"How ironic then that we know absolutely nothing useful at all."

"But we do," Julien protested. "We've got the common link now. Someone is killing whoever finds Nielsen's treasure. Ian, Rocky, Cody, us."

Eli frowned and tried to remember the scents of the cave, his eyes drifting shut—musky air, the warm, tingly smell of old cash, Julien's scent sharpened by nerves, the oily leather of Nielsen's notebook, the husk of Ian Ackman, who had been tucked away for, what, fifteen months?

Eli frowned. "They're all very different, aren't they? We're shot at as soon as we leave the cave. Cody was stabbed and displayed when he got back to the lodge. Someone went to great lengths to cover up Ian's death entirely and—" He opened his eyes and glanced at Julien, who nodded.

"Rocky died over a month later, across the country in what looked like an accident. You think there's more than one murderer?"

Eli shrugged. "I think if it were as simple as one person killing to keep the cave a secret, they would have relocated the contents by now. Five attacks in less than two years is hardly a sustainable business plan."

"What about Sweet Pea?"

"Is that your prime suspect? I suppose we can't agree on everything," Eli drawled.

"I meant, who's setting the fires? Who dug up that hiker's remains? Who was in the kitchen last night carving accusations into the wall? Because if I knew I'd killed someone and his body was hidden on the mountain, I don't think I'd be drawing more attention to myself by staging Sweet Pea's comeback tour."

"I suppose you think it's wolves."

"Well—" Julien shifted around the floor. "Someone didn't want to be seen on that wildlife camera."

Eli bit his tongue, irritated that Julien made a good point. "Maybe. But I don't see what cause a wolf would have to drum up the Sweet Pea legend either. The De Luca pack might want to cause trouble for the retreat, but they wouldn't go so far as to kill Cody just for a territory grab and certainly not for a mere two and a half million dollars. And…" He hesitated, feeling oddly reluctant, but Julien needed to be told. "I can say with near certainty that wolves didn't kill your brother *to protect our secret*. Not the De Luca pack. Not anyone."

"What?" Julien blinked as he shivered. "But he was right. This proves it. He found the notebook and uncovered werew—a conspiracy."

"I'm not saying he didn't," Eli said. "But do you think he's the first one in the whole world to notice? We have a great many nonfatal fail-safes in place for just such a thing. A handful of humans figuring it out here and there will never be a threat. Certainly not one worth killing over."

"Then, what, you don't think his death is related at all?" Julien demanded incredulously. "That it's a coincidence that I just found out werewolves are real and now you and I are trapped with a murderer waiting outside the door?"

"There are a large number of words I'd use to encapsulate our current situation before I got to *coincidence*. But surely you agree what's happening to us and even what happened to Cody are nothing like your brother's death. If someone here knew he'd found the cave, why wait a month to silence him? And for what reason? A copy of a notebook that's half in code that they fail to even collect? Maybe coming to Maudit is what alerted him to wolves, but it's not what killed him. It doesn't make sense. You know that. No one here would have any reason to even know he found the cave at all, the way he left th—the original behind."

"You were going to say the body," Julien said after a moment. "Who would have any reason to suspect he found the cave when he didn't report Ian's body."

"Yes," Eli agreed. "That is the elephant in the tower."

"I've been telling myself Rocky didn't have time to tell anyone, to do anything. But you're right. No one chased him out of Maudit Falls. He wasn't on the run for a month. He went on other trips. He saw friends and family. He tried to tell me about werewolves. He could have told me about the murder right then and there. I would have actually believed that. I would have actually tried to help him instead of—" Julien bit his lip.

"Why didn't he, do you think?"

Julien was quiet for so long that Eli thought he wasn't

going to answer at all. An unpleasant thing, dissecting the wrongs of the dead, particularly the ones who died wrongfully. Particularly the ones you loved.

But suddenly he spoke. "You know, when Rocky was five he almost drowned. Weird, how that works."

Eli hummed. "Live long enough and you can find echoes of anything."

"Don't tell me you've been locked up in a tower waiting to die before."

Eli paused a beat too long and Julien's face began to twist in alarm. "No," Eli said, cutting that look off. *Not in a tower.* "What happened when he was five?"

Julien studied him with a strange look, but said, "We were at this wrap party for one of my stepfather Skip's movies and the director lived right on the beach. The party went late, of course, they always did. Me and Rock were the only kids still there, as usual. I put him down to sleep out on the deck so I could sneak a couple of drinks—I must have been sixteen, seventeen. But when I came back out he was just...gone."

Julien shook his head and his whole body twitched from a particularly intense shiver. "I ran all over yelling for him and no one even noticed. The music was so loud, and I couldn't find Mom or Skip anywhere, and I kept coming back to the porch and staring at the hammock again and again. Like if I could just restart enough times, keep coming out to check on him, eventually he'd still be there sleeping. You don't think very clearly with that sort of panic. It's like looking down and realizing your own body is gone, or that falling feeling right before sleep. It's what dying feels like, I think. Christ, it's freezing in here, isn't it? I mean, it's not just me, right?"

Eli blinked at the abrupt shift in topic. "Did you find him?"

"Oh, yeah. I spotted him in the ocean eventually. Getting pulled out by the tide. I thought he was dead, you know, just bobbing up and down in the darkness like that. I ran out and scooped him up, and of course he immediately starts fighting me. Telling me I'd ruined everything. That the mermaids had been about to take him away to live with them and all I could think was *And then what? Would you have really just left me here for them? Alone? Without even saying goodbye?*"

He laughed. "I guess that's pretty stupid. I mean, he was five years old, what kind of complex empathy was I expecting? But the thing about Rocky is he never really changed. He was so…single-minded. Nothing was ever more important than proving he was right. Than experiencing something spectacular even if it meant leaving everyone else behind to pick up the pieces."

Julien blew out a breath that Eli could see like a plume of smoke. "I want to believe he didn't say anything about Ian's body because he knew it would prove he'd been there, but the truth is he probably hadn't seen Ian as anything more than a prop bit in his own story. Ian was past helping, so what would be the point? A murder investigation would have just gotten in his way. *Ruined everything.* I'm sure he thought I would have, too, if he told me. Just like I always did. And he was right. The last time we spoke I hung up on him. I told him I was done bailing him out, hung up and that's why I wasn't there to pull him back out of the water. Jesus, are you sure you're not cold?" Julien asked, voice shaking. "Because I feel like I'm going to die over here."

Eli moved across the floor to sit beside him and Julien went very still. Or as still as someone could while shivering that much, his wide eyes eerily dark in his too-pale face. Eli took off his coat and pushed it into Julien's hands a bit roughly. "Here."

"You'll freeze," he protested.

"No. I won't." Eli deliberately flashed his eyes and refused to look away.

This time Julien didn't flinch. He just tilted his head slightly, studying Eli with only a tinge of wonder, then slowly put the coat on over his own. "Thank you."

"I suppose you've already been told it's not your fault."

Julien jerked his head, giving that the dismissal it deserved.

"I'm sorry your brother died. No matter how it happened."

"Yes," Julien said. "You see, I've done this part already, though. Unpacking the guilt and the grief. The anger. I have a therapist and a psychiatrist and a grief counselor. I have family and friends and two ex-wives who check in on me every other week. I'm extremely lucky. But every time I close my eyes it's like coming out to that empty hammock again. And every single night I feel like I'm falling and everything in me is just screaming *do something*. I actually thought by coming here, I finally was. I'm so sorry."

"Why?"

"For dragging you into this mess with me. For lying and using you."

"If it meant finding out what happened to your brother, would you do it again?" Julien was silent and Eli shrugged. "So then don't be sorry. I would have done the same thing for someone I loved." If it had been his own family, sister or pack, he'd have done a lot worse. In fact, once upon a time he had.

Julien shook his head as if frustrated. "I made you feel bad. Can I be sorry for that?"

Eli's heart twisted painfully and he didn't know why. Maybe apologies were too close to pity. Maybe something else. "If you truly have nothing better to do," he said in his most pronounced drawl. "Besides, you were wrong before. You didn't drag me into a single thing. I needed to figure out what's going on, too."

"Because the De Lucas are a…rival pack? And they're using this as an excuse to take away your retreat?" Julien asked. "Which is actually a haven for…?"

"Let's not add to the list of reasons why I'm going to be in trouble with *the cabal*, as you put it."

"I thought it didn't matter that I know."

"Not for you. But don't let this delightful countenance fool you, I'm not universally beloved. Or did you think all wolves live in near-complete isolation under false identities?"

Julien's frowned, so maybe he had. "*Who told you about me?* That's what you said when I first woke up. Not who told you about werewolves. But about you specifically. Are you in danger?"

"I'm trapped in a tower with a man I can't trust while an armed gunman waits outside getting, we can only assume, increasingly desperate. I've felt safer."

"But with the cabal or what—whatever. The group of werewolves Nielsen was afraid would steal his work. Do they...not like you either?"

"Nielsen died years ago. Things have changed," Eli evaded.

"I know there's no point saying you can trust me, so I won't," Julien said after a long moment. "But I do promise I won't tell them anything. I won't tell anyone anything about you."

Eli shook his head. "While I appreciate the drama of declaring one's loyalty in the eleventh hour, let's not make promises we can't keep, hmm? You have your priorities and I have mine. Fortunately, those both require living through the night so for now, in here, we're on the same side."

"And after that?" Julien asked. "When we leave the tower?"

"Out there this ceasefire comes to an end and we may trust each other as much as we ever did."

Or ever should have, as the case may be.

Chapter Twelve

It was beginning to feel like the longest night of Julien's life. Considering his insomnia, that was saying something. The only positive was he was so freezing and miserable and *bored* it was difficult to fixate on the killer outside. Guns were a problem of the abstract future. The cold so intense he was straining muscles with the effort not to inch closer to Eli's substantial heat was a problem happening very much now.

What he should really be focusing on was the whole *werewolf* thing. But it had been so long since Julien had allowed himself to even think the word, for fear of the memory of Rocky's excited voice that came with it, that it was almost impossible to break the habit now.

But they're not human, Juley. Inside they're wolves. For real this time.

Of course, if he'd spent less time avoiding and more time thinking things all the way through, maybe he could have avoided these endless empty hours of shivering on the floor in uncomfortable silence, replaying the exact way Eli's voice had cracked when he'd said *you haven't hurt me*, and the fear in his eyes when he'd crawled across the floor to give Julien his coat. Why? What was he afraid of?

And there he went again. Werewolves. Werewolves were real. The most astonishing thing to ever happen and all Julien could keep thinking about was Eli.

Julien opened his eyes and found the man himself staring at him, practically nose to nose. Julien realized he'd shifted closer without thinking about it.

"Sorry," he whispered, and scooched away again. "I'm just—You're really not cold?"

Julien had both their coats wrapped around his body while Eli was still in the same sweater as before. He hadn't even taken it off as a—when the—when he'd turned into a wolf. Julien wondered if that's why he wore such loose-fitting clothes. Maybe he got special outfits tailored for exactly that reason. He imagined the huge black wolf from before wearing a tuxedo and snorted.

Eli frowned. "You may be in shock."

"I can't think of a single reason why," Julien said, closing his eyes. He felt disconnected and dreamy but couldn't tell if it was because everything happening seemed so unreal or if it was the grogginess of night after night without sleep.

A warm hand pressed against his forehead and Julien opened his eyes again eagerly. Sure enough, Eli was feeling around his face almost tenderly.

"You don't smell well," he said after a moment, which sort of put a damper on that. "And I was referring to medical shock. You bled on me quite a bit when I was carrying you here."

"Sorry," Julien said, and Eli's frown deepened. He took his hand away and Julien couldn't stop the whimper at even that small loss of heat.

Eli made a disapproving sound and closed the distance between them until they were sharing air again and Julien could feel the fringes of his body heat. But still he avoided touching him.

Julien tucked his face into his coat's hood in an attempt to warm his nose and was immediately overwhelmed by the scents of Eli. Or at least his shampoo. Something like roses and expensive furs and—Julien sniffed—apricots?

He heard a choking sound and when he turned to look the expression on Eli's face was oddly intense and his eyes were doing that glowing thing again.

"What's wrong?"

Eli cleared his throat. "How does your arm feel?"

"Not bad," Julien said honestly. "Sort of numb." Then the rest of Eli's words caught up to him. "You carried me here?"

"I did mention it before. Were you under the impression you sleepwalked?"

"No, I—to be fair there was a lot to process at the time. That part slipped through the cracks," Julien said. His cheeks were making a valiant attempt at heating, which resulted in a tingle more than anything else. He felt odd. Not embarrassed exactly, but…shy? And something else, too, that he couldn't quite pin down. "I haven't been picked up since—"

Childhood presumably. But even that seemed unfamiliar. Honey had been especially delicate back then and it was difficult to imagine her holding anything bigger than a two-year-old, though surely she must have sometime or another.

"I don't know when," he finished awkwardly. "I must have looked ridiculous flopping around, flung over your shoulder like a big useless lump."

Eli's expression turned abruptly wary. "That upsets you," he said flatly.

"Not upsetting, exactly," Julien said.

"Does it bother you that even when I was on my knees I could have overpowered you anytime I wanted?"

"What? No." Julien shifted a bit on the hardwood floor and his cheeks tingled again. Even just having Eli this close was beginning to help warm him. "Why on earth would that bother me?"

Eli shrugged as best he could while lying curled on his side. "Doesn't really work with the fantasy, does it?"

"The fantasy?" Julien repeated while his brain unhelpfully ran a reel of its own favorite examples with Eli newly cast as the lead.

"You know, man masters the monster of Maudit Falls."

That cut any arousal off at the knees. "Look," Julien blurted. "I wish you'd stop talking about it like that. I don't know what I said to make you think I feel anything but thrilled out of my mind to have gotten to share those nights with you. If I was jumpy or behaving weirdly at all it was because I didn't expect you to come on to me. Not seriously."

Eli made a rude sound. "I've heard the *uncommonly sexy man is surprised people want to have sex with him* parable before and it tugs the heartstrings harder when not coming from someone who's already made a fortune off of looking like a walking, talking wet dream."

"As much as I appreciate the most backhanded compliment of my life, that's not what I meant," Julien said tightly. He was feeling positively toasty now. "When you've been married practically all your life, people make assumptions. And when men do flirt with me, it's always as a joke or just so that they can tell their friends they made some has-been squirm. The truth is I haven't really been with a ton of people. Or much of a, you know, variety. In the gender department…" He sort of faded out at the end realizing he'd said far too much. Maybe he could pass out now and claim blood loss after all.

A small frown line had appeared at the top of Eli's nose. "Please don't be attempting to tell me you're straight as the third plot twist of the evening. Because I may have to opt for the gun, after all."

"No! God, no, of course not. I know I'm bi or—or something like that. And I don't want it to sound like I'm all hung up on a gender binary or anything either, but I'm…well, limited. In, ah, the practical experience of some things."

Eli's eyebrows rose so high up his forehead, Julien half wondered if he was becoming a wolf again. "You're trying to tell me you were nervous not because I'm a supposedly mythical creature who may or may not possess key information about your brother's death, but because I have a dick."

"When you put it like that it sounds silly," Julien muttered. "It's not even about dicks. Not really. I just don't like doing things badly, and this last year I haven't been good at anything at all." He bit his lip. "Usually when I'm not a hundred percent sure of something I avoid it. I'm afraid you've met me at a somewhat unusual time in my life."

"Now, that is surprising," Eli said with a small wry huff, and despite everything Julien laughed helplessly back.

"The truth is I like you. More than I thought I could during—" He flapped his hand as if he could encompass all of grief with one gesture: Rocky, the unwanted withering of his career, the rapid collapse of two marriages, the failing health of parents whose aging had sped up after the loss of their child, the realization that he himself was suddenly closer to the end of his life than the beginning, the feeling that perhaps he might die while still figuring out how he wanted to live. "Oh, you know, the usual. It's true I was nervous. But not because you turn into a werewolf or even because I thought you were some ex–cult member with a criminal past. I just…didn't want to disappoint you." Julien tried to smile, but it came out more like a wince. "We both know how well that worked out."

Eli was quiet for a long time, expression unreadable. Then, "Stop saying werewolves. It's positively archaic. Just wolves."

Julien blinked at him, surprised. "O-okay."

"And I don't *turn into* anything. Sometimes I'm a wolf in skin. Sometimes I'm a wolf in fur."

"In skin. In fur." Julien committed it to memory.

Eli's gaze darted all over his face, studying him, then he slowly bent his knees so that they just brushed the tops of Julien's thighs. "You didn't disappoint me. I enjoyed myself. Very much."

Julien's breath hitched. "I'm glad."

Impulsively he placed his hand on the floor in the scant five inches between them, and only a breath away from Eli's—an offer and nothing else. There was an endless-seeming pause. Then Eli's fingers slid forward, the tips hesitantly resting on Julien's pinkie. His face sharpened to that same intense expression from before and this time Julien had a much better idea as to what it meant.

"You still want me," Eli murmured with no inflection. A simple observation. *It's cold. We could die tonight. You still want me.* But the way he looked up at Julien from under his lashes felt like a question, so Julien answered him anyway.

"Yeah. Of course I do." Carefully, he rotated his hand until the pads of Eli's fingers brushed the center of his palm. "Do...do you?"

"I want..." Eli bit his lip and shook his head. He pressed his fingers down until Julien felt the bite of nails, no, *claws*, along his lifeline. He held very still and a fraction of a second before it broke the skin Eli stopped. "I want to feel different than this."

Hurt? Afraid? Defenseless? Julien wasn't sure he knew how to ask that. Wasn't sure he could hear the answer over the blood rushing through his head.

"How long does this ceasefire of ours last?" His voice was too rough, too intimate for the delicate truce between them.

"Long enough," Eli said, capturing Julien's hand in his and tugging him close enough to meet his lips in the middle.

It was different from before. More honest, for one thing. Their first kiss has been buoyant with possibility, newness and the sentimental illusion that maybe this could be something worth building on.

Now they were two people who had no chance of a future or even a *later today*. They both simply needed a bit of warmth, comfort, and some release from the endless darkness. There was honesty in that, too. Not everything had to be about hope and love and trust to be worth doing. Sometimes it was just the desire to not feel so terribly alone. That was what last kisses were made of. Which didn't mean Julien was going to savor it any less.

When Eli fell backward, Julien followed him over. Rolling until he was between Eli's spread legs and pressing him into the floor. He felt a matching hardness against his own. "Is this okay?"

Eli growled, found Julien's tongue again and sucked on it lightly.

"Fucking hell," Julien groaned, pulling back. "Wait, wait, wait. Same as last time? Pinch me if you don't like something?"

Eli sat up just enough to put his mouth by Julien's ear. "I could quite literally throw you through the window with one hand."

Julien felt another powerful bolt of that same…something from before. "Yes, but I'd rather you pinched me," he murmured back, brushing his lips against Eli's, and then pushed him back down flat on his back, hands on his shoulders.

"Oh," Eli gasped softly, head lolling to the side, eyes closed.

"Yes?" Julien asked, still holding him down. He thrust against him slowly, grinding their clothed cocks together. "Does that feel good?"

Eli hummed and arched into him in response. Julien found his lips again and kissed him briefly but deeply before sitting back on his heels. Eli's eyes fluttered open, looking confused.

"I want you in my mouth," Julien said hoarsely. He tucked his fingers into Eli's waistband. "Can I try? I really want to taste you."

He felt Eli shiver beneath his hands but not from cold. Not with the way he immediately began shedding his clothes until he lay back on the floor naked and pale in the moonlight. Julien took a moment to study him. Soft belly, firm chest, a delicious combination of muscles and fat, he glowed like a marble statue of some ancient hero, tumbled to the ground and waiting to be taken. It was easier than Julien had expected accepting that this beautiful man had looked like a wolf—or rather been *in fur* a few hours ago. Because it was easier to believe in magic when Eli was staring up at him with so much want in his eyes.

Julien caught Eli's left foot in his hand, pressed a thumb into his instep and watched the opposite leg drop open, muscles helplessly relaxing. He hooked Eli's calf over his shoulder and brushed a wet kiss to the inside of his knee. Then a slightly rougher one farther up, and another until he was sucking a definite mark into the soft flesh of Eli's upper thigh as he squirmed, hips twitching up, slowly stroking his own cock flushed and hard against his belly.

"If you have any interest in coming down my throat, you'll keep your hands on the floor," Julien said. Eli's arms shot back, pressed to his sides. "Thank you." Although now he should at least attempt to follow through.

Julien nosed at Eli's balls, lapped at the base of his dick, then traced his way up to tentatively take the head between his lips, suckling gently. Hardly groundbreaking stuff, but Julien's heart still beat wildly and he felt oddly brittle, the way one does when something really matters. This was it. He was sucking his first dick. A completely ridiculous, artificially constructed line in the sand, but life was full of them and god, were they hard to ignore. He glanced up at Eli's face with an expression he hoped was more provocative and less overwhelmed.

Eli was watching him from under heavy lids and panting softly. "Please," he whispered, hands flexing by his own shoulders as if someone were holding them down. As if his body was helplessly pinned there for the sake of Julien's pleasure alone.

There was something so arousing in knowing he could toss Julien around the room but chose to play obedient beneath him instead. To think that Julien might have made him feel bad or shameful about that was unacceptable. Unforgivable, really, ceasefire or no. It seemed suddenly impossible not to take Eli's cock deeper into his mouth. To not do everything he could to prove he saw Eli's eager submission for what it was—the strongest part of him.

Julien licked and sucked and stroked, experimenting with how much he could comfortably take. He did gag and have to hastily retreat several times, but it just seemed to make Eli groan and slap his palms flat against the floor, as if preventing himself from grabbing for Julien's head and shoving him back down again. That image made Julien twitch in his pants, and impulsively he gripped the backs of Eli's legs and pushed them farther and farther back until his ass was raised slightly and his hole was exposed.

"Hold yourself open for me," he said through a gritty throat, lowering himself to the floor, and Eli immediately complied. He was remarkably flexible, although perhaps that shouldn't be surprising all things considered, and it was easy to lick into him, first just enjoying the taste of clean skin and the feel of muscles quivering beneath his tongue, before holding Eli's hips in place and pressing deeper, using lips, tongue and the bare hint of teeth to take him apart.

Well, and why not? He knew he was good at *this* and it was gratifying to hear Eli helplessly trying to muffle his groans. Before long Julien felt the thud of Eli's heels hit his back as he lost control of his legs, thighs squeezing around his ears as he became a relentlessly squirming mess, mindlessly trying to hump Julien's face.

He worked one finger inside Eli's softened hole and felt more than heard him yell as he arched up off the floor. Julien pushed himself back up to kneeling position quickly, suddenly desperate for the leverage he needed to fingerfuck him hard, to push him over the edge.

"That's it. Come on. Ride my hand," he said, working in and out at a demanding pace, and bent to take Eli's dick back in his mouth, seconds before feeling him get suddenly, impossibly harder against his tongue. Making a split decision based on arousal more than logic, Julien attempted to relax his jaw encouragingly and Eli jerked, pushing deep enough that tears sprang from Julien's eyes, and heat spilled straight down his throat.

Julien pulled back, choking, and the second load seemed to flood his mouth, forcing him to swallow with only partial success before Eli released one last time onto his own belly.

Julien sat back on his heels, breathing heavily, and a little out of sorts. It didn't taste bad. Fairly similar to himself, actually. But he'd never had quite so much at once and felt overwhelmed and strange.

Eli was still splayed out on the floor, watching him from beneath cracked eyelids, but sat up when Julien's gaze met his. Silently he brushed his thumb under Julien's eye where a tear was escaping and then kissed him very lightly.

"Not bad. Not bad at all," Eli murmured, and Julien felt ridiculously soothed. Eli's hands dropped and undid Julien's pants, pulling them down just enough to deftly work his neglected cock out into the cool air. He dropped a quick kiss to the head and then stroked him slowly. "How does your arm feel?"

"What arm?" Julien asked, only half joking. Eli huffed and pulled them back down to the floor, arranged so that Julien was pressed against his back with his dick between Eli's thighs, slippery with sweat and spit and spilled come.

There was something strangely arousing about being fully dressed with nothing but his cock and ass out and his boots still on while Eli was entirely naked in his arms. Julien pulled him closer, running his hands over his torso, which incredibly felt perfectly warm.

Eli tilted his head back onto Julien's shoulder, bit at his jaw lightly and murmured, "I want you to pretend you're fucking me."

"Aren't I?"

"I want you to pretend you're splitting me open with your cock, and even though you ate me out so nice and sloppy it's still too much, but you make me take you anyway, because it's your turn."

"Right," Julien croaked, feeling a bit light-headed. "No, yeah, I appreciate the clarification."

He realized he was holding Eli way too tightly and unclenched his fingers from where they'd dug into his chest. The moment he let go, Eli's shoulders stiffened but he didn't say anything. Slowly, carefully, on instinct, Julien maneuvered Eli's arms behind his back instead until he could hold on to both wrists.

"Like this?" Julien asked, giving him a small tug so his spine arched back a bit. "Do you need to be held in place to take me?"

Eli hummed with pleasure and nodded, relaxing back against him once more. "Yes, don't let me move. Show me how you'd fuck me."

Not interested in resisting an invitation like that, Julien tightened his grip on Eli's wrists and thrust between his thighs roughly. There was hardly much chance of hurting him this way, so he didn't bother holding back, pounding against his ass, the sound of skin slapping skin and the faint *clink clink* of his flapping belt buckle echoing around the tower.

"Oh," Eli whimpered every time, biting his lip, face scrunched up like he was actually fighting something. Julien released one wrist to run his hand through Eli's hair, get a good, safe grip and pull so that his head tilted back, and noticed a very faint scar around his neck, silvery and smooth.

Eli's eyes snapped open and they were glowing the tiniest bit. Startled, Julien faltered for a second, hips stilling. Then he tightened his hold on Eli's wrist and hair again and slammed into him once more.

"Going to stay still now and take my come?" he asked.

"Yes," Eli breathed, luminescent eyes still watching him. "Please—please don't let me go."

It was that oddly enough that sent Julien toppling over the edge. Like the clenching in his heart set off a clenching in his belly that moved to his balls until the chain reaction had swept through every inch of his body. A rush of energy like a solar flare whose imprint lingered long after you closed your eyes. He came between Eli's tight thighs and just barely resisted the urge to bury his face in his neck. He still had a bruise from where Eli had bit him the last time and wasn't trying to repeat the experience with his nose. Julien muffled his shout into Eli's hair instead and flopped bonelessly onto his back with Eli half on, half off him, arms still pinned between them.

"Holy fuck," Julien said eventually when he could form

words again. He released Eli's wrists, skin sticky. "Are you okay?"

"Yes, of course," Eli said quickly, though his voice sounded a bit lost, almost confused.

Julien registered that for a moment, then nudged and tugged him around until Eli was lying belly-down across his chest instead. He massaged Eli's shoulder blades carefully where they'd have been strained from having his hands pulled back.

"Are you sure?" he asked after a minute.

"I think I was hoping one more fuck would change things. That it would make tomorrow morning easier. But I feel as tightly entangled as ever."

"What, are you telling me you didn't scare the gunman away with that filthy mouth of yours?" Julien joked.

There was an awkward pause and Julien wondered if he might have misunderstood. But then Eli huffed. "No, unfortunately not. Though I can't hear them moving about, so perhaps they lost consciousness around the time you stuck your tongue inside me. I know I almost did."

Julien's hand rested on Eli's back as he felt an odd wave of protectiveness.

"You should run now," he blurted. "I was thinking it before. I should have said. But there's still time. I could go out on the deck, distract the gunman, draw fire, and you could slip past in fur. You'd make it down the mountain like that easily, wouldn't you? I'm the only thing holding you back. If you—"

Eli reached up and tapped a finger against Julien's lips.

"Shhh. Don't be melodrama itself. Neither of us is going anywhere until all the guns are gone."

"But—"

"Julien. Please sleep. There's nothing else to do right now. Not unless you think you've got another round in you."

Relief flooded through him so intensely it knocked Julien's breath away. "Now that would be supernatural," he said. "Just...don't leave without waking me, okay?"

"Of course not," Eli scoffed. "You still me owe me a life saving, remember?"

"I'm looking forward to it," Julien murmured as some of the last remaining tension in him unraveled. Even if he closed his eyes, Eli wouldn't disappear. They would have tomorrow morning. Within moments, he drifted into darkness.

Julien woke up warm, comfortable and happy. That really should have been the first sign something was terribly wrong. Outside the wind still shook the windowpanes, but inside Julien felt the hot skin of Eli's lower back pressed against his nose where his shirt had ridden up and he nuzzled it softly, feeling the early stirrings of arousal.

He wanted to taste him again. He wanted to try other things. He wanted to try everything. It was almost absurd how much he wanted this man. He couldn't remember the last time he'd felt this...consumed with it. Was it just the newness of Eli's body? Or how long it had been since he'd hooked up with someone? How long it had been since he'd managed to feel any attraction at all from under the heavy, muffling grief? Or was it Eli himself that he couldn't get enough of? Compelling and brilliant. Charming and genuinely terrifying.

Knowing him was bewildering. But touching him like this was the closest Julien had felt to clarity in years.

Eli's hand rested on his shoulder in a stilling motion. "They're moving."

"Who?" Julien asked sleepily and opened his eyes.

Eli was dressed, and half sitting up, leaning back on one arm. He was staring into the near distance with a blank expression as a pink-orange dawn creaked in over the mountains and through the window. It painted Eli's face in vibrant amber, making him seem even more otherworldly than usual.

"The gunman. They're—" Eli was staring into the middle distance, head cocked to the side, listening to something. He frowned. "I think they're climbing that weather dish thing. The one up the hill."

"*What?* Why?"

Eli shot him a critical look, which okay, fair enough. But even imagining climbing the steel lattice of the satellite tower while the wind and snow whipped around them made Julien dizzy. "Presumably so that they may pick us off in here. The sun on the glass is the only thing stopping them from already doing so. As soon as they knock that out, we're toast."

"But they don't have a sight line to the door," Julien suggested. "We could make a run for it now."

Eli nodded slowly. "There'd be some tricky sections on the stairs. But if we find the right time—" His face twisted suddenly. "Down!" he cried out just before the glass shattered over them.

Julien rolled over, shielding his face, and felt Eli doing the same beside him. He glanced up quickly, just before another two loud pops rang in the air and two more windowpanes exploded inward. More glass tinkled around them delicately, glittering in the piercing dawn light. Julien felt a few land like gentle snowflakes in his hair.

Eli tugged at his arm, pulling him toward the door. "It appears our ceasefire's over. Keep your hands off the floor," he added urgently, and Julien registered that just in time. The room was a mess of shards big and small that crunched under their boots as they duckwalked away from the three last untouched windows, just before the gun fired again and one of them shattered outward. The bullet had crossed through the room.

"Is the right time now?" Julien asked.

Eli pursed his lips but nodded. "Stay low on the stairs, keep your head below the metal grating. To avoid the clearing, we'll have to go over the cliff side."

"What is it with you and leading me over cliffs?" Julien murmured, and Eli grinned. For a moment his teeth looked just this side of too sharp and Julien couldn't help leaning forward and pressing a quick kiss to his cheek. When Julien pulled back, Eli was looking at him with slightly wide eyes.

"Be careful," Julien said.

Eli opened his mouth and another three gunshots rang out in a row. Two panes of glass exploded around the room. "Stay close to me," he said, and reached up to flip the bolt. "Ready?"

Julien nodded and, heart pounding, got up off the floor and into crouch position.

"One—"

He glanced over his shoulder and saw the smudge of a dark figure in a snow jacket and hood wedged between the steel lattice of the satellite tower. The long shadow of a rifle propped up on one of the bars.

"Two—"

Julien pinched the back of Eli's sweater as if that would be enough to keep them together, and to his surprise Eli reached back and grabbed his hand instead.

"Go!"

Eli flipped the bolt and yanked them both to standing as he flung open the door. Julien didn't hesitate. He leapt forward and ran right into Eli's back with a grunt when Eli stopped dead.

There on the top step stood Chief Bucknell, gun pointing right at them.

"Wait!" Julien cried out, fear and relief and confusion clouding his thoughts. "Wait, the shooter's out there! They've—"

He glanced over his shoulder at the dark figure in the satellite tower—not shooting, not running, not hiding—just watching. Like a vulture waiting for its prey to die.

Julien turned back to Bucknell, who still hadn't lowered his gun. This time he really saw him. Cheeks red and hair plastered against his scalp, the cold satisfaction in his eyes. He looked like a man who'd spent the night waiting in a shed with nothing but hate to keep him warm.

Beside him, Eli inhaled deeply, and standing this close,

Julien could finally see the way he sniffed the air, the moment wariness turned to rage turned to carefully composed boredom. That's when Julien knew for sure they were fucked.

"Step back inside now," Bucknell said calmly. "Go on."

Julien hesitated, tensing, but Eli squeezed his hand in his and dragged him away from the gun with a shake to his head, eyes darting back toward the shooter on their perch.

Bucknell tracked every small movement with an empty smile, then scanned the tower room. "Sorry to drop by so early. Hope I haven't interrupted something."

"Just our attempted murder. Interrupt away," Eli said. His tone was entirely blasé, but his grip on Julien's was tight enough to bruise.

"Murder? Not at all. We just needed a little incentive so that you might open the door and have a nice, friendly chat."

"And I suppose your friend's just out there to make sure conversation flows," Eli murmured.

"Nobody needs to get hurt as long as I get what I came for."

"Nielsen's treasure? Weren't you just there shooting at us yesterday? If you've gotten lost already, I'm more than happy to play impish forest guide for a cut of the cash." Julien couldn't help himself from making a protesting noise, but Eli continued right over him. "Shall we say seventy-thirty in our favor? Will your gunman be wanting some as well or have you got them on their own payment plan?"

"I don't want the money—I want the notebook," Bucknell snapped. "Cody already told me he left it in the cave. Now it's gone."

"Then maybe Cody lied," Eli said.

"Men don't tend to lie when you stick a knife in their gut." Bucknell adjusted the gun to point at Eli's belly. "I assume the same goes for a bullet."

"I'm inclined to agree," Eli said without flinching. "But that doesn't change the fact that there was no notebook. Granted, we were a bit distracted by the millions of dollars and the mummy and—"

Bucknell fired the gun. The shot hit the floor directly in front of Eli's feet, splintering the wood and kicking up a volley of glass as he and Julien jumped away.

"That's your first warning," Bucknell said when the room stopped ringing. "I don't have the patience for a second. All year I've torn this mountain up looking for that goddamn cave. All year I've had to waste my time at the lodge, indulging Annabelle's bullshit. I'm not going to let you steal that notebook from me now when I'm this close." As he talked, his arm started to shake and his grip on the gun tightened, rising incrementally to point at Eli's head.

"I know where it is," Julien said, stepping between Eli and the gun.

"You?" Bucknell said, frowning. "You don't have anything to do with this."

"No, he doesn't," Eli agreed, yanking Julien back with a hiss.

"I'm telling you I know where it is," Julien said, trying to step forward again, but it was like fighting against the tide itself. "If you don't believe me, ask me about it. I can tell you anything in there. Nielsen, his daughter, Vanessa, how afraid he was the Preservation would steal his experiments." The names rolled off his tongue easily. He'd spent so long reading and rereading those pages that even the words that hadn't made any sense echoed through his brain at night when he was too tired to stop them. "I'm the one who hid the notebook. But if you want to know where it is, you're going to have to let us go."

Bucknell was staring at Julien and slightly lowered the gun, though frustratingly he didn't angle it away from Eli. "All right," he said finally. "I only want the notebook anyway. As soon as I get it, you can walk away."

"You mean like you let Cody walk away?" Eli scoffed.

A strange look passed over Bucknell's face. Surprised, curious and almost pitying. "Do you know why he asked to meet with me that night? He wanted to tell me you were the monster stalking Annabelle."

"That's hardly news. He only told everyone the exact same thing every single day."

"Ah, but this time was different. This time he knew you were the same kind of monster as Ian."

Julien inhaled sharply. But to his right, Eli just shrugged. "I have no idea what you're talking about."

"Don't you? Cody was so excited to tell me all about it. How he'd seen it before with Ian. Seen him *change* at night in the woods. How he'd killed Ian to protect Annabelle last year and now he was going to kill you, too. He even wanted my help."

Bucknell shook his head and laughed. "I should thank you for that, actually. You know, the minute Cody saw that carving, he ran right to the cave to check that Ian was really dead. And where was I? Watching and waiting for Annabelle to do the same thing. All these months I thought she'd killed the fucker herself. I might never have known different if you hadn't gone and shown Cody what you really are in the kitchen. I mean, he could be thick and all, but even he knew when someone was too strong to be normal."

"Whatever Cody thought I am has nothing to do with me," Eli said primly.

"C'mon now, we're all friends here. I know all about you and your little retreat for runaways. I even heard you used to run with a pretty tough crowd. Rebels, right? Before your alpha sold you to some people or something? See, me, I wouldn't bother with the whole alpha thing," Bucknell said. "What's the point of being a rebel if you still have to listen to someone else telling you what to do?"

Confused and uneasy, Julien glanced at Eli and grew more worried to find his face eerily blank. It was so different than his usual, put-on boredom that he almost looked like a stranger. With a jolt, Julien realized he'd been able to recognize Eli more when he was a wolf in fur than right now looking perfectly human and so...empty.

"You're nothing like I expected at all," Bucknell was saying, and his gaze flickered over Eli's body. "You can show me, you know. I like seeing it. I like to watch for the moment when you think it's all done, and there's that last little push more. Go on. Show it to me."

For one full beat no one moved, no one spoke, even the wind seemed to slow.

Then Eli held up his middle finger and his trimmed, clear nail hardened and lengthened into a razor-sharp hook. "This moment?"

"All that power," Bucknell breathed, eyes glinting hungrily. "You could be anything you want and you choose this. What a waste."

"Fuck you," Julien snapped without thinking, and both Eli and Bucknell looked at him, surprised. "I don't know what's going on, but I don't like it."

"Ah, Doran," Eli said briskly. "How rude of us. Allow me to fill you in. Ian Ackman found Nielsen's treasure and was shortly afterward murdered by Cody, perturbed to discover his unnatural nature. Presumably knowing that Ian died with the notebook on him, Bucknell here has been setting fires, staging bodies and generally wreaking havoc across the mountain in order to drive the lodge into bankruptcy and force the killer into revealing the location of the treasure. Unfortunately for him, he's been focusing his campaign of horrors on Annabelle, believing her to have been Ian's killer. Tell me, did she know? Did she know he was a wolf?"

Bucknell shrugged. "Ian never told any of us. I certainly didn't find out werewolves were even a thing until after he was dead."

"Yes, you do have a rather helpful source, don't you? Someone to tell you all about Nielsen and Ian, the retreat and me. The same someone who's been tracking Annabelle's every move this last year, creeping in to search the lodge at night, and frightening the shit out of her. Our second shooter."

Julien automatically looked to the satellite tower and gasped. "They're gone!"

"But not far. She darted down around the time you started reciting all your favorite passages of *Nielsen's Notebook*. Don't lurk behind closed doors, darling. I know you excel at sneaking, but it's a lost cause now."

Behind Bucknell the door creaked open, and the woman from the retreat with the red hair stepped inside.

"Gwen," Eli said simply.

She spread one clawed hand in a conciliatory way, while the other loosely held a long-range rifle angled toward the ground. "Sorry I'm late to the party. David called me last night, but I was unfortunately detained." Gwen sniffed the room delicately, then smiled. "I'm so relieved you found ways to keep yourselves busy."

"Nowhere near as busy as you. I'd chastise you for giving both runaways and rebels a bad name, but you're obviously neither."

"What makes you say that?"

"Because your winged monkey here seems to believe the defining characteristic of a rebel pack is freedom from an alpha, something no actual rebel wolf would believe."

Gwen tilted her head curiously. "Growing up in a ruling pack, we used to hear such romantic stories about life as a rebel. What a pity it isn't true."

"Sorry to disappoint," Eli bit out. "Perhaps the next time you play dress-up with someone else's trauma won't be such a bummer."

She pursed her lips. "Everything I told you was true. I know what it's like to be used, just like you. I know what it's like to want to run. The only lie is I haven't gotten away. Not yet."

"That and the fact that the alpha you're plotting to get away from is Celia De Luca," Eli said. "I suppose that explains how Nia and Brett knew exactly what was happening. You did warn me that spying and setting up wolves was your specialty. More the fool me, to not have listened."

"It was Celia's idea that I pretend to be a rebel runaway and check into your retreat. She thought it'd be a good idea to keep an eye on Park and Dayton's little pet project."

"How fortunate that you were already in the middle of running a year-long coup next door. It must have done wonders for your commute."

"Nothing about this is fortunate," Gwen hissed. "I told you how much I hate being Celia's spy. Doing her dirty work. Uprooting everything to move wherever best assists her obsessive expansion of territory so she can gain a seat in the Preservation. All I wanted was a chance at being my own wolf. The same thing you want to give rebels with your retreat—another choice, a new life, a way out. That notebook is *my* way out." She paused and glanced at Bucknell, almost guiltily. "Our way out. Now, where the hell is it?"

Bucknell pointed his gun at Julien. "He said he knows."

Eli sucked his teeth loudly. "And he was quite obviously and foolishly attempting a bit of chivalry. I see you're not familiar with the concept."

"Don't—" Julien protested.

"No need to be a gentleman. Thanks to your sloppy shooting, Doran was unconscious from cave to tower. I, on the other hand, took the time after delivering him here to sneak back out and secure the notebook somewhere secret. It seemed like a good bargaining chip to have by the by."

"Yeah? How about this." Bucknell pointed his gun at Eli. "If you take us there right now, I won't shoot you. Hard to find a better bargain than that."

"The notebook is somewhere in these woods and believe me, it won't be as easy as finding a whole cave," Eli said. "I covered my tracks and destroyed the scent trail. Kill me and you are never going to find it if you spend ten lifetimes looking. Twenty if your recent track record is any indication of your investigative capabilities. I have a knack for hiding."

Bucknell hesitated a red-faced, breathless moment when Julien thought he might shoot Eli anyway, just from pure irritation. Then suddenly he found the gun pointing at him. "How about I kill him instead?"

"Then you seriously underestimate my ability to hold a grudge," Eli said mildly. "If either of us so much as receives a paper cut at your hands, I will die out of spite and the certainty that you'll have done all of this for nothing will be a better legacy than I ever dared imagine in my most audacious dreams."

"I'm starting to think it might be worth it," Bucknell bit out, shifting his gun back toward Eli's head.

"Wait," Gwen said, grabbing his sleeve and tugging his arm back down. "Just—what is it you want then?"

"That depends," Eli said, "on what's in the notebook."

Bucknell laughed. "Of course you just want your cut. Well, I'm sorry to say it's of no use to you."

"Leave it, David," Gwen said sharply. "He knows more than enough as it is."

"Yes, *leave it, David*," Eli mocked. "In fact, why don't you go back to waiting outside? You make a better guard dog than detective anyway. Remember when you spent an entire year targeting the wrong person? Good times."

Bucknell took a wild, furious swing aiming to knock Eli across the face with his gun, but Gwen yanked his arm and he stumbled backward toward the bench as if weighing nothing more than a child.

"What the hell, Gwen!" Bucknell shouted, slipping on the broken glass. He'd barely been able to stay standing.

Julien blinked and glanced at Eli, who didn't look back at him. He seemed to be staring at a certain spot between where Julien stood and where Bucknell had hit the bench. Julien took an experimental step in that direction. No one even glanced his direction. But Eli blinked once, slowly. *Yes.*

Bucknell brushed the glass off his clothes and walked back toward Gwen, who was murmuring an apology. "I'm sorry, David, but you know he's just trying to provoke you into doing something stupid."

"How fortunate I take pleasure in the simple things," Eli drawled. "You do know he just killed a man, right? Tortured him and threw him over the ledge. And then instead of doing the sensible thing and going to get the notebook right then and there, he decided to take the time to frame me first. I'd be careful there," Eli added in a faux whisper. "I think he's a bit obsessed with me. He was getting off watching me slip."

"That's not true!" Bucknell snapped, and Julien took another small step. "It makes me sick the way you squander it. Power is wasted on people like you and Ian. No ambition, content to watch other people dream and have none of your own. Just going where you're told like a good little pack animal."

"You mean like how instead of handling the situation yourself you sat outside all night listening to us fuck and waited for Gwen to come tell you what to do? Sort of like that?" Eli raised his eyebrows. "Why exactly do you think she involved you in this, I wonder? Your access to the lodge was helpful, or would have been if you hadn't been leading her in completely the wrong direction all year. And of course she needed the cops to not go looking for Ian Ackman until she'd safely gotten the notebook. I suppose you did that right, at least."

"Shut up!"

"Don't tell me you actually think she cares about you. A man with *means to an end* practically tattooed across his forehead. Everyone's second choice. Fourth, in Annabelle's case."

"I said shut up or I'll shoot you!"

Eli just leaned toward Gwen, stepping closer conspiratorially. "Tell me, what exactly do you plan on doing with him once you get the notebook? He'd only slow you down. He'll be useless out there when Celia comes looking for you. Even more than he was here on his own turf, where he managed to let the notebook slip through his fingers three different times. Pathetic. Bumbling. Weak."

"We'll see how weak you think I am when I'm a were-wolf," Bucknell shouted.

Julien gasped. It seemed far too loud in the ringing silence. He turned to Eli, but to his surprise Eli just looked exhausted and little bit disgusted. "What, did she tell you she was going to bite you on a full moon?"

"No," Bucknell snapped. "I know that's not how it works. But Nielsen found a way. And once I'm a werewolf, I'm going to enjoy tearing you up with my bare hands."

"Don't be a fool. Wolves aren't made any more than humans are. What's in the book really?" he asked Gwen, but Bucknell stepped forward angrily.

"If you don't know what's in the notebook, how do you know Nielsen didn't find a way?"

"The same way I know he didn't find a way to turn cats into dogs or you into a charming, astute person. That's not how it works," Eli said. "And if she told you otherwise, she lied. Sorry to be the bearer of bad news. But no title, super strength, special abilities, or gun is ever going to get you the respect or the *power* you crave because in the end you'll always be you."

Bucknell yelled with rage and swung the gun up at Eli, and again, Gwen grabbed him and threw him backward. This time, Julien didn't hesitate. He ran at him before Bucknell even hit the bench. Out of the corner of his eye, he saw Eli move as well, leaping at Gwen, and heard the shot of her rifle go off, but he couldn't pay attention to that.

Julien didn't waste time getting fancy either. He threw himself at Bucknell's knees, toppling him to the floor. Combined with the momentum from Gwen, he went down hard, Julien landing on top of him with a groan and sending the gun clattering across the floor.

To his credit, Bucknell reacted quickly, swinging up and catching Julien in the jaw with a wild punch, but he couldn't get the momentum needed to do damage at this angle. Or he just didn't know how to fight without a gun in his hand. Julien punched as hard as he could down into his lower gut and Bucknell convulsed with a *whoof* of air. It was bad luck only that he happened to grab Julien directly where the bullet had grazed his arm.

A white flare of agony tore through him, and Julien rolled off Bucknell instinctively, anything to get away from the nauseating pain. As he hit the floor, he felt another hard edge press painfully into his ribs. Julien ignored it and braced himself for Bucknell to follow his advantage, but instead Bucknell scrambled to his feet and made a run for the gun, scooping it up off the floor.

Julien lunged and grabbed at his ankle with both hands and managed to grab his boot instead. Bucknell picked his foot up into stomp position right over Julien's face, and Julien twisted the boot in his hand as hard as he could. A stuntman would have twisted his body in the air with the rotation of the ankle. Bucknell just tensed and had his knee wrenched out of place.

Bellowing with pain, Bucknell ripped his foot out of Julien's hands and came down heavy on the weak leg, slipping on the shattered glass. His knee folded and he stumbled back against the empty window frame. *Crack.*

Julien had no idea what had happened. Bucknell was

simply there. And then he wasn't. The room was oddly quiet and Julien realized he was entirely alone.

He stood and walked hesitantly to the splintered remains of the window frame, and peered over the edge. In the snow, the dark shadow of Bucknell lay unmoving. Julien backed away from the window. For a moment he just stood there unable to think. There was nothing in his head but his heartbeat and the horrible, howling wind.

Then, gradually, somewhere below him, Julien heard the clanging and snarling sounds of Eli and Gwen, followed by a piercing yelp.

That managed to slam his brain back into gear. Julien looked around for some kind of weapon, but the gun had gone over the edge with Bucknell. A large piece of glass? He'd be more likely to hurt himself than be of any real help. Could he rip off a hunk of the splintered window frame? Even just the idea of getting that close to the edge again sent a swooping sensation through Julien.

Then he remembered the hard edge he'd rolled on earlier. Quickly he reached into the zippered lining of Eli's coat, but there was no weapon.

Just Nielsen's notebook.

Eli had stood there right in front of them all, taunting murderers, tempting death and lying his beautiful ass off to save their lives while the book was within arm's reach the entire time.

A knack for hiding, indeed, Julien thought, shaking his head, and ran out of the tower room with a half-assed plan. At the bottom of the first flight of stairs, a lone wolf in fur stood on the landing alone, staring down over the edge. Julien swayed in place on the top step.

Eli? he tried to say, but no sound came out. He didn't have the air left in his lungs. Its fur was steely gray with patches of fading auburn, and when it turned to look at him, he saw yellow-brown eyes. *Not Eli.*

The wolf snarled, and behind her Julien saw a flicker of movement. Two furry black paws clung to the edge on the wrong side of the fencing, claws caught in the metal grating of the landing. How long could he hold on like that? *How* was he holding on like that at all?

Julien held Nielsen's notebook in the air. "Gwen! I have what you want!"

The gray wolf took a step toward him, shoulder hunching as if preparing to jump. Julien tore a hunk of about twenty pages straight from the middle of the notebook and tossed them over the edge of the stairs and into the wind. They were carried twisting and flapping like a flock of birds over the cliff side. Julien threw the rest of the notebook after them as hard as he could.

"What do you want more, to kill him or to get those pages before they're lost for good?"

Gwen stared at him, brow furrowed, revealing her front teeth.

"Just go! Bucknell's dead. You have the notebook. Take your chance!"

She took a couple steps backward, hind legs teetering at the stair's edge, rolled her shoulders forward and leapt directly at him.

That was not how it was supposed to go.

Julien instinctively threw his hands up over his face and curled his body away just as he felt Gwen slam into him. It was her breath he felt first, warm even through the coat. Then her teeth sank into his shoulder and Julien sort of lost track of the order of things.

He knew he was no longer standing. He felt himself slammed into the stairs. He saw fur everywhere he looked and heard screaming, probably his own. He felt her biting him again and again and again. Ripping into his flesh.

He kept trying to grab at where she sank into his skin. *Out! Get out!* But his hand just slipped uselessly across her silky coat, muzzle, skull. Once he felt the smoothness of teeth under his fingertips and froze, too scared to reach again in case the next thing he felt was her jaw closing around his wrist, too tired and dizzy to know what to do instead. Then, with a tearing in his skin, a horrible yelp and the ringing thud of a body against metal, she was gone.

Julien forced his eyes open painfully, not sure when he'd closed them, and saw Gwen at the foot of the stairs scrambling back to her feet and staring back up at him. Ears flattened back and head low, she looked...terrified. Gwen let out a high-pitched sort of whine and jumped to the lower landing with a clatter of claws on metal, making her way to the bottom of the tower as fast as she could.

Heart pounding in his shoulder, Julien rolled his head back on the step and saw a dark shape crouching over him. From this angle all he could see was black fur and a wolf's paw on the step by his cheek. It seemed too big. Thick. Wrong. Julien touched it and felt a man's ankle.

It pulled gently away from him out of his darkening field

of vision, and for a moment Julien was alone. Then Eli appeared, kneeling on the steps beside him, so pale he was bordering on blue, blood dripping down his arm from a gash across his hand, eyes luminous, face slightly too angular and teeth far too sharp. He looked like something out of a nightmare.

Julien thought he'd never seen anyone more beautiful in his whole life.

"I thought you'd fallen," he croaked.

"I can be very misleading." Eli's smile looked strange on his pointy face. Much too sad. "Hey. Where do you think you're going?"

I'm right here, Julien said, or maybe he didn't. It was hard to hear himself in this strange, floating hush. He tried to stay focused on Eli, convinced that the moment he looked away Eli would disappear into nothingness, and watching him was the only thing still holding him here. But everything felt too heavy. And the sky was too pretty. It had started to snow again and the flakes looked like pages of paper in the wind.

Julien realized he was wrong. The panic right before falling asleep, the endless grief—they didn't feel anything like dying at all. He closed his eyes and hoped for better dreams.

Chapter Thirteen

Dr. Irving to the nurses' station, please. Dr. Irving to the nurses' station.

Julien's eyes blinked open and he winced. He tried to bury his head into the pillow to escape the fluorescent light, but his head ached like a hangover, his body sloped as if the entire right side was missing, and the paper-thin, scratchy sheet smelled like puree of sweet potato.

"Oh god," Julien groaned, giving up on that immediately. He opened his eyes again, slower this time, and looked around.

The first thing he saw was the flowers. Cheery potted poinsettias. Bouquets of camellias and carnations. There was even a small bundle of floppy pale purple blooms Julien was fairly sure were sweet peas. He barely stifled another groan and turned his head the other way to find a man sitting by his bed watching him. A man he'd never seen before in his life.

"You have a few fans among the hospital staff. The notes are very...*heartfelt*." The man wiggled his finger weirdly as if it was the word itself that was embarrassing and not the fact that he'd been snooping through someone's get-well cards. "I'd try to remember that when you find out one of them told the press you're here."

"You read them?" Julien asked, mildly disapproving before the rest of what the man said caught up to him and the last tendrils of brain fog faded away. Everything crashed down on him at once. Eli. Wolves. Their night in the tower. Bucknell in the snow. Gwen in fur. Her teeth ripping into his skin.

Julien looked down at his arm so quickly his head swam. It was bent flat against his chest in some sort of sling and cocooned in padding from knuckle to bicep to shoulder to chest. So much padding that it might not be there at all. With growing panic Julien realized he couldn't *feel* any of it. Only a heaviness on his chest and a tightness just below his collarbone. Julien tried to flex his fingers and felt a muted, tugging agony, like a charley horse echoing somewhere in the void of his right half. His middle finger managed to twitch, though, which meant the arm continued underneath those bandages. Probably.

"What happened?" Julien asked, tearing his gaze away from the lump of gauze he hoped was still his hand. "How long have I been here? Where's El—"

He stopped himself. The man wasn't dressed like a doctor

or nurse. He wore casual, active-ready clothes, although it was difficult to imagine a person who looked less inclined toward coordinated, graceful action. Noticeably thin with strikingly long legs, he sat perched on the edge of his chair like he didn't quite know how to fold his coat hanger body into a normal, relaxed position, and kept shifting in place and tapping his fingers restlessly on his thigh.

Was he a detective? A Fed? Who else would be sitting here waiting for him to wake up? How could Julien even begin to explain what had happened up there without mentioning the wolf thing? Worse, what if this man already knew the wolf thing? What if this was someone from the cabal sent to find out what *Julien* knew? What if he was one of the people Eli was afraid of sent here to take him away? Unless he already knew where Eli was, because he'd been arrested or hurt or—

"Stop that," the man said sharply, tapping at the bed insistently just beside Julien's leg without actually touching him. It was so bizarre that Julien actually stopped panicking for a moment. "You're supposed to be taking it easy. Your arm got pretty torn up, but you'll recover. You've been more or less unconscious for a day and a half and missed the fallout. Good call."

He didn't say it in an unfriendly way, but there was something about him that made Julien uneasy. He had a pleasant enough face—attractive but not especially so. Long, expressive hands. A gentle, crooked smile. Nothing that should feel intimidating at all. And yet...

"Who are you?" Julien asked.

"*I'm a man who likes talking to a man who likes to talk,*" he quoted, flapping his hand. "Not a man who likes talking to a man who passes out after *hello* like the last three times we've had this exchange. How do you feel?"

"Like my arm might actually have been ripped off but you don't know how to tell me."

The man's smile got a little more crooked. "That does sound like me. Fortunately for both of us, you'll be fine. Your arm's attached. Your doctors said with physical therapy you should regain full motor function. You even got to sleep through your rabies shot."

"Did I need a rabies shot?" Julien asked, startled.

"I guess that depends on who was gnawing on your arm."

It was the eyes, Julien realized. They were a common enough brownish-hazel color, sure, but there was a discomforting sort of intensity to them. As if every minute movement and expression that Julien made was being caught and studied. It was a bit like finding a bird of prey walking around on the ground. Stilted and out of its element—with a gaze still sharp enough to notice a mouse a hundred yards away.

Julien had a feeling he had been cast in the role of the mouse. "I don't remember much about it," he said carefully.

"Do you know what attacked you?"

"No idea."

"Want to make a guess?"

"Not really."

"Who else was up there when it happened?"

"I don't know."

The man looked at him with frank disbelief. "You don't know who you were in the tower with?"

"I don't know who I'm in the room with right now," Julien said pointedly.

"I work for the Trust. Have you heard of it?"

"I don't know, have I?"

The man sighed. "Eli told me you were charming. I assume he's never tried asking you a question."

"Who?" Julien said.

"All right, all right." The man shook his head. "If I'd known you'd wake up swinging, I'd have taken a one-and-a-half-day nap to prepare, myself. My name is Cooper Dayton and I'm an agent with the Trust. We investigate violent crimes against wolves. Would you like me to pause here so you can say something aggressively oblivious about wolves or may I continue?"

"Dayton?" Julien echoed. "*You're* Eli's family?"

The man looked genuinely taken aback. So much so that Julien wondered if he'd fucked up.

"I mean, you're the one who owns the retreat?"

"Yes," Dayton said after a moment. "I guess I am." He rotated what looked like a wedding band on his finger absently.

Julien couldn't remember if this was the ex or the one who'd married the ex. He wasn't sure which he'd prefer him to be. "Is Eli okay?"

"He's fine. I left him playing gin rummy upstairs in the maternity ward and cheating so outrageously that one woman faked her water breaking just to avoid paying up."

"But was he hurt? Can I see him? Is he—okay?" Julien

realized he'd asked that already. But he didn't know how else to ask. *Is he happy? Does he want to see me?* "What's going to happen to the retreat?"

Dayton was looking at him a little strangely. "He's a little banged up, but no one tore his arm off, if that's what you mean. And nothing's going to happen to the retreat. Thanks to Eli's impeccable managerial foresight to spend all of his time elsewhere, the retreat isn't even involved in this latest clusterfuck. Ian Ackman's being autopsied soon, but I'm confident Cody Reeves murdered him last year and that David Bucknell murdered him in turn."

"Is Bucknell—"

"Dead," Dayton said bluntly. "We've asked for a full review of all of Bucknell's previous cases, as well as an examination of the Maudit Falls Police Department as a whole."

"You think he's done something like this before?"

"I'm not expecting to find a string of murders in his past if that's what you're asking. But if he was willing to abuse his power to get what he wanted this time, I think it's fair to question whether he's ever wanted anything before and what happened then." Dayton quirked his lips into an odd half smile, half grimace. "I've never known that sort of entitled corruption to spring up without precedent, have you?"

No, he hadn't. Particularly with Bucknell, who had spent the last year lying to, manipulating and essentially torturing a woman he'd known his whole life.

"Does Annabelle know what happened?"

"She's been informed."

"Is she okay?"

"After finding out how one of her oldest friends killed her boyfriend and her boyfriend killed her partner? Not particularly. Though I think she stands a better chance of becoming okay than she did surrounded by assholes. Eli told me Professor West is planning to stay with her for a while. At least until she decides what to do with the lodge."

Julien bit back a curse as a swooping pain yanked oddly somewhere under his collarbone.

"What's wrong? Do you want a nurse?"

"It's fine. I just squeezed my fist too tight," Julien said hastily. "When did Eli talk to Patrick?"

Dayton gave him another curious look. "West stopped by this morning. Is that a problem?"

"No. You're sure he didn't know anything about...anything?" Julien winced at himself.

"It's ironic, isn't it?" Dayton said after a moment. "The cryptozoologist being one of the few humans not aware. But so far it looks like Gwen Evans only told Bucknell about wolves to have an inside man at the lodge and control the investigation into Ian Ackman's disappearance. Celia De Luca is claiming she knew nothing about Gwen's hunt for Nielsen's treasure and I'm inclined to believe her. Unfortunately she also denies being the one to assign Gwen to infiltrate and spy on the retreat, which I doubt very much. But if there's an upside to all of this, it's that Celia De Luca is going to have to back off from interfering with this area for a while. Whether she was acting immorally under her orders or going rogue, Gwen's actions don't look good for Celia, either way."

"Did you find her?" Julien asked. "Gwen, I mean."

"No. She's gone. Along with Nielsen's notebook." Dayton hesitated. "The Trust is going to want to collect your copy."

Julien had been expecting that. "Aren't you the Trust?"

"Yes," Dayton said, though he shrugged as he said it. "I'd also like a look at the thing. Would Gwen have any way of knowing you have a copy?"

"No."

"Would anyone?"

Julien shook his head.

"Eli told me about your brother," Dayton said so matter-of-factly that Julien's throat caught painfully. "How is it, do you think, he was able to find the cave when Gwen and Bucknell couldn't?"

"I have no idea."

"Did your brother know Ian Ackman?"

Surprised, Julien just stared at him for a moment. "You mean before Ian died? No, not that I know of. Do you... Are you saying you think someone told Rocky where the cave was before he got to Maudit?"

"Those directions on your version of the map, is that the sort of thing your brother would have written?"

"It was his handwriting."

Dayton studied him, and improbably his gaze seemed to grow more intense. Julien looked away, feeling strangely guilty. He had the nagging urge to defend himself. To explain to Dayton about Rocky and the mistakes he'd made. All the things he'd gotten to tell Eli and all the things he hadn't.

Julien flexed his fingers impulsively and was punished

with that nauseating tugging feeling. The pain helped clear his head. There was a sharper center to it now, like squeezing a pillow with a piece of glass buried inside, and he realized the drugs were wearing off. Not a moment too soon, really. He didn't like this erratic feeling. Eli might consider this guy family, but Julien didn't know him. Didn't trust him one bit.

When he looked back up, Dayton was pulling a small card with an illustration of a teddy bear holding a heart on the front from his pocket. He handed it over.

"What's this?" Julien asked, taking it.

"Your medical charts."

Julien resisted throwing the card back at him. Inside there was the usual get-well scripted nonsense, with a hand-written note added at the end in pen:

Congratulations on your find! Happy Hunting!

"Where did you get this?" Julien asked.

"It was delivered with those purple flowers there. Any idea who might have sent you that?"

Julien shook his head.

"What about the message? Do you know what it's referring to?"

"I don't know," Julien said. "The notebook? Or the money? Gwen?"

"But those aren't what you came to Maudit for. And you didn't manage to hold on to any of them from where I'm sitting."

"Has anyone ever told you your bedside manner leaves a little something to be desired?"

Dayton shrugged. "That's fine. Saves me the trouble of

trying to be subtle when I tell you this. I have strong feelings for Eli. Shockingly they're not all variants of exasperation. It's important to me that he's happy."

"Are you threatening me?"

"Please. I—" Dayton started to say when a small knock startled them both. Julien looked up to see a man opening the door. More than anyone he'd met in Maudit so far, this was who Julien would have guessed was a wolf. Tall and muscular, he had an expressionless though undeniably good-looking face and radiated a deadly sort of competence even in a pricey-looking suit.

"Making friends?" the man asked neutrally, speaking to Dayton but studying Julien. Amber-brown eyes that looked a lot like Gwen's flicked curiously over Julien's body.

"You know me," Dayton said. "Unrepentant social butterfly. Doran, this is Agent Oliver Park. He's who's going to threaten you. I just came to read your mail."

Park's lips quirked in a tiny, almost shy smile, and for a moment he looked unbearably handsome. Dayton's eyes glinted with something like satisfaction.

"Where's Eli? I thought he was coming down with you?" Dayton asked, and Julien couldn't help looking at the door and running a hand through his hair. His heart was beating so hard he could almost feel it in his numb arm. Silly. He didn't even know why he was nervous. It wasn't nerves. It was just… Eli. And wanting to see for himself that he was okay. That's all.

Park inhaled and Julien realized he was sniffing him. Considering all the events, good and bad, that had taken place since his last shower, he hoped against hope that someone had sponged him down while he was sleeping. Ideally using some medical-grade disinfectant. From the way Park frowned, it didn't look promising.

"No," Park said succinctly.

Even Dayton looked startled. "Don't tell me he's still raking up in Maternity."

"Eli went back to the retreat. He said he had some things to take care of there." Park's expression had returned to that blankness. "We shouldn't wait for him."

There was an uncomfortable pause and belatedly Julien dropped his hand from where he'd been trying to finger comb his hair.

"All right," Dayton said eventually. "Should we take your statement now or can I finish reading these cards?"

After Park and Dayton left, a nurse came through to ask after his pain and Julien lied. He didn't want to risk another dose putting him to sleep.

When Frankie called, he told her he was tired and promised to tell her everything as soon as he got home. He didn't want to look too busy on the phone to talk.

But hours passed, the hospital shifted over to night staff and still Eli didn't come.

Coming face-to-snout with death should earn anyone the right to a solid night's sleep, but of course it only ever made things worse.

Eli's slipped ears twitched as he listened to Julien's uneven breathing stutter in and then exhale out on the long, forceful push of someone trying to trick themselves into relaxation. Once, twice, three times, before he sat up in bed and carefully sipped some water. Then back down again to try a new breathing pattern—one long inhale, hold, seven, eight, and exhale. Then up for some more water. And down to swear quietly. It had been going on all night.

"This is morbid."

Eli hissed, annoyed to be caught off guard, and picked his head up to glare at Oliver lurking in the doorway. He was backlit by the ugly glow of the fluorescent hospital hallway, but Eli could easily see his arched eyebrow, a beacon of disapproval so strong he wouldn't be able to miss it even if he couldn't see in the dark.

"What are you doing here?" Eli whispered.

"Saving you the future humiliation of having to describe this scene to anyone who asks what the bleakest moment of your life was."

Eli sucked his teeth and flopped back down on the bed. "You're underestimating me, darling. This wouldn't even make the top ten."

Oliver snorted. "It's three in the morning and you've broken into an empty hospital room to listen to the man on the other side of the wall breathe. Just witnessing it is going to make my list."

Eli resisted the urge to growl at him. He always felt safer around Oliver, and back in the tower there were moments when he'd wanted nothing more than the comfort of pack. But right now he just wanted to be alone. "Is there something I can help you with? Or did you just come to mock me?"

There was a slightly too long pause, and Eli picked his head up again in time to catch embarrassment flicker across

Oliver's face. "You haven't been back to the retreat in days. It seemed like a good idea to check there wasn't another hostage situation." He said it like a joke, and maybe someone who hadn't known him for well over ten years would believe it really was.

"I'm not going to run," Eli murmured, and Oliver's shoulders relaxed some. He walked over and folded his big body gracefully into the bed. Eli adjusted so that they were both curled on their sides facing one another.

It was a strange echo of being in the tower with Julien. The positions were almost the same, but the feelings couldn't be more different. He and Ollie were crammed into the same twin bed a hair's breadth away, but the space between them was expansive, softened by a decade of friendship and the quiet intimacy of someone as familiar to him as his own body. With Julien, even stationed as far away from one another as they could get trapped in that room, every look had been as visceral as a slap, crackling, electric.

"Before I forget," Oliver said, reaching into his pocket and pulling out the now rather bedraggled deck of Sweet Pea playing cards. "Here. You said you wanted this?"

"Mmm, all done dusting them for prints or whatever it is you traditional-type sleuths do?"

"I think one revelation per roadside souvenir is more than enough." Oliver watched Eli flick through the cards. "Cooper wants to look into the death of Doran's brother."

"Nosy bastard," Eli said mildly, but his claws prickled and he tucked the deck back into its sleeve. "He believes there's something to it then?"

"He wants to know what exactly happened in that month between Rocky leaving Maudit and drowning. He thinks Doran's hiding something."

"He tends to do that. I assume you're telling me this now because you were both so dazzled by the superior sleuthing skills I've demonstrated this week that you simply can't go on without my aid."

"Not quite that," Oliver said politely. "I just thought you'd like to know that we may keep in touch with Doran after this. Would that be okay with you?"

Eli turned onto his back and stared at the ceiling. "Why wouldn't it be?"

"Oh, I don't know," Oliver said with a shade of exasperation. "Maybe because you refuse to speak with him, but haven't left the hospital in two days. Or that the first thing he did after waking up was start lying to protect you. Or a certain old, familiar scent of yours I couldn't help but notice had dried in his hair."

Eli's cheeks felt hot, but he shrugged. "After what happened to his arm, I think Doran deserves a little reprieve from running with wolves, don't you?"

Oliver frowned. "Is that why you're hiding over here? You think he's going to blame you for what happened?"

"Me?" Eli said incredulously. "I didn't ask him to play the hero."

He hadn't needed to. Julien had come running out onto the steps all on his own. Eli had been hanging on to the platform's edge with slipped thumbs while Gwen swiped at his paws. Unpleasant, yes, but he'd been in worse scrapes. They'd both heard Bucknell fall. Eli had assumed Julien would do the only sensible thing and lock himself back in the top of the tower. He was considering his own hasty exit down when Julien had stepped out onto the platform bellowing Gwen's name, notebook thrust in the air like a neon target that said *Bite me.*

He didn't understand how someone could be that reckless. That...unpredictable.

A man so uptight that he practically choked on his tongue if you called him a thief was throwing men out of windows, doing his backward best to uncover a potentially murderous conspiracy and risking his life for, well, Eli wasn't sure why he'd done it. With Julien, he found himself in the utterly unprecedented position of not being sure of anything at all.

"What's the matter, El? Tell me what's wrong," Oliver said.

Eli bit his lip and scratched restlessly at the thin bedcovers between them with his pointer claw. "In the tower," he began, "Gwen saw me slipping."

"Slipped like this?" Oliver asked, and gently tugged one of Eli's ears in fur.

"No," Eli said, knocking his hand away and slipping both ears back to skin. "Not like this."

Oliver was quiet for a minute. He was one of only a small handful that really, truly understood what that meant, and even he needed time to control his reaction. "Ah," he said finally.

"She was killing him," Eli whispered. "I didn't know what else to do."

"Did he see you?"

"No. I don't know. Maybe. Julien doesn't know what's normal or not for us yet. He was also a tad distracted with trying not to die." Eli's stomach swooped uncomfortably and he ignored it. "Gwen wasn't distracted, though. What if she tells?"

"Tells who?" Oliver said. "Gwen has plenty of reasons of her own not to draw attention to herself right now and no idea that we've got a notebook copy of our own to decode. The sooner we know what she wanted it for, the sooner we'll be able to predict her next step."

"I can't believe she convinced Bucknell it would make him one of us. Imagine. Nielsen's Elixir for the Very Modern Werewolf."

"Maybe I should stake out the local snake oil stalls, just in case." Oliver nudged Eli's shoulder with his head comfortingly. "No matter what, I will find her, El. I promise you it's going to be okay."

Eli hummed, soothed despite himself. "I do so love your baseless assurances of protection."

Oliver snorted just as his phone vibrated. He checked it and his smile softened.

"The whippet's not going to be joining us, too, now is he? He'll have to bring his own bed."

"No, I think Cooper's just about reached his limit for this week."

"Of hospitals?"

Oliver hummed and stood. "Heart-to-hearts. Come on. Let me give you a ride back."

Eli hesitated. Next door, Julien's movements had finally

quieted down and his breathing was even and just barely audible. It was relaxing. Near peaceful.

He shook his head. "You go ahead. I have to do something first."

Eli could practically see Oliver fighting not to bundle him up in his arms and go running for the door, or worse, give him advice. Instead, he leaned over the bed and scented Eli's cheek affectionately. "Call me if you change your mind. Or before you go haring off after any other lost treasures, please."

"So that you can sweep in and return those spoils to their 'rightful owners,' too? Not a chance."

Eli waited until Oliver's near-silent footsteps had disappeared down the hall before slipping into the room next door. In the bed, Julien slept with a small frown on his face and tilted over to one side. His arm was still encased in bandages, but smelled significantly better than it had the night before.

Since the last time Eli had snuck in, someone had packed up all of Julien's things from the lodge and his bags were stacked in the chair by the window. Eli unzipped the top one carefully and tucked the Sweet Pea card deck into an inside pocket.

"Help. Thief."

Julien's tone was dryly amused, but when Eli turned to face him his eyes were dark as pitch, and his scent nervous.

Eli clenched the card deck hard in his hand until his claws slipped back to nails. "What kind of world do we live in where a man can't break into another man's room in the middle of the night to give him a small going-away present without suffering suspicion and condemnation?"

"Present?"

Eli hesitated, feeling suddenly very foolish. He wished he had been caught sneaking in with anything else. Answers regarding Rocky's death. Nielsen's couple million in cash. A brand-new, unravaged arm. He held up his hand. "Something to remember Maudit by."

Julien's gaze rested on the deck of cards and he reached for it silently. Eli had to walk closer to give them to him and their fingertips brushed. Julien didn't react, so neither did Eli.

"That's thoughtful of you. I was a bit worried this trip would blend right in with the others. You know how vacations are." Julien fiddled one-handedly with the flap on top and his voice dropped to a low, urgent murmur, as if worried they'd be overheard. "Are you okay? That man, Dayton, said that nothing was going to happen to the retreat, but I wasn't sure if—"

"I'm fine," Eli cut him off.

"The cabal—"

"Has no reason to notice me at all. It seems a great deal of one's worries evaporate when the pack threatening to sanction you is shamed into silence, the man setting you up for murder dies a known killer, and the wolf you've stuck around to protect runs away with the *cabal's* gaze firmly affixed to the notebook-shaped target on her back. In this situation, I'm practically a footnote."

"I'm sorry about Gwen," Julien said, surprising Eli.

"Sorry you hit her teeth too hard with your humerus?"

"Sorry she turned out to not be who you thought she was."

"There's been a lot of that going around."

"Yes." Julien swallowed like there was something stuck in his throat. "Would it help at all if I promise to tell you the truth now? About everything. Anything you want to know. No half-truths, lies by omission, or misleading."

In that moment, Julien looked so earnest and soft and regretful that Eli almost believed he really would answer anything. Almost. The problem was he had nothing to ask. Nothing he wanted the unencumbered truth in response to, anyway.

Was he hiding anything else? Probably, yes. But so was Eli, and he had no intention of ever telling Julien everything about himself. Didn't want to even risk the possibility of him asking. Anything left to learn about Julien would be through Eli's usual underhanded methods.

Why had he done it? Because he loved his brother. Eli couldn't fault him for that. Nor could he spend his life a relatively unrepentant liar, thief and cad, then clutch his pearls the moment someone behaved the same way. Gwen had used him much worse. He'd been more honest about who he was with her than Julien, and he wasn't half as hurt. It wasn't hard to figure out why. And it wasn't Julien's fault Eli had already begun to like him.

"I'm not angry anymore," Eli said finally. Wary, yes. Tender in certain spots, of course. But not angry.

Julien blinked at him. "Just like that?"

"Well, you trying to save my life a bunch of times helped," Eli drawled, and sat carefully on the edge of the bed. Julien shifted his legs to make room, then hesitantly let them relax back so that the line of his calf just rested against Eli's thigh.

"Right," Julien said faintly. He cleared his throat, looked down at the cards, back up at Eli and blurted, "So can I see you again?"

Eli's heart stopped. "What? See me how?"

"I think... I think I'd be interested in seeing you any way you want," Julien said seriously. "I just don't want this to be goodbye."

"Oh." Eli laughed at his own absurdity. As if after all that Julien would clap his hands and say *shift!* He picked restlessly at the thin hospital sheet. "I don't think we need to worry about that. The way things have gone, I'm half expecting to find you waiting for me in the next room I break into."

"Maybe. But let's not wait till then. Visit me in California. Or say you'll let me come back here."

"Why?" Eli whispered.

Julien frowned like he didn't understand the question. "Why do I want to see you? Because you're brilliant. Because you're beautiful and strange and, well, sort of extraordinary, really. I thought so before I knew you were a wolf and I think it even more now. Because just being around you feels like, I don't know, like I'm finally waking up."

"I'm not sure that's a compliment coming from an insomniac."

Julien shook his head. "When you've been sleepwalking through a nightmare every day, waking up is wonderful. I want to wake up to you again. In any way you'll let me."

Eli looked down at Julien's free hand resting on the bed. He carefully slipped his fingers between Julien's and traced the lifeline with his thumb. The three nail-shaped bruises. And maybe it was foolish. Maybe he'd regret it. A human aware all of two seconds, who lied like he breathed, and was consumed with seeking justice for a brother whose death was almost certainly connected to wolves. It was everything Eli should distrust and he did, oh god, he did.

But somehow while never saying one true thing between them, this had turned into the most honest connection he'd known in a very long time. Eli didn't want it to end. Not yet.

"All right. I'll visit you. As long as we don't do any more amateur sleuthing."

Julien smiled like he'd been given a gift much greater than the vague promise of *not goodbye, but see you later.* He picked Eli's hand up and pressed his lips against the base of his palm. "If I so much as glimpse a red herring, I swear to you we'll both go on the run."

And that Eli could believe. He even sealed it with a kiss.

★ ★ ★ ★ ★

Acknowledgments

Thank you to everyone at Carina for their patience and support. To the best editor anyone could ask for, Mackenzie Walton—I'm not sure there would be a book at all without her. And to my family, who always let me bounce ideas off them to see what sticks when I'm stuck.

About the Author

Charlie Adhara writes contemporary, mystery, paranormal, queer romance. Or some assortment of that, anyway. Whatever the genre, her stories feature imperfect people stumbling around, tripping over trouble and falling in love. Charlie has done a fair amount of stumbling around herself, but tends to find her way back to the northeast US. When she's not writing, Charlie is reading, hiking, exploring flea markets and acting as an amateur cobbler for her collection of weird shoes.

To learn more and stay updated, follow Charlie on the usual suspects!

Website: www.CharlieAdhara.com

Twitter: Twitter.com/Charlie_Adhara

Hunting for big bad wolves was never part of agent Cooper Dayton's plan, but a werewolf attack lands him in the carefully guarded Bureau of Special Investigations. A new case comes with a new partner: ruggedly sexy werewolf Oliver Park.

Keep reading for an excerpt from The Wolf at the Door, *book one in the Big Bad Wolf series from Charlie Adhara.*

Chapter One

The fact that Cooper Dayton was running down the side streets of Bethesda and not driving back to D.C. by now was proof that his father had been dead wrong. His haircut was plenty professional. Too professional, even. How else could Ben Pultz have made him as a federal agent from thirty feet away and taken off running? Not from his jeans and T-shirt. Not from the weapons carefully hidden under his intentionally oversized jacket. It had to be the bureau-regulation hair. Apparently Pultz didn't think he looked like a "boy band reject," though Cooper doubted his dad, Sheriff Dayton, would be swayed by the opinion of a fleeing homicide suspect.

"Freeze!" Cooper shouted. "BSI!"

The few people on the street watched them race past

with mild interest. Cooper wondered if they'd look more excited if he'd shouted FBI. In that case, some may have even tried to intervene. Maybe stick a foot out to trip Pultz, who at five-foot-five, a little pudgy and apparently unarmed, hardly looked intimidating.

When Cooper identified himself as a BSI agent, civilians hardly looked twice. Didn't know what it was. Didn't care.

Ben Pultz knew who the BSI was, though. And from the way he leapt, inhumanly graceful, over a fire hydrant and catapulted down a side alley, he cared who the BSI was, too.

Cooper ran around the hydrant and slowed as he approached the alley. He drew his .38, the feel of it in his hand instantly calming, and turned the corner, weapon raised.

There was a fence at the end of the alley, a dented High Voltage sign tacked on at an angle. Ben Pultz was a good twenty feet ahead and running straight for it.

"Freeze!" Cooper tried again. "It's over, Pultz."

If anything, Pultz just ran faster. His stride changed into an odd sort of loping rhythm and he bent over dramatically, his hand occasionally reaching down as if to touch the street.

Was Pultz about to shift?

Cooper's breath, coming fast and hard from running all over the downtown, caught in his throat. He vaguely hoped there was nothing in the alley to trip over because he could not tear his eyes away from Pultz's quivering form.

Pultz slowed, his steps came shorter and his whole body tensed up as if bracing for something.

Cooper stopped running ten feet away from the suspect. His gun hung limply in his hand and he didn't bother telling Pultz to stop again. Cooper wanted to see. Couldn't look away.

Pultz jumped…

…and landed, still fully human, clinging to the top of the fence. He quickly climbed up and scrambled over the top, sneakers squeaking and slipping against the apparently non-electric metal.

"Shit," Cooper said, running toward the fence again, as Pultz neatly dropped to the street on the other side.

Pultz paused and looked back at Cooper. He was young. He looked even younger than he probably was due to his wide eyes, blotchy pink skin and fine blond hair, which gave him a baby-faced look. A look he'd obviously tried hard to counteract with the angry band T-shirt covered in jagged lettering and snarling skulls and a multitude of cheap chains sporting various tokens hanging from his jeans. Cooper thought he looked like an idiot. But still, a young idiot.

Pultz started to say something through the fence. "I didn't—" He dropped like a stone. Spasms ripped through his body once, twice, and before Cooper could even register what was happening, Pultz's body stilled. He lay unmoving on the concrete.

"Jesus Christ."

"Nah, just me, kid." Jefferson stepped out from behind a Dumpster, Taser gun in hand.

Cooper was torn between being glad for the backup and being embarrassed Jefferson had been there to see him freeze and almost let their suspect get away. Jefferson wasn't his mentor anymore. He was his BSI partner and shouldn't have to be picking up Cooper's slack.

"Nice drop," Cooper said instead, holstering his weapon and climbing over the fence. Not quite as agilely as Pultz, but quickly enough. Having a wiry frame not overburdened with bulky muscle had its benefits sometimes. Sometimes.

He dropped to the other side as Jefferson roughly cuffed the suspect. "I didn't do anything. Let me go," Pultz complained loudly, already recovering from his shock. The Taser guns the BSI issued were specially made to be stronger than any other on the market and could put a human man twice Pultz's size out of commission for hours at least. Pultz had shaken it off in seconds.

"If you didn't do anything, why'd you run?" Cooper asked.

"'Cause you're BSI. I heard what happened in Syracuse."

Cooper's eye twitched. Goddamn Syracuse. Did everyone know about that?

Pultz was still talking, though he didn't struggle when Cooper helped Jefferson haul him to his feet, hands cuffed behind his back. "You're not going to do that to me, man. I'm not going to let you hunt me down."

"Like you hunted down Caroline Tuscini?"

"Aw man, I barely knew that chick."

"I didn't say you knew her. I said you killed her. Tore her up and spit her out," Jefferson said.

"I didn't—"

"Benjamin Pultz. You're under arrest. You have the right—"

"Wait a minute. Are you shitting me? Arrested for what? No way you have anything on me."

Cooper privately agreed. They didn't have anything on

Pultz. They'd technically just tracked him down to a fast-food joint to question him. But Pultz had been seen arguing with the victim a day before she turned up in the river with her throat torn out. And he'd run. As Jefferson said, when a chicken gets killed and there's a fox in the hen-house, you don't have to waste a lot of time and fingers checking his teeth for feathers.

"Let's start with resisting arrest and leave the rest for Bethesda PD," Jefferson said. He pushed Pultz along while Cooper trailed behind as backup. Now that the adrenaline was wearing off, the deep scars across his belly were beginning to burn and he kept an eye on Pultz's cuffed hands, ready for the slightest hint they might turn deadly. But his fingers stayed blunt-nailed and slightly pudgy, twisting around each other anxiously. Under the handcuff he wore a wristband for a local arcade.

"How old are you?" Cooper asked without thinking.

Pultz glared over his shoulder. "Nineteen. The fuck do you care?"

Cooper shrugged. "Young."

"Yeah, but who knows how old that is in dog years." Jefferson laughed.

Cooper watched the streetlights come on as Jefferson maneuvered the car through D.C. traffic. He felt out of sorts. He'd spent the entire two days in Bethesda anxious to get back home and now that he was nearly there, he wanted to be back in Bethesda questioning Pultz.

Why had he killed Caroline Tuscini? Why had he paused

after dropping to the other side of the fence when he could have gotten away? What had he been about to say?

That wasn't really their job, though. The old-fashioned investigative work Cooper had dreamed of doing when he got recruited to the FBI wasn't really applicable these days. Motive didn't have a lot to do with bloodlust, Jefferson would say, and shake it off, ready for the next case. But he was used to it. He'd been working for the BSI for five years. Almost as long as the BSI had existed. Cooper had only been there for six months and wasn't yet comfortable walking away before an investigation was technically closed. After cases like Bethesda he felt like a glorified bounty hunter, and that wasn't why he'd wanted to get into law enforcement. All that time in school, training, everything he'd given up at home, the fights with his dad, for one reason: to join the FBI. And he'd only gotten to stay a few years before moving on to, well, this. And all that this entailed.

But it was too late to get out now.

He'd been warned. Once he accepted a position with the BSI, he couldn't return to the FBI.

"It would present a conflict," his supervisors had informed him. How, he didn't understand. They both worked for the same government. Both went after bad guys. BSI was technically an offshoot of the FBI. Where did the conflict come in?

But he hadn't asked those questions.

After Cooper had woken up in the hospital missing six and a half feet of small intestine, with a tube draining his stomach contents out his nose and an invitation to discuss "possible promotion opportunities" at the mysterious BSI headquarters, the only question he had was what the hell had happened.

The BSI told him they could answer that if he agreed to join their team.

"Isn't that blackmail?" Cooper had croaked, his throat still sore from the intubation, though thankfully the doctors had removed the nose tube and started him on a nutritional IV.

"The U.S. government doesn't blackmail. Unfortunately, the answers you want involve extremely sensitive information that is a matter of national security. Ordinarily, you would get the same cover story as your partner did. But you've showed promise."

So he'd made promises.

And when his recovery was complete he found himself signing away his life in the hushed office of Jacob Furthoe, Director of the secretive Bureau of Special Investigations.

"Monsters are real," Furthoe said, accepting his contract like a pin-pulled grenade and pointing to the chair across the desk.

"I'd rather stand, sir, if that's all right," Cooper had replied. It had taken a month before his rearranged guts started accepting solid foods and he was let out of the hospital, and the weight loss still showed. Cooper didn't want his new boss to think he was weak. Besides, he was too on edge to stay still. What kind of idiot agreed to a job before even knowing what it was? "I've had the pleasure of putting away a few monsters already." He'd seen people do terrible things during his three short years in the FBI. Had grown up with a sheriff for a father who didn't know the difference between home and work, never mind not talking cases at the dinner table. "I'm afraid I already know they're real."

"No, you don't. But you will," Furthoe said. "What do you know about werewolves?"

Cooper frowned and shifted his weight, awkwardly. "Is that a gang, sir? I'm not familiar—"

"No. Werewolves. Sometimes a man, sometimes a wolf. Or woman, too, of course."

"Sir?"

Director Furthoe leaned back and pointed at the chair again. "I really think you should take that seat now."

Cooper sat. And listened, numbly, as Furthoe revealed the best-kept secret of the government.

Werewolves were not just in books and movies, cartoons and games. They were real and they had "come out" five years ago to governments around the world, represented by a group that called themselves the Trust. The Trust had explained werewolves had always existed, living amongst humans, but due to persecution had slipped quite intentionally into hiding and mythology.

Until now.

They'd revealed themselves to the government in order to request certain rights that were increasingly tricky to work around in the modern age. The ability to decline certain antibiotics, avoid certain tests, receive certain allowances that would help them continue to move through the world without public detection.

Because, as the Trust explained over and over again, most wolves lived totally normal lives. They were teachers and writers, doctors and secretaries. They ate the same food, watched the same TV, had families, and looked like everyone else. Most of the time.

The eensy-weensy difference was they could shift their human bodies into wolves' bodies whenever they wanted.

Seemed like a pretty major difference to Cooper.

"That's not all that's different, of course," Furthoe had explained. "You see, they don't have to completely change shape to grow claws or fangs, and *that* is what makes them so dangerous, as you well know, Agent Dayton."

Cooper's hand twitched to his stomach. The stitches had been removed but the skin was still raw and tender, and the indigestion daily. His doctors said they had "high hopes" that what was left of his small intestine would adapt. And if it didn't? He wasn't ready to talk about that. "What does the BSI do exactly, sir?"

"Simply put, we specialize in wolf crime. Any crime the FBI picks up that's flagged as peculiar gets passed on to us. Our home office will either confirm or disprove wolf involvement. As a BSI agent your job is to track down and bring in the guilty wolf. Track and capture."

And that's what he'd done with Benjamin Pultz. So why did he feel so dissatisfied?

Cooper ran a hand through his hair. His dad was right, it was a little long on top and had a tendency to flop into his face. It certainly didn't look federal. So what had made Ben Pultz look up from his cup of fries and stare with such horror and...fear? Why had he run?

Guilt, Cooper supposed, could make anyone see things that weren't there.

Jefferson interrupted his self-reflective pity party. "You're quiet. Stomach bothering you?"

"I'm fine," Cooper said quickly, which of course his guts belied immediately with a painful twinge. Jefferson was always checking in on his injury. Cooper appreciated it, he did, but still wished he would stop bringing it up. At Cooper's last checkup his doctor had told him there was no medical reason he should still be experiencing sharp, burning pain in his belly. Then he'd referred him to a psychologist. Cooper had not gone, stopped the checkups with his doctor and not told anyone about the whole thing, including Jefferson.

"What's on your mind, Dayton?"

Cooper shrugged and watched the people swarming the crosswalk. A typical D.C. Friday evening crowd of business folk and government employees. A sea of black and gray heading home. The troubles of the workday already locked away for the weekend.

He wanted that, to be able to leave the job behind. But when your job changed your entire outlook on reality, how could you ever walk away? What would they think, these suit drones, knowing mythical beings walked and worked amongst them?

The public could never know about werewolves, though. That was one of the few things the BSI and the Trust agreed on. The panic, the prejudice, the senseless violence that would surely come if the truth was revealed, it was too much to contemplate. So Cooper's job mattered. Even if it didn't always feel...right.

He realized Jefferson was still watching him, waiting

for an answer. "Just thinking about Pultz, I guess," Cooper said finally. "Why do you think he did it? Kill Caroline Tuscini, I mean."

"Motive is the least important factor, you know that," Jefferson said. His hairline was receding, but the color was still a stubbornly dark brown and his face looked younger than forty-six when he smiled, which was often. He had been Cooper's first and only partner at the BSI, and almost everything Cooper knew about wolves he'd learned from Jefferson. He was lucky to have him. "What I may think constitutes a good motive isn't going to be the same as what Pultz thinks. Or even you, for that matter."

"Yeah, yeah," Cooper sighed. "I know. It's just, it's got to be him, right? I mean, it's not some other wolf or—or whatever," he finished lamely. *Or what?*

"He's the only wolf who came into contact with Caroline Tuscini," Jefferson said, giving him a strange look. "We got him, Dayton. And if Bethesda PD find it's not him? There must be another wolf and we'll go back."

"Right," Cooper said, looking out the window again. He knew the deal. Nine times out of ten in a wolf killing, the closest wolf was the guilty one. Jefferson didn't like wasting a lot of time proving it. It worked out most of the time. Only in a couple of cases had they needed to go back and rework the case. It wasn't the most efficient process, but then neither was a job recruitment that couldn't explain the details of the job until after the contract had been signed. It made for a limited number of new agents. The BSI was stretched thin. This was the best they could do.

"Trust me," Jefferson said. "We caught a monster today, kid."

"Right. Just the weekend blues, I guess. Feels weird to sit home when there's so much to do." Unlike other agents, Cooper disliked when his free days fell on the weekend. It only seemed to emphasize the fact that he didn't have a social life to speak of.

"With that attitude you're going to burn out before you even get to my age." Jefferson laughed, but he looked almost approving. "You're way too young to act so old. You need to get out there, have fun, get laid, make mistakes."

Cooper snorted. Jefferson made it sound like Cooper was twenty-two and not rapidly approaching his mid-thirties. Though, to be fair, at twenty-two he hadn't been doing a lot of that sort of stuff either.

"What are your plans this weekend?" Jefferson continued.

Cooper gave some vague response and quickly tried to turn the question back on his partner. Truthfully his weekend plans consisted of catching some old noir films on TV and drinking a couple of bottles of wine with his cat, Boogie. Well, he'd be drinking. Boogie would be judging. But Boogie tended to judge everything he did. Even if he did go out and manage to find a guy he wanted to bring home for the night, Boogie would be appalled and annoyed. It was his basic look. Not that Cooper was projecting. Much.

Soon enough Jefferson dropped him off in front of his apartment building with the final instruction to "Live a little!"

"Only a little?" Cooper called back. "No problem!"

Don't miss The Wolf at the Door *by Charlie Adhara,*
available wherever Carina Press books are sold.

www.Harlequin.com

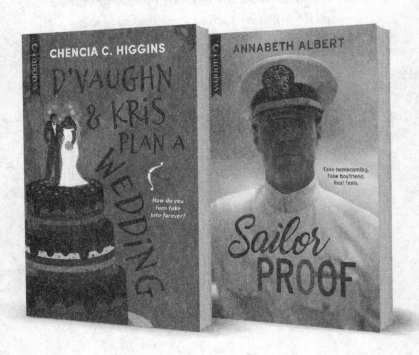